1. Joe Calls In

Ru-DIN-ski!

Rudolph Barnes looked at the name on his phone. Joe Normal calling. *Again.* Whenever Joe's I.D. popped up, Rudolph knew that damn silly nickname would be the first thing out of the man's mouth. Rudolph was one of Joe's best friends, but that wasn't saying much. Joe Cool's behavior had grown so squirrelly in the last few months it was doubtful if the man had enough friends to even stretch it out to a Good, Better and Best.

Rudolph cautioned himself. *I shouldn't mess with this. Not now.* He braced himself and poked the button on his smart phone anyway.

"Ru-DIN-ski!" Joe chirped.

"Joe, hell. You're supposed to say hello first." He said it in the sassiest tone he could come up with and still not come off as pissy.

"Hello first," Joe said, being stupid. Just to have a little more fun with the man, he tacked on another, "*Rudinski.*"

Rudolph exhaled his frustration long and heavy into the phone to make sure Joe know he was getting on his last nerve. It was mostly just for the helluvit. "I don't know about *your* damn clock," he said, putting a playful edge on his voice, "but mine says ten forty-nine p.m." He came down hard on the 'pee-em.'

"Couldn't be better, thanks," Joe answered, totally immune to his friend's problem with the time.

Rudolph sighed again. Joe was so spaced lately he wouldn't know an attitude if it bit him on the butt

"Take it easy, Rudinski," Joe said. "I'm not calling to cry on your shoulder."

Rudolph could see that easy enough, with The Coolster doing a one-eighty with his happy-happy routine.

"Why don't we talk about it tomorrow," Rudolph said. "I got better things to do on a Friday night—if you get my drift."

Joe wasn't anywhere close to getting his friend's drift. "I'm telling you, Rudinski, this isn't about Franki. I've accepted it."

That was fine with Rudolph. Joe's late wife had hardly been kissy-huggy around him, anyway. Always seemed to be riding with her foot on the brake whenever he was around, truth be told. Woman seemed to put her husband's work pal in his own special category. Joe's Best *black* Friend.

"I've got a great idea." Joe said, "but I need you to help me."

"*Help* you."

"I'm talking a quest!" Joe said.

"A *quest*?"

"You know, a search, a hunt, a way to..."

"I *know* what a freakin' quest is," Rudolph said. "Hell, give me a *little* credit."

"I want you to help me find somebody, Rudinski."

"Try Facebook."

"I mean it. We can do this!"

"How many beers you had, man?" Rudolph asked.

"She's a girl," Joe said.

"A girl. Go find a *girl*?"

"Correcto. From college," Joe said. "I mean, from when I went to college."

"*College!*"

"Right."

"That was what—a hundred years back?"

"Ha-ha. Try thirty-five. Nineteen-Eighty-one."

Rudolph couldn't believe the man. Joe all juiced about about hunting down a girl from *college*. He tried to shame the man back into being real. "Mighta *been* a girl, but now you're talking about an old woman."

"Hardly," Joe said.

With that bullet bouncing off, Rudolph tried a harder angle. "Anyway, she might not even be alive after all this time." He wasn't bluffing on that one. Rudolph knew a string of women College Girl's age who had already passed. Bad drugs, bad men, bad luck, you name it. Hell, Joe had a prime example right in front of him—the man's own wife Franki, shot dead going on a year ago at age fifty. All because for one split second some yahoo with a hunting rifle thought a female hiker bent over to pick wildflowers just *had* to be a white-tailed deer.

"Uh, not to be rude," Rudolph said, "but go find her then."

"I will, but there's a complication."

"Damn right. Thirty-somethin' *years'* worth of complication, I'd say."

"Naw, something else," Joe said.

Rudolph took a pained glance back at the clock on the nightstand. It read *11:14.* "Just *tell* me, Joe," he said.

"Love to," Joe answered. "She was black."

2. So She's Black

Rudolph ran it back in his head.

Man wanted him to help find his old girlfriend. Who just happened to be black. Who Joe hadn't even seen in thirty-some years. Which sure made her not a girl anymore. And do it for a white guy who up until twenty minutes ago had never shown Sign One that he had a thang for sistuhs.

"So she's black," Rudolph said, just to be sassy about it. Mixed couples weren't weird anymore, not in 2016. Different maybe, but not like the old sideshow. "Hold up a sec," he said.

Joe heard Rudolph's baritone muttering something away from the phone. He assumed the man was talking to Denise, the woman he'd moved in with. The muffled female voice said something that sounded a lot to Joe like "some luck." Rudolph came back to the phone and said wearily, "Headin' to the kitchen."

"So my idea is giving you an appetite!" Joe said.

Rudolph ignored that nonsense. In a forced whisper, he said, "Let's wrap this up quick. Dig?" Rudolph said it, but he knew that Joe most assuredly *wouldn't* dig, not the way his head was floating around lately, out there somewhere in La-La Land. A picture popped into Rudolph's head: Pink-faced Joe back in the day, hooked up with a Hershey Bar-colored sistuh. Back when a two-toned couple in Kentucky could get seriously hurt for pulling that stunt.

"You telling me you dated a black girl thirty-five years ago," he only half-kidded, "and you didn't get shot by anybody?"

"I didn't just *date* her, Rudinski," Joe corrected him. "I *went* with her."

"Oh," Rudolph said. He spread the sarcasm thick. "'You *went* with her."

In a way, Rudolph really *could* picture Joe Cool back in the day, sniffing around a cute little brown-faced shawty. In the five years they'd worked together, Rudolph couldn't help but notice the way Joe liked to challenge his bosses at Maxi-It Imaging. Joe didn't do anything major that would get him fired—say have his hand caught in the break room's dollar bill changer. He just nibbled at the edges. Dared The Man to get worked up over penny-ante stuff, like who got stuck with mandatory overtime, or who had to work every single holiday. Stuff that wasn't about to get changed, anyway.

Joe was rolling with his great idea.

"Here's what I'm thinking, Rudinski," he excitedly explained. "Go to some black neighborhoods. Check out the beauty shops, churches, bars, that sort of thing. Ask around. Whadd'ya think?"

What Rudolph thought was that he didn't need a white man telling him where to poke around in the 'hood. Blacks had their own beauty shops and churches and joints, sure. *Theirs.* He cleared his throat.

"So what you're telling me is, you need somebody with Negra skin to go run *interference* for you."

"You got it!"

Damn, Rudolph told himself. He couldn't even insult the man off with *that*.

"I figure some people might be hesitant to talk to me, so, yeah—that's where you come in, Rudinski." Then, in an effervescent delivery, Joe added, "You da Man, Rudinski!"

Rudolph let loose an involuntary snort. "Hesitant, hell! You just don't want to get your butt kicked for nosin' around in the 'hood." He said it, but Rudolph knew there was a good chance a sister that age wasn't even in any damn 'hood. Could have got herself a nice job or a rich husband and moved on up.

"Wrong!" Joe chirped. "I'd go with you."

"Main!" Rudolph came back. "In other words, you're *using* me."

"Come on, Rudinski" Joe said. "You know I wouldn't use you unless you were a great friend. A *top-drawer* friend!"

Rudolph heard the word "drawer" and his head zapped back to Denise back in bed, primed for action and wearing that tiny African print thong that was just begging to get itself tore off of her.

"Listen Joe," he whispered, "If I don't hustle back pronto, that stuff Denise been heatin' up for me *all night long* is gonna be ice cold, thanks to you. Later."

"Come *on*, Rudinski," Joe whined. "Tonight." His voice soared. "She was my Nubian Prin-*cess!*"

Rudolph double-clutched on that one. "Your *which?*"

"My Nubian Prin-*cess.*"

Rudolph leaned back against the sink and rubbed his forehead. "Okay," he finally said, drawing the word out to make it sound like he was making a big sacrifice. "Give me a little time to take care of business here."

"Fifteen minutes?" Joe asked.

"Something like that," Rudolph said. He hung up and beat it back to Denise and her hot little heart-stoppin' thong.

3. Rudinski Comes Over

An hour later, Rudolph stood on Joe's front porch, muttering to himself. The man who insisted that Rudinski come over quick hadn't answered the pounding on his front door.

"Now ain't this somethin'," Rudolph said, keeping his voice low. He shuffled his feet impatiently. At least he'd arrived here at Joe's house a halfway sassified man. That was Denise' pet word for being sexually satisfied: "sassified." It was obvious from the thumping bass notes coming inside that Joe was home. Rudolph tried the door knob. *Unlocked.* He didn't need any nosy 'Burb Family catching sight of a black man standing in front of a white guy's house at 12:30 a.m. He made sure he didn't have an audience and nonchalantly stepped in.

Rudolph was hit full force by a rogue wave of Bee Gees high-pitched harmonizing. He stood rigid while his eardrums adjusted to the decibel level. Joe wasn't here in the living room. A fourth voice leaped out at him from the tight blend of Bee Gees harmony, one that definitely didn't fit with the rest. *Joe's voice.* When Joe's old stereo went silent as it changed over from *Lonely Days* to *Stayin' Alive*, Rudolph placed Joe somewhere down the hallway. The man was talking to somebody.

"Now what," Rudolph whispered to himself. He took a few steps and craned his neck to look down the hall. There was Joe—no, there was Joe's *reflection*—in the bathroom mirror. Rudolph's mouth pursed into a mischievous smile. He slid into the hall closet and pulled the door behind him, leaving just enough of a crack for him to peek out. He could see Joe, no shirt on, twisting his white flour self from side to side.

"Not exactly Mister Universe," Joe told the mirror, in the

same upbeat voice Rudolph had heard on the phone. "But okay... no big belly, anyway."

Rudolph had to admit that The Coolster, for his age—fifty-three, fifty-four—did have a fairly decent build. As for himself, six months' worth of playing house with Denise had him well on his way to a pot belly and love handles.

Suddenly, Joe yanked his shirt back on and was charging out of the bathroom. Rudolph, taken by surprise, jerked back and clanged against the empty coat hangars. If it weren't for the BeeGees' high-volume wailing, Joe would have surely heard the racket. Instead, Joe breezed on past him.

Rudolph wasn't ready just yet to give up the free entertainment. He nudged the door open a few inches wider and watched the man go to the living room, boogying or doing whatever dance Joe thought he was doing. Joe picked up a bottle of beer, took a sip and joined in the singing again. Rudolph could swear he was listening to a cat getting itself run over by a forklift.

"Stayin' a...LI, I-I,I-I-I, I-IVE!"

After a second refrain, Rudolph's threshold for pain hit its limit. He hustled out of the closet. "Yo, Joe! Joe!"

Joe spun around, startled. When he saw it was Rudinski, he gave his friend a big grin. "Rudinski!" he piped out. He was still so deep into his Bee Gees Zone that he didn't wonder why Rudolph was coming at him from down the hallway instead of the front door.

"Most people knock, Rudinski."

"I *did* knock," Rudolph came back, answering with some attitude of his own. He pinched his eyelids against the noise. "Back at my building, half the tenants would've jumped your case over all this racket."

"Correction, Rudinski," Joe said. "They call it music. Top of the charts, back in the day." Out of consideration, he went over to the CD player and turned the volume down. When he returned to Rudolph, he saw the man was holding his palms up. A *What's up* expression was on Rudolph's face.

"So you gonna tell me why I'm here at twelve-thirty in the morning?" Rudolph asked.

"Got something to show ya," Joe said. He asked Rudolph if he wanted a beer.

"Still ridin' a rum-and-Coke," the black man said, waving him off.

Joe took a last gulp of his Corona and set the bottle down on the coffee table, next to another empty. While he was bent over, he took hold of the large book.

"College yearbook, Rudinski" Joe explained, stepping closer so the man could appreciate it up close. "Haven't had it out in like forever."

"So?" Rudolph said.

"The first time I pulled it open tonight," Joe said, ignoring the man's remark, "it cracked like a board." He glanced over to his buddy. "The pages are stuck together. That's how long it's been since it's been looked at." He held it closer to his friend and read the words on the cover. "*Splenditus. Nineteen-Eighty.*"

"Aww, come *on*. Don't tell me you got me out of bed to show me a damn *yearbook*," Rudolph said. He made the aggravation in his voice hard to miss, even for Joe.

"Wanna see something beautiful, Rudinski?" Joe asked, oblivious to Rudolph's complaint. He didn't wait to find out if Rudolph wanted to see something beautiful.

"You're not taking your shirt off again, are ya?" Rudolph

cracked. As soon as the words were out of his mouth, he knew he screwed up. Now The Coolster would know he was down the hall spying on him.

Wrong. Joe was too caught up with the book to catch Rudolph's little dig. He held the book tight against his midsection and braced it at the top of his belt buckle. Yearbook secure, he tried to insert his fingernails where the bookmark was. It took four tries before he could pry the pages apart. The book opened with a loud, sticky *RRRIP*.

"Bam!" Joe sounded out. "Page one-seventeen."

Rudolph looked down through his bifocals at the head-and-shoulder shots of several dozen students.

"Whadda'ya think?" Joe asked.

Rudolph squinted at the little faces on the page—all but one white—and decided to pull the man's chain again. He pointed to the only African-American on the page, a female.

"*There?*"

Joe gave him a double-take. "You're hilarious, Rudinski. Of course there."

4. Nubian Prin-*cess*

"So that's your Nubian Prin-C*ESS*," Rudolph said coolly. He took in the girl's bright eyes and wrinkle-free beige skin. Natch, he thought. Sister was still a kid, like all the rest. One thing, though. Her eyes were different, kind of oriental. Still, no way did girlfriend rate any 'Nubian Prin-*cess*.'

"Just *look* at her, Rudinski," Joe gushed.

Rudolph's eyes went to the name at the bottom of the photo. He made his voice into a monotone and read out loud, "Bernadette Armstrong Averytown Kentucky."

"Bernie," Joe purred.

"I'll give her a 9," Rudolph offered. The girl wasn't *anywhere* close to that, for real, but maybe that was all the man needed, let him see his friend's two thumbs up and then Rudolph could hustle himself back to Denise.

He might as well have kept his "9" to himself.

"Look at that *neck*," Joe swooned on. "You ever see a neck like that, Rudinski? Long...graceful..."

"Huh," Rudolph dissed, knowing Joe wasn't listening to him anyway.

"Eyes straight ahead. That's pure confidence, y'know," Joe pointed out.

Rudolph stifled a yawn.

"Everything's rounded, see? Brow, nose, cheekbones. There's not a hard edge *anywhere*. Do you know what that *means*, Rudinski?"

"Good makeup?" Rudolph joked. He knew he could forget any more playtime tonight with Denise, not from the way Joe was humming along. He folded his arms and let Joe give him his damn answer.

"It means, *this* is real kindness. *This* is real beauty."

In the eye of the beholder, Bro, Rudolph thought. Seriously, the girl was a 5—and lucky to get that from him.

"She has these long arms you can't see in the picture...and this little waist. Not exactly super-sized up top, but it's plenty for me."

"Well, you know what they say," Rudolph said, not caring how the second part came out, 'If it's more than a mouthful, it's a waste.'" That was easy for him to say—Denise had lots to waste.

"And she has these thighs," Joe said. "Long, athletic thighs."

Rudolph felt the hairs inside his ear give him an unnerving tickle. It was a sensation that came over him whenever he recognized that something weird was happening. There it was. Joe was talking in the *present tense* about this girl in the thirty-five-year-old picture. *Has* sexy thighs. *Has* a little waist.

"Gotta take a leak, Rudinski," Joe said abruptly. He shoved the big book into his friend's own gut and headed down the hallway.

With his eyes stinging from fatigue, Rudolph became even more cynical about this Prin-*cess*. Sista-girl come to college looking for a husband—any man, any color. That's the way he looked at it. He got a notion and went to the sophomores. He unstuck the pages until he found *Joseph E. Normal*. Joe looked like a real kid himself. Black eyelashes and long, reddish-blond hair blow-dried and brushed back over his ears. Nice-enough looking guy. Seeing that, he cut the girl a little slack. If Joe was anything then like he was now, he would have stood out, back in the day. Maybe sistuh-girl really had fallen for him.

He heard Joe coming back and quickly flipped back to the Bernie page.

"Was that girl ever crazy about *me*," Joe said, taking his book back. "I was a sophomore, Rudinski. Called her after her dorm closed, *every single night.* It was locked to men, if you can believe that. Pay phone at the end of every floor. I can still hear this one girl who picked up, Jeezy, Beezy, something like that. Yelling at the top of her lungs. "Hey Bernie! Yo white boy callin'!""

That line perked Rudolph up. "Oh, hell."

"I can still hear Bernie's flip-flops smacking against the concrete," Joe said. "She always made this full sprint to get to the phone." Joe turned his eyes on his friend. "It was like winning this big grand prize, Rudinski," he said. His voice dropped. "And then I lost my nerve and gave her back."

Rudolph stood there thinking, *Poor, pitiful Joe. You are so damn trippin'.*

5. Lunch Tray Fight

Back in high school, Joe's dealings with blacks would have been best described as not very damn likely.

In 1978, Squire Boone High, thirty miles south of Louisville, had an enrollment of roughly eight hundred and ninety-three students. All but forty-three were white. Up until then, virtually everything Joe knew about those forty-three—all of them African-Americans—came from watching the samples offered on TV. They were pop singers, ballplayers, and actors. The actors mostly played pimps, prostitutes and gang members. In his four years at Squire Boone, Joe had came into direct contact with a grand total of two of them. One of the experiences lasted an entire school year. The other ran for something like thirty-seven minutes. Both of the blacks happened to belong to the same family. The girl's name was Angel French. The boy was Angel's younger brother, Marquis French III.

Joe met Marquis for the first time in the cafeteria.

The trouble started when Marquis, a tenth-grader, walked up to the roller stand to send his used lunch tray on to the kitchen. A male voice in the back of the cafeteria yelled out, "Hey French! Have a fry!"

Joe looked up just in time to see something sail high over his head and then, like a heat-seeking missile, *splop* onto Marquis brown cheek. Joe and every other person in the room saw that a large fry had been smothered with packets of mayonnaise until it resembled a vulgar lump of male ejaculate. The boy stood there, immobilized by the yelling of his name and then the sudden shock of being struck by something. The obscene mess soon succumbed to gravity. It slid down his cheek and fell to his tray.

A raucous chorus of hoots erupted from the bad-boys behind Joe. He didn't have to look; he recognized the voices. They were coming from Gil Barstow, "Butt" Heinert and that bunch. Their big fun was enhanced by the squeals of the girls sitting with them.

A few righteous kids who had seen the shitty act tried to counter the punks' celebration with half-hearted boos. Their voices were easily drowned out by the troublemakers, who would gladly trade one hour of detention for some boredom-busting yucks. Barstow, the ringleader and the actual fry-thrower, cackled, "Look at that! Hey French Fry! What you got running down your face!" The girls went to each other's ears, giggling over what the mayonnaise looked like.

Racial slurs weren't exactly new to Marquis.

"You go tone deaf," his father, Lawrence French, had told him back when his boy started fourth grade. "Ignore all the junk, 'cause there's plenty of it out there. Besides, you get mad and it'll be *you* who gets in trouble. And *they'll* win."

Until now, Marquis had managed to do just that, dodge all the mess. But this time, he couldn't pretend he wasn't humiliated. Not when he saw what slid off his cheek. Eyes half-blinded by embarrassment, he heaved his tray toward the voice.

Unfortunately for Joe, Marquis didn't have much of an arm. Joe was just turning back from taking in the jokesters when Marquis' tray T-boned the bridge of his nose. Joe was overwhelmed by a blinding flash and heard a lunch tray clatter hard on the floor.

Seeing that, the punks erupted with an even louder wave of hooting. "Holy shit!" one of the young rednecks howled. "He done hit a junior! Gonna get his black ass beat now!"

Joe, head sagged toward the floor as he tried to collect himself, noticed the bright red dots on the floor. They puzzled him until he saw another one of them fall through the air and land on the tile. It was blood—his own blood—dripping from a cut on his nose. His new Hilfiger shirt, the first really nice shirt he'd bought with his own money, had blood and food smeared all over it. *Ruined.* Joe sprung up and threw his tray back at the black kid. It missed Marquis' head, ricocheted off a concrete support column and flipped against the chest of Joycell Ann Berry. Until the moment she saw Marquis fling his tray, the new volunteer lunchroom monitor liked being around teens at Squire Boone. Tomorrow's future! At least that was what she used to think. She grabbed the two bastards and marched them across the hall and into the office.

In the end, both boys' good grades and spotless conduct records got them off the hook. J. Richard Spradling accepted Marquis' description of his being attacked, which was verified by a substitute teacher. The real instigators were the usual suspects. Spradling was only in his second year at Squire Boone and sure didn't need any race war over a goofball food fight. He offered to buy Berry a new blouse with his own money. She declined just before she quit. The issue was officially dropped after Marquis and Joe followed Spradling's orders and went through the totally bogus charade of shaking hands and making friends with each other.

Angel French gave Joe his first hint that African-American teenagers might actually be like other kids.

It was owing to Joe's own penchant for being a directional idiot, even here in his senior year. Ten minutes after his very first *Humanities* class got underway, here came Joe, bursting into Room 302—lost in the huge building again. The veteran teacher, Mr. Oliver, hardly missed a beat. Midway through his annual Intro to *Humanities* speech, he gestured the red-faced Joseph Normal to the last unoccupied desk in the room. It was next to the black girl.

6. Angel

He didn't know her name, but she wasn't a total stranger. Joe had seen her around school, most often in the third bus line, the one that the black kids stood in after school. Joe slid into his seat.

Angel had seen him before, too. Up close now, she saw he had pretty eyes for a boy—long, curling eyelashes—and as far as she knew, he didn't hang out with the punks.

"Hey," she said in a half-whisper, cocking her head toward him as Mr. Oliver continued his monologue. "I'm Angel."

He gave her a cheap chin wave. Put off by that kind of response, Angel dialed back her bright-white smile and turned to focus on her teacher.

The seating layout was totally rad. All of the desks were set side by side, creating one continuous row that snaked along three walls. Mr. Oliver's desk was in the middle of the big U that their desks formed. In effect, all of the students had a front row seat to their teacher. It was as democratic a classroom layout as any teacher at Squire Boone had ever dreamed up—no more back row full of slackers and self-appointed losers. No more front row stuffed with achievers and suck-ups.

Inside this theater-in-the round, the bearish Mr. Oliver shared his passion for the classics. Homer's "Odyssey." Debussy's heart-melting piano chords. His love for the subject material showed in Oliver's florid face, a face made even more ruddy by his long, slicked-back white hair. Most of the students actually paid attention to the man.

There was another big surprise in store for Joe. At the end of class, Mr. Oliver threw out a directive: "Ladies and gentlemen," he said, "this is the time when you need to determine your philosophy of life."

The words stopped Joe cold. Up until then, schoolwork had been about tests and homework and grades. The man was telling him *he* could decide what his own life would be about. The new concept blew Joe's mind.

Day Two came, and Joe entered late again. Late, but not *as* late. When he saw that the students were all in the same seats as the day before, he realized to his sour displeasure that he would be sitting next to the black girl for the whole semester. It wasn't anything personal. It was all just a total unknown to him, not having any idea how black people studied or thought or, for that matter, what they thought of *him*.

At lunch, Fitzer, a friend of Joe's who sat on the other side of the U, clued him in on something. "I ain't believin' who you're sitting next to," he hawed at him in the cafeteria.

"She's sitting next to *me*, okay?" Joe said defensively.

"That's not the person I'm talking about, Stooge," Fitzer snorted. "Didn't you recognize him? That's Richard Hazel. The Walking Time Bomb."

Joe had heard of the guy but thought it was just a myth. "He's real?"

"Well, *yah*. A real psycho."

Fitzer clued Joe in while they ate. Word was, with his parents' blessing, Hazel dropped out of Squire Boone the day he turned sixteen. Up and joined the Coast Guard. It took Hazel less than a month to get into it with another recruit, beat him up and locked him into one of the ship's food storage bins to teach him a lesson.

"The Coast Guard gave the guy the choice of either serving time in the stockade or getting his can shipped back to Squire

Boone," Fitzer explained. "So here he is."

"Truth?" Joe asked skeptically.

"C'mon, Normal. You think I could I make something like that up?"

Hazel hadn't pulled an Angel on Joe and tried to make friends with him. Joe saw the guy was way too preoccupied for that. Hazel sat there with his classbook, "Anthology of World Literature," standing up on his desk, while his eyes ate up what was tucked inside it—his *Field Weapons Guide*.

It took three days for Joe to do something about his growing curiosity about her. Having never seen a black person at close range before, he started sneaking peeks. He saw she had deep dimples when she smiled—at other people—and her skin was brown as a baseball glove. Shiny black bangs hung over her forehead, and longer hair curled down to her shoulders. The brown on her arms wasn't dirt, like some of the other kids used to say. It was more like a dye. He even noticed she smelled good. Perfumy.

While Joe was pulling in his freebies of her, he had no idea that Angel was blessed with some exceptional peripheral vision. Her big brown eyes could be aimed straight at Mr. Oliver, and still she could be aware of Joe on the fringes of her lateral range of vision. She knew Joe was stealing looks at her.

A week into the school year, she'd decided Joe was not only harmless, but kind of cute. She tried a new tack. Every day, at the start of class, she greeted him with a big cheesin' smile and a chirpy, "How *are* ya, Joe?" Joe dummied up, as the old folks used to say, doling out his short, curt, "'kay's" and "Jus' fine's." But the girl was relentless. Under her holding smile, Joe began adding a sheepish little grin to his "'kay's" and "Jus' fine's." He discovered there was a side benefit for him. It gave him a chance to take good long looks at her, without having to do it anymore on the sly.

That was all Angel needed. One day, out of the blue, she asked, "What's your sign?" And then it was, "What do you think of Michael Jackson?" Joe's stingy answers turned into phrases, and then whole sentences. Angel had her act down, where Joe was concerned. Making with the big teeth and shiny, attendant brown eyes, she acted impressed over anything that came out of his mouth. Joe could have been talking about President Carter's underwear and her face still would have lit up. At the end of class, day in and day out, her parting words became, "Tomorrow, Joe. Same time, same station."

Then the day came when Joe actually arrived early to class. He walked over to the other side of the "U" to kill five minutes with Fitzer and another friend, "Check" Checjek. Joe told the two of them a really lame joke, one that went all the way back to the Marx Brothers. Fitzer responded with his typical stone-face while Check, a tall drink of water, pushed his glasses up with his middle finger at Joe and grinned, "That's so damn spastic."

Out of nowhere, they heard a high-pitched burst of a female voice, followed by a whooping belly laugh. They all turned toward the door and saw Angel, juggling her books with one arm and trying to cover her giggling mouth with her free hand.

"That was so *clever*, Joe," she beamed to him as they sat down.

Joe spent the entire fifty minutes in a light-headed daze. *She thought he was funny!*

As soon as the bell ended class, Joe, heart hammering in his chest, blurted out, "See ya tomorrow, Angel. Same time, same station." Before she could pull her jaw back up, he was out the door and gone.

The following Monday, Angel made a point to hustle to *Humanities* early. She sat down next to Joe and angled her body toward him just enough to get his attention, and then she took her leap.

"Dig this, Joe," she smiled. She proceeded to tell Joe *her* joke, the one she'd spent an hour rehearsing at home the night before, after she shoo'd her sister out of their bedroom. Her little funny came from an old, water-stained riddle book she'd dug out of the school library.

"Why was the ink sad?" she recited to him in a straight face.

"I don't know," Joe played along, seizing the chance to let his eyes roam her brown face. "Why was the ink sad?"

"Because his mother was in the pen—and he didn't know how long her sentence was going to be!"

This time, *he* laughed, and Angel joined in with her own hearty brand of laughter. With her shaking, Joe noticed she had breasts.

Anybody else, Mr. Oliver would have shut down the fun and games before the clowns took over his class. This time, though, the flaming liberal stood there and allowed the cozy race relations scene to play out. The class saw Mr. Oliver's own amused countenance and added to it, breaking into a mushrooming mass laugh over the way Joe and Angel had their eyes locked on each other. *Lost in space.* The two of them finally were distracted by the cascades of laughter. As it died down, the master teacher cleared his throat and said, "And now, Mr. Normal and Miss French, if we may move away from your one-on-one stand-up routines..." They both straightened with embarrassment and then nosed themselves back into their *Anthology* books.

That night, at home, Joe replayed the scene over and over

in his head. So did she.

After that day, Joe even began stopping at her locker to gab and joke. Angel happily returned the favor. Their get-togethers offered an unusual sight at Squire Boone, a black girl and a white boy hanging out together. If the other students didn't see flirting, they saw something close to it. Hard looks came from some of the students. Joe put up with the stares. For him, Angel had become the coolest thing in school.

7. Blacks

The next year, when Joe headed off to college, he saw a lot more African-Americans than forty-three. It was unreal. Right there on the campus of Rolling Flatts State College, there were *hundreds* of them among RFSC's six thousand students.

The only reason he was enrolled at RFSC at all, which was on the far eastern side of the state, owed itself to the essay contest he'd entered and won. His "Why I Dream of Appalachia"—the essay shamelessly targeted entries from students elsewhere in the state—only brought him a $250 scholarship. It was the ego-boost of winning a writing contest, *and* knocking down help money from a college, that was huge to him.

So there he was, far away from the city of Louisville, in the foothills of the Appalachians. There were no fellow students from back home.

One thing he noticed right off the bat was that nearly all of the African-Americans kept to themselves. They didn't get involved in all the small-college hoopty-hoop, such as flag football games in the mud to celebrate—mud. And nearly always, the blacks did things in homogenous packs. Walked to class together. Gathered in one virtual clump to eat their meals in the Student Union. Sat together at concerts and ballgames. As far as Joe could tell, the blacks seemed happy enough with that arrangement, free to joke and enjoy each other's company.

The gathering place for the first-year black students was the sidewalk in front of McAfee Hall, the freshman women's dorm. Three weeks into the fall semester, on a warm evening, Joe came into their midst. As he approached them to pass by, all the happy talk and giggling muted down. One of the brothers, seeing the apprehensive white guy passing through, chided the feistier members of the group with a, "Come on now, act right."

Bigger laughs.

A skinny girl perched on the low stone wall heard the brother's bossy order and busted out with her own laugh. Somebody else said, "Y'all need to behave." *Group laugh.* That line struck Joe as funny, too—*people his age being told not to laugh by one of their own.* His sedate expression gave way to a little smile. The skinny girl saw the white guy had a sense of humor and decided to get bold. She pointed her thumb at the girl whose laugh started all the silliness and told the white dude, apologetically, "She don't know no better. She from Owensboro."

They were all surprised by what happened next. Instead of cranking up his walk to hustle away from them, the white dude *stopped.* With that, the skinny girl on the wall, Mareesha Stebbins, tried some jive on this guy with the blond hair and green eyes.

"*You're* not from Owensboro, are you, Baby?" she teased.

Joe felt the heat sear across his face after being called a sultry, "Baby." His only response was a "Nope." He tagged it with a polite smile.

Another female let out an admonishing, "*Girl!*"

Mareesha's chestnut eyes stayed on him. She was amazed that the shy guy got any words out of his mouth at all. When the silence hung, Joe got the feeling he was butting in on their private get-together. He threw out a "See ya later," and waved a casual goodbye with one of his textbooks. As he walked on through them. Mareesha kept her eyes on the nice-looking guy. "Dude might be worth gettin' to know—if he ever comes back," she mouthed to the girl next to her.

It took a little more than a week for Joe to pick up on their pattern—the same group of students gathered at the wall on Tuesday and Thursday afternoons. On his second Thursday through, Joe decided to try and make friends. He summoned his friendship with Angel French to bolster him. Angel had thought he was pretty funny, he reasoned. Maybe these people would, too.

Ahead of him, he saw a couple of white guys pass through the knot of blacks and keep going. Following on their heels, apparently for protection, a white coed hustled through the same bottleneck, arms clutching her books to her chest to protect her boobs.

Think of Angel, Joe reminded himself. *Graduation Day.*

That was easy enough for him to do. He'd gone looking for her right after the ceremonies were over, shouldering his way through the happy mob of students and relatives. He saw her through the glass exit doors. She was outside, talking to well-wishers. Angel had spotted him quickly and motioned him to come outside. He came out, but then hesitated, seeing that her family was drawing in, surrounding her. She saw him hesitate and high-heeled her long purple gown in his direction. When she got close enough for him to hear her above the din, she had some fun.

"My brutha!" she shouted.

The come-back was automatic.

"My *sistuh!*"

She latched onto one of her black girlfriends to take their picture. Joe and Angel had stood there, arms around each other's waist, and proudly posed.

Picture taken, she kept her arm where it was and beamed at

him, "We're practically related now, my fellow Squire Boone alum." Joe couldn't miss the quiver at her chin. She made a small lean over to him, and when he didn't kiss her on the cheek, she grasped the tassels on his graduation cap and pretended to straighten them. Joe at last relaxed enough to respond to her hug. It was his first hug ever with a black girl. Angel was so delighted with Joe's reciprocating that she held him and turned it into a rocking embrace. When she offered her cheek to him again, he went for it. For the first time in his life, Joe planted a kiss on a black girl. He didn't know how long he was supposed to hold it, but Angel certainly did. With her family looking on, she pulled back quickly and let out a syrupy "Awww." Then, abruptly, she followed her own impulses and gave him a quick smack on the cheek.

Joe backed off and let her relatives take her over again.

"Forget Rolling Flatts, Joe-Joe," she'd yelled over them in a tease. "Stop by UK if you ever want to check out a *good* school!" She held her eyes on him for a second longer. "I'll show you the hot spots."

"Sure thing!" he yelled back, not meaning it. The super-intelligent girl had a full ride, and was going places.

So Joe's vision of Angel had come in handy here on the sidewalk in front of McAfee Hall.

He saw that skinny Mareesha was on that wall again. This time, Joe stopped dead in front of her.

8. Joe Makes Friends

"Hey," Joe said in a soft, easy voice to Mareesha, then turned to share the greeting with everybody else. Those with their backs to him jolted, caught off guard by the return of the lone wolf white guy. Mareesha answered with a, "Hey back." She was thrilled that she hadn't scared him off.

"My name is Joe Normal," he said.

"He said Joe Normal," a voice mocked.

"Shut up," Mareesha smiled, turning toward the critic. Then, looking back at Joe, she introduced herself. "Pleased ta meet'cha, Joe Normal," she said, acting just as formal as Joe had. She offered him a hammy handshake. "My name is Mareesha Stebbins. Everybody calls me Stick." She hadn't forgotten his first visit. "I'm not from Owensboro, either."

Several of the others—they were almost all freshmen, like himself—contributed a few lame "Hey's" of their own. No other handshakes were offered, but Joe gladly accepted their greetings—despite one that sounded totally snide. Joe guessed it came from the brother he had noticed the week before, the one who had given him the bad eye when he passed through them.

"C'mon, now," Mareesha implored the group. "Show the man some love."

When no one walked away, Joe took that as an invitation to stay.

"Anybody here from Louisville?" he threw out. "I'm from right outside, Boonesville."

He got back four nods and a "Yo." Plus a stare from the hateful guy. Stick piped up, proudly telling Joe she was from

Maysville. Pronouncing it like the native she was, it came out,"Maysvull." She gave the white guy a little test. "You ever hear of Maysvull, Joe?"

"Sure," Joe said. "Rosemary Clooney's hometown, right?"

A few bust-out laughs. A low voice tittered, "He said Rosemary Clooney."

"Yeah, that too, Joe," Stick helpfully. "But I was thinking more about the Underground Railroad. Maysvull was one of the places to cross over." She had some more fun with him. "You know what I mean when I say 'crossing over,' right Baby?"

"Sure," he said. "Crossing the Ohio River. Slaves escaping."

Stick turned to the others. "See?" she said. "Some white folk know what time it is." *Assorted laughs.* She gave a flirty pull at her long neck chain and said, "Bet you never met a Mareesha before, have ya Joe?"

He shrugged and said, "Nope."

"Any time you want to discuss the Railroad in detail," she performed, "you look me up."

Joe heard a couple of low whistles and snorts. The girl who stood behind Stick sneaked a hard pinch on the girl's butt. Stick let out a squeal and then noticed Joe's red face. "Just messin' with ya, Baby," she said.

Joe gave her an easygoing, "No sweat." That cool remark scored style points with a few of them. Even the hostile guy, the one who had pretended to study the dorm's windows while the white dude was there, turned around, impressed by the way the dude was hanging.

Joe went with the joke he'd heard his first very week of school. "Welcome to Rolling Flatts State College. Set your clocks back twenty years."

The freshmen had all probably heard his ragged-out line five thousand times by then, but the polite laughter came anyway. The next ten minutes was chit-chat, anything that hit common ground—first year in college, Louisville connections, oddball faculty members. And of course RFSC's Stone Age dorm rules that required women to be in by eleven on weeknights, one o'clock on Friday and Saturday and Midnight on Sunday. With no males allowed past the lobby, *ever*. When the small talk dried up again into long pauses, Joe got the message—time for the white guy to move on so they could get to some straight-up rap. He gave them a loose "See ya later." Several responding "Laters," plus a "Later, Baby" from Stick, sent him on his way. Joe walked away, thankful as he could be for his Angel.

The following Tuesday, he returned to their hangout and *really* stunned them—he stayed for over twenty minutes. After three weeks of Joe's checking in, some of them were beginning to think this Joe Normal was the real deal. Joe learned their names. It was work, since it seemed like everybody in the group had a nickname. For example, there was "Heavy" (Drew Williamson) "Wheelie" (Georgella Griffin) and of course "Stick" (Mareesha Stebbins).

Joe had his handful of white friends, too, but if he saw one of his sidewalk friends sitting alone in class, Joe took a seat next to the brother or sister. That move earned him some bonifieds all by itself. By winter, virtually all of the campus' African-American students knew what the heck a Joe Normal was.

"Why don't we give this group a nickname?" he asked one chilly afternoon. "I'm thinking, 'The Stonewall Gang.' Get it? *Stone? Wall?*"

Boos—good-natured, but still boos—pelted him. Joe had Option 2 ready to go.

The "Loud Crowd," he shouted. "How about that?" Now

that they liked. "The Loud Crowd" was born, with Joe right in the middle of it.

When Joe returned for his sophomore year, he found that most of them were back. But now, they collected on the brick terrace at the entrance to the Student Union building—no reason to act like a bunch of rookies and stand in front of a freshman dorm again. Heavy, the big guy from Covington, Kentucky—just across the Ohio River from Cincinnati—was now a soph, like Joe. His weight had climbed to a good three hundred jolly pounds. Stick, now his girlfriend, didn't appear to have put on a single ounce. "Hurtt Man," aka Isaiah Hurtt, was there for his second year, too. Hurtt, a slick dresser from Louisville, had the Hollywood looks and jeri curls. He was anxious to check out the new crop of freshman girls.

By then, the Loud Crowd had made Joe as legit as a white guy could be with them—they gave *him* a nickname. It was pulled straight from the *Star Wars* movies. They called their street-quality stand-in for Luke Skywalker, "Jedi Joe."

Joe had an open invitation from a few of the brothers in his dorm to stop by their rooms and shoot the breeze. For their amusement as much as anything else, roomies Heavy and Hurtt Man had got into the habit of asking Joe his opinion on things. Sports, politics, whatever. Joe didn't know any more about current events than they did, but that wasn't the point. It was a real novelty for brothers like Heavy and Hurtt Man to get straight-up answers from a white guy.

"Lay the white take on us, Jedi," they said.

They didn't mind pulling Joe's chain from time to time. "Who's smarter, blacks or whites?" Hurtt Man once brazenly asked him. By then, Joe knew a Hurtt Man set-up when he heard it.

"Oh, African-Americans, by far," Joe played along. He made his answer sound as official as he could. "Tests prove it."

That b.s. drew snickers, which grew into hoots and hand slaps.

"I *told* you the dude was a brother," Heavy wailed at Hurtt Man as he reveled in his own laughing fit.

"Here!" Hurtt Man grinned, raising his own hand to demand a Joe Normal high-five.

Females were a big topic of conversation, of course. Who was the most bootylicious, who had the best rack, et cetera. Joe backed off that topic. The brothers didn't ask his take on the sistuhs, anyway.

It was the Prentice Gray Incident that reminded Joe how some people really were. It played out at lunchtime in the Student Union.

Gray was the student council president, just a semester away from locking down his business degree. Gray's career goal was to graduate and immediately slide into a cushy administration job. Preferably something like, "Assistant to the Dean of Students." At a starting pay of say, twenty-five thousand. That would be sweet. Especially since the job didn't exist yet.

Joe knew Gray. He had run into him the year before, when Gray campaigned for office. Candidate Gray asked the freshman where he was from and, lo and behold, Joe's old high school was right down the road from his very own Big Elm. *Rival.* Learning about the Squire Boone connection, Gray had really swelled up. "Man," he told Joe, "we *owned* you. Sports-wise, academics-wise, cheerleader-wise, you name it." Then he hustled on to the next potential voter. With his walk-off, Joe had made a mental note. *Prentice Gray: Moron.*

Now Gray was up there in the raised dining area, the one that was reserved for administration and faculty. As usual, Gray was shlepping to the power brokers, re-filling coffee cups. He had a pot in each hand, right for regular, left for decaf. As he topped off Dean Chester's cup, Gray took a glimpse at the students below and nearly sloshed hot decaf on the Dean's privates. Here was that loser, the Normal guy from Squire Boone. Jim, John whatever. *Eating with the blacks.* Gray's eyes bulged. Dean Chester, wary over Gray's pot-handling skills, followed Prentice's gawking expression out into the dining area to see what the problem was. Feeling the Dean's eyes on him, Gray thunked his coffee pots down and went into action.

By the time Gray came down the riser steps and crossed the floor, Joe was done with his meal and heading for the door. Gray got to him in just enough time to stick his palm straight up in front of Joe, in a traffic cop STOP gesture. He gave Normal—he still hadn't remembered the turkey's first name—his trademark smile. Joe came to a halt, wondering what Gray was up to.

Gray moved in so close that Joe could smell the garlic from the cafeteria's Special of the Day: "Roman Rolling Flatts Holiday."

"Hi, Prentice" Joe said. He waited the guy out.

"How'd you do that?" Gray said.

Joe looked at him, puzzled.

Gray gave a little motion of his head, back toward the table Joe had just left. "*You* know," he said in a secretive tone. "*That.*" He screwed his eyes down a little harder on Normal, bad-ass style, in case the Dean was taking this in.

When Gray's head tilted back toward Joe's lunch table,

Joe knew exactly what Gray was asking. By then, with his freshman year under his belt, Joe had taken in plenty of dirty looks from people, just for hanging out with the black students. He proceeded to act as dense as a bowling ball, curious to see how Gray would put this attitude of his into words.

"Do *what*, Prentice?"

Gray let out a frustrated breath, then came back hard and accusing. "*You* know," he said. His eyes scanned the area slowly for eavesdroppers, found none, and returned to the loser. This time his jaw was so tight his mouth could barely grunt out the words. "Sit with *them.*"

Joe was enjoying this perverse exchange. He took his answer straight at the guy. "I just asked them," he said. He shrugged his shoulders to show Gray what an easy thing that was to do, ask actual black people if he could share a meal with them.

Gray's face couldn't mask his annoyance. He blinked at Normal, waiting for a *real* answer. When he didn't get one, he huffed, "Thanks a fuckin' lot," and headed back to the admin dining territory. If Chester asked him what the hell the white guy was doing down there eating with the Negras, he'd just shovel Dean-o some b.s., tell him the Normal kid was taking a student poll. Was asking them something like, "*What do African-American students like best about Rolling Flatts?*"

Joe's answer burned at Gray for the rest of the day. As for Joe, he filed the question—How did he manage to eat with the blacks?—away for future reference. He couldn't believe it. *Having to explain treating blacks like real people.*

For weeks after that, whenever he sat down here with his friends, he was reminded of Gray's amazingly brain-dead question.

9. A View from the Street

Joe saw her for the first time on a Friday afternoon in September, along Pine City's 25 mph main drag. He had been walking on the other side of the street, mumbling out the future tense forms of the verb ganar (*"to win, to earn"*). On his way to his last class of the day, Intermediate Spanish, in the recently renovated and re-named Abraham Lincoln-Terryella R. Bottoms Language Arts Building. The second part of the name had been added, thanks to a generous contribution to RFSC ($1.4 million) from the J.T. Bottoms Construction Co.

J.T. Bottoms, Terryella's husband going on four years, was one of the state's ascending road contractors and campaign contributors.

Everything about Terryella Rainey Bottoms was big or poofy or both—eyes, lips, hair, boobs, rear end. She was fourteen years younger than. J.T., but after two angry marriages, he had finally come to the conclusion that, if matrimony was so much of a pain in the ass, he might as well get himself a trophy wife and enjoy the scenery.

Joe was just a few steps from taking a running jump over the sidewalk's wall and trotting over to what the Rolling Flatts' students had already labelled "The Trophyella Building." That's when he glanced across the street and saw the bloc of young black women. There were seven or eight of them, walking the sidewalk two-by-two, approaching from the other direction. He could tell they were freshmen, from all their giggling and gawking. There wasn't a single book among them—a sure tip-off that the coeds were done with classes for the week and out to kick up their heels a little.

They planned to hit every shop on Main Street—all four stores—and after that, they'd slide into the town's only semi-authentic pizza place, Tony and Bitsy's Italian Pizzeria and Dry Cleaning. And of course, they were all up for checking out whatever buff guys they found along the way.

Joe took in a mix of faces, hairstyles, body shapes. It didn't occur to him, after spending so much time with the Loud Crowd, that these ladies would be offended by his staring. There at the front of their group, Jelise Henry and Ameya Kendricks were the first to pick up on the white weirdo. RF student, they assumed, since the dude was toting a couple of books. Jelise, eyes aimed his way, elbowed Ameya. "Whitey out winda shoppin'."

Ameya, the tallest female in the pack at five-ten, gave the guy a glance. "God, he's even talking to himself," she whispered out of the side of her mouth. "Total psycho."

"'Nuther damn White Lech," Jelise spat out.

They had no idea that Joe was working on, "*ganaré, ganarás, ganará.*"

Ameya suddenly gave out a shriek. Her big shopping bag of a purse had slipped off her shoulder and when she grabbed at it, it went upside down. Everything was tumbling out, rolling and skittering across the walk.

Ameya blurted out an "Oh, Shit!" and hopped back from the debris, trying not to step on anything. There it all went—lipstick, mirror, hairbrush, wallet, deodorant, breath mints, tissues, play rape whistle, makeup case, personal feminine products, extra pair of panties. The girlfriends who were walking behind them, lost in their own mini-conversations, plowed into Ameya and Jelise like bumbling police in an old silent movie.

Ameya dropped to her knees to go after her things.

The others saw the huge mess—*Purse crisis!*—and followed

her to the pavement, whooping and laughing, pajama party-style. Joe couldn't help but break into a grin.

Ameya felt her face flush with embarrassment, as she stretched toward the gutter to retrieve a tampon. She cried out in mock panic, "Save my cork! It's my last one!" As the girls crouched and bent down to help, Joe saw the girl in the back. He couldn't take his eyes off of her. She had honey-colored skin, high cheekbones, and an oversized upper lip. But what made her truly different were her eyes. The eye fold made her look slightly Asian. He could tell from the way her jeans fit snug at her thighs that she was athletic, might have even been, like him, a runner on a track team back in high school, or even here at Rolling Flatts. She was wearing a Yankees ball cap, with a short tuft of frizzled ponytail that poked out the opening in the back. Tiny ears made her hoop earrings look huge.

"White Lech gettin' his jollies lookin' us over," Jelise puffed as she took another look across the street while at the same time she threw Ameya's stuff back in her purse. The other girls' eyes came up, searching. "Pervert across the street," Jelise instructed, tipping her head in that direction. "Probably start jerkin' off any minute."

The girl with the Asian looks followed the eyes of the other women. The white guy didn't look like a pervert to her. In fact, he was looked pretty good.

Ameya's purse re-loaded, one of the other young women, Kym Suggs, yelled out, "Come on, Ladies, hell. Let's shop!"

They resumed their walk. After traveling less than thirty feet, the girl who thought Joe didn't look like a pervert had a notion. "Rock," she announced to no one in particular, faking a limp. She went down to one knee, pretending to dig something out of her sneaker. When she looked across the street again, she saw he was taking her in. She liked his blond hair and reddish mustache that was trimmed to show off the notch at his lips. Caught, he turned away, faking a look at something down the street. Sexy boy, she saw, was interested in her.

"Earth to Bernie Armstrong!"

Bernie looked up the sidewalk. The others were a good fifty feet ahead of her.

"Get a move on, girl!" Ameya yelled at her roomie. "We'll find you something a lot better than that White Lech at the dance."

"We're wastin' time!" somebody else barked.

With that, Joe remembered his Spanish class and hurdled over the wall, he jogging toward the Trophyella Building. He had no idea that the girl on the sidewalk with the shoe problem had turned in his direction again, just in time to admire the nice, narrow buns that disappeared through the door.

10. The Deal

"No you didn't!"

Denise tossed her dirty underwear, including that African print thong that made Rudy drool all over himself, into the washing machine. Her comment was aimed toward the kitchen—which was just on the other side of the washing machine.

"Yes I *did*," Rudolph shot back, giving some of the woman's sass back to her. "I told him I'd help him look and I will." He wasn't exactly thrilled about joining Joe in his search for Mystery Girl, but his word *was* his word.

Here it was, eleven-thirty on Saturday morning, and Rudolph had just woken up from his late-night visit to Joe's. Denise had blown into the bedroom and given him a booming, throaty "Mornin'!'" As soon as he sat up, she got to stripping the bed, tugging the bottom sheet right out from under him. Rudolph glumly knew what clean sheets meant. *No playtime for at least two nights.* Keep things fresh and clean!

After pouring his cup of coffee at the little dinette table, Rudolph was ready to give Denise the play-by-play of his funky middle-of-the-night visit with Joe. Denise's fine mess of a dog, Sir Pepi, lay curled up at its Mama's feet.

Denise leaned back against the washing machine as it chugged and sloshed away. Her arms crossed just under her pink sports bra. Although the only other articles of clothing she was wearing were a pair of fresh pink walking socks and a generic pair of panties, she felt more or less safe from Rudy, after giving the man some the night before. Her eyes held on him, waiting for him to detail his visit to Joe's.

"I'll check out a few places, ask some questions," he said.

"No biggie."

In the ten months since she met Rudy, Denise had never understood why this white dude was near the top of her man's friends list. When it came to weird, Denise considered Joe Normal *Exhibit A.*

Denise took her pink sweats from the dryer and began pulling them on. "You know how crazy this sounds?" she said, grunting and wiggling until they were finally up and over her behind. She anticipated a smart remark about her growing booty, so she caught his eye and came in with a preemptive strike. "Don't say it."

He didn't. What he did say, was, "Well, that's because Joe *is* crazy," Rudolph chuckled. Then, getting serious, "Not really. His head's still shook up, that's all."

"I know," Denise said. "You told me enough times." She leaned back against the washer again and rehashed it. "Wife shot dead by a cross-eyed hunter."

"Legally-blind," he corrected her again.

Her next comment was going to sound bitchy, but she couldn't help herself. "You've spent enough time letting him cry to you about it." She regretted her words as soon as they came out of her mouth. She hadn't wanted to sound like a bitch. Besides, Rudy was going to do what he was going to do, she knew that. She came back bitchy *again.* "That doesn't make it *your* problem, Rudolph Barnes."

He heard the *Rudolph Barnes* and tightened up. Whenever Denise called him *Rudolph Barnes* instead of Rudy, he knew the woman was heated. He tried another sell.

"Guy's just lovesick over an old picture," he said. "I'll only tag along with him until his fever passes."

Denise's pessimistic stare stayed on him, so he threw

something else out.

"You wouldn't believe how he was eyeballing her picture in that yearbook," Rudolph said. "Like he was hypnotized."

"What's he going to do if he *does* find her after all that time?" Denise said. "Ask her if he can carry her blood pressure pills for her?"

"Cute," Rudolph said. He let his eyes travel like a Mars Rover, all over Denise's hills and valleys. "He asked. I said yes. End of story." He stepped over to the sink and got a glass of water. "Tell you what I'll do. Before we hit the road, I'll lay some tough love on him."

She went to a hook on the wall and pulled down her lavender windbreaker. It was perfect for power walking on cool April mornings like this one, when the sun had become strong enough to make up the difference. "Tough as in *what?*"

Rudolph dredged up some points that had occurred to him over at Joe's. "As in, this girl just might've found herself a husband in the last thirty-somethin' years. As in, reminding him the girl might not even be *alive* by now."

"You don't think that's occurred to the guy yet?" Denise said.

Rudolph could ogle her all day in her loaded-up bra and sweats, especially now that they were easily one size too small. "Maybe not," he said.

She rolled her eyes on that comeback.

"I'm telling you, Denise, he was standing in his living room, talking about this Bernie like she was still a girl! I told him, 'Girlfriend might not be much to look at after all this time, anyway. Hell, she's gotta be close to fifty.'"

The only sound in the apartment came from the industrious churn of the washing machine.

"*Really*," Denise said. "*I'm* almost forty-six. What does that make *me*, Rudy?"

Rudy thought about that, and came back with a little diplomacy. "Girl could have had a hard damn life, that's all I saying."

"You're going on fifty-one, yourself, y'know," she pointed out.

Rudolph, the comedian, tried some humor to smooth things out. "You know what I told him?" he said, offering a tentative grin.

"What?" she answered, deliberately yanking her jacket zipper up to her throat.

"I said, 'Hell, Joe, If all you want is a quick hook-up with a sistuh, I can fix you up there. There's plenty'a young thangs out there who need help with the rent."

Denise gave that remark an unamused expression and checked the time on her phone. Scootie would be waiting downstairs. She waited for him to throw her a compliment--*any* kind of compliment.

Rudolph immediately stepped on another land mine. "I'll take experience over youth any day," he said. He tried to pat her hip but Denise pinched the top of his hand so hard he snatched it back.

"Thanks a lot, Mister Barnes," she said, gritting her teeth. She grabbed her water bottle off the kitchen counter and bounced on the balls of her feet out the door.

Scootie was waiting down on the second-floor landing. Denise greeted her with a determined, "Let's do it" and a fist bump, and they headed out.

Scootie lived on the second floor, just beneath Denise's

place. The woman didn't have a live-in, but she had two grown sons—twins Martin and Luther. She didn't see much of them, unless they got in enough hot water to send them back to their mother's crib to crash for awhile.

The women's "weight management summit"—Scootie's tongue-in-cheek term for their walks around the neighborhood—had helped Scootie hang on to her hourglass figure. The only thing was, Scootie owned a big hourglass. The woman was only five-two, but she easily weighed one hundred and nine-five pounds. As for Denise, her dress size had zoomed from an 8 to a 12 and sometimes even a 14, thanks mainly to her late-night shenanigans with Rudy.

The ladies' walking route, a series of straight lines that made a four-block rectangle, took fifty minutes to complete—as long as they didn't run into any other friends who just *had* to chat with them along the way.

Scootie waited until they reached their first red light and then, true to her own taste in conversation, went straight for the juicy stuff.

"Heard a lot of racket coming from your place last night," she said in her screechy, suggestive voice.

Denise ignored her, walking in place while she waited for the light to change. Scootie was just getting started. "You sure you're good to go, after all that *exercise* you two got in last night?"

This was Scootie's lucky day. Denise was still trying to cool down from Rudy's *I'll take experience over youth* remark. "I took care of him," Denise allowed.

"I could tell, girl," Scootie said. "Together for what, five months? And still plenty of screamin' and moanin'. Who was on top, him or you?"

"Which time?" Denise joked. Scootie laughed and the two of them put together a hand slap. "Six months. The problem is, when we get back home, he'll want some more."

That tidbit kept Scootie's motor revved. "Oh yeah?" she said, raising her eyebrows to Denise for more.

Denise's lips loosened with her frustration over Rudy. "Man'll get all grabby again. He'll blow out something like, (Denise took on a mock-baritone voice) 'Hey Baby, now this is *on time*. Here you are, all sweaty, and so am I."

"Hoo!" Scootie egged her on. "That's a man for ya. Can't never get enough."

Denise kept her rap going, twisting her torso toward the other woman each time she thought of a new complaint. "Don't get me wrong, Scoot," she said. "I like it with him. But it's like, if I let him know I want to do it, and then, for whatever reason, I wind up *not* doing it, he gets a damn *attitude*."

"Umm-HMM."

"*And*," Denise added, going to a rhythmic sistuh head bop, "just because I don't do it when I *said* I would, he thinks that means he got a *free play* comin'."

"Aayyy-men!" Scootie seconded.

"You hear me?" Denise said for emphasis. "It's like I *owe* him one."

"On damn *credit!*" Scootie came back.

They both laughed.

Scootie was absolutely loving this. Denise and Rudy's lovemaking the night before had provided the only entertainment of the night for her. And then there was the drama that unfolded right after that, when she looked out her bedroom window and saw Rudy drive out of the parking lot, headed who knew where.

"I don't care how dumb or smart or rich or poor they are, Girl," Scootie told Denise. "Every man I ever met had his brains hangin' between his legs."

Now *that* was downright on'ry to Denise, but, on'ry or not, she had to nod in agreement. Tired of that subject, she put another complaint out there, Rudy's new project. In less than three blocks, Scootie knew all about Rudy's promise to help his middle-aged white friend find his one-time college squeeze. His *recently widowed* white friend. When Denise put that fact out there, plus the bonus—the girl they would be looking for was black—Scootie *really* drilled down.

"What's this old geezer Joe look like?"

"Green eyes, salt-and-pepper hair."

"Beer gut, I guess?"

"Not really. Okay build for his age, for as little as I see him," Denise said. "Fifty-ish."

"Good-payin' job?"

Denise caught on to Scootie's interrogation and a strange possessiveness came over her. She tried to tamp Scootie back down with a, "Nothing special about him, really."

"I *said*, good-payin' job?"

Denise shrugged. "He's been working at Max-It a lot longer than Rudy, plus he's a manager or somethin', so—probably so."

"*Lord Jesus*," Scootie said, making a faint whistle between her lips. "And you ain't never told me nuthin' about him?"

"I just told you everything I know."

"Girl, I don't care if he's white, black or polka dot. Damn, throw a sistuh a rope! Gimme his number." She tried to be funny. "Don't they say white meat's better for ya, anyway?"

Denise walked faster, kicking herself for opening her mouth to the girl.

"Wida-man, with no woman," Scootie lobbied. *"Has* to be looking for a port in a storm. You tell him I got his port right here. He don't have to go off on some damn time-trip lookin' for an old broken-down girlfriend."

Denise gave her a dubious look.

"I *mean* it girl," Scootie said. "Give him my damn number."

"I'll do it," Denise said, just to put a clamp on the girl's mouth. No way was she going to pass Joe on to hot-box Scootie.

11. Joe Calls

When they arrived back at the Valley Vista Apartments, Denise didn't waste any time "Later'ing" Scootie. The 1.4-mile walk she'd just finished with her girlfriend, plus that teeth-rattling hookup with Rudy the night before, had taken their toll. She unlocked the door to Apt. 307 and Sir Pepi raced to meet her.

She forced her body to bend down far enough to pet her dog's curly head. Rudy was parked on the couch in front of the TV, locked into a twenty-year-old football game being played all over again on cable. She went catty with him. "Who's winning?"

Rudy got out a, "Pittsburgh just kicked..." before he caught on. He hit the pause button and looked up at her. "Looks like your walk wiped you out."

"It did," she admitted. "So did last night," she added, just in case the man had another hook-up in mind. She couldn't wait to slide into a tub of steaming-hot bubble bath. "Your boy call yet?"

"Naw," Rudy said. It was curious to him that she should even ask, after the way she'd bad-mouthed him an hour ago.

"I thought the man was on fire for Mystery Sistuh," she said.

Rudolph ho-hummed it. "I'm just chillin'. If the man calls, he calls."

"Okey dokey," Denise said, not believing the man for a second. She began to step toward the master bath but stopped long enough to say, "I had a thought while Scootie and I were out." She unzipped her jacket to make sure Rudy was paying attention. The only dry area of her sports bra was a thin vertical l pink strip that ran up and down her cleavage; the rest of her bra was dark burgundy *wet*. Rudy paid attention.

"Why don't you let me help out with your buddy?" she asked.

"Say *what*?"

"I mean it, Rudy. You really don't want to spring this guy on her *stone cold*, do you? After all this time?"

"I thought that was the whole idea," he said. "Find her, hook the two of 'em up, then get on with my life."

"Think about it. Girl hasn't seen her boy in thirty-something years—and then one day he shows up and knocks on her front door? She'd have a heart attack, Rudy!"

"I didn't think of that," he confessed.

""It takes a woman to read a woman, right?" she pitched. "Even if you do find her, you can't just walk up to her and say, (Again, using her Pretend Rudy Baritone) 'Hey Baby, what up since Nineteen-Eighty?'"

Rudy's smile turned into a chuckle. Denise could always kill him with her impressions. Once the ball got rolling, he was gasping for air between volleys of cackling. He shook his head at her.

The Charge of the Light Brigade sounded from the phone on the coffee table.

"Speak of the devil," he chuckled to Denise.

Denise's damp muscles were calling for hot water but she stayed put.

Rudolph answered and made some yadda-yadda before cutting Joe off. "I got this idea I want to throw at you, Cool," he said. "What do you think about having Denise help out?"

She gave his shoulder a push, irritated by the way he put it. *His* idea.

"Sure," Rudolph said. He hung up and smiled at Denise. "He'll be here around eight."

"*Tonight?*" she asked, surprised.

"Tonight. Like I told you, he wants to get this rollin' ASAP."

"I suppose I could get in a nap this afternoon," she said. She got another wild comic hair. "News Alert! White guy coming to black folks' apartments—at night!"

"C'mon," Rudy said, "He's been here before."

"Not after dark he ain't,'' she said. "White guys don't come to this side of town unless they want to buy something."

"Bad," he smirked. "You're bad."

She moved on to the bathroom, where she had to wrestle the clingy, cold bra off. Something occurred to her and she pushed the bathroom door open just wide enough for her voice—and not any bare skin—to get out. "I was talking about white guys coming here to buy *drugs*, not the other thing."

"If you say so," Rudolph's voice came back.

12. At the Dance

Rolling Flatts' students stayed on campus for the weekend whenever the Fighting Pioneers had a home football game, and RFSC's Friday Night Dance came in as a nice prelude to the fun. Other than The Fightin' Pioneer theater downtown, which showed first-run movies, there was little else for students to do. Especially if they didn't have a car. That being the case, most of the freshmen and sophomores wound up at the Friday dance.

There was a good crowd on the Friday that Joe had stared at the sisters on the sidewalk. There to entertain them was a live DJ, who offered a spinning overhead disco ball, a stop-action strobe light and plenty of tapes—both 8-track *and* the new cassettes.

Joe went to the Student Union's cafeteria/dance hall by himself, more out of boredom than anything else. An hour after he arrived, he was still standing there holding up the wall that led to the restrooms. It was his own fault, never having learned to dance worth a lick.

The DJ, a radio major from the hills of western Pennsylvania who billed himself as "The Bomb," played his tapes from the elevated dining area—the same location where Prentice Gray did all his meal-time sucking-up to the admin and faculty. The Bomb followed a format of running four up-tempo disco and soul songs, followed by a slow dance so couples could get up close and personal.

Most of the black first-and second-year students showed up for the dance, since so few of them went home on weekends. They not only craved the socializing; fewer than half of them had this kind of deal back home—safe, clean streets, cozy little grills to hang out in, a campus that was manicured like a city park. They formed a black island in a sea of white dancers. Hurtt Man saw Jedi Joe braced against the wall and motioned *over here.* Joe wagged his head and mouthed out, as he had the year before, *Can't dance.* Hurtt Man made a face and threw his hand at him before turning back to his friends.

Joe was thinking about heading back to his dorm when the glaring white light splashed in from the lobby—latecomers. He recognized them. *The girls from Main Street.* He picked her out while they stood there getting their bearings and adjusting their eyes to the darkness. The women were all decked out now, had makeup on and wore flashier clothes than what he'd seen out on the street that afternoon. Sequined tops, fancy sandals, high-waist jeans, all that. The slender girl with the Asian eyes had bumped up her game, too. She wore lip gloss that matched her red leather jacket and had gone upscale with sequined jeans. She wore even bigger hoops than he'd seen out on the street. She'd ditched her ball cap. Now her hair was gelled shiny, with a hard part to one side. That, he *really* liked.

The girls went to the cluster of blacks and stood in a loose circle, then goofed to the song, lipping the words and doing some uninspired arm spelling to *YMCA.* The beat helped them loosen up while they mingled and checked in with their other friends.

Bernie Armstrong was moving to a mild personal groove of her own, all the while scanning the room. She saw the boy and hesitated just long enough to make sure it was him, the guy from Main Street. She cleverly positioned herself so that as she danced with her girlfriends, she could look past their shoulders and keep her eyes in his direction—and he would be able to see her. She saw he wore snug black jeans and a nice pullover that showed off a trim build. At first she thought he was waiting for a date or a girlfriend to come out of the restroom. Two songs later, she felt a lifting relief—he apparently was here by himself. With that thought, she picked up her happy chatter and got even more animated with her girlfriends, just so he could figure out she wasn't there with a guy.

The Bomb called for another slow song.

Just as Kenny Rogers was getting into *Lady*, Joe entered the blacks' territory. Most of the Caucasians did a double-take, seeing the whacked-out white dude wade in with the blacks. Heavy, who was in a slo-mo embrace with Stick, stopped his swaying long enough to send out a surprised smile and a two-finger *peace* sign. A sistuh gave Joe an encouraging shout. They all kept their eyes on Jedi Joe to see what he was up to. Ameya and Kym, with their backs to the white side of the room, stopped dancing when they saw Bernie go into a stare. They looked back to see—*God*—White Lech headed their way. Things got crazier for the freshmen girls. Blacks, both male and female, were *beaming* at Lech, grinning, trading soul shakes and hugs. The guy walked right into them and stopped.

"I'm Joe," he smiled to the black girl with the Asian eyes. "Wanna dance?"

Bernie heard "Sure" come out of her mouth, and then, in more control, she told him, "I'm Bernie." Without touching her, he lead her to the sliver of open floor between the two races.

Bernie's friends gawked like bumpkins.

"What the *fuck*?" Jelise grunted to the others. It was a rhetorical question.

Joe squared up with Bernie, and placed his hand at the warm, firm spine of a black girl. *Another first.* He gently pulled, and she let herself come against him. When she offered her right hand, he grasped the delicate fingers and brought them to his chest. He tilted his head down to her and she let her cheek go lightly against his. Joe breathed in the sweet scent of her hair and neck, and they began to move back and forth with the music. Joe couldn't slow dance with a hang, but Bernie didn't care. The flutter that came into her chest when she first saw him walking toward her had grown to a thumping so strong she was afraid he would hear it.

There were less than ten seconds left in the song.

Forty feet away, Mimi McKinley stood gaping at the whole pitiful scene. Like Joe, she was a sophomore, starting Year Two of trying to find a way to get green-eyed Joe hot for her tail. Joe had been friendly to her in their freshman English class, but he'd deflected her flirting. He just wasn't interested in the big-boned girl who looked like Rocky Balboa in drag. Regardless of how huge her boobs were. Just a few weeks ago, she had given it another shot. She'd jumped in the student flow in the Trophyella building just after class, had worked herself beside him as they walked out into the sunshine, and said, brassy as she knew how, "Hey Joe. Did you know that when they hang a man, he gets an erection?"

A witty reply came to him easy enough: *That sure would make him well-hung.* He wisely kept that sexual reference away from the girl. Instead, he'd given her a quick laugh and a chilly "Later," and taken off for his dorm. Mimi had stood there, stunned by the guy who brushed her and her big tits off like that.

Now Mimi stood on the dance floor, so angry her scalp felt like it was on fire, watching Joe cozy up to the black girl. So what if she didn't look like a cover girl. Mimi still had the brains, the big hair, the ass. Plus her boys, her 36Ds. Here was fine Joe Normal slummin' after a skanky ho, even though Mimi

McKinley was there for the taking. And the fool was doing it in front of *the whole fuckin' room.*

13. Sort-of Dancing

Bernie felt the electric current surging through her. The cute white guy had walked across the room, just to dance with *her*. After the last notes of *Lady* had faded away, they still clung to each other, while all the other couples had broken their clinches, set for another fast number. Donna Summer's voice drifted in with her lilting prelude to *Last Dance*, as The Bomb bellowed, "Okay gang, let's see ya...bust a move!"

Joe released her, assuming she would head back to her friends, but it was her turn to surprise him. She placed her hands on his shoulders, brought her lips up to his ear, and said, "We got cheated, Joe. Didn't even get a whole dance."

He took the liberty to go to *her* ear. "Sorry. I didn't hear you."

She came back to him, amping up her voice as the song's beat kicked in. "What?" she said.

I could do this all night long, Joe told himself. It was incredible, feeling her breath on him, being so close to her that he could smell her lipstick. *Cherry. Sweet.* He pulled back and tapped his lips with his finger to let her know he wanted to say something back at her. Bernie grinned and tilted her head to the side, so his lips and that cute mustache brushed against her cheek.

"*What?*" he said.

Bernie liked this game as much as he did. This time, she pulled in so close she left some of her lipstick on his ear. "I said I didn't hear *you*," she repeated.

He went back to her. "Never mind."

She laughed at this sorry exchange, he laughed with her,

and this time she stayed at his cheek. Joe inhaled the tantalizing scent that rose from the hollow just below her throat. *Moist and sweet and musky.* He pulled his hand from her spine. That caught her off guard, but then he put it back, this time a little lower. His palm rested on the soft, gentle swell where her bottom began.

She pulled free of him, making a big smile so he wouldn't be alarmed, and let her slim hips make some toned-down moves to the beat. "Like this," she said in her soft voice.

Joe reacted by doing the unthinkable. He tried copying her moves. He picked up her first couple of steps, going with her, but then lost the beat and went off kilter badly. With that, he gave up and turned his missteps into a silly dance.

She covered her burst of laughter with her hand and—*what the hey*—started copying *him.*

"Joe, you are such a hoot!" she laughed. She threw her head back and laughed.

It was the strobe lights that rescued him. The Bomb flicked a toggle switch and the room was suddenly filled with staccato flashes of light. When Joe saw that Bernie's moves were frozen into still pictures, it dawned on him that his pitiful lack of rhythm didn't matter anymore. He goofed his way through *Last Dance,* then Spinners' *Workin My Way Back to You* and then Queen's *Crazy Little Thing Called Love.* With another slowdown, this time *Endless Love,* they came together tighter than before.

Joe pulled back far enough to take in her exotic eyes. "I saw you on Main Street this afternoon. The spilled purse."

Yes, Bernie told herself. He *had* been checking her out.

"Really?" she said.

"You're beautiful, Bernie."

Her chest felt as if it would burst. "You're making me blush, Joe."

As the voices of Lionel Ritchie and Diana Ross wafted toward them, she brought her arms up around his neck. She let her body drape against him.

At the next break, the girls huddled up to fume.

"I see it but I ain't believin' it," Kym broadcast to the others. "Armstrong leaves us for one dance and here it is, almost eleven-damn-thirty."

"Girl should have her butt spanked," Ameya huffed.

Jelise came down hard with her own mouth. "Lech really working huh. Aimin' to jump it tonight, guaranteed."

When The Bomb came back to his control board and kicked off another set with *My Sharona*, the girls saw Bernie heading back their way.

"About damn time," Ameya greeted her, nice and bossy.

"Hey," Bernie said. She was absolutely dreamy-eyed.

"You miss us?" Jelise said.

"Just wanted to let y'all know Joe's gonna walk me back to the dorm."

They stared at her, then among themselves, then back to her.

Ameya jumped in first. "That's the lech from this afternoon, in case you didn't recognize him."

Bernie stiffened at that. "He's a nice guy. *Really* nice."

"Yeah, wants to be nicer, too," Jelise said.

"You pop your pill today, girl?" Ameya asked, adding some private sarcasm. Bernie played it cool and didn't answer. Her virginity was one of the first secrets Ameya had pried out of her lonely roomie in their first month of school. Ameya knew her roommate didn't have a reason yet to be on any pill, unless it was vitamins.

Joe walked up and offered a smile at the glowering girls.

He turned to Bernie. "Ready?"

Her girlfriends lasered their stares at her.

"Sure," she smiled to him. She flashed her eyes at her stupefied friends. "Later."

The three girls watched as Bernie took the white guy's hand and followed him through the crowd. Along the way, Joe saw Heavy's big thumb go up. Hurtt man, standing near Heavy, gave Joe an admiring nod that said, *Pretty damn slick, wallflower.*

Lots of eyes followed them out the door, including Mimi's. After watching Joe with his head up his ass all night long, she was working on her third rum-and-Coke. Some frat guy had supplied the rum, he was so jacked up by those knockers.

Outside, they took the wide concrete path across the middle of the campus green and strolled toward the women's dorms. In front of McAfee Hall, Bernie surprised him by taking the lead. She pulled him on past the steps.

"Let me show something," she said in an anxious breath. She guided him across the lawn and around the corner of the dorm. A towering maple tree stood there, arched between McAfee and Taylor women's dorms. The tree's limbs still held enough leaves that they blocked out nearly all of the light from the dorm windows and the nearby lamp posts. Bernie went to the darkest area beneath the tree and stopped at the concrete bench. She released his hand and held her arms out, as if she were a realtor showing off a backyard.

"Like this?" she asked him eagerly. "One of the girls told me about it."

"Maybe," he played. He went to her, but then sidestepped and came behind her, bringing his arms around her waist. She placed her hands on top of his.

"Do you realize we've spent the whole night standing up?" he said, putting his cheek to hers.

She gave out a little giggle. "Why do you think I showed you the bench?"

Joe unwrapped his arms from her and she let him turn her to face him. He took her head ever-so-gently with his hands and kissed her. Bernie took handfuls of his sweater and held on, opening her mouth to his. When they finally broke, Bernie was so lightheaded she went to the bench. He sat next to her, and they went into each other again.

When they finally came up for air, Joe said, "This is a first."

"Me too," she said, knowing what he meant.

She tilted her head back and let Joe run his fingers through her gelled hair. Then, when she complained about the cold concrete, he took her onto his lap. They would've gone on with it until the 1 a.m. curfew, if it weren't for the yelling.

"BER-nie!"

Bernie pulled her mouth away from Joe's and listened.

"Is that you in there, Bernie? Hey!"

Joe felt the girl's body go rigid.

"Bernie Armstrong!"

There in the shadows, Bernie took an exasperated breath and turned toward the shouting.

"It's me!"

Joe helped Bernie to her feet and she shook her clothes straight. They stepped into the light to see girlfriends, guy friends, Heavy, Stick, Hurtt Man, practically the whole Loud Crowd, all standing there.

Joe's complexion had given them away. Despite it being long after midnight, the fair white face had been nearly luminescent, even in the shadows.

Her girlfriends girls were nervy enough to gawk, looking for any noticeable damage to the sister.

Joe started out with a sheepish expression but eased up when he heard Heavy's voice yell out, "Let the Force Be with You, Jedi!"

Scattered snickers.

Joe escorted her past their audience and up the wide steps to McAfee's double doors, where other couples were also playing the clock down to the last minutes before curfew. Bernie looked at Joe under the coach light and gasped. She went to her jeans pocket, pulled a tissue out and, to assorted catcalls, proudly started cleaning up her man.

"Lipstick, Joe," she explained to him as she worked.

"Wonder how that got there," one of the girls cracked.

That done, she went to Joe's ear for the final time that night. "Call me," she said in a low whisper of a voice. She stuck a Good Little Girl peck on his cheek and he responded by giving her a neighborly pat on the shoulder.

"Maybe we can go to the game tomorrow," Joe threw out in front of the others. He made it sound as formal as he could.

"Cold shower, Jedi!" Heavy yelled out. "Or *somethin'*."

Bernie turned and floated into the lobby.

Heavy broke with Stick long enough to offer Joe a hand slap. Joe enthusiastically made it pop and then bounded happily down the steps. He picked up icy glares from one or two couples, but as soon as he hit the sidewalk, he went into a joyous lope down the street.

Heavy was ahead of any skeptics. "Five dollars says he's back here tomorrow."

He didn't get any takers.

Jelise, who was working some kind of whiskey drink in a plastic GO PIONEERS cup, didn't care who heard her when she declared in a cutting voice, "He'll be back, all right. White Boy won't quit 'til he gets hisself a piece. Y'all know it."

14. Denise and Rudolph Get Ready for Joe

Rudolph sat at the dinette table and waited for Joe to show up. He looked down at Denise's baby, that sorry canine dust mop. When she and Rudolph had met last summer, Denise had described Sir Pepi as some fancy crossbreed, a "Poodle-loodle-stroodle" or whatever it was she told him. He wasn't impressed.

She was at the kitchen counter pulling together some snacks. She wore a 2X Pittsburgh Steelers jersey and the baggiest jogging pants she had. Denise wasn't going to put on a show for another man, especially a white one. And definitely not in her own place. She did enough of that on her job at the Hotel Kentuckian.

"We're probably going to need a notebook for this, Rudy," she called to him from over in the kitchen, which was just around the wall. Then she instructed Sir Pepi, in baby talk: "Now doan Suh Pep get all wowd when da dobell wings. *NO.*" There would be no real baby for her to baby-talk to at her age. Pep was it.

"Hell, just put it in its cage right now," Rudolph said.

"Him," Denise set Rudy straight. "He's a *him,* not an *it.*" She reached down to pet Sir Pepi's baseball-sized skull and then took a seat across from Rudy.

Hell of an arrangement, Rudolph sat there and thought. Sharing Denise with her idiot mutt. He moseyed to the bedroom—*at his own pace, by damn*—and plucked his spiral pocket notebook from the nightstand.

Denise pulled out her big plastic bowl and filled it up with pretzels, wheat crackers, M&Ms and broken cashews (two dollars off at Walmart). She set it down in the middle of the small, round, oak table she took such joy in admiring. It was a real find—ten dollars at a yard sale. She'd stripped it and refinished it all by herself.

"Stay out of the goodies until he gets here," she ordered Rudy. "Now tell me again. Why are you going to all this trouble for your boy?"

Rudolph helped himself to the snack bowl before Denise could smack his hand away. He took his time as he crunched at it, not to aggravate Denise, but to run his answer through his head one more time before he delivered it to her.

"Man's like a ship without a rudder," he said.

She blinked at him. "But why does Rudolph Barnes have to be the rudder? Why can't he go find somebody else to help him out? Like one of his white friends?" She was still mildly irritated by what Rudy had told her, about Joe going with a little lovesick sister for nearly a whole school year, and then throwing the poor thing under the bus. Rudy didn't put it quite like that, but she could see it going down like that, back in the day.

Rudolph considered that cut, her *white friends* dig. "For one thing," he exaggerated, "he don't have any." He gave an ironic laugh and tacked on a, "He's pretty short on black friends, too." Rudolph hoped his light mood would be infectious. It wasn't.

When Denise gave him her insistent expression, he fell back to the nitty-gritty.

"I *told* you why," Rudolph said. "He's looking for a black girl, and he thinks I can help open some doors for him. You know."

"Um-hum," Denise said, studying his tight-bearded face. She suspected this was partly a leverage thing from work, since Joe was front office and Rudy worked out on the floor.

Rudolph went to the kitchen, and while he was pouring out two highballs, he thought of something else to say before Joe showed up. "How many white friends *you* have?" he called back her.

She shut her eyes dismissively and kept them shut as she gave him her answer. "I work with all kinds of people, Rudy," she shouted back, not able to say it without a touch of condescension. "That's my job."

He came back to the table and took a long pull on his drink. "You have your little night out with them every month. *Some of 'em must be your friends.*"

"By the way," she said, seeing the man was draining his glass fast, "you might want to slow it down a little."

Rudolph made a raspy grunt and set his glass down. He didn't need the woman to start carpin' again about his drinking. Denise slid a cardboard coaster under each of their glasses.

"My *point*," he said, "is this. I work mostly with a black crew at work. Then I come home to these apartments, which are full of nothing but black folk. I go to an all-black barbershop. I shop at all-black liquor store, I go to an all-black church..."

"Like you go to church often enough to notice."

Rudolph responded to that little cut by scooping up a handful of trail mix. "Well, when I *do* go," he said, "it's what? One hundred percent black."

"What's wrong with that?" Denise said. "That's our choice." She hauled up Sir Pepi with one hand and set him on her lap.

"Here's the thing," he said. "When you leave this apartment, you're around white people all the time. But look at me. Joe's the only white friend I've got, for real." He threw some more of the mix into his mouth. "So why *wouldn't* I help the man out?" He figured that would at least score some compassion points with her. Instead, she kept up the hardball.

"Your choice," she said dryly. "He's weird."

"Sure he's weird, but he's a straight shooter, too, straight-up as they come." He poked around to find the last of the red M&M's. "So you take the weird along with the rest. Plus, he likes *you*." That was a given. Everybody who met Denise liked her from the get-go. *Denise Jackson, Ms. Personality-Plus.*

After taking a sip of her own drink, Denise made herself sound as powerless as possible. "Whatever."

Rudolph rapped his empty glass down hard—on the coaster.

"I thought we were going to wait until he got here before we started drinking," she said.

"Too late for that," Rudolph said. He quit worrying about when Joe was going to show up and went ahead with his story.

"There was this new guy at work a couple of months ago," he said, "name Hoyt Phillips. Came from somewhere down South. Well, 'Too Much'—you know him, one of the press operators—Too Much was taking a break outside, shootin' the breeze with Joe, when this Phillips barges up and horns into their conversation.

"Everybody at work knew how good Phillips was at *that*. After about ten minutes' worth of saying a whole lot of nuthin', Phillips looks over at Joe. He's trying to score some brownie points with the gravy guy from up front, so he says, 'Sorry to hear about your wife.' Phillips don't get anything from Joe but a nod, so then he says—being so *sensitive* to Joe's feelings—'We got a nice singles club out my way, the *Rid'em Hard Saloon*. Dances every other Thursday.' And then he tells Joe, right out there in the open, 'And the best thing about our dances is—*no niggers*.'"

Denise's face instantly pulled tight, stung first by the n-word itself, and then by its vile social message. "Delightful," she said sourly.

Rudolph busted into a laugh. It was a screwy thing to do,

Denise thought, until the man came back with his kicker.

"Joe looks this Phillips dead in the face and says, cool as ice cream, 'What's wrong with *them*?' Well, *that* sure as hell knocks Phillips back. And while he's takin' Joe in, all *speechless*, my man Joe says, '"I mean, if you had black girls at your place too, my odds would double, right?"'"

With that punch line, Rudolph went into a laughing fit. Denise gave him a disapproving smile. Just like always, she thought. Men and sex.

"Ol' redneck Phillips stares at Joe for the longest, and then says, 'You're effin' sick, man'—except he don't say 'effin—and then he huffs off!"

'Rudolph repeated it, laughing hard again. "*'My odds'll double!'*" He made it sound like the Quote of the Century. "Now, how many white dudes do you know who would do *that*? And Phillips ain't no hundred-pound weakling. My man Joe *shut him up*."

"Good for him," Denise said, giving a mild shrug of her shoulders. She was impressed, but not by much. Joe sounded to her like he was more interested in scoring with a sister than working to improve civil rights.

The knock at the door made Sir Pepi go ballistic. He yapped and charged his scrawny self toward the door.

"There he is," Denise said. The bourbon gave her voice a nasty edge. "Your straight-up white friend."

Rudolph stood up and tried one more time to lighten her up before he opened the door. "Aw, you're still mad over him cuttin' us short last night."

"Oh, *please*," she shot back at him. She gave her baby a look of pretend sadness. "Suh Pepi haffa go ta jail. Po Pep." She carried the dog toward the bedroom while Rudy checked the peephole.

How was it, Rudolph asked himself, that a woman who looked like she did, didn't have more romance in her than that?

He slid the deadbolt and pulled the door open.

15. Denise Gets Interested

Denise returned to the living room just as Rudy was putting Joe's jacket on the coat hook. She forced herself into a weak, buzzy smile and stepped up to offer her cheek to the man; she didn't need Rudy coming down on her later about—*Oh tragedy!*—totally dissing his *one and only white friend.*

"Great to see you, Denise," Joe smiled. He meant it. The man was sky-high over this plan of his.

"Have a seat, Cool," Rudolph said, showing him to the table.

Denise was amazed when, instead of sitting himself down, Joe stepped to the side and pulled her chair out for her. She double-clutched, looked back at the white man and then at Rudy. Rudy was as stunned as she was. Surprise surprise, she thought. So the man knew something about old school manners. She lowered herself onto the chair, and this time she smiled at Joe like she meant it. "Thank you, Joe," she said. Already, she regretted going all sloppy-butt with her sweats.

"I was just about to get that chair," Rudolph joked, covering his own embarrassment.

"Pretty as ever," Joe smiled to her.

That compliment was a bit much from a man who hardly knew her, but she cordially accepted it, after the man's smooth move with her chair.

"Why, thank you, Joe," she said, not pulling her punches.

"Wow, Denise. Haven't seen you since what—the employee picnic?" Joe asked.

"It's been a minute," she said. She asked him how he was doing, offering a concerned brow. When he only returned a terse "Fine," she knew to leave it alone.

"What do you want to drink, Joe?" Rudolph asked. "Beer, pop, coffee?"

The booze was Denise's suggestion. *Get the man's tongue loosened up so he would open up a little.* That was a common practice in her sales job at the Hotel Kentuckian—share some spirits with show planners and sometimes that stimulated some deal-making. Rudolph was all for pushing the beer. He'd just as soon save his expensive Woodford Reserve for his next mattress-wrestle with Denise. "How about a Corona?" he suggested.

"I'll have whatever it is you two are drinking," Joe said. "Bourbon and Coke?"

Rudolph felt Denise's *Told-you-so* eyes on him. He made a highball for Joe and another for himself. He cut Joe's amount of bourbon by a finger.

Denise sat there and took the strangeness in. *Surreal.* She had sat at tables with plenty of Caucasian men on her job. But never in *her* apartment. Never at *her* table.

The HK's sales director, Nancy Pat Rollins, had four sales managers under her -- two white women, one white man and one black woman. Having a Denise Jackson out front told the world that the HK was downright *progressive*. Yes, her African-American sales manager had put on some pounds after nearly a decade of wining and dining clients, but the girl's figure was still fetching. And Nancy Pat was absolutely amazed at the woman's face. Mid-forties, and Denise hardly had a wrinkle showing.

Since eighty-percent of the convention and trade show decision-makers were men, Nancy Pat had a simple directive for her three female managers—flatter 'til you drop. Do the legwork and research required, sure, but laugh at the mens' dumb jokes. Bat the 'ol eyelids. Put in some extra wiggle as they walked folks around the building. With some booking deals worth tens of thousands of dollars, staff was expected to act downright *enchanted* with meeting planners.

Looking accommodating was where Denise drew the line. Since she turned eighteen, she'd worked so many jobs—day care helper, barmaid, restaurant hostess, sales associate in an athletic store, and now this, the heads-in-beds business—she'd become an expert on how to deflect men who hit on her.

But here she was, sitting in front of the oh-so-proper white guy and regretting being covered up by her Steelers tent. Joe was a different kind of man, that was for sure. He was a little too perky, a little too cable guy, but here he'd been ballsy enough to go looking for a sister, back in the day. He was a fairly attractive man. Had some gray creeping into his full head of reddish blond hair, but that wasn't a negative; the gray complemented the pink face, just as his stubble growth did. And as she had stupidly blabbed to Scootie, Joe didn't lug a pot belly out in front. She knew some men who acted like a watermelon-sized gut was their prized possession. But looks-wise, it was the green eyes, with the girlishly-long dark eyelashes, that impressed her the most. They were beautiful, for a man.

With her drink nearly gone, she asked if he wanted to see her "baby." Rudolph's eyes pinched down at that invitation but he kept his mouth shut.

"Sure thing!" Joe told her.

She came back with Sir Pepi cradled in her arms.

Joe delighted her by making over the thing. Sir Pepi responded by bracing himself against Denise's arm, fearing another attack by a man. Joe sat back with a little "Awww" and gave the animal its space. Rudolph thought he was going to lose his M&M's, watching Joe act so damn lovey-dovey with the mutt. When Denise started to sit down again, Rudolph leapt to his feet and held her chair for her. Not expecting *that* move, she almost missed her seat.

"Aren't you polite," she said to her man. She allowed Rudy to push her toward the table, but only part of the way. She wanted to leave enough room for Sir Pepi to sit on her lap.

Their Joe-grilling began. Denise, as planned, used the most gosh-golly sales manager voice she had:

"Wow, how did you meet Bernadette, Joe?" she said.

"My Nubian Prin-*cess*?" he corrected her.

"Yeah, that's *right*," she said. "Rudy told me. Your Nubian Prin-*CESS*." I'll be blessed, Denise said to herself. Rudy really hadn't made that up.

Joe gave Denise essentially the same narrative he'd given to Rudinski. Met his perfect girl in college, fell for her, then made the biggest mistake of his life and broke up with her.

"She must have been all that," Denise said.

"She *was* all that, as they say," Joe said. He left it there.

With her head taking on a pronounced buzz, Denise decided to take a another run at Rudy's good-looking white friend. "Must have had it *all* goin' on," she said with a head shake. "She must have been a real beauty."

Rudolph sighed. He had already told the woman what this college girl looked like. Plain. Real plain. Women, he concluded, just *had* to size each other up.

"She is," Joe jumped in, suddenly seizing on a faraway image. "Has the most beautiful face."

"Oh wow," said Denise, pumping him along. She sneaked a glance at Rudy. He opened his lips just enough for her to read, *No way*. Might just be a *Yes Way*, she told herself. Hey, hadn't Joe just described her—Denise—as "pretty as ever?"

"A real beauty?" Joe said to Denise, backtracking on her

comment. "I'll tell you how beautiful she is."

Rudolph felt another Joe Monologue on the way. He got up from the table, ostensibly to refill the snack bowl, and looked over at Denise and yawned, letting her know she was in for a speech. That was fine with her. She angled her chair closer to Joe and re-balanced Sir Pepi between her legs.

"The second or third week we're dating," Joe said, "she asks me to go to church with her. And I'm thinking, *church*? But I tell her 'Sure, why not,' because I'd go anywhere with her, you know? Just to be with her. I asked her what kind of church she went to, and she gave a little laugh, like I was asking a crazy question, and said, "Baptist, of course!"

"We're Undecided ourselves," Rudolph called over, making a little quip. He heard Denise clear her throat.

"What happened then?" Denise pushed. Rudolph sat back down.

"I go to her dorm to pick her up. There are only a few people who are awake that early, it being Sunday morning on a college campus, right? Well, the first girls I see in the lobby are wearing house slippers and sweats. You know, kind of grunge."

Denise thought about her own outfit and felt an embarrassed flush.

"Well, while I'm waiting for her to come down from her room, I see a few black girls walking down the hall. And *they're all dressed to the teeth.* Pretty soon here are some black brothers coming in the front door—boyfriends or whatever—and I see these guys are decked out, too. I mean, sharp suits and ties. And here I am, good 'ol Joe, wearing the only slacks I own— khakis—and my best coat, which is my safari jacket." Joe smiled and wagged his head. "I thought I was pretty decent until *those* guys walked in."

Joe eyeballed Rudinski and Denise to make sure they were with him. They were. Especially Denise.

"So this is blowing my mind," Joe said. He took another sip of his highball. So did Rudolph. So did Denise. His eyes went to a vague spot on the ceiling.

"There's a set of French doors that lead to the upper floors," Joe said, getting louder from his drink. "I've got my back to them, admiring these brothers, and I see Kym, one of Bernie's friends, come into the lobby. She's wearing a nice long skirt, nothing too tight, all respectable for church. She's meeting up with one of the brothers, and she recognizes me—because why wouldn't she, she's seen me around Bernie every single day— and for some reason she throws me this strange little smile. And while I'm standing there wondering what that's all about, I notice everybody in the lobby is staring at me and grinning. And I realize *somebody's* coming up *behind* me.

"Before I can turn around, I feel a little tap on my shoulder. I swing around and...*Oh, wow.* It's Bernie. *In a dress.* She's smiling that knock-out smile of hers, and while I'm standing there, mouth hanging open, she says, playing it all formal, 'Morning, Mister Normal.'

"She can't help but see my eyes are practically spinning out of my head, admiring her up and down. She takes a couple of steps back and then does a slow turn to let me take in the whole package. Her dress is a kind of mint green and it has these padded shoulders...the neckline has this little ladylike high scoop to it...belt that goes tight to show off her little waist. Her sleeves come about two-thirds of the way down, making her arms look longer and more graceful than ever...the hem of her dress stops a couple of inches above her knee and she's wearing these matching green high heels."

Nuh-uh, Denise sat there and told to herself. No way does a man remember all that, not after thirty years. Not after two days. Not unless...he's still crazy in love with her.

"This is the very first time I've seen her legs, since she's always in jeans around campus. And they're...*my God*. Tiny little ankles and then strong, slender legs. And just enough dimple on the calf to give her that sexy athletic look, you know?"

Joe looked over at Denise and deadpanned, "This isn't too graphic for you, is it, Denise?"

"You shut up," she laughed, waving off his silliness. "Keep going, Joe." *Keep going, white boy.*

"Her hair is different, too. It's been curled, and pulled back on one side to show one of her cute little ears—which have little pearl earrings. She has a lot more makeup on too, looks like she belongs on a magazine cover. It's amazing. All this—the pearl necklace and dress, the shoes—plays off her skin, makes it glow like liquid caramel. She's holding a Bible in one hand and a little green purse in the other. While I'm standing there being blown away, one of the women yells, 'Spin it for him again, Bernie—we'll sell tickets!' But somebody *else* says, 'Gotta get to church, y'all. Somebody get Jedi pointed out of here before he melts into the floor!'

Joe brought his eyes down from the ceiling and back on Rudinski and Denise. "When we get to the door, Bernie tells me, 'Green's my favorite color—like your eyes, Joey.'"

Joe sat back. "You know, I think I could have stood there the rest of the semester, getting all I ever needed to live on, just by looking at her."

Sir Pepi let out a sudden, sharp yelp and the two men jumped. Denise's thighs had given the creature a hard, tight squeeze. The men didn't have a clue.

16. Denise Turns On

Denise covered her sudden stab of arousal by clutching Sir Pepi and bolting to the kitchen sink.

"What the hell got into *him*?" Rudolph called to her in a dull voice.

"Must have spilled my drink on him," Denise shouted back, as she opened the faucet to full torrent. For more show, she threw a few of handfuls of water on the dog's head and then set him on the floor. Sir Pepi shook it off and stared bug-eyed at his Mama over the way she was treating him.

Denise held her cool, wet fingers to her throat and then moved them to her cheek.

"I guess spilling your drink on the dog means I hit my limit," she chuckled, looking over her shoulder in their direction. As soon as she got herself and her dog back to the table, she mouthed another prompt to Rudy. *Married?*

Rudolph took her cue. "Listen Man, how do you know this girl's not already married?"

Joe frowned at him.

Rudy rephrased his question.

"I don't mean, *already* married, 'cause hell, we're talking about thirty year-some years. But, you know, married *already*." He shifted his shoulders up and down for a response. Denise shut her eyes, not believing how the man butchered *that* line. She jumped back in.

"Oh *Rudy!*" she said, playing out their good cop-bad cop thing. "Have some *sensitivity*."

Rudolph didn't remember her laying it on so thick when they rehearsed it.

"She's not married," Joe said. "No way."

Denise sent a stare at Rudy to keep it going.

"But...what if she *is*?" he asked.

Joe's eyes dropped and he fingered the rim of his nearly empty glass. "I can't think about that."

Rudolph looked over to Denise for some backup.

"Okay, Joe," she said. "Let's say she's *not* married. Lots of things could have happened since you saw her in college. This Bernadette..."

"*My* Bernadette," Joe said.

"Okay, *your* Bernadette. She just might be involved with somebody else, you know."

"Doubt it," Joe said in a crisp voice.

Denise let that unreality of his slide. "She could be living in another part of the state, or even *another* state."

"We'll find her," Joe said.

Rudinski got up and made his third highball. When he returned, he slapped a playful, inebriated hand against The Coolster's shoulder. "C'mon Joe," he said. "Get real. For all we know she's a nun. With some weird disease. You know, something they can't cure. So she's like, gone off and hid to wait it out."

Denise bit on her lower lip and stared at Rudy. *Disease? Runaway nun?* Where did *that* come from?

"WRO-ong!" Joe said, making it a two-syllable response.

Sir Pepi sat up and stretched, pushing his stringy wet head back against Denise's jersey. Within seconds, the wet material sunk into the deep valley of the woman's cleavage. Rudolph noticed. Joe didn't. Denise felt the clammy coolness on her chest and looked down to see the deep crevasse marking her Steelers logo. Fine, she told herself in her buzz. Remind the guy I'm a woman. Snaps for me.

"Straight up, Joe Cool," Rudolph said. He spoke like an older brother, although Joe had a couple of years on him. "As wonderful as you must have been back in the day, she *just might* have forgot you by now."

That made Denise cringe. She knew brothers who would pull out a weapon over an ego-buster like that.

Joe laughed so hard he blew his drink out of his nose. "*Forget?*" He held his empty glass up and tilted it toward his friend. "Half a glass, Rudinski?"

"How about some coffee, instead." Rudolph didn't need Joe wrapping his car around a tree before his big search even began.

"I give, make it coffee," Joe said. Rudolph wobbled his way out of his chair and went to the kitchen cupboard to get the instant coffee. Joe raised his voice, despite Rudinski being a whole twelve feet away, just around the wall. "Read my lips, Rudinski. She's *crazy* about me! All we have to do is go find her."

Rudolph handed Joe a cup of hot instant coffee and gave in to a yawn. "We've been burnin' it again, bro. Two nights in a row, stick a fork in me."

Joe looked at his phone. "Is it really midnight?"

"Really," Rudolph said.

As the two guys headed toward the door, Denise entertained some private thoughts. Would she have fallen for a white man like him, back when she was Bernie's age? A college guy who had such a huge crush on her, he didn't care what color she was? Would she have given it up to a guy like Joe back in the day? *Ooh, Baby. Put it on a platter.*

She hustled over to catch Joe before he got away. She gave him her best goodbye hug, bringing her wet chest against him. Joe felt the cool sensation and jerked back. "Sorry, Denise," he told her respectfully, taking his eyes away from the damp spot. "I forgot you're still wet."

She was amused by that. The man had finally looked at her below her neck. "The next time you come over," she smiled, "you're not a guest, you're family."

Rudolph wasn't expecting such a drastic change in her attitude, but he'd take it. Girl was definitely on board with their Bernie search.

As Rudolph walked Joe out to the man's Jeep, he joked, "Hope nobody sees us. Don't want anybody to think we let any bad elements set up here all night."

"True that," Joe played along. He took a last sip of his coffee and handed the mug back to his friend. Rudolph felt a burning in his stomach when his friend looked at him and said, "I gave her up, but it was just temporary. That's the beauty of all this, Rudinski. Love never really dies." The man's eyes had literally brightened when he said that. Rudolph would have sworn they did. By the time he returned to the apartment, Denise had decided not to put her big question to him—the reason for Joe and Bernie's break-up:

Pregnant?

17. Long Work Day

Monday morning.

Rudolph was out of the shower first, since he had to be at Max-It by eight. Denise didn't have to deliver her fine self to the Hotel Kentuckian until nine. He was stepping into his navy Dickies when she returned to the bedroom from her bath.

"I was thinking," she said. She sat on the foot of the bed and waited for him to acknowledge her comment.

"Yeah?" he said, irritated. His mood fouled by the start of another work week, he wished the woman would just say whatever it was she wanted to say.

"How can we get Joe to ask me to help?"

"He *did* ask," Rudolph said.

"No he didn't," Denise said, bending over at the waist to load her breasts into her bra.

"Sure he did. That's why all three of us were at the table."

"But that wasn't *asking* me."

"You're *in*, Baby. Otherwise he wouldn't have opened up like that in front of you." He did his impression of a swoony Joe. 'Her dress was...kind of...mint green.'" Rudolph laughed at his trippin' Joe voice.

Denise didn't think it was so damn funny.

"*Quit,*" she said in a sharp tone.

"I sorry," he said. "Truth be told, I think it's pretty damn impressive, remembering the color of a dress from that far back. You believe that guy?"

Denise mumbled to herself, "I'd *like* to." She sorted through the wide collection of expensive blouses and picked her alluring sage green. "Surely he understood the drawbacks we were pointing out."

"Plus she's *old*," Rudolph said. He let his belt come out one notch looser. His swelling waistline had become a daily reminder to him of what high living with Denise could do to a body. "Anyway, you're on the team. Joe's the General, I'm the Lieutenant General and you're my...aide."

"And you're a nut," she said, smiling. She stepped into her size 12 sales manager skirt and fought with the zipper until it was up and over her booty. She took a long breath. "Okay, I'll consider myself in—but only for a while." She stepped closer to the dresser mirror and brushed her bangs in place. Nancy Pat went out of her way to compliment the daylights out of her when the girl wore her bangs like that. Cornrows she could forget—Nancy Pat wouldn't tolerate those, or, for that matter, most braids. Way too ethnic for the HK.

"Life be movin' on," she said, "long-lost love or not."

Rudolph, who had gotten into his poetry thanks to Joe, heard the wordplay. "Alliteration," he said, happy to educate her. "That's what they call that. All els. 'Long-lost love.'"

She ignored Rudy's English lesson. While she worked on her makeup, she asked another question that had been gnawing at her. "Has Joe had any lady friends since Franki?"

"Doubt it," Rudolph said. He gave it some more thought. "Let's just say I never saw any panties hanging on the lampshades."

Five minutes later, makeup done and blouse on, she started to head to the kitchen to get to her new breakfast fare—a cup of black coffee, artificial sweetener, and a banana. One way or another she *was* going to lose weight. She wheeled back to ask him, "What's our next step?"

"Go to work," he said in a curt tone, still ticked off for her ignoring his literary insight. He buttoned up his short sleeve polo shirt, the one with a red logo on the pocket that read "Max-It Imaging."

"Trying to be funny," Denise sniffed back. She went ahead and brought the other thing up. "Ever think there was love child? That's why he dropped her?"

Rudolph swung a disbelieving look at her. "Not a chance. Joe wouldn't have left her high and dry like that." Then he added, "We're not getting into that, with me halfway out the door. We can talk about it at dinner tonight." He paused for effect. "At *Mister J-Bones.*" He'd been waiting ever since he got out of bed to lay that surprise on her.

"Mister J's!" she said, pulling her head back to look at him incredulously. "You win the lottery or what?"

"What."

Denise knew Mister J's like the back of her hand. She'd ushered potential HK clients there for years. Four stars, in the heart of downtown Louisville, with a terrific view of the Ohio River. The place had the city skyline, the bridges, the river hustle and bustle. It even had a grand piano, with a live grand piano player. She and Rudy had been there together a grand total of once—for what Denise labeled, "Our three-month anniversary." It marked the exact date Rudy had moved in with her. The two dinner comps had been a gift from Mister J's management, a thank-you to Sales Manager Denise Jackson for steering all kinds of business their way.

Rudy smiled at her. It was a thrill for a working man like him to stand there, invite his woman to the upscale Mister J's, and say "I got it."

"You're *sure*," she'd asked again before he left for work.

It was an economic question, not a put-down.

"I'll just take my lunch to work for the rest of my life," he joked.

"And drink nuthin' but water," she tacked on. She was curious how he could suddenly afford such a pricey place—maybe he had a lottery ticket pay off—but she let it slide. This was his deal.

Both of them had gone off to work energized by the thought of wrapping up the day together in a fine, luxurious restaurant.

At six o'clock, Denise trudged back through the squeaky old door of Apartment 307. Rudy was ready to go, styling in a nice pair of slacks and a sharp open-collar shirt. That's one of us, she told herself. She'd just finished eight hours of beat-down.

Around nine-thirty that morning, almost as soon as she'd made her cup of green tea and sat down at her desk, an event planner phoned the HK. The guy introduced himself as Anson L. Huey, of Moline, Illinois. He told Denise he had a "real nice" convention that was looking for a new city and a host hotel. Huey identified himself as the chief executive officer of the American Antique Glass Bottle Collectors Association. He talked it up to Denise: As many as eight hundred attendees and spouses, nearly all of them from out-of-town. They would overnight the three days of the show, maybe four.

With the October show dates and other particulars jotted down on her notepad, Denise had waited out the man's ten-minute speech of a good-bye and then checked him out to make sure his outfit was legit. She'd never heard of his group, but hey, there were thousands of associations around the country she'd never heard of. There was no reason for her to make a beeline to Nancy Pat's office and waste the woman's time if this was a little bottle-collecting club that wanted the entire hotel for a dollar and a half. She flipped through the sales office's huge directory of national associations and found them soon enough. *American Antique Glass Bottle Collectors Association (AAGBCA.) Check*, Denise told herself. Moline, Illinois. *Check.* Membership: 1,098. *Whadd'ya know. Legit.*

If the man wasn't blowing smoke at her with his attendee numbers, the payoff for the host hotel would work out to a nice piece of business for the HK. Then, there were the potential add-ons: action for the HK's bar and grill, ballroom and meeting room rental. The 23rd Annual AAGBCA Convention might actually do what Huey had fluffed out there to Denise—generate at least two million dollars in economic impact.

"We might even be bigger than that," Huey's rough voice had said, as he threw out more bait.

"How's that?" Denise asked him.

"If Ambeca decides to partner with us—and we're pretty darn sure they will—that's another three, four hundred people, plus spouses."

At the risk of sounding ignorant, Denise asked.

"*Ambeca?*"

"The Antique Milk Bottle Exhibitors and Collectors Association," Huey said. He spelled it for the girl. "A-M-B-E-C-A. He sensed her embarrassment and said, charitably, "Don't feel bad, Hon. A lot of people still don't know they're out there. That's why they gave us a call. Get some exposure by partnering with us."

As soon as Denise hung up, she'd quick-stepped it to Nancy Pat's office. She watched her boss lean forward in her leather executive's chair and stick her hand into the crystal dish in front of her. Nancy Pat fished out one of the peppermints, removed the cellophane wrapper imprinted with the letters "HK," and popped it into her mouth. She released a knowing little smile and a nod. "How about that. Convention bureau told me a couple of months ago that Agbeca was out shopping for a new home."

The nature of Nancy Pat's job required her to make a sort of phonetic nickname—a red-haired acronym—out of the hundreds of association names she had to deal with. Otherwise, she'd wear herself out just saying their full names. "Agbeca, how about that," she said. "It's not exactly a Vegas electronics show, but it's still a decent payday for us. Maybe throwing in this Ambeca'll get 'em over the hump." She sucked her mint and said, "If they're pushing for some numbers by end of day, get to it, Honey."

So Denise had penciled out her to-do list and then knocked the tasks down one by one, all before heading home:

Check how many of HK's three-hundred-and-seven beds would be available for October 19-23;

Determine the availability of the assumed move-in and move-out dates;

Make sure the ballroom and meeting rooms weren't already booked for stand-alone events;

Make sure no unannounced major maintenance work was planned;

Come up with a starting point to negotiable room rates, based on Nancy Pat's guidelines.

Huey had already done what any competent event planner would do—had gone to the websites of hotels in several cities to compare their basic information—number of meeting rooms, floor plans, utility services, sound and lighting capabilities, media room, show office, public transportation, etc. Then he'd contacted their local convention bureaus to get some early competitive buzz started—the kind that he was reasonably sure would get back to Nancy Pat.

The Hotel Kentuckian had more goodies to throw in later, if it was forced to further sweeten the pot. Things like discounts on video conferencing, WI-FI, a portable dance floor. If the show's choice of host hotel appeared to be razor-thin, the HK could even offer up the freebies, like guided bus tours to Churchill Downs.

The starting-out objective was to get the Kentuckian on Agbeca's short list of two or three hotels. If that happened, a site visit would come into play. Nancy Pat would do the actual contract-haggling if things got that far. Denise would be expected to sit by her side at the negotiating table, ready to supply not only the crunched numbers and moral support, but the eye candy.

So that had been Denise's day. She'd spent the final hour of it back on the phone with Huey, confirming HK's stats and answering more questions. She hadn't walked out of the sales office until quarter after six, just after she'd fed her last page of details into the fax machine and sent it to Agbeca's home office in Moline.

That was why she came in dragging when she finally reached her Valley Vista apartment. There wouldn't be any wardrobe change for Mister J's—she didn't have the energy to get into the fun clothes she'd set out that morning, the v-neck gold tunic and red slacks. Rudy was fine with what she had on. In fact, he loved her fancy office getup. Everybody she worked with got to enjoy Denise in fine blouses that busted out here and skirts that went up to there. Why shouldn't *he*?

18. Dining Out

It had been virtually a u-turn; Denise gave her dog a, "How Pep-Pep today, him aw-wight?" Ten minutes later, as soon as she freshened up, she and Rudy were on their way to Mister J-Bones.

Mister J's might have sounded like a rib haven, but out there overlooking the Ohio, it was about frying and grilling anything that came out of water, short of a car tire.

In the time it took to walk from the parking lot to the etched glass entrance doors, Rudolph had changed his mind about eating inside. A warm breeze came off the river and it looked like a dazzling sunset was on the way. For this kind of money, no way was Rudolph going to be stuck inside a gloomy restaurant, listening to some local piano crooner.

"Fine with me," Denise told him. For what was left of the day, the biggest decision she wanted to make was which fork to use.

The sniffy male greeter had given Rudolph a miffed expression before he scratched the name *Barnes* off his inside reservations list. Twenty minutes later, a young guy wearing a black shirt, black slacks and two wire rings in his eyebrow greeted them with a "Hey guys, how's it goin'." Rudolph's eyes went to the name tag and read, "Brenden." He guessed the fella's age at twenty-seven. Brenden led them through the dining area, toward the glass wall on the far side of the room. Beyond it, out on the sprawling deck, Rudolph and Denise could see a forest of big, burgundy table umbrellas in the late sun. As soon as they stepped outside, Brenden took a hard left and stopped at a table against the glass wall.

"Here we go, folks," he told them.

The Ohio River, hidden by all the umbrellas, might as well have *been* in, well, Ohio. And their table wasn't even big enough to rate an umbrella. Denise knew a crappy deal when she saw one, but she kept her mouth shut. This was Rudy's dime, his thrill. Rudolph stood there and slowly licked his bottom lip in frustration. He was tempted to tell her, Screw this, we'll just go to some soul food place. His balking turned out to be a stroke of luck. Arete Winslow was working over. When the restaurant's day manager looked out and saw Denise Jackson and her man being steered to the pitiful table, she thought she'd pee her pants. Arete almost strained a hip getting herself out there.

"Hey you!" she called out in a sugary greeting. "Di— NEESE!"

Denise recognized the voice before she located the woman. With a remarkable adroitness, Denise shifted from weary diner into supercharged HK sales manager mode. She put on a huge smile and spun around. "He-e-e-y Arete!"

Rudolph watched the two women exchange their best business hugs and happy faces. Denise introduced, "my guy Rudy."

There were a number of strong reasons why Arete was day boss at Mister J's. Here was one. She was already cha-chinging the clients Denise would surely bring back, if she were just treated right. She also made a mental note: *Have a little talk with Brenden.*

"I *know* you two want a nicer view of the river than this," she told the couple. The brunette brushed her long hair away from her face and set off to find one.

Rudolph's face had brightened with the offer of *any* relocation, but his eyes soon narrowed when he saw the woman was dealing with Denise, not him.

"Oh, *could* you?" Denise said. She placed a hand to her chest.

"Sure thang," Arete answered, going ethnic. "In fact, you guys are going to get a bonus. The *Belle of Louisville* is going to be passing by here pretty soon. Evenin' cruise. *Awesome* sight." As she led them on a snaking route through the other tables, she turned to ask Denise how things were going at the HK. Denise translated Arete's code and gave her some love.

"Spent the whole day talking to a new show," Denise said. She spread it on extra-thick. "They would absolutely *love* J's, Arete."

With that boost, Arete didn't stop walking until she came to the tables that had nothing in front of them but a wrought iron railing and the wide Ohio River. Rudolph was in awe. To their left, he saw the skyline of downtown Louisville. It clung to the river, bending along with it as the water curled to the southwest. Across the river and beyond the bridges stood the more modest view of two neighboring Indiana towns, Jeffersonville and Clarksville.

Denise had taken in this panorama far too many times to be wowed by it, but she played along. "Oh *wow*! This is *fantastic*, Arete!"

When Rudy's voice rammed in to say, "Now this is *somethin*,'" Denise had no problem picking up on the aggravation in his voice. She'd used her connections to take charge, and he was pissed about it. *He'd get over it.*

Rudolph wasn't going to be a butt-hole about it, certainly not in public. He reminded himself why he brought Denise here in the first place—to talk about Joe's Girl Search. He would back off, have a great meal and forget Denise's playing big-shot.

Arete hung with them just long enough to instruct their new server to bring a bottle of Mister J's house chardonnay. "Consider this your own personal happy hour, on me," she told Denise. She gave the striking black woman another hug and an air kiss and left in a giggling, *"Enjoy!"* She took a few steps and pivoted back around to tack on, "That goes for your handsome guy, too!"

Rudolph pulled out Denise's chair for her, but before he sat down, he took in the impending sunset like a tourist. To his left, the orange sun was hanging above the river's bend on the western horizon. In a matter of minutes, it would look like a dark red beach ball doing a sizzling float on top of the water, then sink into the water. To his right, upriver, the eastern sky was already turning lavender and melding itself into the wide, silver stretch of water that flowed down from Cincinnati. Along the riverbank, yellow dots began to glow from the streetlights. Nearby buildings lost their shape to the night sky, replaced by the small rectangles of light coming from offices being cleaned.

By the time the server poured their chardonnay, Rudolph— not Denise—had selected their appetizer from the menu. Although he'd never had "Escargot Phillipe" in his life, for $18.95, it had to be good, right? He went comical for Denise and their new server, a tattooed nymph-like female named Zoey. "Start us off with one of your Cargo Fill-ups, ma'am." He raised his menu and put his finger on the words, just so they'd get the joke. "Cargo Fill-ups, see?" he said. He let out a chortle.

The two women stared at his menu and then giggled together. Denise was relieved that the man had lightened up. Zoey thought the black man had a retarded sense of humor, but she wasn't about to lose a tip over it. She smiled big as Rudolph continued to the entrees. Alaskan King Crab for both of them.

"I'll get that Fill-up right out, Sir," Zoey smirked. She looked at Denise. "Your guy has quite a sense of humor."

"Tell me about it," Denise laughed.

As soon as Zoey left their table, Rudy lifted his glass of Northern California chardonnay to Denise. "Toast," he said. "To our Bernadette project." They clinked their glasses together. Rudolph took a big sip and she took a tiny one.

She surprised him by immediately bringing up Joe. "Time for bidness. Give me the long version on Joe Normal."

Rudolph was happy to sit out there and be invited by her to give Joe his props. He scooted closer to her and began.

"Let's see," he said. "When I started out at Max-It four years ago, I thought Joe was gonna be your run-of-the-mill white guy. He's salary, I'm on the clock."

"10-4, Brother," Denise said, as she picked at her first snail.

"But the very first time I hit the break room, I can see the man's different. He's at the vending machines, standing around cracking jokes to anybody who'll listen, us folk included. And I go '*Hmm*' —because you know how perceptive I am."

"Right," Denise said, thinking, With men, maybe.

"Then one day not long after that, I go to the break room for lunch. It's hump day, so talk's extra dull by then. Us minorities are taking up most of the tables, everybody lookin' half dead... and in comes this Joe."

Rudolph shoved his untouched escargo to the side—one taste was plenty—and lowered his voice. "Usually, when a white person walks in and sees that the color scheme is against him, he does a one-eighty, right?"

"Word," Denise said, feeling slangy with Arete gone.

"Well, I figure that's what he'll do. Smooth over to the pop machine, like that's what he really came in there for—and then skedaddle. But Joe starts looking around for a place to *sit*. And dig *this*. Two or three of the brothers *come alive* when he walks up to them, and the next thing I know it's, 'Yo Mister Cool! Get on in here!'" He tapped her hand to make sure she was with him. "Then, Baby, they tell me—*me!*—to slide over to make room for *him*! And all of a sudden everybody's all loosey-goosey, like a party's started, just because this Joe shows up! You understand what I'm sayin'? I'm supposed to be one of the talkers in this crowd, and here I get sent to the back of the bus!

"Well, after the man wolfs down his little carton of chili he got from the roach coach, he stands up to leave. And as he's goin' out the door, one of the brothers cracks, 'Back to the plantation, huh, Mister Cool?' I wiggle a little on that one, tell myself, Are you *kiddin'* me? Talkin' like that in front of a *white* guy? But instead of getting all bent out of shape over that, this Joe laughs like he's heard it a thousand times before! He yells back, 'I hear ya'—and he's gone. And I turn to one of the other brothers—"Specs"—and say, 'Got some enlightened white folk around here, huh?'"

Zoey came out of nowhere with their crab and Joe zipped his lip.

"Like the Fill-up?" Zoey smirked.

"Delish," Rudolph faked her. "Best fill-up I've had all week. How about a to-go for it?"

"*Awesome*," Zoey said, before heading for the take-out box.

Rudolph resumed his story.

"Specs tells me, 'Joe Cool's all right. He's front office, but he's still all right. I don't know if he got dropped on his head when he was a baby or what, but the dude's for real."

"So you and Joe hit it off right away, huh?" Denise asked.

"Not that quick," Rudolph said. "I watched my mouth

around him the first few weeks, yes I did. But it wasn't long before I picked up on his game."

A question came to her.

"So...while his wife was alive, was he still carrying a crush for sister-girl from college?"

"Who knows," Rudolph said. "He never mentioned Bernie to me before. Frankie and him were a tight couple, judging from what I saw—which wasn't much." He took the shiny pliers and cracked a crab leg in half. "Anyway, after Franki died, he didn't seem to be interested in women. And they came after him at work. Oh, *did* they. Nice-looking guy making good money. He even showed me a note that said—I swear—'Hey Joe: Guess what color panties I'm wearing and you get what's inside.'"

Red, Denise answered to herself.

She followed an impulse. "Any sistuhs give it a shot? I mean, since he obviously isn't turned off by brown."

Rudolph shifted his eyes around to see if any of the ninety-percent white crowd heard her. If they did, they were playing deaf.

"I'd say a sister or two might have come on to him, yeah," he said. "But Joe just wasn't interested."

While he was thinking of sex, he noticed she'd barely touched her drink.

"Wine don't agree with you?"

"It's fine," she said. "Taking it slow, that's all." She brought the glass up and wet her lips, just to please him, and then set it back down.

"How about giving me a thumbnail on his personality," she said. "Twenty-fi' words or less." Her second wind had come with the Joe talk, but now she was losing energy fast. She couldn't wait to get home and sink into her mattress.

"Twenny-fi, huh?" Rudolph said, repeating the girl's slang. "Let's see...he's funny...fair...smart..outgoing personality..." He gave up counting the words in his head. "Likes poetry... super-friendly at work but, from everything I've ever seen, a real loner when he leaves the place."

"Did you see him today?" Denise asked.

"Sure," Rudolph said. He looked over the rail as the *Belle of Louisville* went by. The old steamboat's paddle wheel was pushing it upriver, slow as glue. Its deck was festooned with lights that seemed in the night to be luminescent pearls, their number doubled as their reflections played off the water. Happy passengers stood at the rails and waved at the Mister J.'s crowd. Rudolph waved back at them. Then he turned to Denise and said, in a big, bursting laugh, "Who do you think's paying for this meal?"

19. The Search Begins

Long before they got back to the apartment, Rudolph saw there wasn't going to be any playtime with Denise tonight. The girl barely had enough steam to make it—with his help—up the two flights of stairs. And the sexiest thing she could manage to say to him when they got in the door was, "Pep needs to go pee-pee."

Rudolph hated this routine, but it was what it was. He clipped the leash on the mutt and the two wound up in Sir Pepi's usual spot, the little patch of grass near the bus stop sign. Eight minutes later, they were back. Sir Pepi, anxious to return to his Mama, went to the bedroom as fast as his little legs would take him.

Rudolph stayed in the living room. With the dog out of his hair and a belly full of buttery lobster and chardonnay, he let himself down into the red leather recliner Denise had bought him for his fiftieth birthday. With his inhibitions liquored down and chair tilted back until he felt like an astronaut at lift-off, he decided to make some phone calls. The last thing he wanted to do was drive to the girl's hometown with Joe at his side and cruise a bunch of black beauty parlors. Wouldn't that be a tub of fun. And if they went to a joint, he could just see some angry brother going off on him and his white friend. *"What the HELL? Where you think you ah, niggah? This bah ain't heah for no honkies..."*

He thought about Joe's dead-in-the-ground wife. Looks-wise, Franki had it all over Nubian Prin-*cess*. Even if she wasn't a sistuh, Franki was still plenty dark, when she got her tan on in the summer. Why couldn't Joe just be satisfied finding another brown Eye-talian?

He held his phone up in the air above his face and moved it forward and back until the numbers came in focus. He punched up "Averytown, KY" in the White Pages and then typed in *Bernadette Armstrong*. The results popped up ridiculous-fast. "2 matches," the screen read.

"Found her already," he kidded with himself. He mumbled them out loud. "B. Armstrong, age 55." And then, "Philomena B. Armstrong, no age."

These women probably wouldn't be overjoyed to hear their phone ring at 10:30 at night, but Rudolph was going with the feeling. "Into the valley of death rode the six hundred," he recited in the baddest Tennyson bravado he could muster. He dialed "B. Armstrong."

"Barry Armstrong," the man's voice answered.

Rudolph saw he shot himself in the foot on that one, but he asked about a Bernie Armstrong anyway, just to save face. He received a courteous, "I'm sorry, no Bernie here."

Wake up, he told himself. *Initials*. He went back to his White Pages screen. At least he knew *Philomena B. Armstrong* was going to be female. He went for it.

A black woman answered.

Woman: (In a sharp tone) Hel-LO?

Rudolph: (Making friendly) Hey, how 'ya doin'. My name is Rudolph Barnes...

Woman: Wha' the hell you want?

Rudolph: (Knocked out of his easy-going delivery) Uh, I'm looking for a lady. Name Bernadette Armstrong? Got a friend who wants to...

Woman: (Interrupting) Lookin' for a *what*?

Rudolph: A lady, Ma'am. Name's Bernadette Armstrong.

Woman: (Hostile) *Who* is this?

Rudolph: (Hears children laughing and screaming.) (Repeating) Name's Rudolph Barnes. From Louisville. I'm looking for...

Woman: (Turning from phone, screaming) You kids shut the hell up!

Rudolph: Ma'am?

Woman: (Coming back to phone) He don't live here.

Rudolph: No, a *woman*.

Woman: (Sassy) Well *she* don't live here neither. (Pulls away from phone again) Debray, I'm gonna bust yo ass! (Back to Rudolph, over the noise) Now *whut?*

Rudolph: (Voice rising in frustration) I need to get in touch with a Bernadette Armstrong, soon as I can.

Woman: What the hell for?

Rudolph: (Taking a wild stab) Are you her, Ma'am?

Woman: (More racket from the kids) Shakia! Get in here and shut ya kids the fuck UP!

Rudolph: (Massaging his forehead) Friend of mine wants to find a girl he went to school with. From college.

Woman: (Snorts bitterly) College! (To loud kids) Granny says shut...the hell...UP!

Rudolph: (Giving it one last try) So you don't know a Bernadette Armstrong?

Woman: Dumb shit! (Slams down the phone)

Rudolph tossed his phone over to the couch and lay back. This helping Joe put him in a foul mood. He closed his eyes. *Easy money, sure.* Mr. J's had already wiped out half of it. While he was trying to think of his next move, he heard the heavy gunfire coming from the bedroom. The TV was on. Denise had somehow come back to life. Despite the girl's fatigue, her brain apparently was wired to alert her when her favorite show was on.

Rudolph grunted his way out of the recliner and went to the bedroom. He saw her propped up in bed with her long robe on, sitting cross-legged. She had her contacts out and had slid on her yellow frames, the ones that made her look so smart he called them her "genius glasses." Rudolph's head swung over to the flat screen. There they were, more of Denise's damn zombies, all staggering around making their fitful zombie moves. This time they were in a toy store, biting and grunting at all the customers and their kids.

Rudolph raised his voice to get her attention.

"So much for the easy way," he said.

"What's that?" Denise said, eyes riveted on the TV.

"I *said*," Rudolph repeated, zombie disapproval in his voice, "I just struck out. There were only two names in the white pages, and neither one of' em was close."

That didn't surprise Denise. She concentrated on the ghoul getting his eye stabbed with an Army bayonet. "It's not likely she has a land line these days. I'll go online and try one of the dedicated people searches."

He stood there and took in her exciting TV show. The star was an anorexic-looking female with pipestem arms, chicken legs and boobs the size of volleyballs. Half of her grimy top had been ripped off her frame to give the viewers some gratuitous cheesecake. She was dodging right and left, turning back every few seconds to shoot at the pursuing fiends. Zombie guts splattered with every shot she took.

"I didn't want it to be easy anyway, Baby," he said. "Just make it that much sweeter when we *do* find her."

As soon as her show was over, Denise went into a long, spontaneous stretch. She fuzzily reassured herself that Rudy's futzing around with the White Pages would actually be a plus for her, would give her more time to find the girl herself. And find out a lot more about Joe, while she was at it. She was asleep as soon as her head sunk into her pillow.

20. Free Advice

"You're gonna tell us *way* more than *that*, Girl," Ameya ordered her roommate in McAfee women's dorm. Her head hung upside down from her top bunk as she eyeballed Bernie below her.

"Hail *yay-ah*," Jelise joined in with her country twang. Her butt was perched on the corner of Ameya's desk, the rounded corner between her legs. "You should thank us for coming up on you when we did. Another five minutes white boy would have had his tool between ya legs."

Kym came back from the bathroom and joined the piling-on. She walked over to Bernie, who was sitting on her bunk, nightshirt in her hand. Kym gave the little girl a hip bump to move her over. Bernie, who couldn't have weighed more than a hundred and fifteen pounds, let out a melodramatic cry and relocated herself down the mattress.

"That little love tap ain't *nuthin*," Kym told her as she had a seat. "If boy-boy had got his white stinger in ya, then you woulda *really* felt something."

That line set off the other two girls, who backed her up with whoops and "uh-*huh's*." They were ready for some get-down-wid-it cutting on the girl who had traded them for, of all things, White Lech from Main Street.

Bernie tried to stay cool with their silly sex talk. In a way, she liked them messing with her, now that she had a boy of her own. In another way, she was counting the minutes until Jelise and Kym cleared out for the night. Then she could lie alone in her bunk, free to play her amazing night back to herself, over and over.

The girls weren't showing any signs of leaving. Or cutting her any slack.

"Well?" Kym said to her, this time giving Bernie a slight elbow-poke in the ribs. "Did white boy put a trance on you or what, *Miss Thang*?"

Bernie began to say something, but Kym bulldozed in. "He comes out of nowhere, and the next thing we know girlfriend here is following him around like a puppy dog."

"*Lap* dog," Jelise threw in. "Lech got balls, I'll give him that. Walks right into a crowd of black folk, picks a cherry, and then runs off with it to get hisself a taste."

"He's not a lech," Bernie said. She gave Jelise a hard look.

"Weird," Kym said. "Who would have thought your boy was super-cool with black folk."

"Amen," Ameya said. She busted into a laugh. "Dude knew more Negroes than *we* did."

"That's right," Kym said, giving Bernie a pat on her little shoulder. "We won't call Lech no more."

Ameya looked down again at her roommate. "Observe," she said to the other two, as if she were a psychology professor offering up Bernie as a specimen. "Thanks to being worked over tonight by a white boy she *just met*, Rolling Flatts freshman Bernadette Armstrong has lost her fuckin' mind. And now she's going to attempt to tell us how the hell it happened."

Kym and Jelise hooted it up.

"Let her get on with it then," Kym said, sounding like a cop. She jumped up, squared herself with Bernie and made a little grind. "Give us some hot sex talk, Bernie. You know you want to."

"Inter-*racial* sex talk," Ameya yelled. "Woo! You go, Girlfriend."

That set off an enthusiastic, cadenced chant of "GO Bernie...GO Ber-nie..."

"That's crazy and you know it," Bernie said, still feeling the ache from Kym's hip bump. As if she were testifying at a trial, she said, "All we did was dance—and talk."

"*And* play rub-a-dub," Ameya said. "*And* work some major tongue." She shouted out to the others, "What do they call it, Sistuhs? 'The Make-out Maple'?"

High-fives again, all pointedly bypassing Bernie. When that subsided, Kym gave Bernie a solemn look. Her eyes pulled down and she paused, ostensibly weighted down by the gravity of what she was about to say. Timing the silence well, she said, "Seriously, Girl...did he really taste like vanilla?"

More whooping.

"*French* vanilla, Baby!" Ameya said, throwing in some of her own wit. She stuck out a nasty tongue and wiggled it down at Bernie.

The laughs and slaps came louder than ever.

Bernie looked over at the wind-up alarm clock on her desk. It was nearly two o'clock. At least she could lie in bed all morning, if she wanted to. The football game wasn't until tomorrow night.

"I *like* him," Bernie said. "He's nice." She could've added a lot more. Could've told them how his green eyes took her breath, how good his lips felt on her, how safe his arms felt around her. She could have told them how exciting it was to do things you weren't supposed to do with a white boy. But she didn't. All that was for *her*.

Ameya let out a groan. "'He's *nice*.' Shit. Be sure not to tell us how turned on you got, Bernie Armstrong. "One little Friday night dance and you are so damn hung up." She looked at the other two girls, "That's it. No more men for her. We're locking her up 'til she graduates."

Jelise took on what was for her a softer edge. "Free advice, little one," she said. 'Really nice' will get you knocked up just as fast as 'really an asshole.'"

Kym and Ameya let out testifying *"Umm-hmm's!"*

"What you know 'bout this white boy, really?" Jelise kept it up, shifting to hard-ass again. "I mean, since you met him for the very first time about an hour and a half ago?"

Bernie supplied more general information, hoping that would be enough for tonight. "He's from around Louisville, I know that. And he's a sophomore, undecided. And..." She searched for words that wouldn't get her in more trouble, "And he's funny, and interesting. And he's into music and sports, too. Ran cross country and track in high school, just like me."

"He *said*," Jelise wisecracked.

"*And* he can't dance," Ameya kicked in. "We saw him. Sorry as hell."

"I'm telling ya this for gospel right now, Girlfriend," Jelise said. "Yo 'nice' white boy is just like any other male. All he wants is somethin' to stick it in."

"That's what *you* say," Bernie came back. "And I don't believe all men are dogs, either!"

Kym let out a huge yawn. She was played out for the night. "Just keep them knees together when you're around the dude, that's all we're sayin'."

Ameya cupped her hands to her mouth and pretend-megaphoned her words at her roomie. "We love ya, Girl. Otherwise we wouldn't bother."

At two-thirty, Jelise slid off the desk and said, "Right. We just don't want Miz Armstrong to be the next freshman Mama— compliments of White Lech." She was halfway out the door, following Kym, but she just had to say more. "There's plenty of white boys out there who'd *love* to get them some chocolate stuff," she sneered. "As long as it's in private. Trust me."

As soon as Kym and Jelise went back to their room. Bernie went to the bathroom to finally get herself cleaned up and ready for bed. By the time she slid under the covers and reached to the wall to snap off the light, she could hear Ameya above her, asleep and breathing hard. At last, alone with her thoughts, she closed her eyes and played it all back, starting with the moment she saw him coming across the room for her.

Before she gave in to sleep, she let her dream play out. White men fell in love with black women in Nineteen-Eighty— sometimes. Even married them—sometimes. Look at her own parents, a black man and a Korean woman. They were happy, weren't they? She really *could* have her own white boy.

21. Joe Brings the Book

The next morning, Rudolph was at work loading blank paper into a digital printing press when he heard the *boop* from his personal phone. *Text message.* He pulled the phone out of its holster and read:

Wht nxt re Joe nrml?

Rudolph frowned. *More text-spelling crap.* Denise must have been in a sales meeting. Otherwise, she would've called instead of sending him this Swahili. He did have an answer for her question, though. He hit the reply button.

Got an idea, he said. He began spelling his answer—all the way out, like he'd been taught to do in school.

u stil ther? she buzzed in.

He told his phone, "Hell yeah" and kept on typing until he finished. He sent: **Got an idea. Go over his yearbook with him. have him identify people who knew her. Try calling them.**

Denise came back with **y not. BTW thats not how u tex-spel! lol.**

Rudolph looked at her reply. Wasn't that cute. He had another thought. **Will ask him to bring it to work tomorrow.**

Coo, Denise answered. **hows he doin?**

Joe was fed up with this back-and-forth. **Fine except he's already asked me twice today when are we going to Averytown.**

So he realy meens it, she came back.

One-track mind, he replied.

I kno thats rite, Denise said. **oop gotta go. L8tr. xoxo**

At the mid-morning break, Rudolph used a company phone

to call Joe, who was up front in his cube. Joe sounded like he was going to do somersaults ("*Great* idea, Rudinski!") when he heard his friend's suggestion to bring his *Splenditus* to work.

At the end of his shift, Rudolph stood in his customary position, near the front of the line leading into the time clock room. He saw Joe approach, lugging his yearbook, and cussed to himself. *Damn man just couldn't wait one more day.* Joe must have gone home at lunchtime, driven there and back like a bat out of hell.

When Joe shoved it into his hands, Rudolph went tart in front of the other employees. "Tomorrow turned into today, huh?"

"Never put off tomorrow what you can do today," Joe said cheerily.

Rudolph did a few mock two-handed barbell curls with the heavy book.

"Right now is as good a time as any," Joe said.

"Wrong. Time to go home."

Joe's face took on a hurt look. "That's why I went home at lunch."

Rudolph was about to put up an argument with the man when he saw Phillips join the line. Phillips saw the two of them talking, being real friendly with each other, and glowered through his safety glasses.

"Not here, Joe," Rudolph said.

Joe gave him a halting look. "How about my car, then?"

"Oh no." Rudolph dug in. "Tell you what,"I'll meet you at Taco Bill's. Fifteen minutes."

"I'll get my keys. Fifteen minutes."

At 4:08, Rudolph steered his car out of the employee lot and called—not texted—Denise.

At her desk at work, Denise heard her ringtone for Rudy—Kylie Minogue's "I Can't Get You Out of My Head." She could make time for a quick chat. Thanks to the one-hour time difference between Louisville and Moline, Illinois, she had a few minutes to give Rudy and still get back with Anson Huey, like she promised.

"Hey Text Master," she answered. "What's up?"

"Jack jumped it up on me," Rudolph said, with a pained expression in his voice. "Went home at lunch and brought it back to work, if you can believe that."

"His yearbook?"

"His yearbook. I'm on my way to Taco Bill's. Wanna meet us? Have dinner while we take a look at some prospects?"

"Won't work," she said. "The bottle collectors are *this close* to choosing us for a site visit. I'm getting ready to call them and throw in the kitchen sink."

"Cool," Rudolph said. "Do what you have to do. I just figured you could use that women's intuition of yours to pick out some of the females for us."

Denise heard it—*an honest-to-God compliment from Rudy*—and it had nothing to do with her body. "I'll try to make it," she said, "but don't let your tacos get cold. This guy in Illinois talks like he gets paid by the minute. If I don't show, just ask Joe if you can bring it home. Then we can go over it together."

"Right," Rudolph said.

She glanced up at the clock and her voice rose. "*Whoop.* Gotta make this call. Wish me luck."

22. Rudolph and Joe meet Up

Rudolph hung up his phone just as he pulled into the parking lot of *Taco Bill's*.

Taco Bill's had been open for about two months and its owner was hoping he could keep that name under the radar a lot longer. If the big boys at Taco Bell had their attorneys—who surely had better things to do—send him a threatening letter over something as minor as trademark infringement, well, Ace Wallingford would just change his cheap little sign, make it "Taco Mel's" or something.

Rudolph saw that Joe was already out of his vehicle, waiting for him. Joe pointed to the empty space next to his Jeep.

"Look who's here," Rudolph smarted off to himself. Although Rudolph had pulled out of the Max-It employee lot before Joe did, Joe's Jeep had caught up with him and then blown by Rudolph's old Maxima. Joe had the advantage there. Rudolph was obligated to stay under the posted 35 MPH. He didn't need to give some high-strung Popo an excuse to pull over another brother and start World War III.

Joe took a step toward Rudinski's car to open his door valet-style, but Rudolph lowered his tinted window and said, with annoyance, "I know how to get out of a car, Cool."

"I'm feeling good about this, Rudinski," Joe told him. "*Really* good. This is a great idea of yours!"

Rudolph gave him a bland look and and then rammed his beefy left shoulder into his door to get the thing open.

"Slow down," Rudolph grunted, as he got out. "Miss Wonderful's been out there for thirty years. She can wait five more minutes." He walked to the other side to haul out the big book. Just before they went through the restaurant's door, Rudolph asked Joe under his breath, "We *are* gonna be customers, correct?"

"You bet," Joe said.

"Then you got this, right?"

"I've got it, Rudinski," Joe said. "In fact, I *insist*."

That was all Rudolph needed to know. After setting the *Splenditus* on a booth table, he headed with Joe to the counter. A teenage girl wearing an orange Taco Bill T-shirt greeted him. Rudolph tilted his head toward Joe and told the girl, "He's got this." The counter girl gave him a dubious stare and her eyes went to the white guy for confirmation. Joe gave her a smile and a nod. Rudolph ordered two burrito supremes, a chalupa, a taco salad and a taco.

"Y''all want drinks with that?"

Rudolph caught her. "That's *my* order. He hasn't give you his yet." He added, "Coke. Biggest you got."

She punched in the drink on her touch screen. "*Awesome*."

A few minutes later, they picked up their food and headed for their booth. Rudolph slid in, and when he realized Joe was trailing behind him, he stopped cold and stared at him.

"*What* are you doin', Joe?" he said.

"What do you mean?"

"I mean, what are you *doin'*?" Rudolph repeated. He wasn't about to sit side-by-side in a booth with another guy, looking at a picture book. "Tell ya what, Joe," he instructed. "You sit over there on that side with your book, and when you find a prospect, just spin the thing around and I'll take look. We can go back and forth like that."

"Brilliant," Joe said. "*You* look and then *I* look."

"Damn skippy," Rudolph said. "*Hell.*"

Joe crunched through his two-taco meal in no time. Rudolph, on the other hand, was determined to enjoy his meal. With a tray piled high with free, greasy goodness, he was gonna *sava the flava.*

Ten minutes went by, then fifteen, and Joe couldn't wait any longer. "If you don't mind, Rudinski," he said, "I'll go ahead and get started."

"Go ahead, Cool," Rudolph said. He took another long slurp from a plastic cup that was almost as big as a table lamp. "I'm wrapping it up right now."

Joe opened the book. It made that sticky, ripping noise again. The noise made a few of the other customers look over and gawk for a minute. Then they went back to their food.

"Since your bookmark is already in the freshman section," Rudolph bossed, "check out the other people in her class."

"Alrighty," Joe said. He unstuck his way along, until he reached the H's. "There!" Joe said. He pointed at a black female. "That's one."

Rudolph followed Joe's finger and spun the book toward him.

"Something Henry." He looked over at Joe for help. "I give. How do you say it? *Jelly*? *Jealous*?"

"Ja-leese," Joe said. He got cute with his friend. "Don't you know how to pronounce black names?"

"Who says that's a black name," Rudolph smarted back.

"She was the girl I told you about," Joe said. His voice got louder, being *informative.* "The one who yelled, 'Bernie, yo white boy callin'. "Remember?"

Several heads turned to them.

Rudolph ignored the eyes and mumbled sarcastically to his

friend, "Why don't you say it louder next time, Joe. I don't think the folks back in the kitchen heard ya." He looked under the girl's photo. Hometown: Lexington, Kentucky. Rudolph gave the freshman a quick size-up: Short Afro. Almost a blue-black, African kind of face. Big round cheeks, thick neck. Had a rough look in her pose, even in her official Be Nice Yearbook Smile.

Rudolph took the pen and notebook from his shirt pocket. The cover of the pad read, "Max-It Imaging. We Print it, You Profit." He began jotting down notes. The two of them moved through the freshmen and then the sophomores. Gradually, Joe found the people who knew Bernie. Among them were Jelise Henry, Ameya Kendricks, Kym Whaley, Isaiah "Hurt Man" Hurtt and Drew "Heavy" Williamson.

By nightfall, Rudolph had his fill of being in the fishbowl with Joe. He stood up, saying, "That's enough Who's Who in the Zoo for me." In all, his notebook had a list of eleven names, including eight females and three males.

"Denise can at least get an idea what these women looked like before she calls 'em," he told Joe.

Joe hung with him as he set the *Splenditus* back into his car. "A woman's touch never hurts." He smiled, more encouraged than ever.

As Rudolph pulled out of the lot and away from Joe, he took a tired breath and blew out, "Crapshoot, crapshoot, crapshoot."

23. Joe and Bernie Go to Church

He took her arm as soon as they walked out the door of McAfee dorm. No reason to take a chance on Bernie breaking her neck on Joe's first go at church with her. The old limestone steps, worn concave by decades of students, were far too risky a descent for an exhilarated freshman wearing mint-green high heels.

When she was safely on the walk, he released her. Joe wasn't about to flaunt the two of them in front of the town, and that was where they were headed. Bernie was fine with him letting her go—for a little while. In the two weeks since they'd met, it seemed as if they'd spent more time together than apart. Hanging out in front of the Student Union with the growing Loud Crowd; sharing their dinners there; studying every night in the library.

They were definitely working against the grain. Over the years, the few interracial couples who popped up at Rolling Flatts State disappeared fast. Either the novelty wore off for the pair or they couldn't handle any more of the ugly looks. That was fine with the school. The Admin office didn't need any examples to suggest that the region's center of higher education was headed in *that* direction.

Bernie happily strolled alongside her boy, staying just close enough to him to let any ambitious females out there know they were a couple. The eleven black students and the one white one headed down the street. The way Joe and Bernie were kept in the middle of the procession, one with an imagination could have likened it to elephants on the march, guarding their young from danger, front and rear. The only time Bernie and Joe made physical contact with each other came when Bernie's

heel caught in a crack in the sidewalk. Off balance, she'd gasped
and fell against him, and of course he'd caught his ravishing
girl with both hands. Bernie quickly broke from Joe and let out
an embarrassed laugh.

"Shit, Bernie—that was *so fake*," Kym's voice sounded out
from behind them.

Then from Ameya, "Ooo, good thing Joe *saved* you, Girl."
More laughs.

Kym and Ameya had mellowed toward Joe by then, after
seeing the white guy dote on her for two solid weeks. Jelise, on
the other hand, didn't mind shooting the white guy her bad eye
every now and then. Bernie'd take two out of three.

The line of young black folk was a weekly Sunday morning
sight for those who lived along their church route. The men
and women joked their way along Main Street, here on a crisp
autumn morning that was quickly giving way to the climbing sun.
They continued past a string of student-dependent businesses—
second-hand stores and comic book-and-record shops and the
like—and then took the side street into a neighborhood. That
was where the full-bore gawking would start. Just ahead of them
was the run-down bungalow with the three white guys. As usual,
the trio was standing there all puffy-eyed, wearing ragged jeans
and undershirts. They took lazy drags on their cigarettes while
they picked up the empty beer bottles and plastic cups from their
Saturday night blow-out. A girl wearing only a man's flannel
shirt came outside to help. She made slow, angular moments, as
if she had a rough night. When she saw all the blacks and then
the mixed couple, she placed her hands on her hips and joined
the guys in frowning at them.

The black students had wised up to them after their very
first Sunday, had learned not to bother offering up any smiles.

They kept their eyes straight ahead.

Across the street, a middle-aged woman in a housecoat picked her newspaper from the edge of her flower bed, banged it against her leg to knock off any loose mulch, and gave them all a quick, indifferent glance. Up the block, a middle-aged couple, dressed for church themselves, saw them coming and hustled out to their car. The man gunned it out of their driveway and down the street as they rolled toward a different church. From the open door of a well-kept Cape Cod, a forty-ish woman with analyzing eyes—possibly an RFSC faculty member—saw the white guy with the black girl and gave them a thumbs-up. Most in the group, including Joe and Bernie, smiled and waved back, glad to respond to any friendly gesture that came their way.

They crossed a wide intersection that was spanned in the middle by railroad tracks. "Hang onto your butt, Jedi," Heavy yelled back at Joe in a mischievous grin. "Headin' to the other side of the tracks." The houses almost immediately began to change. Many of them shrunk to shotgun style. There were fewer brick homes and more frames. A good number of them were tidy, but others needed serious attention, with cracked windows, flaking paint. Here and there, high weeds grew where a house once stood.

Suddenly, every body was black. Joe understood Heavy's "other side of the tracks" announcement. But here was a stunner for him: this black neighborhood was barely fifteen minutes' walking distance from campus. *As if it was a secret.*

Two blocks later, the church, a dingy, white clapboard building, came into view. Joe saw its stained glass windows were done on the cheap -- they were squares of bright-colored plastic. The faded black letters on the plywood sign out front read, *Second Missionary Baptist Church.*

Joe had never been in a Baptist church before. His parents took him and his three sisters to church once a year, on Christmas Eve. Joe's folks had put their day-to-day inspirational stock in one simple directive: "If you just follow the Golden Rule, God *has* to be on your side." Joe and his sisters grew up believing that.

From the other direction, a small clump of the local church members approached. The students stopped at the steps leading up to the wide front doors and respectfully gave way to them. "Mornings," and "Amens" were warmly and enthusiastically exchanged. Then a couple of "Mornings" came out shaky, as the white student was spotted. The Rolling Flatts students followed the town folk on up the steps, with Heavy in the lead. At the door, Bernie shifted her Bible to her purse hand and surprised him by putting her free arm through his. She gave his arm a little tug, looked over at him, and softly asked, "Are you okay?"

The Hammond organ inside suddenly began playing, pumping deep-throated gospel chords all the way out the door. The Harmonious voices of a choir joined in. Joe bent over and whispered into the pretty ear decorated with small, ladylike imitation pearl earrings, "Sure I am, Baby—I'm with you."

She high-heeled herself in with him, trying to hold herself down.

Joe thought the Rolling Flatts church-going students were something with the way they dressed, but here, he saw a whole building's worth of people decked out in super-fine clothes. The women here were the main attractions, for sure. Hair and makeup just so, sporting gleaming jewelry. They wore killer outfits, all of them tasteful, not a disrespectful mini skirt or pair of slacks on any of them. The male members of the church weren't slumming, either. They'd rolled out in nice suits and sports coats. Even the old prayer warriors whose backs were bent by age managed to look sharp.

The choir—seven women and three men—was on one side of the pulpit, swaying their burgundy robes to the beat. Joe was amazed that so much sound could come out of such a small number of people, until he realized the singing wasn't coming just from them. In here, not only the choir, but *everybody*—the pew-sitters, the preachers, the ushers—*everybody* was singing and clapping and hallelujah-ing like nobody's business.

An usher, a short woman wearing a white blouse with a dark blue cravat, greeted them just inside the door. She made a slow, graceful sweep of her white gloved hand and guided them into the aisle that went down the middle of the building. The Rolling Flatts contingent followed her toward the front. As the college students marched into view, the worshippers took notice, one pew at a time, paying out lots of smiles and nods. They wanted to be sure to let the college students, far from their own hometown churches, know they were welcome.

And then the white guy came into their view. The one with the beaming black girl on his arm. Some eyeballs locked up. Mouths fell open. Up in the choir stand, one of the older sopranos was knocked so far out of her rhythm she forgot the lyrics to *Battle Hymn of the Republic*. Up until then, the only time the congregation saw a white male inside these walls was just before an election. And none of the politicians had *ever* entered wearing a young sistuh on their arm. The sight of the mixed couple charged up more than a few spirited "Ayy-mens" and "Hal-le-LU-yahs."

The only bitter look came from the refined-looking man in the graying goatee and matching wool suit. He gave Joe a hard stare, not caring if his obvious dislike offended the white kid or not. Joe didn't know the man's name, but he recognized him. He was one of only a handful of black professors at RFSC. The man's telegraphed glare told Joe, *Cute stunt, white boy. Showing up in church with a gullible little sister hanging on your arm.* His nasty look bounced right off Joe. By then, *every* mean look bounced off Jedi Joe.

When the usher gestured to the second pew, Bernie pulled her arm from Joe and sidestepped her way in. Joe followed her. Worshippers scooted down to make room for them. As Joe lowered himself to the worn cushion, he heard a powerful, resounding, "Ayy-MAHN!" His head swung up in the direction of the voice and he saw a tall, thin preacher at the pulpit, grinning his approval down at him. Bernie gave the man of God a big smile and then arched herself over to Joe's ear. "Reverend Winter," she whispered helpfully.

As Joe and his white self had stood out to the blacks, it was the other white faces that jumped out at him. There were three of them, all female. The oldest was sitting next to a black man who had his arm stretched behind her, resting on the top of their pew. Sitting on the woman's other side was a teenager with toffee-toned skin. The girl's violet eyes matched the woman's. Daughter, Joe told himself. Joe had noticed the third white female as soon as he entered the building. The raw-boned woman was sitting by herself on the back row, close to the door. She had frizzed-out hair and oversized eyeglasses that covered most of her face. Her incredibly bony frame was swallowed by the exploding colors of a Bob Marley-style T-shirt. Rebel in the mountains, Joe told himself. He guessed *graduate student.*

Eventually came the call for visitors to introduce themselves, if they liked. Joe stayed mute on that one.

"His name's Joe Normal!"

Joe flinched at the sound of Heavy's big, gleeful mouth, and looked down the pew to see him grinning and pointing him out to the whole room. The congregation laughed as they smiled warmly, taking in Joe and the young sister sitting next to him. That wasn't good enough for Heavy.

"From some town called Booneville!" he added in a teasing tone. "Near Louisville."

The congregation gave Joe a final charitable laugh and respectfully removed its attention from him. A few intrigued high school girls from the neighborhood held their eyes on Joe and the girl next to him. *The white college guy who had a thang for the sister.* Down on the pew cushion, Bernie reached for his hand and intertwined her fingers with his.

Later, as the preacher hunched over the pulpit and began his sermon, Bernie opened her Bible and held it up to Joe, pointing at the verses to be discussed. When he looked down past the book, he was blown away. Bare, sexy thighs were jumping out from her hiked-up dress. He hadn't seen them before, since she was always in her jeans. They were supple, creamy, moist chunks of hot caramel. Instantly, he felt himself get excited for her.

She saw his eyes weren't on the Bible verse and gave his hand two rapid squeezes—their secret signal that the other person wanted to share something in private. Joe kept his eyes on her incredible legs as he bent to her. In something just more than a breath, she told him, "Welcome to ch'uch."

Joe had no idea church could be so wonderful. The following week, he went back with her and the others, partly to hear the sermon and partly to be treated to those fabulous melting-hot thighs.

The screaming came on his third visit.

An older woman, one with a large hat with white feathers, was sitting in the pew just in front of them. The woman heard the old spiritual, and without warning, her rocking turned into violent lurches. At the top of her voice, she screamed, eyes tightened shut, "Thank ya Jesus! "Thank ya Jesus! Thank ya JE-sus!"

Joe was horrified, thought the woman was having a seizure. He turned to motion someone to help—to call a damn *ambulance*—just as the short usher rushed up. The usher waved at the woman's face with a handful of church bulletins. Joe was amazed by that pitiful attempt to help the woman. He was also amazed that the choir hadn't quit singing. He was flat astonished when he turned to Bernie to make sure she wasn't freaking out. The girl hadn't changed her expression at all. Like the rest of them, she was taking the old woman's delirious scene in stride.

"Ay-men," Bernie coolly said with a steady voice, sticking with the song and looking past the woman to the choir.

As the song ended, the woman with the emotional fits settled down, once again a coherent member of the congregation. Joe sat there, crisis over, and told himself he couldn't imagine himself *ever* losing control like that, over anything.

That night, in a break from massaging tongues with Bernie, there under the Make-out Maple, a totally bizarre thought came to Joe. Bizarre, because for some strange reason it now appeared obvious to him. *If a person can't get excited enough about his religion to go crazy every now and then, then maybe he needs a different religion.*

He kept that rogue notion to himself and went back to sucking face with his hot-tongued, hot-thighed black girl.

24. Together

November came, and when the night air grew so cold that frosty love clouds rose above Joe and Bernie with every kiss, they headed indoors. Their new winter necking headquarters was the RFSC library, second floor.

They had a system. Around nine-thirty, right after Bernie's foot tapped against Joe's sneaker, she headed for the stacks. Joe gave her a couple of minutes and then followed, leaving his own book open on the table as well, as if he was taking a restroom break. Nobody but a campus idiot could have missed their game. Then again, there was only half an hour left before closing time. All but a handful of students had cleared out for the night.

Once Joe and Bernie were alone in the back row of the stacks—Biographies, that was their getaway section—they had it made. At first it was treating each other to light, daring kisses, lips barely tickling lips. Then, privacy all but assured, they went into a tight clinch and helped themselves to long, deep exchanges. That was the reason Bernie didn't bother wearing lipstick after dinner.

Neither of them went home for Thanksgiving, and after they spent those four entire days together—minus the hours of her curfew—they were an inseparable couple. Soon after school commenced again, Bernie's girlfriends began calling them, "Bernie 'n' Joe." Not to be outdone, the Loud Crowd played off that and made it, "Joe 'n' Bernie."

Back at McAfee Hall, whoever happened to be working the front desk knew what to do when the mustached guy with the green eyes and long blond hair showed up. Before Joe could even offer up a "Hey," the tinny intercom was calling out, "Bernie

Armstrong—he's here."

Unlike some of the other girls at her dorm, Bernie didn't make her guy wait on her, didn't pretend she was oh-so-busy with other things. She'd already taken a good ten minutes doing her customary prep work for him—fiddled with her hair, checked for any incoming zits and covered them with concealing foundation, swished around a mouthful of Scope wintergreen. With her yell-back of "Okay!" Bernie bounded—always bounded—down the steps to meet her boy.

Bernie's classroom threads were nearly always comprised of a pair of snug, plain jeans and her *Fightin' Pioneers* sweatshirt. And her big hoops. Those were a given, too. Joe loved the way hoops made her look sexy and super-feminine at the same time. "Be *presentable*." That was what Bernie's Army father had always preached to her and her sister before they went out in public. But whenever she was hid away with her Joe, it was a different story. Tucked back in the stacks or standing deep within the Maple's shadows, she let him handle her however he wanted—as long as he didn't get carried away and try to get into *that*. But oh, how she would let him go at her hair. Joe loved to squeeze it between his fingers. He was fascinated by the coarse feel of it, loved to stroke it and crush it and smell it.

On one of those relatively mild early-December nights, when they were back alone under the Make-out Maple, he had played a game with her.

"Do you trust me?" he asked.

"You know you don't have to ask that," she said, her eyes open wide.

"Close your eyes."

Eyes shut tight, she felt his fingertips move lightly across her brow. Slowly, they followed the rounded bone to the side of her face, as if following a trail. Then they descended, brushing at her temple before moving on to her wondrous, high cheekbones. Her face turned up to him, as she drank in the exquisite sensation of having him caress her. His fingers lingered there, making slow circles on her cheek, as if he were signing his initials on her. That done, his fingers slid down to her delicate jawline, leisurely played along it, and then slid up to her lips. A single fingertip rubbed back and forth on the swell of her upper lip. When it began to do the same at her bottom lip, she sucked it into her mouth. The sudden erotic spark forced Joe into a low grunt of carnal pleasure. Soon, he pulled his finger away from her wet, tight lips.

"That's all of *that* I can stand," he said, taking short, rapid breaths.

She looked up at him and said, "Now close *your* eyes." Her fingers petted his face and then went him one better by applying a lingering, warm kiss to every place she touched. And then she worked his finger again.

They were blown away by each other.

25. Jelise Corners Bernie

Bernie was in her room, packing for the Christmas break, when Jelise yelled out a "Knock!" and barged her way in. Her bullhorn of a voice startled Bernie, who was straddled over her duffle bag and shoving her dirty clothes into it, daydreaming about Joe.

"Jelise," Bernie reluctantly said. She looked up and made her greeting a cool one. Bernie already had her hair wrapped and her bedclothes on—her pink T-shirt and purple "Fightin' Pioneers" sweatpants—but she saw bedtime wasn't going to happen anytime soon, not now.

Jelise, like Bernie, wouldn't be catching her ride home until the next day. And with Ameya and Kym already gone home, Jelise knew she had all kinds of time to biz the buzz with Lil' Ms. Goody-Goody. "Packing up," she observed. "Be good to go home and get some home cookin', won't it?"

"I know that's right," Bernie said. She ducked her head and scooped another mound of funky clothes across the floor and into the mouth of her Army duffle. Jelise' uninvited drop-in suggested to Bernie that the best thing about Christmas vacation would be not having Jelise Henry to put up with. Bernie punched the last of her things into the bag and slowly began to bring her feet together to stand up.

"Watch the legs," Jelise said. "You had yourself unfolded pretty good."

Bernie pulled the duffle up on its bottom and bounced it up and down to make the overload of clothes settle as well as they could—and to show Jelise that Bernie Armstrong was a wiry sister. She tied it off.

Jelise walked over to Ameya's desk and took her favorite

sitting position on the corner, shorts opened wide.

Bernie was so sorry that Ameya was already gone. After she had spilled the beans to her roommate that she was still a virgin, Ameya had seemed to grow closer to her, turn more protective. Ameya was a former high school volleyball player with deceptively strong arms, and at the end of them, she sported long, sharp nails. Any run-in between Ameya and Jelise over Bernie would have been a real scratch-and-dent, that was for sure. Now Jelise had her all to herself.

"Guess Bernie's gonna miss her White Boy, huh?" she said.

"Things are going to be different for a couple of weeks, that's for sure," Bernie responded. She glanced at Jelise but quickly shifted her eyes away.

Jelise's lidded eyes studied the girl. *Silly Little Thing was dope over the white guy.* "I guess he's gonna come see you over the holidays, huh?" she pried. She held the rude stare on the girl while she waited for an answer.

"Don't think so."

"Yeah," Jelise came back darkly, "That's what I thought."

Bernie felt the fire burn into her cheeks. "What's *that* supposed to mean?" she snapped. She wasn't aware she'd made fists out of those pretty hands of hers.

"Aw, girl, take a chill pill," Jelise sneered. She pushed down on the desk until her elbows locked, lifting her bottom until it hung in the air. The move was just to let Little Girl know that Jelise was one strong bitch. Exhibition performed, Jelise lowered herself and asked, in a sly voice, "You give White Boy his Christmas present?"

"I got him cologne, yeah," Bernie replied. She stood behind her duffle, crossing and uncrossing her arms. "Chaps." Before Jelise could ask, Bernie added, "He gave me a really nice top."

"Cologne, that's not exactly what I meant," Jelise said. She paused. "Girl ain't been popped yet, has she?"

The words stung Bernie, made her feel like she'd committed a crime. Jelise seemed to *know*. Bernie wanted to let out a shriek and tell the girl it was none of her damn business, but she held the words in the back of her throat. She swallowed, and in a voice as even as she could make it, she said, "You don't know that."

Jelise smiled. She figured if the girl had given it up, she wouldn't have been so up tight about the question. Maybe would've even been up for a little crowing. Jelise was happy as a pig in mud sitting here talking sex to Sweet Polly Purebred.

"C'mon, Sista-girl, don't get all bent, hell. Everybody knows you were clean as Windex coming in here."

Bernie knew Ameya wouldn't have blabbed anything. Jelise was just yanking her chain.

"Girl changes after the first time," Jelise harped on. "You can see it in her eyes. But you—well, *you* look like you're still on the Good Ship Lollipop."

Bernie's voice went harder. "What I do with Joe is my business." She glanced at the alarm clock next to Jelise's big butt. It read *11:59*.

"Take my word for it, I know some things," Jelise said. Then, out of character, she let her voice go mellow. She licked her lips to prep herself. "Mind if I tell you a story? You cool with that?"

What if I'm not, Bernie said to herself. Then, out loud, "Go ahead."

Jelise stood up and propped her rear against the desk like an instructor kicking off a lecture.

"I started out all boy-crazy too, like most any girl does when she comes of age. Was about thirty pounds lighter, had a real nice figure. Gave it up when I was sixteen. After that, it was like somebody put up a billboard, know what I'm sayin'? The brothers come waggin' after me like dogs. When my senior year started, I was *really* hot to trot. My mama wasn't blind, so she put me on the pill. *Smart.* Hell, I did all the parties, had fun with my share of brothers. Even had one fool chase after me, wantin' to get married, just because I gave him a little piece 'a heaven. Shee-it. Jelise was gonna *enjoy* her senior year."

Bernie had a seat on her bunk. Jelise dropped her head to the girl.

"This is the part you're really gonna like, so listen up, Little Maid."

Bernie crossed her arms, but paid attention.

"Friday night," Jelise said, "after a football game. I'm at a party—plenty of booze and smokin'. And it's really mixed, lookin' all Oreo, if you can believe that. Well, this white dude comes up to me with a couple of cold brews. I remembered him, he was a year ahead of me. Weightlifter. He told me he was in college. Well, that hooks me, college guy checking *me* out. His eyes are all over me while he's making with the chit-chat. But I'm cool with that. He's even a comedian. Tells this crowd, 'I was thinking about pledging for a fraternity—*'Ioughta Eata Thigh.'* That scores some laughs, and I feel myself actually startin' to heat up for him. Before I know it, he's coming back with another round for the both of us, and now I'm checking out *his* stuff, and not caring if I look interested or not."

Bernie sat motionless.

"Guess what. He complains about how hot it is in this house, and asks me if I want go take a ride in his car and cool off. And I say to myself, why not, he's got okay looks and one studly body. So what if he *is* white. So I leave the party with him. We wind up on a dead end way out near the park. Well, we're making so much steam in the back seat all the windas are fogged up. When we're done, I tell him he's the first white guy I ever had and he says,'Congratulations.'

"I go ahead and let him puff himself up—why not, if that floats his boat --- and before you know it, he's back up and we're doing it again. He fires off another round, and I'm lying there, all played out, but still ridin' on Cloud Nine. He looks down and gives me a big, sweaty grin, and when I smile back at him—*Oh God,* he slapped me hard. My eyes went all blurry from the tears, and when they more or less clear up I can see he don't even look like the same guy anymore. Got this snarlin' face. Says, 'Thanks for the free fuck, nigger.' And then he says, 'Oh yeah, *two* fucks,' and hits me *again.* I start to gag, and I feel his hands squeezing at my ankles. He's dragging me out of the car. I'm trying to put my hands behind me so my head won't bust on the ground, and he's yelling, "You ain't upchuckin' up in *my* car, Bitch!'

"He left me laying there in the weeds. Panties gone, my capri's covered with dirt from him throwing them out with me. And all I could think of was, *They warned me.* And then I *did* throw up, puked my insides out."

The tears welled up in Bernie's eyes.

"So that was what it was like between me and a white guy," Jelise said. "I shut down right after that. Quit school, quit boys, quit everything. My head was so screwed up I had to repeat my senior year." She narrowed her eyes at Bernie. "I ain't never gonna let another white man get near me again. *Ever.*"

Bernie felt the cool, wet sensation from a tear sliding down her cheek. She didn't know what to say to Jelise, so she offered a simple look of sympathy. She was startled when Jelise's voice came back sharp again. "I'm telling you. Sooner or later, your white boy's gonna skip on you. Guaranteed."

With the insult, Bernie's compassion for the girl disappeared.

"No he won't," she insisted. She stood up and held her door wide open. "I'm going to bed, Jelise."

"Right," Jelise said scowled. "Your white knight would *never* do that." She butt-strutted past Bernie but turned around and stopped. "How long he been sniffin' around it now, Armstrong? Three, four months? And all you give him was a whiff?" Jelise gave the girl a parting shot. "In case you ain't noticed, there's dick-crazy females all over this campus. How long you think he's gonna wait for *your* precious stuff?" She paused, as if another thought just came to her. "Unless he's been gettin' it someplace else. And he's just bidin' his time with you, waitin' til he can sample hisself some chocolate."

"'Night," Bernie said, stronger.

As Jelise walked away, she raised her voice and said, "You *don't* give it up, Baby Girl, he gone. You *do* give it up, he's yours for a month or two, and then he's *still* gone."

Bernie wanted to slam the door as hard as she could, but she caught herself and instead slowly pushed it until it clicked shut. She pushed the knob lock in. *Discipline,* she heard her father say.

Even after she slid under her covers, she felt the assault of Jelise's story. Her anger came up again. She wasn't Dorothy in The Wiz and she wasn't going to be treated like a child. Joe wasn't anything like that monster Jelise ran into. When the day came when they made love, it wouldn't be two drunk strangers pounding away at each other in the back seat of a car.

26. Denise Checks Out the Yearbook

Denise smiled at the canine cradled in her arms and started up with her baby-talking.

"Woodee home, Pep. Evva-body home now. Yay!" The dog looked over at Rudolph and yawned. "So that's the book," she said, downshifting her voice to make it sound as if she was barely interested in it. She put the dog on the floor and extended her arms to Rudy. "I'll hold it. Get enough fine dining at Taco Bill's?"

"Just enough," he said. He lowered the weighty book onto his woman's open palms. "Watch it, thing'll throw your back out."

Her arms drooped with its weight. "Whoa, you got that right," she said, puffing her cheeks out. She looked over the dull gold letters. *Splenditus*. And under that, *1980*.

"How'd your phone call go?" he asked.

"Phone call?" Denise gave him a blank look.

"Yeah, your phone call." He was surprised he had to repeat the question. Any time Denise's hotel was in the running for a site visit, she'd always brought the play-by-play home with her. But here she was, and not a word of business talk coming out of her. "*You* know," he prompted her. "The guy from Minneapolis or wherever. The bottle people."

Denise pulled her head up from the book and her mouth dropped open as she became aware of her brain freeze. "Oh, them. Moline." She threw him again by giving him a shrug that almost bordered on indifference. "I'm ninety percent sure we're in," she said. "Huey said he'd take it to his board and get back to me by Thursday." Her eyes dropped again to check out the book.

Rudolph's eyes stayed on her. *Really weird, Denice.*

She put down the book and stepped into the kitchen to get him a soft drink and her a water. "Any luck on your end?"

"Got some names, some notes." He stepped toward the couch and saw that Sir Pepi was in front of it, blocking his path. With Denise around the corner in the kitchen, Rudolph made a smooth, back-legged swing with his work boot. The dog, shoved more than kicked, gave out a little woof and relocated itself to the other side of the room, looking back sullenly at the man. Rudolph let himself drop to the couch. He wasn't about to work overtime and then come home to ask a damn canine piece of shag carpet to move, pretty pretty please.

Denise came back, set the drinks down and had a seat next to him. She extended her hands to take the book back. "We can go over your notes in a minute," she said. "First of all, let's see this Nubian Prin-*cess* of Joe's." She placed her thumbs on the pages and pulled. It didn't open. She tried again. *No-go.* She twisted to him with a *What's the deal* look.

He milked the joke for another few seconds and then grinned, "Trick book. You have to use your fingernails."

"No."

"*Yes.* You got a thirty-something-year-old book here. I almost broke one of my own fingernails trying to pry it loose." She wasn't amused, so he suggested, "Try where the bookmark is."

Denise found the scrap piece of notebook paper and sliced her thumbnail along the pages it marked. That done, she pulled as hard as she could. The sudden cracking sound was so loud she leaped back. A partial shriek sprung from her throat. Sir Pepi ducked.

With her reaction, Rudolph busted out with one of his

convulsive, full-blown laughs.

As soon as Denise saw there weren't any spring-loaded rubber snakes jumping out at her, she let loose a sharp "Rudy!" and threw a shoulder into him.

He took the hit and laughed, "I *told* you it was a trick book."

Denise collected herself, anxious to get back to business. Her eyes darted over the head shots and went to the only black female on the page. There she was, the girl who'd sent Joe over the edge, way back when. Bernadette Armstrong wasn't quite the "Plain Jane" Rudy had described. The girl was definitely different, with those rockin' cheekbones and oriental-ish eyes.

"What did I tell ya," Rudolph said. "Plain Jane all the way."

"Hardly," Denise said. She looked the girl over again. "So she wasn't Tyra Banks. Girl was a freshman, didn't have any polish yet."

"*Plain*," Rudolph obstinately repeated.

Her eyes stayed on the picture. "What do *you* think it was?"

"*What* was?"

She tapped her forefinger on the girl's face. "What did she have that made Joe go off the charts after all this time?"

"Besides him trippin', you mean?"

"C'mon," Denise said. "Give me a real answer."

"Umm—puppy love?" he tossed out.

She gave that guess a quick rejection. "Puppy love goes away when the dog grows up."

Rudolph tried to think of a believable answer.

"She was just different to him. Brown-skinned little girl who batted her eyes at him."

Denise kept her eyes on the photo.

"Why not?" he reasoned. "The guy had a'hold of something

he never had before."

"Maybe," Denise said. "Some couples say they fell in love the first time they laid eyes on each other. You know, felt the magic and that was that."

Rudolph kept his mouth shut on that one.

By the time they went to bed, they had the beginnings of a plan. Rudolph and Joe would try to run down the men Joe had marked in the *Splenditus*; Denise would track the women. If nothing panned out from Denise's search app, she would travel to Averytown with Joe and they would see what they could dig up in person.

The next morning, while Rudy was in the shower, she unstuck the *Splenditus* and studied the girl closer. Physically, there wasn't anything special about her, other than her eyes. If the rest was all Joe was looking for—brown skin, wide nose, black hair—she could supply those easy enough.

27. Rudolph Tries Some More Calls

The next Saturday morning started out *mahvelous* for Denise. It was raining. That meant her weekly eight-thirty walk with Scootie wasn't going to happen. Denise could park herself at her dinette table and spend a couple of unmolested hours on her laptop looking for Mystery Girl.

At eight thirty-five, her phone rang.

Denise's words of greeting came out sharp, just like she meant them to. "Didn't you get the memo?"

"*What* memo?" Scootie's voice shot back, just as hard.

"It's *raining*, Scoot."

"*Girl.*"

"C'mon Scootie, who wants to walk in the rain?"

"*I* do," Scootie said, getting agitated. "Hell, we start lettin' a little rain scare us off, we'll never hit a routine. Grab a K-mart bag and let's go."

Denise shished into the phone. "We've been doing this for seven weeks. Sounds like a routine to me."

No way Scootie was going to let the girl off the hook, not when she had lots more questions about Rudy's white friend. "Aw, Girl," she chided. "Don't be a such a candy-ass. Besides, it ain't even raining now."

Denise's eyes shifted toward the window. Her face fell. The gray clouds were beginning to give way to patches of blue sky.

"Remember the deal," Scootie said. "Every Saturday for three months unless one of us dies. Then re-up if we're still feelin' it."

The girl was stressing Denise out. Here she would have

to give up a good hour and a half putting up with Scootie and her meddlin' instead of working on her Bernie Project. "Okay, okay," she said. "See you in five."

Scootie was ready in one. Rudy's white buddy didn't sound too shabby to her. Had some gray hair, but she wouldn't hold that against him. White men with gray hair and a good job usually translated into plenty of green.

Moving it with Denise now, Scootie Simon started off doing almost all of the talking. As usual, it was heavy on gossip. As soon as they bread-and-buttered around a big puddle and came back side-by-side, she got to it.

"When's that guy coming to visit—Joe."

"Hard to say," Denise stonewalled. She made an unenthusiastic shrug.

"I could do some lower body exercises with him," Scootie said, thinking surely Denise would have something to say about *that*.

Denise kept walking.

Abruptly, Scootie stopped. From under her vinyl bucket hat, she glared at the other woman and barked, "You got some kinda *problem* today?" Then, not getting an answer, she asked, "Why you actin' so stingy-lipped, Jackson?"

Denise cooly stroked the back of her ball cap. "I don't have a problem. I'm just preoccupied with work." Then she added, "I just don't see the point in screwing up a good workout talking about some man."

That answer was so outrageous Scootie couldn't help but let out a snicking, explosive laugh.

"What do we talk about every Saturday?" Scootie demanded, "The freakin' stock market?" She didn't get the girl. Denise already *had* her a man.

"Since when do we rap about *white* men," Denise said, cool as a lawyer.

"Like I said before, D, next time you get word that this Joe is coming over, do a sister a favor and ring me up. I ain't got nuthin' against havin' me a vanilla shake."

Just to change the subject, she asked, "How are Martin and Luther?"

"So-so," Scootie replied about her grown-up twin sons. That was it. If Denise could play dumb, so could she.

28. Digging

Denise quickly showered and took herself and her iPad to the dinette table. She expected her job to be more complicated than Rudy's, what with dealing with women's married names, divorced names, following their partner's' jobs to other cities, that sort of thing. The seven female names supplied by Rudy after his sit-down at Taco Bill's included a girl she tagged as a main player, Bernadette's freshman roommate Ameya Kendricks. Denise was hoping she could hit a home run off her, even if the girl happened to do no more than touch base with her old roomie with an annual Christmas card.

Among those on Denise's list was another possible from Rudy and Joe's sit-down at Taco Bill's—Jelise Henry, the 'Yo White Boy callin'' girl. Denise had gone online to *FindYourPeeps* and plugged the names in. Six of them produced results. Her iPad read like this:

*Ameya Kendricks, Mt. Sterling, KY. (Bernie's freshman roommate, very tall.)

    Peeps Listing: A. Kendricks, Tempe, AZ

*Jelise Henry Watts, Covington, KY. (Stocky, smart-mouth.)

    Jelise Henry, Lexington, KY

    J. Henry Thompson, Massillon, OH

    Jessica Henry, Aurora, Colorado

*Kymberly Suggs-Whaley, McKeesport, PA. (Jelise's roommate)

    Kristen Whaley, Pittsburgh, PA

*Anita Galloway, Hodgenville, KY: (Soph. Terrific eyebrows and makeup, *Dark* skin, with-it look)

    A. L. Galloway, Hodgenville, KY

*Joelia Ann Turner, Maysville, KY: (Soph. Big poof cut, button nose)

    J.A. Turner, Seabreeze, FL

    Jacquelyn Turner, Louisville, KY

    Joseph R. Turner, Prospect, KY

*Valerie Moses, Hazard, KY: (Soph. Mid-length Afro, petite, silk blouse)

A couple of hours later, she fetched Rudy out of the back bedroom and the two went to the kitchen table to update each other. She joked to Rudy that she expected him to cover the $1.99 *FindYourPeeps* fee for each search.

"Chicken feet," Rudy had said with clownish generosity. "Any luck with your calls?" he asked.

"You first."

Rudolph pulled his chair close to the table and flipped through his notebook. "This won't take long," he said, scratching his beard.

"Got some good news and some bad news." He waited to hear her choose.

Good news," she said.

"Landlord says he's sending his bug man over on Wednesday." As soon as her body fall into a droop, he wisely followed it up with a quick laugh. "Just kiddin'!" he said.

"Rudy!"

He sat up straight on the couch. "The bad news is, I tried three of the guys on my list, and only one of them even answered the phone."

"So who's the one?"

"Name is Isaiah Hurtt. Found him right here in town, in the White Pages. I had to go over things a few times before Joe's name clicked with the guy. Talked to him about three minutes. About the only thing he remembered about Joe was, he hung out with him some. And he had a nickname. Seems the brothers at college called our boy 'Jedi Joe.'" Rudolph repeated the name and grinned. "You know, from *Star Wars.*"

Denise wasn't impressed by the silly name.

"He couldn't remember Bernie at all. Even when I told it to him—Bernadette Armstrong—he still couldn't make a connection."

"That's all your good news?" she asked.

"That and the fact that I didn't have any old Philomena hassling me like I did last time."

It was looking better to Denise all the time, her being able to track the girl down before Rudy did.

Her exercise reminded her that now she had an extra job, too—beating Scootie off of Joe.

"Your turn," he said.

"Eliminated a couple of contacts, if you want to call that progress," she said. "One main source is already shot down. I thought her roommate might be a biggee when she answered her phone—Ameya, the name you gave me. Poor girl has problems."

"Like what?"

"Like Alzheimer's. Or some other kind of dementia. I started off asking if she knew a Bernadette Armstrong from college, and

she said," 'Oh, yeah. little Bernie, Rolling Flatts. Go Pioneers!'
But then I said, just to be sure, 'Went to Rolling Flatts State in
Nineteen Eighty?' And she says, 'I never went to college!' "

"Oh hell."

"I go 'round and 'round with her," Denise said, "and finally
a younger woman takes the phone and says, 'I'm sorry, but my
mother is really *forgetful* these days'. And that was that."

Denise dragged her finger down her pad screen. "Left
messages for a Joelia Turner and a Kymberly Suggs-Whaley.
Oh, and a Anita Galloway. She went back and found another
note. "I got a number and left a note for this Jelise Henry Watts,
too."

Rudolph sank back on the couch. It was definitely *not* a fun
way for him to spend his Saturday.

29. Home for Christmas

The next morning, Bernie, her suitcase and her duffle were on the bus, splashing in the rain out of Pine City. The next two weeks, full of Christmas and family and the loving embrace of home, promised to be the most miserable time of her life. There would be no Joe to kiss, no Joe to talk to, no Joe to get lost in.

Velvette met her sister at the bus stop, which in Averytown amounted to a sign that read **BUS** in front of the old *Sinclair* filling station. 'Vette jumped out of their father's Lincoln Continental Mark VI and hugged her older sister as if the girl had been away for twenty years. With it, Bernie noticed the girl's build was rapidly catching up with her own. 'Vette, fifteen months younger, would also keep her boyish straight-line hips. And, like Bernie, she would be compensated for them with a high, full booty. Up top, her bosom was small, too. But if the girls followed their mother's track, their boobs would get bigger once they got married and started having their own babies.

At the curb, 'Vette popped the trunk and watched in amazement as Bernie jerked her duffle off the asphalt, balanced it on top of her right quad, and then used a piston-like thrust to send it flying on top of the spare.

"He-e-ey, Wonder Woman!" Velvette grinned, impressed by her sister's demonstration of Girl Power. Here was something new to admire about her sister, along with the smarts and self-confidence.

"'Conditioning class,'" Bernie explained.

"Have you dated lots of hunks?"

Bernie knew that was coming. "All the time," she said, just to play along with the girl's silliness.

Velvette gave her a loud "Woo!" She couldn't wait until she

could do her own thing like Bernie, bust out of Averytown and be surrounded by good-looking, smart brothers in college.

When they pulled into their parents' driveway, they saw their mother standing at the front door. Her real name was Mi-Cha, but she'd long ago given up using a Korean name that Americans couldn't say or spell. "Mee'ch," she learned to tell people. "Just call me, Mee'ch." She brought herself up on her sandals and gave her older daughter an extra-tight welcome-home hug.

Just inside the door, Master Sgt. (Ret.) Harold Armstrong impatiently fidgeted and waited his turn. When his turn came, he gave his daughter a warm but proper military man's hug.

By the end of her second day at home, 'Vette had waited long enough. She was dying to hear more about Bernie and her new world of college men. That evening, she powered up the early Christmas present her parents had given each other—the high-tech "microwave oven." As soon as the kitchen filled with the smell of scorched popcorn, Velvette hustled a bowl of it to the living room, where the parents were watching *The Jeffersons.*

She popped a second bag and hurried with it to the den. After turning *The Jeffersons* up loud on the little portable, Velvette hopped on the love seat next to Bernie, shoved her bare feet under the gold afghan and turned her hips so she could face her sister. She held out the bag of popcorn to Bernie, who wrinkled her nose at the burnt-corn aroma but took a handful.

"So," 'Vette began, wiggling her shoulders. "Like, on a scale of one to ten, how many college guys are really the bomb? Eight out of ten, nine...?"

Bernie's lips stretched into a wide grin as she listened to her sister's clumsy attempt to get into her personal life. "You are so stupid," she said. She snickered, loving it.

"Come on, Bernie!" 'Vette wheedled. "Just give me a rough estimate."

Just to amuse the kid, Bernie threw out an off-the-wall number. "Three. How's that? Three out of ten are really the bomb."

"Oh, psyche," Velvette grinned. "*Really.* Eight?"

Two whole days and nights without Joe had been tougher on Bernie than she'd expected. Now, with her sister's invitation, Bernie couldn't hold it in.

"One," Bernie said.

"*One?*" Velvette asked, puzzled.

Bernie said the number again, pointedly, waiting for 'Vette to catch on. The studio audience was busy hee-hee'ing at George Jeffersons' come-backs when Velvette's eyes went wide. She threw a hand up to each side of her face and her vocal cords went off the charts. Bernie stuck her hand over the girl's pie hole, but Velvette pulled it away.

"You got a new boyfriend!"

'Bernie made a "Shhh!" and faked a slap toward her sister's mouth. "Don't you tell anybody, either."

Velvette responded with a hokey, shoulders-back military salute.

"Clown," Bernie laughed. That out, she couldn't help but release her second piece of news. Boyfriend bulletin out of the bag, she was more excited about what she would tell her sister *next.* "There's something really special about him, too," she said. She allowed her words to hang out there.

'Vette gave her a searching look again and then joked, "Married!" Her face went mock-serious. "You oughta be ashamed of yourself, Bernie Armstrong. Going with a married man!"

Bernie looked down at one hand and with her other hand rubbed her fingers over it, as if she were cleaning something off her skin.

Velvette's brown eyes studied the hand and her eyes darted from side to side in thought. Then they went huge.

"No you didn't," 'Vette said.

"Yeah buddy. Sho' did."

"*White?*"

"Very."

"Teacher?" Velvette guessed. "I mean, like a graduate student or something?"

Bernie shook her head from side to side.

"Professor. Is he a professor?"

"Get real. He's a student. A sophomore."

"Ooo," Velvette said. "A *SAH-fa-more.*" Her smile brought out the Asian fold of her eyelids, which was more prevalent than her sister's. Bernie told her sister the story of her and Joe, starting with that day out on Main Street.

An hour later, after they finally called it a night and tiptoed upstairs to their separate bedrooms, Bernie looked at her little sister and made a locking key motion at her lips.

Christmas vacation rolled on, with the girls spending most of their days together. 'Vette even joined Bernie in her jogs around the old high school track, just to learn more about Bernie's Joe Normal. All the chit-chat helped Bernie get out from under the crazy doubts that Jelise had stuck in her head.

Bernie's parents couldn't help but pick up on their college daughter's peculiar behavior. Bernie made very few phone calls to her old girlfriends, and she didn't even try to connect with her high school steady, Dexter Metcalf. The only familiar routine Bernie had stuck to was shopping with 'Vette and their mother. A couple of days after Christmas, Harold had grown so mystified over Bernie that, at bedtime, as soon as he settled in alongside Mee'ch, he said in a strained, gravelly voice, "Okay, Baby, what's up with Bernie?"

Mee'ch placed her small hand on his chest. Although Harold was only five feet ten, he was a giant lying next to the Korean woman.

"I think our daughter is in love." She wasn't smiling. Then again, she wasn't frowning, either.

"Some kid from school," he deduced, waiting for her to confirm that much.

"'Vette told me," Mee'ch said. "That's why she didn't come home for Thanksgiving."

Harold just had to say it. "You don't think she's pregnant."

Mee'ch blew at that nonsense. "Of course not. She *would* tell me that." Then, to assure him further, she said, "She hasn't been with *any* boy, as far as I know. But she *is* in love, Sarge. Your other daughter has been acting off-the-chart goofy ever since her sister got home. Like she's celebrating something *big*."

The man let his head go back on his pillow and rubbed his face, then turned to plant a goodnight kiss on his wife. "I just hope she tells us about this new boyfriend of hers before she goes back."

"She better," Mee'ch said.

30. The Parents Find Out

On December twenty-seventh, as the Armstrongs headed back to work, Mee'ch sat in their car and out of nowhere informed her husband, "Bernie got a nice phone call on Christmas Day. Young man from school."

Harold's hands made a slight involuntarily jerk and the big car pulled toward the center line. He finger-tipped his new land barge back into its rightful lane and contemplated the news while he chomped down harder on his Juicy Fruit gum. Non-stop Juicy Fruit-chewing was the trick Harold hoped would help him quit smoking for good.

"Phone call, really," he said.

Given the fact that both girls would be around the house until their schools started back, the Lincoln VI was as good a place as any for the parents to have a private, wide-awake conversation about their college-age daughter. Both of them had jobs at the VA hospital at Ft. Knox, just fifteen minutes from home. Harold, the forty-seven-year-old Army retiree, was in charge of grounds security. Mee'ch had a good-paying civilian job testing blood specimens in the lab.

"So that's who she got her hair cut off for yesterday?" Harold asked.

"Shortened," she corrected him. "Probably."

"Why didn't you tell me about the phone call?" he asked, being a little snippy about it.

"Take it easy, Sarge, I just found out myself yesterday afternoon."

Harold analyzed those words. *Found out. Found out from...* It took four seconds of drive time for him to fill in the blank. "Velvette," he said. "And that's why you were so sure there's no baby business here."

"I knew that anyway. All I had to do was give 'Vette a long look and it gushed out of her like Old Faithful."

Harold automatically reached in his shirt pocket for another piece of gum, exactly as he used to go for his cigarettes when he chain-smoked. "I'll buy that," he said, peeling the foil from another stick. "So the new boyfriend's been their little secret."

"Their little secret," Mee'ch confirmed. "Velvette said they talked for two hours on the phone on Christmas night, while we were watching TV."

When they came to a stop at a traffic light, Mee'ch turned to him and said, "There's just one more thing." Harold's hands wrung at the leather grip on the steering wheel. *Mee'ch and her 'Just One More Thing' Columbo impersonations.* His question came out raw. "*What* more thing?"

Mee'ch held to her customary unemotional demeanor. "I just found out last night. He's...another race."

The Lincoln lurched to the left again. Harold brought it back and immediately said, "White." That much he'd bet the house on. If the kid was anything else—Mexican, Vietnamese, Arab—his wife wouldn't have been so dodgy about it.

From a biological standpoint, of course, their two girls were just as much Asian as they were black. Products of a young black American G.I. serving in the Korean War and the girl he brought home with him in '53, Mi-Cha Oh. After two early miscarriages, the girls had come much later, seven and nine years down the road. Master Sgt. Armstrong's final stop had been at Fort Knox, Kentucky. Knowing he would likely serve out his last eight years there—which he did—they'd bought a house nine miles down the highway in Averytown.

By the time the girls started grade school, their parents had informed the girls how the one-drop rule worked, how one drop of African blood in their veins made them black in America's eyes—end of story. Harold's little sacrifice of fighting the Commies along Korea's 38th Parallel in '52 and '53 hadn't delivered much improvement in the way he was seen back in his own country. In Nineteen-Sixty-One, their newborn Bernie would be stamped as a Negro girl. A *colored* girl. With all the rights and privileges listed therein.

Harold unwrapped a new stick of gum with one hand, a skill he was getting quite good at, and shoved it into his mouth. He was certain he'd heard tacit approval in his wife's voice. "A *white* boyfriend," he said. He gave a long exhale that sounded like air being let out of a tire. He drove on and steered toward the back entrance of the hospital. The sign said 10 MPH. His car was going 20. His gum was going 50.

"Thumbing your nose at The Man is easy when you're on a college campus in the middle of nowhere," he told Mee'ch. "Yippee, what fun. But in the real world, where can Bernie take *that*?"

"We got stares when we came here from Seoul," she pointed out. "And times are changing."

"*Changing*," he said, twisting the word into a mocking sound. His gum was getting in the way of his debate with her. He pulled the super-sized wad out of his mouth and found a fast food napkin to bury it in.

They pulled into his parking space, which happened to be wherever Master Sgt. Harold Armstrong (Ret.), Chief of Security, wanted it to be. Today it was in front of the NO PARKING sign just to the left of the big automatic entrance door. He turned off the engine and sat there, thinking. Here they finally had their first girl in college, and damn if Bernie wasn't already begging for trouble. The Chief of Security felt a sharp stab of anxiety. He'd known there would be boys—of course there would be boys—but how was he supposed to protect her now?

The early-bird vets arrived in droves, anxious to latch onto a space close to the back door. It wasn't unheard of for Harold to have to deal with some kind of silly confrontation over a handicapped space. Some days that was Chief Armstrong's biggest job, playing referee, deciding who got to park fifty feet closer to the door.

Harold turned off the ignition, started to open his door, and right there, facing the busy sidewalk, he got a wild urge. As the vets and their supportive loved ones streamed by, he pulled his Korean wife to him and stuck a big, long kiss right on her mouth. Did it for any haters who might be out there on the other side of his windshield. Deed done, he pulled back and confidently addressed his startled wife. "Happy holidays, Baby." He let her catch her breath while he pulled on his VA SECURITY ball cap, just to let any hardcore bigots who might be watching know that what they had just seen was performed by a black man. A black man with a badge and a gun.

Mee'ch gaped at her husband. It had been years since he'd gone after her like that in a car.

"I thought we were talking about our *daughter's* love life, Sergeant Armstrong," she finally said, patting her black hair back in place.

"Let's just say I needed to do that," Harold said.

Mee'ch kept her eyes on her impossible man. Her daughters could consider themselves blessed if they found men half as loving as their father.

As they walked into the building, the chief of security went showy again, taking her hand and holding it until they reached the first intersection of hallways. When they arrived at his base of operations, the long counter with TV monitors, he released her hand. Mee'ch continued walking straight ahead, on to the main elevators. As she walked on, her mind went back to her daughter's college romance. Betraying her own reserved nature, Mee'ch turned and shouted back through the thickening mass of incoming vets, "Love conquers all, Sergeant Armstrong!"

The Chief of Security had looked up and cracked a little smile to his beloved wife. *Love conquers some.*

Morning, New Year's Eve, arrived, and there were Harold and Mee'ch, still waiting to hear Bernie's big announcement about her new boyfriend. There were only two days left before they were to take Bernie back to school, and the girl hadn't said word one about him.

"Well, why don't we just *ask* her?" Harold said before they left their bedroom.

Mee'ch looked at him incredulously.

"*Ask* her if she has a new white boyfriend we're not supposed to know about?"

"How else are we going to find out?"

"No. She's in college. Let *her* decide when."

Harold drew a sigh. "I'll tell you this much. She won't leave us in the dark all dang winter. Look at her. Her head's been up in the clouds her whole vacation. Crazy, don't you think?"

Around seven that evening, Velvette's friends picked her up and they headed for the local roller rink. Her parents had granted a special New Year's Eve dispensation for the daughter who was halfway through her junior year: she could stay out until one.

Bernie, on the other hand, was still at home, still sitting in front of the TV with her parents. They assumed she was content to stay put, without having her boyfriend around. At ten, Harold sent up a flare anyway. "If you're going to go celebrate with your friends, you're gonna have to move it, Bernie."

Bernie gave her parents total bull when she replied, "Oh, I'm not into that countdown stuff anymore." And then she added, with a pseudo-sophisticated college air, "It's all kind of silly, anyway, cheering for numbers." The parents let it ride.

At eleven-thirty, Bernie gave a little cough to get their attention and said, "I'm going to hit the phone and check in with some school friends. You know, just to wish them Happy New Year's. Mind if I call long distance?"

Mee'ch played it wonderfully. "Sure, Honey," she said. "As long as you're not going out, cheer up a lonely friend or two. They'd appreciate that."

"Yeah," Harold jumped in. "We'll just sit here and wait on the ball."

"Happy New Year," she wished them, "just in case this pers...any of these people need to talk for awhile." Bernie had moved slowly, making her departure as nonchalant as possible, but then betrayed herself as soon as she was out of sight. Her parents heard the sock feet thumping to her room, and then her bedroom door banged shut.

Harold turned to his wife. "That's the friskiest she's been since she's been home."

Upstairs, Bernie sat on her bed, wedged a pillow behind her back, and worked herself against the headboard. She nervously pulled out the wrinkled scrap of paper from the rolled-up cuff of her sweater. Joe's home number, in case she had to call him. At 11:50, right at their agreed-on time, her phone rang.

31. Phone Call

Bernie picked up the phone and said, kitten soft, "Hello?" There was no voice on the other end of the line. She knew it was Joe, playing with her. After a few seconds, he said, "Is this my beautiful black girl?"

Instantly released from her aching loneliness, she swallowed and said, "Yes it is. Yo' black girl. You're right on the money, ten 'til."

"Solid. Did you think I'd miss this, Baby?"

Bernie soared. "Say that again."

"Solid."

"Fu-NEE. Say it again."

"Baby," Joe repeated. "Baby Baby Baby Baby Baby Baby, *BAAAY-BE*. How's that?"

"Oh yes," she purred into the phone. "I like that a *lot*."

She shut her eyes, pretending he was sitting next to her, sharing her warm bed while they talked. Then, eyes open again, she confessed, "I'm all alone in my room and about to go bananas without you."

"Me, too. Everybody here's out partying." He tried to lighten her mood. "I've been thinking. Know what I'm going to start calling you?"

"What?"

"My Nubian Princess."

She tried to suppress a laugh but couldn't. "Oh, Joe-Joe, *no*."

Hearing her wonderful laughter, he ran with it. "Naw, make that my Nubian Prin-*cess*. Sounds even *more* special."

"Don't you *dare* call me that!" she said, in a muted squeal.

"I'll settle for Baby." When his end of the phone went silent, she gave in. "Okay, I'll be your Nubian Prin-*cess* whenever we're alone together. Okay, Baby?" She loved him so much.

"Deal." Joe felt like Sir Lancelot when he then assured her, "Day after tomorrow." He made another joke for her. "Back to being bestus buddies."

"You shut up, Joe Normal," she came back, definitely *not* joking. "It's been ten long days—and nights."

Joe heard heavy knocking on Bernie's end of the phone and then a man's muffled voice. Her phone made a jostling noise. Half a minute of silence went by before Bernie's giggles came into the phone.

"Everything's copacetic, Baby," she laughed. "My father just came upstairs. Says, 'The ball's starting to drop, Bernie. Dick Clark, the whole shootin' match! You're gonna miss it!' He was acting *so* silly. He knew I had a lot more goin' on than watching that ball."

Joe laughed along with her until he heard the soft sniffling.

"I miss you so much, Joey," she said, catching her breath before snifling again.

Joe had had girlfriends before, two in high school and one briefly during his freshman year at Rolling Flatts. None of them, as far as he knew, had ever done any crying over him.

"I guess it's Nineteen-Eighty-One by now," he said, thinking about that grabbing, kissing-crazy Times Square celebration. "Happy New Year, Baby. You owe me a kiss."

Bernie took a big breath and blubbed out, "You'll get it, Baby. I promise."

They spent the next hour gabbing about school and friends and each other and whatever else came to mind. When the conversation lagged, they were content to just listen to each other's breathing. Around one, Joe told her, "You'd better hang up and get your rest. You're going to need it in roughly...oh... forty-one hours, six minutes and fourteen seconds—not that I'm counting."

She loved that he was just as anxious as she was. "All right, all right," she said reluctantly. "But I won't like it."

"Go wrap your hair before you fall asleep," Joe said, acting bossy to his girl.

"What do *you* know about black women's hair?"

"I know I like to touch it, and smell it, and get myself all in it," he said. He heard a high-pitched swoon come from her. "I know that you wrap yours every night before you go to bed. You told me so—or did some other girl tell me that?" He paused for her come-back.

Bernie's voice was solemn as a funeral. "Joe Normal, don't you *ever* joke about that."

"You're all I need and you know it," he said as a closing remark. "Now get some sleep."

"Yessuh," she said dutifully into the phone. She pressed her lips together to stop their quiver. With a huge breath, she said, "Happy New Year, Baby."

"Happy New Year, my Nubian Prin-*cess.*"

She waited for him to say it first. He didn't.

"I love you," she said.

Her words made him feel like he was being lifted into the air by angels. "I love you too, Bernie."

They talked for another hour.

32. Bernie Comes Clean

Bernie figured the best time to break the big news about her white boyfriend would be at breakfast on Sunday morning, and here it was—time to eat. With church coming up next, the folks would be in as charitable a frame of mind as she could ever ask. That would be a lot easier on her than holding it in for over a hundred miles back to school and then dropping it on them like a bomb.

Velvette jounced herself into her sister's bedroom, dispatched by her mother to get Bernie downstairs for breakfast. She saw Bernie making herself up big-time, 'way more than her usual look for church. The biggest change was her new pixie-look hair. Slick, short, sharp. "He's going to freakin' collapse when he sees you, Big Sis," she said. Bernie kept her eyes in the little round mirror on her dresser and gave her sister's reflection a grateful smile.

Velvette got down to it. "When you tellin' Mama and Daddy?"

Bernie deposited her tube of lipstick into her makeup bag and twisted around to face 'Vette. "Soon enough, Miss Ma'am," she said. "Be cool."

"Back at school? Yeah. They won't be able to do anything about it then but go back home then."

"How does five minutes grab you?"

'Vette let out a low-volume "Woo-wee!" and with that, Bernie held up her hand to lay a popping soul slap on her little sister's palm. They both burst into a punchy, nervous laugh.

Bernie leveled off quick and said, "You let me do this, 'Vette. I mean it."

"Will do, General Armstrong." 'Vette couldn't wait to get downstairs.

Bernie closed her eyes, went silent for a few seconds in a personal prayer, and then opened them back up. "Ready-Freddy."

Downstairs, Bernie ducked into the living room to slide a chirpy "Mornin' Daddy" to her father. She stayed there just long enough to hear him crow, "Hey, Miss America's in the house." She laughed modestly with that line, gave him an "Oh, Daddy," and took a hard left into the kitchen. Her mother was standing at the stove, cooking what was likely her daughter's last big meal at home until Spring Break. It was the works: country ham and eggs, gravy, grits, fried potatoes, buttermilk biscuits, orange juice.

Mee'ch glanced at her and did a quick double-take over the girl's made-up face, "Woo, all done up for church," she said facetiously before returning her attention to her meal.

"Well, Sunday morning," Bernie hedged.

Bernie started in on the mealtime prep jobs she and 'Vette were raised to do—set the table with silverware and napkins, fill the juice glasses, put out the plates and vitamins. Those done, she sidled over to her mother and placed a light hand at her shoulder.

Mee'ch flickered her eyes over at Bernie and she asked, ""Happy with your new look?"

"Oh yeah," Bernie smiled, putting her hand to her pixie. "I can get up for class and just go. Super-practical."

Mee'ch's eyes returned to her stove. "Practical is good," she said, tongue in cheek.

Harold came into the kitchen with a bogus stroll and asked his wife, "Need any help?"

He was lucky Mee'ch hadn't fallen into the frying pan after

hearing that question. Mee'ch hadn't needed any help from her husband in the kitchen since the girls were big enough to walk. "I think I've got it," she said. She swung her eyes over to Velvette. The girl was leaning against the arched entrance to the dining room with a strange smile on her face.

The meal was prayed over, and the talk started with checklist-type questions from the parents. *Did she have everything packed? What time were the dorms going to be open for the returning students? Did she remember to take an umbrella this time?*

Ten minutes in, after hardly touching her food, Bernie set her fork down on her plate. She folded her hands in front of her like an adult, and her eyes went to her parents to make sure she had their full attention. "I've got something to tell you," she said.

Velvette's eyes went down to her scrambled eggs.

If Bernie hadn't been so keyed up, she would have had no problem noticing how awful her parents' play-acting was.

"Something the matter, Dear?" Mee'ch sweetly asked her older daughter.

"What's *that*, Bern?" Harold said, stiff as concrete.

Bernie let fly.

"I, uh...I've got a new boyfriend."

"*Really?*" Harold Armstrong said. He picked up his napkin and wiped the mouth he'd just wiped. "No more Dexter, huh?"

"History," Bernie said, clipping it short.

"A new *boyfriend*," Mee'ch said. She gave her Bernie an intrigued gaze.

Bernie began to tell them all about her Joe Normal. Sophomore. Funny. Smart. Sociology major. Blond. Green eyes, *amazing* green eyes. "Actually," she said, "we've been going with each other since September. Practically since school started."

"He sounds...*interesting*," Mee'ch said.

Harold nodded, waiting for the rest.

Bernie went over her next line in her head and then just said it. "Umm, there's just one more thing."

Harold twitched. *Was Bernie her mother's child or what.*

Bernie didn't dare stop. "He's white."

'Vette's eyes flipped up. She *had* to see how her parents would play that.

"*Really?*" Mee'ch said, open-mouthed.

"You don't *say*," Harold said.

Her parents' ridiculously-stiff reactions to that news might as well have been performed with cue cards. Bernie sent a stare to her sister, who quickly rolled her eyes away from her and then self-consciously rubbed her chin. Bernie's alarm slacked off when she realized that hey—her parents seemed to be cool with the whole thing. Her big-mouthed sister had unwittingly done her a favor, giving the parents time to deal with it.

Harold had enough of the game-playing. He made a long, low guttural sound, which was his recognizable signal to the family that he was about to say something important. "*White,* huh?"

When he didn't get a prompt response from Bernie, he fired off his question. "Why'd you do *that?*"

Bernadette knew he would ask that. "I *like* him."

"What I *mean* is," he said to her in a stern, analytical delivery, "do you see any *other* black girls dating white boys?"

Bernie hadn't rehearsed the answer to that one. Nevertheless, she delivered her answer with a strong, clipped voice. "Haven't looked."

"Do any of your friends date white boys?"

Velvette jumped in. "Oh, I know some kids in school who..."

The head of the household gave her a hard look that cut her off in mid-sentence.

"Why should that matter?" Bernie asked. "I mean, who's counting?"

"Maybe we could discuss this more on the way to church," Mee'ch offered.

"Forget church," he said in a heavy tone. "We've got something to talk about here."

Once again, Harold gave his Race Speech, the one that covered everything from slave ships to being following around in shopping malls. To bring it home, he made it local. "Me and your mother caught our own kind of hell," he told his daughters. "But it wasn't a tenth of the junk that you and a white boyfriend would get thrown at you."

Harold was taken aback when he saw she kept her eyes on him, jaw set. He'd never seen her look so determined.

"We've been out there since school started," she said.

"And nobody said anything nasty to you two yet?"

Bernie was certainly ready for *that* question.

"Oh yeah." She tried to sound worldly. "It happens." Harold's brow wrinkled. Bernie caught herself and she added, "Not very often, though."

"Not very often," Harold said skeptically.

Mee'ch reached across the table and rubbed her daughter's arm. "We just want you to be safe, Bernie."

Bernie was ready for that one, too. "I've never felt safer in my life than when I'm with Joe."

Sensing that the storm was passing, Bernie opened up a little more. "He makes me happy. *Really* happy."

"You just met this boy a few months ago, Bernie," Mee'ch said. "Maybe you should just go easy." Running alongside that thought in her head was her recollection of how safe Harold Armstrong had made *her* feel, back when she was a year younger than Bernie.

"How long did you know Daddy before *you* fell in love?" Bernie came back. She gave herself a mental pat on the back for using the L-word.

"That was in a *war*," he said. "Things were more intense."

"Things can get pretty intense *these* days," Bernie replied.

You go girl, Velvette silently cheered.

Harold looked up at the clock. Bernie'd put them in a trick bag. In a few hours, they would be leaving her with a white boy they knew nothing about. He had no choice but to back off. "Keep your eyes open. That's all I can say. Keep your eyes open."

"We just want you to be happy," Mee'ch said, stroking her daughter's arm again. She looked into her daughter's eyes and saw the young girl back in Seoul who found herself head-over-heels in love with a black American soldier.

Five hours later, Harold double-parked his Lincoln in front of McAfee Women's Dorm. The trip had been mostly conversation-free, as they sat in their own spaces and mulled over Bernie and her boyfriend. Harold's jazz tape provided the background music. He turned off the ignition and surveyed the returning students darting all over campus. They were greeting each other and laughing and dealing with luggage and boxes crammed with food. *One of these ballsy white boys had turned his little girl's head upside down.*

"Mister Armstrong? Mister Armstrong?"

The guy's voice came at him from just outside his car window.

33. Rudolph Passes Joe to Denise

"Rudinski!"

Shortly after two in the afternoon, here came Joe into the Max-It Imaging's press room. Joe had just tried calling the number for a third "D. Williamson" and run into his latest wall. This one was named *Deborah*.

Rudolph had just finished stacking 3,000 sheet-fed brochures onto a heavy steel wagon and was about to lug them over to Finishing when Joe caught his eye. He took out one earbud and watched his friend approach. Joe had a gravy job, no doubt about it. Spent most of his time up in the front office where, at the end of the day, he could leave Max-It nearly as clean as when he arrived. And Joe's salary beat Rudolph's paycheck easily by half again.

Thanks to Max-It's status as a "preferred vendor" with the state, Joe wasn't so much a salesman as he was a well-paid order-taker.

Here was Joe's job in a nutshell: Whenever a honcho from one of Kentucky's state agencies sent out an RFP—Request For Proposal—Joe looked at the specs and worked up the production costs. At the state capital in Frankfort, the chances were pretty good that Max-It's bid would get kissed with the seal of approval. After that, Joe performed the relatively painless task of bird-dogging the work from one Max-It "team member" to the next, until the job was completed.

"When are we going to Averytown, Rudinski?" Joe shouted over the roar of the big web press churning along at production speed.

Man was relentless, Rudolph thought. He took off a heavy glove and slapped it against the cart handle. He held up an index finger for Joe to just hold on a minute. Aloud, Rudolph joined along with the wind-down of the poem. "You're a better man..."

Uninvited, Joe joined in. "...than I am, Gunga Din!"

"Helluva man," Rudolph told his friend, pulling the remaining earbud as he savored the one-and-only Kipling. He owed Joe for that one, putting him on to Kipling and some other no-nonsense poets. Men who talked about *real* men.

Joe got to it. "We're getting closer, Rudinski," he said. "I can feel it. One phone call, one old friend, that's all it takes."

"Possibly," Rudolph replied. This was still needle-in-the-haystack territory as far as he was concerned, but why argue with the man? Especially since he still had some of Joe's Search Money in his pocket.

"What do you say we drive over to Averytown this Saturday?" Joe said. When Rudolph hesitated, Joe put his foot on the corner of the cart and bent down to look over the cover of *Southeast Arrow*.

Rudolph saw the danger and quickly threw his glove over the photo of the elk. All he needed was for Joe to see the animal—close enough to resemble a deer—and go into another funk over Franki. He ran with Joe's question. "Averytown, huh?"

It worked. Joe brought his eyes back up to Rudolph. "People win the Kentucky Lottery, don't they, Rudinski?" His face was bright with optimism. "Our odds *have* to be *way* better than that."

Our odds, Rudolph repeated to himself. Now it was *our* odds. "Why don't we give it another week or two?" he said. "We just started making our phone calls."

"Onward rode the six hundred," Joe said, hoping Kipling would pump up Rudinski.

"There ain't no *onward* in that line, Coolster," Rudolph said.

He did a quick visual of the surroundings to make sure none of his fellow workers were honed in on Rudolph Barnes debating a project manager over any damn poetry. With no witnesses around, he issued his correction. "*Into the valley of death* rode the six hundred."

"Into the valley of Averytown, then," Joe countered with a cheery smile.

Rudolph had no desire at all to do this with Joe. With the sparkle of a bright penny, Denise's suggestion came to him.

"Hey, Denise had a point," he said. "Let a woman break the ice. Girlfriend might not go into shock like she would with one of us."

Joe thought it over. "Yeah, maybe," he said. Then, "Okay, that works."

The plastic box clipped to Rudolph's belt squawked. "Rudolph! Waitin' to fold your brochures, Man."

"Hey Boxcar!" Joe happily yelled at Rudinski's hip.

Rudolph snatched the radio up to his mouth to screen off Joe's impending Happy Talk.

"On my way," he answered. He motioned for Joe to take his foot off the cart and began tugging it toward Finishing. Other than wrestling with Denise in the sack, handling big stacks of paper was practically all the exercise he got.

"I'll have Denise call you," he shouted back to Joe. Joe nodded enthusiastically and waved.

As Rudolph tugged the wagon along, he congratulated himself. Let Denise hold the man's hand for awhile, since she was all of a sudden so hot to help him find this girl.

34. Denise's Dating Highlights

Denise felt like a gold-plated present had fallen out of the sky and plopped right in her lap. And it definitely wasn't her period.

As luck would have it, she was at home burning some HK overtime when her time of the month kicked in. She'd propped herself up on the sofa, Sir Pepi providing some soft fluff at her bare feet, and spent the afternoon cramping in front of the TV. She had prudently called Rudy during his lunch break and given him the heads-up about her monthly visitor. Otherwise, if he walked through the door and saw her splayed out like that...well, long robe or not, the man would automatically think *Afternoon Delight*. That was just the way the man was wired.

When Rudolph rolled in a little after four, he gave her a compassionate *Hello* kiss and a mild look-over. After seeing to his lady's request for a refill of green tea, he departed for the shower. Within minutes, even with the water spraying out full blast from the master bath, Denise could hear him reciting along with one of the poems that blared out of his audio player.

When Rudolph came back to the living room, he'd been transformed by the shower and the poetry into a fairly content man. That lasted until he reached down to give a supportive pat to Denise's exposed ankles. Sir Pepi went for his hand, nipping furiously. Rudolph jerked it back just in time.

"Damn ya!" Rudolph yelled.

"Well, you made a sudden move," Denise said, gently nudging Sir Pepi off the couch so Rudy could take his place. "He thought you were trying to hurt me."

"Right," Rudolph said. "Been under this roof half a year and

I ain't assaulted you yet. Dog's got a screw loose, Denise."

"Whatever," she said, tired of having to defend her pet again. "Thanks for the tea."

"You're welcome," he said. He got to it. "What do you think about going over to Averytown with Joe? I mean, you instead of me. Like you said—'Give it the woman's touch.'"

She heard it and temporarily forgot her cramps. "Did you say *with* Joe—not by myself?"

"Right," he answered. "You can run interference for him, instead of me having to do it."

It was better than she expected, but she managed to play it coy. "One time. I'll go with him one time."

Rudolph felt like jumping up and clicking his heels. "You're on, Baby," he said.

"First things first," she said, lightly patting her stomach. "I have to get past all this fun I'm having—and the bottle people." She considered the enticing prospect of spending a whole day alone with Joe, but deftly turned it into a whiney, put-upon request. "All right, give me his number."

"Max-It," Rudolph answered. "Just call work and ask for him."

"*Tomorrow*," she said. She laid it on thick. "But only if I'm up to it."

The following morning, as soon as she got to work, she punched up Max-It's number.

"Yeah, Rudinski mentioned it," Joe had replied.

She repeated the 'woman's touch' spiel she'd given Rudy, then held her breath until he said, "I like it, Denise. The beauty shops, all that, it makes a lot of sense." The prospect gave him a jolt of fresh energy. "It's a date!"

Denise wasn't going to argue, if that was the word he wanted to use.

Going all the way back to the ninth grade, when her body started to swell *up here* and *back there*, she learned how a girl's blossoming figure could draw attention. Her gym teacher made sure Denise Jackson tried out for cheerleader. She was a shoo-in. She managed to stay intact through high school. It hadn't hurt that she lived in a Section 8 apartment that had been crammed since middle school with her mother, her grandmother, a sister and a brother. At age six, her father had been killed in a drug deal gone bad. After graduation, she was more than ready to start drawing a full-time paycheck somewhere. *anywhere*, so she could move into her own apartment. She began with the counter gigs at fast food places. When she was nineteen going on twenty, she knocked down her first "grown-up" job: barmaid in a beer and hot wings place. She knew nothing about making drinks, but that was a minor drawback, as far as the manager of *Lickin' Good Wangs* was concerned. One look at her brick house did it for Juan "Don Juan" Farringer. She would do the place proud in one of his server's super-tight *Lickin' Good Wangs* V-neck tee shirts. The girl could learn to mix drinks as she went. She was still a year shy of legal bartending age in Kentucky, but that didn't count for much. The po-po didn't exactly make a habit of visiting any tar paper African American food shack to check for bartender licenses.

Within three months of being there, Denise fell in love. Not with Juan, but with one of the regular customers—Digger Jones, he with his heavy-lidded bedroom eyes. She gave it up for the very first time in the back seat of his slick powder blue Chevy Caprice. The love affair didn't last long. Digger showed her soon enough that he cared more about his *purple drank* than he did for her. She could share small sips of the mix of beer and codeine syrup with him, but that was her limit. What *really* hurt was, the night she broke it off with the addict, it didn't even faze the man.

"I can always find a new bitch to drink with," he'd told her in a haze.

By her twenty-first birthday, Denise had had her flings. Unfortunately, her choice of brothers all seemed to have the same view of women as Digger had. She'd also became sick of putting her body on display every night in a stinking, smoky joint, and on top of that, being hit on by every other man who sidled up to the bar. She took a day job, cashier work at a discount store. That didn't last long. It took no time at all for the cruel reality to hit her—unskilled service jobs, jobs that required women to be fully clothed, didn't pay diddly.

She wound up job-hunting at a nearby mall. Her insecurities ironically proved to be the ticket, since she reverted to a tight top and a pair of stretch pants to get some attention at the athletic shops. The first was a wash-out, but only because the manager of *Ball Cap Man* thought she was so hot she'd be a distraction. But then she visited *Play of the Day Sports Gear*.

Ben Bowala, the silver-haired Indian owner, had a sales team made up of trim-looking young guys and, more important, young, curvy females who wore super-tight, bright-red volleyball shorts and long-sleeved black stretch tops. Denise had done nothing more than stand there near the entrance and ask the man if he was taking applications. Inside of ten minutes, Bowala was astounded to see the effect the stunning black female had on men. Sure, her body and her face turned their heads, but there was something else, something *genuine*, that came out of her eyes. Something that said she *cared*. Men veered into the shop, most of them smiling, not leering, at the stunning woman.

She was hired on the spot.

In her fifth month—she'd already been bumped up to assistant manager—Denise had the misfortune of catching the eye of Percy "Quick" Perkins.

The thirty-eight-year-old black man was the son of Epper Perkins, the founder and CEO of Perkins Cleaning Services. PCS was one of the largest minority-owned businesses in the state. Quick was Deputy Director and the company's *de facto* CEO-in-waiting. PCS had a broad clientele, providing housecleaning and janitorial work for business offices, retail stores, factories, warehouses. Quick, married with two kids, didn't give a rip about the cleaning business. It was the $64,000 salary plus perks that kept his interest up. That, and the out-of-town business trips. He loved traveling on the company dime, driving his company-owned Mercedes and staying in lux hotels—especially if he was accompanied by any foxy, lively female who happened not to be Mrs. Quick Perkins.

Quick had come into Denise's store looking for a pricey University of Louisville team jacket, red-and-black leather. His eyes immediately spotted the svelte legs standing tiptoe on the stool. He followed the curves on up and saw a girl with looks to match her body. Armed with the confidence of having a handsome face and a roll of cash that would choke a rhino, he left the store with the four-hundred-dollar U of L jacket, a pair of hundred-dollar Air Jordan V's and most important, Denise Jackson's phone number.

Their first date was at one of the most expensive restaurants in Louisville. As they enjoyed their filet mignons and the fifty-dollar bottle of wine, Quick sat there listening to a good chunk of the girl's life story while he looked for openings. He found them in spades. Here was a young, smokin'-hot piece of tail, no daddy and no boyfriend, limping along on a little nickel-dime mall job. *Father Figure* came to mind. He'd run that play before. He spent the entire evening lending a compassionate ear to any and all of her stories—no matter how fucking boring they were to him. By their second date, he'd pushed so many of her buttons they'd wound up in a king bed at the upscale Hotel Kentuckian.

For his part, Quick wasn't about to bare his soul to any empty-headed girl who sold basketball shoes for a living. The only honest information he turned over to Denise was his job title. After that, his facts got a little bent. For example, he told Denise that he was married (which was true) but extremely unhappy (which was not true). The fact was, he wasn't happy or unhappy with his wife Jaquel. After fourteen years of marriage, Jaquel and their two boys were no more meaningful to him than the wallpaper in their three-hundred-thousand-dollar house.

And that thin scar that ran from his left cheekbone down to his jawline proved its worth again. He told wide-eyed Denise it was from his old college football days at the University of Tennessee, when he was tackled and fell on a first-down marker. "Not to brag," he lied to her, "but it was right after I caught the winning touchdown against Notre Dame." Truth was, the man hadn't played football a day in his life. The dull purple-white scar came courtesy of a city housing bureaucrat named LaClaraine Barksdale.

In exchange for her providing him with some inside information on city cleaning contracts coming up for bid, he'd forced himself to bed down with the homely LaClaraine. Quick's game would have gone on for no telling how many more contracts, if LaClaraine hadn't found out that Quick was also shagging Albertina Davis, an assistant superintendent in the Sanitation Dept. The scar came from LaClaraine's nail file.

It was only a matter of time before Denise began to be troubled by the hushed phone conversations he made when he stepped away from her and the furtive, familiar looks he exchanged with other attractive women. Her hookups with him dwindled from nearly every Thursday afternoon to one a month. His invitations to join him on his out-of-town trips dried up. Toward the end, when she called to tell him the AC at her apartment had broken, he's snarked, "Try ice cubes."

On their last night together—he'd stopped by her place for a quickie—she'd told him, "I'm starting to feel cheap." It was a ridiculous thing for her to say to a playa, but it finally gave him the exit door he was waiting for. There in bed, Quick play-acted some morality for Denise.

"Me too," he told her, straight-faced. "From now on, I'm going do the Christian thing, try to do right by my marriage."

"I hope to God I never marry anybody like you," she had come back at him, eyes red, sheet pulled up to her throat.

"I could take you again," he'd retaliated. He ripped the sheet from her hands, exposing her nakedness. That done, he pulled on his briefs and said, "To be honest, Denise, your stuff don't even heat me up anymore."

She lunged toward him to slap him but he easily caught her hand and bent her fingers back until she cried out. Quick threw her hand back at her and sneered, "What makes you think anybody would want *you*, huh? You're so damn ig'nant it's a joke."

Not long after that, when Denise's Mama got on her case for the thousandth time about going back to school, she registered. She would go to school and learn a skill and finally get paid for her brains, instead of trotting herself out in public in some triflin' costume.

35. A Real Job

Denise knew she was "ig'nant" about some things—Quick Perkins, for one—but she knew just as well that she wasn't stupid. Her little bit of savings helped pay for classes downtown at River City Community College. She'd picked a field that sounded like it had a real future,"Hotel-Motel Management," and eighteen months later, in the summer of 1996, Denise had her associate's degree.

She was so anxious to get on with her new career that, four months before her August graduation, she was already making the rounds of local hotels. She always wore her "interview outfit"—her pretty red blouse and snug gray skirt. She started with the bigger places, the hotels that offered the "amenities" she'd studied in school—luxurious rooms and suites, ballrooms that seated hundreds of people, exercise gyms, spas, retail shops, work stations. She learned soon enough how often it felt like her old *Wangs* job. An interview with a man could amount to nothing more than filling out a meaningless application in exchange for her providing him with twenty free minutes' worth of leer time.

One red-haired fellow in his fifties, Duke Henderson, left no doubt how this would work. After pointing her to his office love seat, he quickly had a seat behind his desk and turned his eyes on her. When Denise sat down, the yellow cushions sank like marshmallows. Her knees came up so high and fast that she'd had to throw her hands on top of her skirt to avoid giving the man a real show. After scanning her paperwork for two implausible minutes, he'd given her a greasy smile and said, "Judging by everything I've seen, Ms. Jackson, I don't see anything *not* to like." When she responded with an uneasy thank-you, he said,

"I don't have anything right now, but opportunities come up fast in the hotel business—practically overnight." His eyes flitted down to her legs again. "Sometimes the job just goes to whoever wants it more."

Denise couldn't get out of the man's office fast enough. She drove two miles before her rage forced her to pull her junky old Corolla over to the curb. She screamed, and then channeled her anger by taking her marker and notebook and rubbing at her list of hotels so hard that Henderson and his hotel was soaked in a puddle of red ink.

But 'joy comes in the morning,' as her Mama liked to say. One month after graduating, Denise got a phone call. The Hotel Kentuckian had a job opening. Nothing big, just counter help in the gift shop. Could she come in and discuss it? Of course she could.

What Sharon Fincastle, the hotel's HR Director, didn't tell her was that the HK's only black employee in the front office, Ralph Ford, had quit his assistant concierge job two months ago. The man had taken his commercial license and gone back to driving a tour bus. Longer hours with out-of-state trips but a bigger paycheck. The Hotel Kentuckian was desperate to get another African American face out in public view again.

Denise had shown up for the interview wrapped like an expensive present. Nice jewelry (all fake), immaculate makeup (her own doing), and a new interview outfit, a swank gold blouse and black skirt (bought on layaway). The more the two talked, the more impressed Fincastle became with her. In fact, Fincastle was overjoyed. Here she was, interviewing a black female who didn't have the first hint of an *attitude.* And on the flip side, the woman hadn't delivered any shuck-and jive performance, either. Denise Jackson was smooth as butter, easily dancing past Fincastle's leading questions. *Would you be driving to work or taking the bus?* ("Depends on the weather.") *From what part of town?* ("I'm moving into a new apartment.") *Would you be able to dress appropriately five days a week to represent a top-flight hotel?* ("My wardrobe goes up from here.")

When she left the building that day, Denise had herself a job.

"Praise God!" her Mama's voice rose when she brought in the news. "Got your *foot* in the door!"

Denise felt blessed, she really did.

In late November, things finally clicked for the girl. Folks from the Forty-Second Street Baptist Church, Savannah, Georgia, came to town. The Rev. Richard Crenshaw and his wife Brenda had followed a Louisville Baptist preacher's suggestion to take a look at the Hotel Kentuckian to stage its 53rd Annual Southeast Regional Convention. Theme: "Fired Up for Jesus!"

Nancy Pat had given the two of them and Deacon Milner— the Reverend's right hand man—the grand tour. That done, Brenda Crenshaw surprised her by asking if she could take a look at the gift shop. That was just fine with Nancy Pat. She knew these Baptists wouldn't be farting around over a dinky gift shop unless they were already okay with the facility.

"Why sure!" Nancy Pat had answered. The two women heel-clicked to the far side of the lobby while the men stepped to the other side to take a closer look at the eye-catching display window that played up all the food items made with Kentucky bourbon.

Brenda Crenshaw had her reasons for wanting to look over the gift shop. If the Crenshaw's attendees had to deal with magazine covers showing off half-nude women every time they went to buy a pack of breath mints, well, that could be a *big* problem.

Nancy Pat gladly led the Reverend's wife into her hotel's glitzy, cornily-named, "Horse-of-Course Gifts, Gadgets & Sundries."

Sister Crenshaw immediately spotted two good things. One, the magazine rack was as clean as anybody could expect for 2016. The most offensive headline being, *Give Him A Brain Freeze in Bed!* And Two, here was a striking black sister standing behind the counter. The enthusiastic young woman was dressed well—black bolero jacket, red silk blouse and a black skirt, all of which showed off her substantial curves without being vulgar about it. Brenda Crenshaw recognized the obvious—the lady was 'way too fine to be working a register in a hotel gift shop.

Being a professional's professional, Nancy Pat noticed what Brenda noticed. She took a glance down at the sales woman's snug black skirt. *Thank God this church lady didn't see something that was slit halfway to Canada.* Still, Nancy Pat felt mildly uneasy. Nobody told *her* about any new hire at the gift shop. And a black one, at that.

The visitor's eyes grew bright as she sized up the polished, presentable sister who seemed to have her act together.

From her side of the counter, Denise took in the fine designer clothes Nancy Pat's guest wore. She couldn't help but notice the well-manicured nails, the eye shadow, the lip gloss. And the wonderful hair. It was permed and tinted just so, certainly by a high-class salon.

"Good morning," Denise smiled to the stranger. "May I help you with anything?"

Rev. Crenshaw's wife was pleased to see a young sister

who could step out. "Oh, just looking," she smiled, returning the friendly greeting. "Admiring this lovely hotel of yours."

"Please do, Ma'am," Denise said. "I'd be delighted to help you with anything while you're here."

Nancy Pat may not have known who the counter help was, but Denise sure knew her. *Nancy Pat Rollins. Director of Sales. Boss Lady.* Had an expression that could go from Wicked Witch of the West to granny-sweet, depending on whether she was lecturing a staffer or trying to pitch potential clients like this woman probably was. The tumblers in Denise's head turned. The Hotel Kentuckian didn't have a single black out front, let alone one on its sales force. She bowed slightly to the visitor and said, "That's a lovely outfit you're wearing. I've never seen anything like it."

"Why, thank you so *much*," the Reverend's wife had responded with an encouraging smile. She turned to Nancy Pat and raised her eyebrows. "I *like* this young lady."

Nancy Pat, in new territory, produced the only communication she could think of. The modulated chuckle came out, "Ah-mmm-MMM-mmm-ah-hmm-hmm!"

Brenda turned back to Denise and said, "Well, we're from Savannah. I guess we have some different choices down there."

"*Are* you!" Denise said. She could feel Nancy Pat's eyes flitting between her and the other woman. Denise Jackson, counter help at $8.16 an hour, kept playing her hand.

"How are you enjoying Louisville so far...if you don't mind me asking?" Denise said.

"Very well, actually," Brenda said in a voice that was now softer and less guarded than it had been with Nancy Pat. She looked at her host and nodded before turning back to Denise. "We're becoming...quite impressed with Louisville."

Nancy Pat's eyes opened like a tigress.

"I'm so happy to hear that," Denise carried on, braced by the the positive vibes from the woman—and the apparent approval from Nancy Pat. "We have a wonderful facility here. All the amenities. Plus a fabulous Sales Director, if you don't mind me saying so."

Nancy Pat chuckled and rocked back and forth in her heels, which were killing her. Her eyes went to the badge clipped on the girl's lapel. *Denise Jackson.*

"Oh, Denise is a *wonderful* ambassador for the Hotel," Nancy Pat said. She grinned at her guest. "We just *love* her."

"Denise..." Brenda inquired. She waited for the pretty girl to fill in her last name, rather than her be gauche about it and read it out loud for herself.

"...Jackson," Denise courteously identified herself, tipping her head to her badge. "Assistant Gift Shop Manager."

"Brenda Crenshaw," the woman said. She extended her hand to give the young woman a cordial shake. Denise took in a thick yellow bracelet and wondered if it was real gold. On the elegant woman's other hand was the biggest diamond wedding ring Denise had ever laid her eyes on in her life.

"Delighted to meet you, Mrs. Crenshaw," Denise said.

"It's Brenda," Mrs. Crenshaw said. "Pastor Crenshaw's wife," she smiled. "We're with Forty-Second Street Baptist in Savannah. Taking a look at your fine hotel here for our convention."

In her years of setting up their annual Southeast convention, the pastor's wife couldn't help but notice the still-laughably small number of blacks in hotel sales. She delivered a point-blank hint. "It looks like you've got a natural sales person here, Nancy Pat."

Denise didn't put up a fuss, hearing that compliment. She didn't intend to stand here in this trinket shop selling breath mints and Derby souvenirs for the rest of her life. She saw her opening and went for it. "Oh, I don't know about that, Mrs. Crenshaw—Brenda—" she said modestly. "I just got my hotel-motel management degree a couple of months ago."

Brenda brought her cheeks into a big *Wow* shape. "Oh, you go, girl!". She offered a high five to the fresh counter girl.

Denise came up with one more super-sized brownie point. "Well, whatever God wills," she said, in a saintly voice.

Damn she's good, Nancy Pat told herself. *Denise Jackson.*

Brenda nodded at Denise and said, with a quick glance to Nancy Pat, "Who knows? Maybe we'll see you over in somebody's sales department one of these days, Ms. Denise."

Nancy Pat let out another of her ready-made, effusive giggles.

After Nancy Pat parted company with Brenda and the other two Baptists, she returned to her office and stretched out on the couch. She wasn't smiling. She had the bible-thumpers figured to sign a contract before they left town. She replayed that scene in the gift shop. The reverend's wife really got charged up seeing a black woman on the HK staff. *Really* charged up. The lightbulb went on in her head. Having a black woman on her sales team just might be the deal-maker. She thought farther out of the box. The Baptists could be the tip of the iceberg here. The HK had never chased after black religious groups before, but hey, the Crenshaws sure looked like they had money.

The next week, Nancy Pat called over to the gift shop and invited Denise to come to her office. Denise hoped she wasn't going to get her butt chewed out for getting too chatty with the church woman.

"I had Human Resources share your resume with me, Denise," Nancy Pat told her, noticing that once again the attractive young woman was dressed to beat the band. "Congratulations on your associate's degree." That said, Nancy Pat then made HK history. "We'd like to add you to our sales team, if that's all right with you. Effective immediately."

Denise was thunderstruck. Tears came to her eyes. She couldn't speak.

"You'll be my fourth Sales Manager," Nancy Pat said. She handed the girl a tissue. "You'll make quite a bit more pay than at the gift shop. And I'll see that you'll get a little something extra, right off the bat—if you can help get those darn stubborn Savannah Baptists on board!"

She sat there and watched her new manager tremble with the glorious news. "I see big things here for you here," she said to the black girl who a week ago she wouldn't have been able to pick out of a police lineup. Nancy Pat gave her a business card from the Baptists and asked her to check in with the Crenshaws. "Make it nice and friendly," she said. "Like you did last week. Just ask them if the HK is still in the running." As soon as she was alone and had settled herself down, Denise made the call. Brenda Crenshaw picked up. She was elated to hear that, virtually overnight, the impressive gift shop girl had been made an entry-level sales manager. She gave herself a little pat on the back for that. "Praise the Lord!" she told Denise.

A few minutes later, Reverend Crenshaw came to the phone. "Looks like your place is the winner, Sister Denise. We're going with the Kentuckian."

Before she ran the news to Nancy Pat, Denise went to her office and had herself a good cry.

Later that afternoon, Nancy Pat gathered her sales team in

the meeting room.

"Two announcements, people," she told them. "First, the HK has added a fourth sales manager—Denise Jackson, from the gift shop." As a round of mild applause was made, Nancy Pat added, "She had a hospitality degree and we didn't even know it!"

"And second," Nancy Pat said, "Cha-Ching! The Baptist folks are coming! Not for one year, but *three*!" That three-year part was news even to Denise, per Nancy Pat's follow-up dealing with the Reverend. "Our new staffer Denise helped get' em in!" This time, there was louder, campaign rally applause for the black woman and her obvious value.

Happy task done, Nancy Pat went back in her office, sat down and kicked her heels off. She set her feet onto her guest chair and reveled in the moment. Her first-ever black religious convention was nailed down, with more likely to come, thanks to her new hire. Nancy Pat Rollins felt like a freakin' genius.

36. Take Off

With any luck at all, Denise told herself, she was here doing her last Saturday morning with Scootie. Three blocks into their walk, her head danced with the prospect of spending the whole afternoon with Joe.

Scootie had no problem picking up on the girl's *bizarro* behavior. First it was the abrupt, unexplained change in their starting time, from eight-thirty to eight. Then it was the jacked-up pace, with Denise barking out a, "Let's really push the cardio today." That had really put Scootie in a mood, the way Denise came off as some jive-ass push-push coach. They wound up doing their route in record time, arriving back on their street by 8:45. She was about to get in the girl's grill about it when the red Jeep pulled over.

"Da-neese!" Joe shouted out his passenger window. "I'm here!"

Denise took a reflexive bite at her lip. Joe wasn't supposed to show up until nine-thirty. There he was—OMG—seeing her sweaty, nappy, rough side. Even worse, Scootie was taking it all in. Denise gave Joe a forced smile and threw up a limp hand as a wave-back.

Scootie made her own wave, one big enough to flag down an aircraft carrier.

"Gonna pull in," Joe shouted out to them. He rolled into the parking lot, got out and met the two women at the door. Joe leaned in to kiss Denise's cheek as he had back at her apartment, but this time Denise quickly took his hand and shook it.

That didn't bother Joe any.

"Ready to hit the road?" he smiled at her. He sounded like a bird chirping in springtime.

Scootie gave Denise a *Well lookee here* pose. So that was what Denise's hustle was all about—girl had to get her walk done and hurry back in time to pretty up before Sexy Whitey showed up.

"Uh, not quite," Denise said.

Scootie did some walking in place while she checked out Joe up close. Dude's age made him a C-plus, maybe a B with those green eyes and kickin' lashes. Had a nice face under that trendy little stubble. The man had to have some Presidents in his wallet, what with the Jeep and the *muy* expensive leather bomber he was wearing. She didn't see any reason to play Miss Shy.

"Shoot, Denise," she said nice and smooth, "you don't even have enough breath left to introduce me to this handsome friend of yours." She gave Joe a genteel handshake and held on. "My name's Scootie," she said, giving her voice a honey-glaze. "Denise's exercise partner." Before she let go of his firm hand, she threw in an extra little squeeze. She lifted her sunglasses to let the guy appreciate her pecan-browns.

"Scootie!" Joe said, pronouncing it with a grin. "Now that's a nice, fun name."

"It *is* fun, Baby," she came back.

"I'm Joe," he said. "Any friend of Denise's is a friend of mine."

"I was just about to introduce you two," Denise blurted out.

Scootie ignored that shit. "You like to work out, Joe? You look like you do."

"A little bit," Joe said, still smiling.

"You could join us sometime," Scootie said. She rubbed her flat palms slowly on her thighs. "Give us some tips on how you keep your body rockin' like that."

Denise fumed. *Why don't you just lick him right here, Scoot?*

"Exercise pays off in the long run," Joe said, pointing an instructive finger in the air. "You ladies have the right idea."

Scootie nodded up and down and smiled big. She couldn't believe how Boy Scout he was.

Denise had her fill of The Scootie Show. "Hey, time's moving on," she said. She motioned for Joe to follow her into the building. As Joe and Denise headed on up, past Scootie's floor, Scootie shouted up after him, "I wasn't just being polite, Joe. Join us sometime." As the pair's footsteps faded down the hallway, Scootie mumbled out a nasty, "Now ain't you somethin', my Sistuh."

Rudolph had his earbuds in when they came through the door. "Boots, Boots, Boots!" he greeted them, keeping up with the infectious, onomatopoeic beat of Kipling's poem about soldiers marching. He was loving this. It was Joe who had shown him that men poets didn't have to be limp-wristed types skipping around writing about butterflies. Rudolph had been so impressed by some of Kipling's poems that he went online and bought recordings of other poets' work—Robert Frost, Carl Sandburg. He really got into Robert Service too, after reading the man's rhyming tales of the wild, frozen Yukon. But for him, Kipling was The Man. Somehow, Kipling's writings made Rudolph feel like he was right there in India *with* those soldiers.

"Look who I found," Denise told Rudy.

In the bedroom, Sir Pepi heard Denise's melodic voice and went into a barking, squealing frenzy. Denise's mouth fell open. "Rudy! You didn't lock Pep up!"

Rudolph was straight-faced when he said, "Just thought he'd like some quiet time."

She held her disapproving look on him and then took off

for the bedroom to give her dog his freedom. Rudolph turned to his friend and said in mild surprise, "You're a little early, ain't ya, man?"

"Didn't see any reason to waste any daylight, Rudinski."

Rudolph didn't care one way or another—he wasn't the one who signed up to lead Joe around Averytown.

Denise came back with Sir Pepi happily bouncing alongside her. She stayed just long enough to let the boys know she was off to take a bath. Now that she was in the warm air of the apartment, she felt more self-conscious than ever of being all smelly around Joe.

"Be back in fifteen," she said.

As soon as she left, Joe began bending Rudinski's ear again about finding his Bernie. Rudolph let him make his run, knowing that within minutes he was going to be off the hook.

Denise bathed and dressed in twenty-five, which still was quick for her. It helped that she had her Averytown wardrobe ready to go before she began her walk with Scootie. She wrestled herself into her black jeans and pulled her light blue turtleneck over her head. It stretched so tight over her chest, her bra cups stood out like a pair of torpedoes. That was where the black leather vest came in. It did a good job of concealing her chest after she snapped it shut. She tied on her pair of color-coordinated light blue sneakers and returned to the living room.

Although Rudolph was the one who pushed her to do this Averytown trip, he gave her an evaluating once-over. He knew that plenty of brothers would be scoping her out. That was a given with the girl. She could handle herself, he had no worries there. If she walked into a strange place and felt any bad vibes—sexual or racist—she had the good sense to clear out fast, and take Joe with her. As for Joe, Rudolph had zero worries about him doing any funny stuff around Denise. Joe Cool was so hung up on his perfect Nubian Prin-*cess* that Rudolph would have bet the rent that even Beyonce in a bikini couldn't have budged the man's needle.

37. On the Road

Denise, all fresh and sexy now, went up on her tippy-toes and daintily slid her bottom onto the Jeep's leather passenger seat. Joe's chivalry had surprised her again. This time he'd escorted her to the passenger side of the vehicle and opened her door for her.

For the first time in her life, Denise found herself sitting alone in a car being driven by a Caucasian man. The excitement pulsed through her. She thought back to the night before, hearing Rudy laugh as he assured her, "Don't worry about Joe hittin' on you. He's so caught up with his old flame he won't even give you a second look." When she responded to that comment with a cold stare—*Insult, Rudy, that's known as insult*—he diplomatically tacked on, "But the man would *have* to be trippin' not to see what a fine..."

"Enough, Rudy," she'd cut him off. Secretly, though, she admitted he was probably right about Joe and this obsession of his. He was dialed so tight into finding his Bernie it was unreal. Out here on I-65, the old insecurities returned. Here was Joe—smart, real good job, tons of education. And here she was, with nothing but a high school diploma and her puny little hotel-motel certificate. Joe was a project manager, knew about the printing business and how to work with all kinds of people. She stopped herself and pulled back on that one. *She* knew how to deal with people, too.

Indeed, Denise had come a long way since signing on with the HK. As the years went by, she had accumulated some serious offers to work at other hotels, one of them all the way up in Pittsburgh. Thankfully, she had the preacher's wife as a combination client and mentor for her. Denise had called Brenda after a rep from a big chain hotel in Nashville had met her on a fam tour ("familiarization" tour for convention and tourism organizers) and made her an offer to be vice president of sales. Brenda Crenshaw had advised her to stay where she was, unless the increase in salary was huge. It wasn't—ten percent. So Denise had stayed put, with her secure job and decent paycheck. "Fancy titles don't buy groceries," Crenshaw had wisely advised the young sister.

As things turned out, Nancy Pat made sure Denise's salary notched up every year, anyway. Other big hotels had taken notice of the black conventions that became a staple at the HK, and in response had begun hiring their own black sales people. But even now, ten years in, Denise was still the gold standard for sales managers of color in the entire region. Didn't matter how she was graded—looks, personality, poise, brains.

Even so, here on the road with Joe, she listened to the voice in the back of her head. It whispered, *Be careful, Girl. Don't do anything in front of him that's gonna make you look like you just walked out of your old Section 8.*

She leaned back and took some slow, deep breaths. It was a trick she'd learned back in her hotel-motel training. *Don't let them see you tighten up.* A few miles after Joe pulled onto I-65, she unbuckled her seatbelt and did something that Rudy definitely would *not* have appreciated. As inconspicuously as possible, one at a time, she popped the snaps of her vest open. That done, she casually pulled the flaps aside so Joe could take in her high, full bosom.

Joe noticed, all right. He gave her a neighborly smile.

"Getting warm, huh?" he said. "You forgot to click yourself back up."

Denise made a wry smile, thinking *unbelievable*. Not a single leer from the man. She re-connected her belt, making sure to make a show of yanking her belt up and over her right boob and letting it pull down deep between her peaks. She sat back and watched the suburbs of Louisville quickly turn into open farm land and then wooded, rolling hills. As Denise and Joe small-talked, she alternated between watching the road ahead and trading friendly glimpses with him. She admired the gentle, lightly-bearded face that back in the day somehow summoned the gumption to go out and get tight with a sistuh.

Joe tapped his brakes. "Whoa," he said. "I was doing almost eighty. Sure didn't feel like it."

She smiled at that and looked over his hands. They were placed at ten and two on the steering wheel, just like the old driver's manuals instructed.

On down the road, she had an odd realization. Joe had no scent at all, not even at this close range. Every man she'd ever known wore *something*. Rudy had his "Unforgivable" by Sean John. Pricey, yes—that was why he only used it on their party nights, when sex with her was virtually a sure thing. That scent of Diddy's was oh-so-effective. Her mind went back to earlier that morning. If she'd let Joe kiss her hello in front of Scootie, she would've found out for sure if he used cologne, and what kind it was. She made a mental note to allow Joe to put that little peck of a kiss on her cheek when they got back home. *Then* she'd smell him good.

She admired the masculine hands, and the graceful way they handled the wheel. They weren't meaty and callused from manual labor like Rudy's were. But still, they were strong hands, covered with a thin layer of reddish-blond hair. She saw that he wore no jewelry at all, other than his old wedding ring. She wondered if he had the same color hair on his chest.

After a lull in the conversation, Joe said, "I really appreciate you doing this for me, Denise."

When his eyes went back to the road, she kept her eyes on him. He had little crow's feet beginning at the corners of his eyes. She liked the creases, thought they made him look—what—*distinguished*. She took in the reddish skim of beard on his face. Now that, she *really* dug. Totally smooth faces did nothing for her, especially on a white man.

Ten minutes from their exit, she decided to go fishing again.

"Rudy says you...kind of let her get away. Bernie, I mean."

Joe's perpetual smile faded. "Yep. Biggest mistake I ever made. *Ever.*" He quit talking and concentrated on the road.

She regretted opening her mouth about it, but within seconds, here he was, brightening up again, sun breaking out of his clouds. "Anyway," he smiled, "that *is* why we're doing this. To make things right."

He didn't seem real to her. The only times Denise ever heard a man talk about a woman like Joe talked about his Nubian Prin-*cess* was in the movies, or in a thousand love songs—of which not a single one rang true, as far as she was concerned. Anybody could *make up* a song about love. Rudy had been good company, a decent man, and was an earth-shaker of a lover. But Rudy as much as told her she wasn't his *everything*. She pulled her shoulders back against her seat and re-adjusted her seatbelt to give him another chance to look her over. He kept his eyes on the road. If he was turned on by her, she told herself, he sure knew how to hide it.

"I hope we find her, I do," Denise told him. As they neared their exit, she pulled her phone out of her shoulder bag and punched up her list. "Several black beauty shops out there," Denise told him. "There's a *N'ella's B.S.* and, not too far from that one, there's a *Brenda B's Cuttin' Up*."

Her detailed itinerary surprised Joe. Here he thought they were just going to play it by ear, tool around and drop in on whatever place felt right.

"I'm following your lead, Denise," he smiled enthusiastically.

If only, Denise told herself.

38. Joe Meets the Folks

"That's Joe!"

Bernie's voice called out from the back seat of her father's Lincoln as she smacked her hand up and down on his seat. "That's *him!*"

Harold and Mee'ch had no problem hearing the boy's voice. They turned toward Harold's side window and saw a slender white guy standing there. The young man was proof that, although the low sun was still shining, it was growing colder outside. Joe's nose was bright red and his hands were jammed down into the pockets of his rinky-dink cloth jacket.

"Lower your window, Daddy," Bernie said anxiously. "He wants to say hello."

"I know what he wants," Harold gruffed. As the window came down, he could literally hear the kid's teeth clicking in the frigid Ohio Valley air. He looked over the kid that his daughter was so crazy about. His reddish-blond hair was in style, long enough to be brushed back across his ears until only the earlobes were showing.

"He's got a mustache like you, Daddy," 'Vette observed from the back. Harold ground away on his Juicy Fruit. He gave the boy a chewing smile that was civil without treating the kid like he was some kind of rock star.

Velvette clutched her mother's headrest and pulled herself toward Bernie's side for a closer look. Shoulder-to-shoulder with her sister, she saw that Bernie had been on the money. Joe really *was* fine, really *did* have dreamy green eyes and nice hair.

Despite her exhilaration—smile stretched as wide as her heart could make it go—Bernie managed to keep cool in front of the folks. What she *wanted* to do was throw open her door and leap out of the car and wrap herself around him for the rest of her life. It was their fault he was so cold. She'd told him on the phone that they would be at the dorm between three-thirty and four, and here it was, bearing down on five. At least Joe knew what to look for, a white Lincoln Continental with a front vanity plate that read ARMY.

Bernie's father checked his side mirror, saw the street was clear and slowly pushed his door open. He unfolded himself with the mild groans that came from a man his age spending too much time behind the wheel of a car. He hadn't intended to show any physical weakness in front of his daughter's boyfriend, but his sound effects couldn't be helped. Finally upright, he saw that he stood about the same height as the boy, but he was easily forty pounds heavier. That was the price he paid for quitting puffing, after doing it virtually non-stop since he joined the Army.

"I'm..." Joe began his introduction.

The chief of hospital security cut him off. "Let's get out of the street, Son," Harold said. He saw Bernie's door begin to open and he flicked his thumb toward the sidewalk. She was to get out on the curb side with the other women. As soon as he lowered his hand, Joe grabbed it and began shaking away. Harold tightened up, but then allowed the kid to go with it, impressed by how hard he was trying. Since their hands were already clutched together, he pulled the boy out of the street with him. When they joined the females on the sidewalk, Harold looked at the boy and said, "I'll bet your name is Joe."

Joe grinned politely at the imposing black man and said, "Yessir. Pleased to meet you, Mister Armstrong."

Velvette, who was standing in front of Joe with her mother,

liked Joe's voice. He sounded sure of himself. Respectful, too.

When Joe shook hands with Mrs. Armstrong, he found himself for the first time ever standing face-to-face with a real Korean. Her black hair, Asian eyes, and tons of cheekbones all said *Bernie*.

Bernie decided it was high time she had her turn. She made a gentle nudge past her mother and then, with only 'Vette in her way, she gave her little sister a little push. "*Mine*," she said in a kidding but firm voice. She gave her boyfriend's arm a friendly tap and said, "Hello, Mister Normal." She deposited a lipsticky kiss on his cheek.

As Velvette let out a syrupy "Awww," Joe bent down to give the same to his girlfriend. Relationship validated for her family, Bernie was back in her college comfort zone. She turned to the three other Armstrongs and joked, "Well, I guess y'all can all go home now."

Harold and Mee'ch ha-ha'ed that one off in an indulgent, parental way.

Joe fell into another round of teeth-chattering.

"Oh, you must be freezing to death, Baby," Bernie said in a nurturing tone.

"Not anymore," Joe said valiantly.

That was enough of the Young Love for Harold.

"Let's load up before we *all* freeze to death," he said. He zipped up his heavy sweater and headed to the trunk. With Joe dutifully helping, the two of them pulled out Bernie's small suitcase and then a bigger one, followed by a trendy new student backpack and then, from a wheel well, Bernie's duffle, now packed full of clean clothes. The sisters grabbed what was left—two paper grocery bags spilling over with school survival staples, from Raman noodles to jars of peanut butter to toilet tissue. Because Mee'ch insisted on carrying *something*, the daughters handed their purses to her, plus the umbrella Bernie forgot to take to school in August.

Velvette and Bernie climbed up McAfee's steps together, following behind the others. About halfway up, Bernie heard a little "Pssst." Her younger sister had stopped, two steps below her. 'Vette wore a wide grin—identical to that of her sister's—and brought her eyebrows high. "Yeah?" she asked in a hushed voice.

"*Oh yeah,*" Bernie said. She loved having a sister like 'Vette.

After Bernie's cargo was unloaded, Harold took them all out to eat. Joe had butted in to tell Mr. Armstrong that he would be paying for his own meal, but he was wasting his time. Bernie's father insisted on picking up the boy's tab. The more Joe argued, the more Harold thought the kid really meant it. "You'll just have to be mad, then," he told the kid, as he chewed his after-dinner Juicy Fruit. Harold had his own reasons to invite Joe to go eat with them. It would give him a little more time to reconnoiter the boy, see if there were any early warning signs to pick up on. If Master Sgt. Harold Armstrong Ret. didn't do his checking, didn't look for trouble spots on behalf of his daughter, then shame on him. By dinner's end, he hadn't seen anything resembling a red flag.

It was nightfall by the time the big Lincoln rolled out of Pine City and pointed toward home. Mee'ch and Harold would save their opinions of the boy for later, when they were alone. 'Vette was enjoying having the back of the car all to herself. Her head sank into a pillow mashed against one window, her legs stretched to the other end of the seat. Twenty miles down the interstate, she couldn't hold it anymore.

"*Well?*" she called to the front.

"Well what?" Harold said in a stiff voice.

Mee'ch knew what her daughter was asking. "He seems to be a very likable young man," she said. Mee'ch knew that whatever she said to Velvette would be passed on to Bernie at the first opportunity—probably quoted word for word—as soon as 'Vette could get to her bedroom and grab the phone. "They seem to be good friends."

"Mama!" Velvette yelled. She went into a screeching hoot. "*Friends?* Did you see the way they looked at each other? They are totally *into* each other."

The parents couldn't help but notice how tight Bernie and Joe were, but they weren't about to break it all down in front of 'Vette.

"Your sister has a long way to go before she gets out of school," Harold threw out, hoping to nip the girl's over-the-top celebration.

Velvette couldn't believe her parents. They just met their daughter's Prince Charming—anybody could see that—and they were acting like, *Hmm, maybe Bernie and this Joe can be pen pals some day.*

"Well, *I* thought he was cute," she informed her parents. "Those eyes, and his hair. Really nice."

"And really *white*," Harold said, using a word that had been begging to come out. He brought up an excerpt from his breakfast speech. "Might be fine back there on campus, where everything's make-believe. But not in the real world."

'Vette had been so inspired by her sister's standing up to their father at the breakfast table that she pulled her own Bernie.

"Well, I totally disagree," she said. She saw her father's eyes zero in on her through his rear view mirror. She softened her tone. "I mean, everything went okay today. *Right?*"

"Not exactly," Harold countered. If his younger daughter wanted to cheerlead her version of reality, he'd give her something to think about. "Did you see the stares they were getting while we were eating?"

"Maybe they were for *us*," Mee'ch jumped in.

That wasn't the back-up Harold wanted to get from his wife. He gave her a quick eye and a loud gum-chew.

"Yeah," Velvette said, bolstered by her mother siding with her. "You two get looks all the time."

"So it's the women versus Daddy," Harold said drily. He stopped the chewing. "I'm telling you, Bernie dating a white boy is asking for trouble. I don't care if it *is* Nineteen Eighty-One."

"Bernie's just a freshman," Mee'ch said, hoping to appease her husband. "She might wind up with half a dozen boyfriends before she gets out of school." She said it, but she didn't believe it herself. Not after studying Bernie's sullen behavior during Christmas break and then today, witnessing the phenomenal way her daughter's spirit had changed when she was re-united with her young man. Harold hit the radio and let some R & B soothe everybody for the ride home.

Later that night, Velvette did call her sister. Whoever answered the pay phone went to Bernie's room, but before the girl came back to tell her Bernie was out, it dawned on 'Vette that this was a wasted call. No way was her sister in her dorm room. She was out somewhere lip-locking the beautiful boy she'd gone without for two long weeks. *Fer sure.*

When Mee'ch shut the door of the their room and came to bed, she deliberately took up the awkward English she used when she first met her handsome black soldier.

"Bernie love this boy," she told him. "She has same look in

eyes I had for you when I was girl. Bernie very happy."

That departure from her normal speech grabbed Harold. He came to a full stop, one leg out of his pants, and watched her.

"I talk like this when we first meet, remember?" she went on. "We different, too."

Harold didn't want to go there. He *wasn't* going to go there. "Infatuation," he said. He lifted his other leg out of his trousers. "She's got a new toy—one called a white boyfriend."

"Like I had a toy, a *black* boyfriend?" Mee'ch said gossamer-soft. "Handsome black man who was most gentle man I ever met? Black man who gave me everything he had?"

With that, Harold ditched his controlled, military-man behavior. He flipped his pants up in the air. They came down all akimbo over one of the bed posts.

Mee'ch slid out of bed and went to get him. With her tender kiss on his neck, he settled down.

"This just scares the hell out of me, Mee'ch." he told her. "And it should scare you, too."

"I know," Mee'ch said, dropping her broken English routine. "But she's on top of the world, Harold." Then she told her husband what she *would* have said on the way home, if 'Vette hadn't been with them. "Your little girl is a woman—in college. Some day, whether you like it or not, Bernie is going to get married. Whether it's to this Joe or somebody else. She'll have her own man to love, just like I do." She took his hands in hers. "When that happens, her husband will be the most important man in her life. And you will be the *second* most important man in her life."

His face tensed with that thought.

"We should blame ourselves, Sarge. She sees all kinds of doors opening for her—because of *us*."

Harold sighed heavily. "You know as well as I do what people are like."

"Yes," she agreed. "*Some* people. And we still have a wonderful life, now don't we?"

He conceded that truth. "We do." He pulled at his wife. "Get in on my side," he said, having fun with her. She crawled over him, just to give her weary man a cheap thrill.

The last thing Mee'ch said to him that night was something Harold could have done without. "Not to worry you dear," she said, "but your *other* daughter is already more rebellious than Bernie ever was."

He made a long, heavy sigh. Despite the beat-down from all the day's driving, he had a tough time getting to sleep.

39. In Love

Bernie stood there, at last under the Make-out Maple, and the two of them heated each other up with kisses. She went from his left cheek, on to his mouth, and over to his right cheek, then reversed directions. Along the way, she told her boy, "I didn't think...they would ever...leave."

As soon as the Lincoln VI was down the street and out of sight, Bernie had hustled to her bed in Room 212 to grab her knit hat and the "emergency" jacket that her father had handed to her just before they pulled out.

"You'd better hang onto this, Baby Girl," he'd told his daughter as he pulled it out of the trunk. She saw that the XL was big enough to swallow her up. "Might need it when the weather gets super-cold," he'd said before giving her one last hug. She knew the jacket wasn't for her. The corny, quilted thing, with elastic cuffs and waistband, was intended for her teeth-chattering boyfriend.

She'd hurried back down to the lobby and handed it to Joe. It fit fine at the shoulders, just as it did on Harold, but it hung like a window drape over his butt. Despite its looks, Joe gladly made the trade for a coat that was ridiculous-warm. Bernie ran his paper-thin safari jacket back upstairs to her room and hung it in her closet. She was thrilled with the prospect of having a piece of him there in her room. It would be there for her whenever she was alone, and needed to touch him or smell him.

Out there under the big tree, Bernie had her hands back where they belonged—inside Joe's new jacket. Her hands slid inside his flannel shirt and held against his bare ribs. He chose to play with the shiny jelled hair that was chilled by the night air. "You got it cut," he said.

"I was waiting for you to notice."

"Oh, I noticed, all right" he said, stroking it with his fingers. "I just decided to wait until we were alone."

"Too up close and personal for you, in front of my parents?"

"Nope. I just wanted to wait until until I had a chance to do something about it."

"Then do something about it."

He took the short, black hair between his fingers, then bent to kiss it here and there and there against her pretty head.

She laughed over his fascination with it.

"Low maintenance," she said. "Wake up, hit it with a brush and go to class." She stayed on his eyes to see if he bought that, like her parents did. When he responded with a bogus, "Uh-huh," she gave him the real reason. "See, I've got this boyfriend who likes to play with it all the time."

"Anybody I know?"

Her white teeth flashed in the shadows and she leaned back against the tree. She took up her pig Latin and said, "How about we ix-nay the alk-tay." Her hands dropped behind the bottom of his droopy new jacket and she took a handful of each cheek. She gave him a long, hard squeeze, and felt him grow against her.

"You feel so *good*," she moaned.

Joe pressed back and said, "I'm going to have a hard walk back to the dorm, y'know."

"I'm sorry, Baby," she said. She backed off and dug into her coat pocket. Softly, she said, "Hold out your hand." As soon as he did, she deposited her present in his palm.

Joe looked down. "A candy kiss?"

"A *chocolate* kiss. That's to makeup for the candy I couldn't give you at Christmas, Baby."

"Can I eat it now?"

"You can eat it anytime you want."

Joe unwrapped it and popped it in his mouth, smiling at her gratefully. Within seconds, he blurted out, working his tongue around the candy, "I should'a shared it w'you."

"Not too late," she said. She laid an enormous open-mouthed kiss on him. They stood there and let their tongues swirl in the chocolate sweetness.

Just before her Midnight curfew, they dragged themselves up the McAfee steps. A half dozen other couples were scattered around the porch, making up for lost holiday time themselves. One pair, seeing that the black-and-white couple was still together, relayed their disgusted looks. Harold Armstrong's words came back to Bernie. *Not in the real world.* She let that bitter thought go. They would do just as her parents had done, would just say *to hell* with everybody else and hold tight to each other.

Ameya was sitting up in her bunk, listening to some disco on her brand-new Walkman—Christmas present from the folks—when Bernie walked in. The time was one minute past twelve, the Sunday curfew time.

"Why'd you come back so early?" she said, sitting up. She added a second quip. "Monitor must have had to use a crowbar to get you two apart."

Bernie smiled and took a big, exhausted breath. She pulled her unused knit hat from her pocket, tossed it on her desk and waited. She knew Ameya would have *lots* to say after two weeks.

Ameya looked down and studied her. "Hey-hey—pixie 'do.

I *like* it." She let her long legs slide off her mattress and made the short drop to the floor. She stood amid Bernie's unpacked stuff and noted, "Except it's going ever-which way. Plus the lipstick's all *over* your face...lots of whisker burns...sweater twisted up good from him playing with your breast-esses...pants on backwards..."

"*Ameya*", Bernie said, shaking her head at her roomie.

"Yep," Ameya went on, deadpanning it all the way. "Looks like you and Joe can still stand each other." With that, she reached up to her bunk and took something from under her pillow. She faced Bernie and held out both of her long-nailed fists. "Pick a hand," she said.

Bernie was too tired for games, but she played along. "Left."

Ameya showed her a wrapped condom.

"Time you used a little protection, Girl."

"We haven't done anything yet," Bernie said.

"I know," Ameya said, mocking her. "I'm still saving it, blah-blah-blah."

Bernie smiled to herself. *Ameya, Big Sister.*

Ameya went educator on her, pointing to the ring-like object in the package. "And this is called a what?"

"I know what a rubber is, Ameya," Bernie said. "Come *on*, Girl!"

"Take it, then."

Bernie delicately plucked it from the girl's palm, gave it a closer look, and joked, "I don't have to sleep with it, do I?"

"Smart-ass," Ameya said. "You get what's in *this* hand, too." She opened her other hand to reveal a second condom. "Take two and see me in the morning," she joked. "Seriously, once a brother gets himself going, lots of times he's gonna expect a second helping. Joe probably won't be any different, from the looks of you right now. Anyway, you got yourself a back-up, just in case."

Bernie picked up her purse and found a good hiding place for them. For *her man's* rubbers.

After the two shared the trivial news from their holidays, they turned in for the night. Ameya's voice came to Bernie in the dark. "Not to be a know-it-all, B," she said, "but if your boy ain't come out with this routine yet, he will. He'll complain about how worked up you got him, and then you don't let him do anything about it. How much he *hurts*." When Ameya's mattress springs took a violent squeak, Bernie knew the girl's head was pitched over the side, eyes aimed at her. "He'll tell you, you need to help him, since you're the one who got him that way." She waited for some feedback.

"I know."

"You know, right," Ameya said sarcastically.

"He loves me. He told me."

"Then that makes it more important than ever. He's gonna want it pretty damn soon. Especially after this lay-off, and especially because he *loves* you."

"I know," Bernie said again. She'd do right by her Joe. She'd been thinking about the When and Where ever since New Year's Eve.

40. More Kisses

It turned into a running joke, Bernie's thing with the candy kisses.

On the fourth or fifth time she sprung it on him, Joe was sitting in one of his elective courses, *Renaissance Art.* Joe was a real rookie when it came to watching the slide show and listening to a professor *explain* a great painting, instead of letting the class just sit there *ooo* and *ahh* over it. Joe spent the class in perpetual motion, crossing and uncrossing his legs, then his arms, leaning up, leaning back.

The lecturer, Peter Ursury, was a burly assistant prof with lots of fluffy black hair and a necktie wider than a file cabinet. He looked up at the one hundred young faces in the fine arts auditorium, followed the rising tiers of seats, and began asking prompt-questions. *Why did Raphael use two angels instead of three? What did the lone tree 'stand for' in the atmospheric Titian orgy?* Then it was on to Rembrandt and more questions.

It was clear to Joe that there was more to Rembrandt's *The Anatomy Lesson of Dr. Nocolaes Tulp* than met the eye, what with its half dozen or so men gaping at the physician and the blanched corpse. But just exactly what that was, was anybody's guess. His nervous energy prompted him to shove his hands deep into the pockets of his quilted *Harold Jacket*, as he called it. When he did, he felt the small, familiar cone shape. Bernie and her candy kisses. No, her *chocolate* kisses.

He knew the thing wasn't in his pocket an hour ago, when he did a super-quick meet-up with her in front of the Student Union. She must have slid it in his pocket while she gave him her reserved *for public consumption* good-bye hug. Sneaky Little Girl, he thought. As cool as he could make it, he peeled the foil away and inserted the sweet lump of chocolate into his mouth. He smiled as he reflected on the crazy, caring girl who'd left it there for him.

Ursury turned away from Botticelli's *The Birth of Venus* just in time to catch the only person in the whole room with an appreciative smile on his face. *Mr. Normal.* In a huge mis-read, the man congratulated himself. *Tell Pete Ursury naked women don't fire up young bucks about art. Right on, Botticelli.*

The truth was, the only effect Ursury's selected nudes had on Joe was, they made him more curious than ever about what Bernie looked like under *her* clothes.

After class, Joe went to the Student Union to re-connect with her. She was sitting at the back of the grill with Kym and several members of the Loud Crowd. As soon as Bernie saw him start making his way through the cafe tables toward her, she sent out her private smile. Joe met that with a stone face. She saw right through *that*. Joe *never* had a stone face for her. When he got closer, he gave his jacket pocket a subtle pat with his textbook and then his face crinkled to a close-mouthed smirk. She smiled big and rocked in her plastic chair. He'd enjoyed her latest kiss, all right.

She gave him a kitten-soft, "Hi, Baby" and stood up to stroke his arm. Then, in his ear, she breathed, "Need another kiss?"

"Right now," he mumbled back.

The others sat there and took it in. There it was, the next installment of The Joe 'n' Bernie Show. Chairs were clattered around to make room for him to sit next to his girl.

There were glares from a few haters, too, but Bernie had her own thick skin, thanks to that biracial upbringing of hers. Now that she was in college, in some ways it was easier. She had her dorm friends. She had the Loud Crowd. She had the town's black church. But it was Joe, self-contained Joe, who could absolutely amaze her. He acted as if nothing could hurt him, even when he was hanging with his black buddies. It was if he were standing behind bulletproof glass. Now *that* blew her mind.

Early in February, she decided.

Valentine's Day. She would give herself to him on Valentine's Day. Everything would be perfect.

41. Far-Out

"Have you noticed," Harold Armstrong asked his wife at their booth-style breakfast table, "how much our college girl talks about her boyfriend? She'd probably go to the bathroom with him, if she could."

"Oh, *Harold*," Mee'ch reacted to his hyperbole. She set her cup of tea in the microwave to heat it up.

The two of them heard a sharp laugh pierce through the ceiling. '*Vette* was on the phone with her sister. Her second-floor bedroom was just above the kitchen, which worked out great, as far as the parents' private conversations were concerned. With the sound effects overhead, Mee'ch and Harold knew their daughter was preoccupied and their own information was safe.

Mee'ch cautiously nudged the start button. Her parents would have never believed it back in Korea, not in a hundred lifetimes. *Using a metal box to heat up a tiny cup of hot tea.*

Harold waited until she looked back at him. "Joe, Joe, JOE!" he sing-songed it, making the last *Joe* sound like a bothersome, aggravating word. "That's all that ever comes out of the girl's mouth anymore." The microwave hummed industriously in the background, and after it made its loud ready *buzz*, Mee'ch brought her steaming tea back to the table.

"Here's my point," he said, with the return of his audience, "If Bernie is really hung up on this kid, don't you think we should be trying to find out more about him?"

"More as in what? His grades? His blood type? *What?*"

"Thanks to our daughter, the boy knows plenty about us, you know he does," he said.

Mee'ch took a tentative first sip from her mother's teacup, the heirloom bone China cup with the pastel pink and blue flowers painted on it. It was still comforting, after all these years, to take sustenance from the same cup that spent so much time in her mother's hands. "That's because she's proud of her family,"

"I'm glad," Harold said. He bit into his chewing gum and then shoved it to the side of his mouth. "But what do we know about *his* family? Zilch, that's what. Zero."

An outrageously-long roller coaster ride of a teenage girl giggle broke over their heads.

"*Think* about it, Mee'ch. No background check, no nothing. For all we know he's an orphan."

"*Harold*," Mee'ch said, rejecting his nonsense.

That kind of response really killed him. His suggestion would have brought a rise out of most people. All he got from his wife was a *Harold*.

He motioned at her cup and she pushed it to him. Harold took a sip, and with his throat wetted, he said in a stern voice, "We need to find out what kind of parents this kid has. And what *they* think about all this."

"Why now?" she said. "Let's give it 'til Spring. See how things go."

"*Why?* Because, for all we know, the boy's parents might not even know he's going with a black girl. If they have a problem with that, what's *that* going to do to Bernie?"

Mee'ch motioned for Harold to give her tea back to her. She took another sip and gave the man a steady gaze with her impenetrably-black pupils. "You honestly think this boy's parents wouldn't treat Bernie right, the way she says he worships her?"

Harold sucked at his gum. ""All I'm saying is, the girl needs to keep her eyes open."

Mee'ch had a thought. "Saturday is Valentine's Day. We

could make our regular Sunday call a day early. Maybe work in a question about his family then."

"Okay. On Saturday, we play her like a fiddle until we get some real answers."

Mee'ch shook her head at him. Her husband had a real way with words.

After Bernie hung up with 'Vette, she allowed herself to daydream *way* ahead. In two more years, she and Joe could rent out one of the apartments that Rolling Flatts had set up for married students. Get part-time jobs if they had to. Or at least she could, while Joe, the sociology major, scouted job prospects. Rent would *have* to be cheaper if they were sharing one bed, right? *Their* bed?

She had even checked out married housing. Back on the last Tuesday in January, she had skipped her Psyche class and gone on a fact-finding mission. It began with John "Officer Johnny" Settles, the main campus cop. He happened to be standing in front of the Admin building, scoping out the hot coeds from behind his aviator sunglasses. The thirty-four-year-old really enjoyed the best perk he had going for him.

Bernie had hurried up to him and courteously pulled up her shades and asked him how she could find Hardesty Hall.

"For *married* students?" He wondered why the slender black chick was asking a question like that.

"Yep, married."

When he held his attention on her for more information, she fudged. "I got a girlfriend who asked me to come over and visit."

He nodded and then blew what he considered to be two extremely sexy plumes of cigarette smoke out of his nostrils.

"Can't miss it," he told her. He sucked in his gut in front of the colored girl and motioned toward the north side of campus. "That way." He took another drag. "You on your way now, walkin'?"

"Right this second," she said, glancing at her watch to let him know she was in a hurry.

"Follow the yellow brick road," he grinned.

"*What?*"

"Just a joke, Young Lady," he said. "Hardesty is the only yellow brick building on this whole campus. Was the very first Admin building. Go over to College Street and stay on it. It's just past the tennis courts."

Bernie thanked him and did a quick pivot to start her hike. Officer Johnny's eyes stayed on her, admiring the swing of her high rear end as the girl made double-time down the sidewalk. If there were any married black folk over there, he'd never seen them. He watched her cross the street and then take off in a quick, snappy jog.

Even with her high school cross-country, Bernie knew time would be tight. She guesstimated she would have just enough time to jog over there and maybe find a building manager to give her a quick peek inside one of the units. If everything clicked, she would still have time to beat it back to the Student Union to meet Joe for lunch.

She pulled up in front of the place, still light on her feet, barely panting. She stood there and stared dumbly. If the name *Hardesty Hall* hadn't been on the side of the building, she would have sworn she was at the wrong place. Here at the front, on the shade side, the yellow brick building was ugly, splotched with a sick-looking green-gray mold. Yellow paint flaked big-time from the eaves. The lawn was nothing more than thin grass that was reduced even further by the dirt path that led to a common front door. Still, she held to the positive. She'd take it over the dorm world, with its constant girl chatter and thumping boom boxes. Would in a heartbeat, with Joe as a roommate.

She cut across the yard to see what the sunny side looked like and beheld a minor plus; the wall wasn't stained nearly as bad as it had been in the front. Eyes off the building, she noticed the blonde sitting on a sagging park bench that had been dragged into the sunlight. The woman had just pulled her shirt open to begin nursing a baby. The young mother's eye caught the shadow that flickered across the yard and instinctively covered both breast and child. She was startled to see the black girl standing there.

Bernie gave the woman a friendly smile and a wave, not intending to chat. The young mother had been bored with her surroundings, but now was curious. She'd never seen a black girl around Hardesty before.

"Hey," the woman said, keeping her voice down so she wouldn't startle her sucking baby. "Looking for somebody?"

"Oh, just checking it out," Bernie said, giving a cursory look at the decrepit building while she approached the woman.

The blonde looked her over. The girl didn't even look old enough to even be in college, let alone be married. "This is all married housing here, you know," she said.

"Yeah, I know," Bernie told her. Wanting her conversation to sound more imminent than wishful, she threw out, "One of these days."

"Far out," the mother answered. She pulled her shirt back open. "This is Shiloh," she said in a doting voice, "and I'm Judy Pelky. I'd shake hands, but..." She chuckled.

Bernie introduced herself, first name only, and glanced at the textbook on the woman's bench. "So you're a new mother *and* a student," she said, buoyed by that thought.

"*Was* a student," Judy said. "I'm on break, you might say." She jiggled her baby into a new position. "My husband's a grad student. I'm actually reading one of his assignments right now. You know, save him some time and trouble."

Bernie stepped closer to admire the baby. "She's beautiful. How old?"

"One whole semester and counting. I can't believe it." The woman's eyes went to the black girl's left hand. *No wedding ring.* "I don't want to sound nosy, Bernie, but...you look so darn young!"

Bernie pictured her guy's handsome face. "Well, I'm a freshman," she said. "But my boyfriend's almost a junior."

"Super," Judy smiled. "The world needs more black power couples, that's for sure."

Bernie heard the woman's words and the air left her lungs. She'd been getting looser with this girl, was on the verge of blabbing to her about her fantastic white boyfriend. No way, not now.

"I know that's right," Bernie flung out there, just to keep the conversation simple and stupid. With that, Bernie turned on her heel and split. Bernie's harsh "Have a nice day" was shouted back at the woman as she rounded the corner. Judy sat there, mouth open, wondering what the devil she did to offend the black girl.

Bernie's jog back to the Student Union was even faster than she planned, fueled not only by the depressing Hardesty building, but her anger over the blonde girl assigning her a mandatory black husband. There was that rude message again: Couples here at Rolling Flatts were white-white and black-black. There was no mix-and-match.

The sight of Joe waiting for her in front of the Student Union renewed her again, healed the wounds from *Hardesty Hall.*

Now, bolstered by this latest phone call with 'Vette, here she was, daydreaming again.

Bernie Normal. Mrs. Normal. Mrs. Joseph Normal. Mr. and Mrs. Joseph Normal. Joe and Bernie Normal. She played with the new titles. She would be overjoyed to wear them all.

She organized things in her head. In the beginning, their marriage would be all about studying—and enjoying each other. Making love. Going to concerts. Doing all sorts of new things together. They wouldn't have kids for at least three more years, when both of them were out of school. When she *did* start having babies, their children wouldn't be raised in a slum like Hardesty Hall, where backward people put races in separate boxes that weren't meant to touch each other. It would be in a progressive city, not where people were stuck in Nineteen Sixty-Eight. And oh, how overjoyed her parents would be when she gave them their first grandchild—a beautiful, latte-skinned, olive-eyed treasure of a baby!

42 . Make-out & More

Just six days from Valentine's Day, the Sunday morning troupe of Rolling Flatts students arrived at church wrapped in enthusiasm. In another two hours, they would be walking out of these doors into air that would feel downright balmy for early February in Kentucky. The weather forecast was for warm air to come up from the Gulf.

The morning's church service carried an added flair. An enthusiastic young visitor, a Rev. Ernest Gamble, from Cincinnati, was in the house.

Reverend Minter began his message. "If we look in the book of Hebrews, eleven and one..."

Rev. Gamble: (His voice sounding out powerful) "Hebrews eleven and one!"

Minter: (Flinching from Gamble's echo) "...we read, 'Now faith..."

Gamble: "Faith, Amen!"

Minter: (Sighs) "the evidence of..."

Gamble: "The evidence! YESSUH."

Minter: (Pursing his lips and pushing on)"...things not seen."

Gamble: (Even louder from his chair, stomping a foot down with conviction) "Yessuh! NOT Seen!"

Some preachers, Joe guessed, appreciated the back-up. Minter wasn't one of them. But the man of God braced himself and rode Gamble out.

At one o'clock, the benediction made, the church-goers stepped outside and were thrilled. The breezy air was close to sixty degrees. Barely out the door and down the sidewalk, Bernie moved closer to Joe, and said, "How about a picnic up at the lake?" She stroked her Bible against the small of his back, then brushed Joe's ear with her lips and whispered, "We could take a blanket." She pulled away and let her steady gaze tell him she meant it.

"Earth to Bernie 'n' Joe!" Kym yelled, out of patience. "Light's changed!"

The other students relaxed the charitable standards they'd just been reminded of at Second Baptist and had their own fun with the two of them.

"Damn, let's move it."

"Gettin' sunburned here!"

"C'mon, honeymooners, we hongry!"

"Start your family after lunch!"

The group went to its usual Sunday lunch destination, the only Kentucky Fried Chicken outlet in town. At two o'clock, they virtually had the place to themselves. Before anybody got too busy placing their orders, Bernie faced the crowd and made her announcement.

"We're taking ours up to the lake."

That swiveled some heads. Word was the girl really *was* still intact, and maybe Joe was too, despite the two of them buzzing around each other day and night. A surprised Ameya looked back at Bernie from the table she was laying claim to. She gave her roomie a supportive chin up and patted her shoulder purse. Bernie sent back a smile and a nod.

Joe ordered two-piece combo meals. Heavy got cute and asked, "Gettin' all dark meat, Joe?"

Assorted giggles.

That bust-out inspired Stick. "You forgot to order the dessert, Jedi. What'choo gonna do for dessert, stuck 'way up at the lake?"

Woofs and cackles.

"Hot fudge Sunday!" came another throwaway line.

More laughs.

When the couple left, chicken in hand, all of their friends' eyes went to the big glass window. Bernie 'n' Joe would be on their own up there.

Back at Bernie's dorm, he helped her clip-clop her high heels up to the door. While she went up to her room to change clothes, he hurried on to his own dorm to do the same. Fifteen minutes later, he was back. Both of them wore jeans and sweatshirts. He carried the chicken and she held her father's green Army blanket.

Their three-quarter-mile walk to Fightin' Pioneer Lake began smooth as Sunday morning had, but their pace soon picked up with their anticipation. Finally, at the top of the rising street, they looked down at the water. The lake—technically a reservoir that served Pine City and the surrounding area—was the largest body of water within thirty-seven miles.

They took the gravel path that led down to the shoreline, with Joe holding tight to Bernie's hand and leading the way. Several white couples were down on the gravel beach, hanging with the late afternoon sunshine. One hot-blooded pair had been stretched out with a comforter beneath them, he stripped to his chest and she down to her halter top. But now, prompted by the approaching mixed couple and the evening's cooling air, they began pulling their sweats back on. Another pair gawked at them just before Joe made an abrupt turn to the right and began to climb the thickly-wooded hill. No way would it be as warm up there as it was on the beach, Joe knew, but the trade-off would be well worth it. They would have a secluded spot of their own, among the bushes and trees.

"There used to be a fire trail up near the top," he said to her.

"Sounds like you've been here before," Bernie said teased.

"Actually I have," he said. "Hiking last year, just looking around." He looked back at her and gave her a bemused look. "*Alone.*"

"I'll bet."

He came to a sudden stop. Facing the hill above them, he said loudly, "Dang, forgot my camera. *Now* what are we gonna do for fun?" He got the kind of response he was hoping for.

She climbed up close enough to put her chin at the back of his neck. "Your hands will be plenty busy, Boy-Boy," Bernie said enticingly, after catching her breath. When he began climbing again, she swung the Army blanket and thumped it against his nice butt.

They came to the trail. Sections of it were a more-or-less flat, creating an undulating strip that followed along the tops of the ridges that ran from hill to hill. Joe picked an area in the middle of it, behind a dense stand of pines. He turned around and scoped the area. He played with her some more. "Ain't this a shame. We can't see the lake from here."

"Let's eat," Bernie said. "I'm starved."

Joe bent down and threw the bigger pebbles and limbs to the side, before flapping the Army blanket on the ground. She went to her knees on it, happy to rest her legs, and began taking everything out of the Colonel's bag. It included not only the meals, but stuff she'd rounded up at the restaurant. Things she knew that Joe, worked up as he was, wouldn't think of: napkins, extra plastic forks, straws. As she leaned forward and began putting everything in place, Joe noticed that the letters on her RFSC sweatshirt were billowed out. *She wasn't wearing a bra.*

Bernie took his hand and asked him to give thanks.

"Thanks for Bernie Armstrong," he said, admiring her.

She wrinkled her mouth at him. "And bless the food. In Jesus' name we pray, Amen."

"There's something different about you," he smiled, eyes back on her chest. "I can't quite put my finger on it." He reached for a boob.

Bernie poked his hand with her plastic fork. "After lunch, Joey," she said, then gave her boy a loving smile.

The two of them sat there, hip to hip, facing the lake they couldn't see, and ate. By the time they finished, the sun's rays were nearly gone, glinting weakly through the pencil-like trees on the other side of the lake.

Bernie pressed herself closer to him, knowing it would take a pair of eagle eyes for anybody to see them now. She reached into the hand-warmer pocket of her sweatshirt and said slyly, "Oh, almost forgot. Our dessert." She pulled out two silver-wrapped candy kisses, showed them to him, and then lay back on the blanket. "One for you and one for me." She stood them up on her sweatshirt, positioning them as close to her nipples as she could without them falling off her chest. That done, she carefully turned her head to him and said, "I take it back. You can eat both of them."

Joe bent over her and used his teeth to pluck each of them off of her, flinging them away like a hammy cat. Her breaths were short and rapid from her excitement.

"Gimme some," Joe said in a mock command. She shut her eyes and offered a prim, close-lipped kiss. He laughed at that pose and ran his finger along her lips. "Your father was in the Army. Didn't he teach you how to follow orders?"

She opened her eyes and set them on his face. With both

hands, she yanked her sweatshirt up to her chin. "Is this what you wanted?"

The blackness of her nipples stood out in full contrast to her sepia-toned modest breasts. Her nipples were raised, not only from the rush she felt from giving Joe his first look at them, but by the chill air that suddenly descended on them.

Joe could hardly defy nature. The crotch of his jeans became painfully tight, pinching at him. "They're beautiful," he offered.

She allowed him to suckle her, of course. And lie on top of her, with his own sweatshirt off. There in the fading light, he kissed her and then ground himself against her, sharing his heat with hers. She pushed back at him with her own strong hips. He tried to unsnap her jeans, but her hand clamped on his hand and held it away from her. It was too late for Joe, anyway. He gave out an intense groan and convulsed against her. She held herself tight to him, matching up with his rhythm, and when he was finished, they both went limp.

In the murky veil of twilight, Joe smacked kisses on whatever flesh he could get to.

"I love you, Baby," she said.

"I love you too, my Nubian Prin-*cess*," he huffed. Their perspiration soon had both of them shivering. After they put their sweatshirts back on, she draped a leg over him. Joe pulled at the blanket and covered her as best he could.

"Feel better?" she asked.

"Uh," he said in a flat voice. "Better."

She knew what he meant. Better, but not there yet.

"Do you realize this is our five-month anniversary?" she said.

Joe hadn't kept up with that one.

"You mean today?"

"Two days ago, actually. Our first dance was on Friday, September Ninth."

"Wow," he said. He gave her a lip-nibbling kiss. "Happy Anniversary, Baby."

She stroked his arm up and down. "My parents really like you, Baby."

He went silent on that one. For the past hour and a half, parents—*anybody's parents*—had been the farthest thing from his mind.

Before they stood up to collect their things, she stroked his neck and asked, "Do you think your folks will like *me*?"

"Of course they will."

She brought herself against him again and with eyes clear and fixed on him, "Valentine's Day, Baby. You can have it then. I promise."

That nailed him in place. He honestly didn't think their first time would be out here, on an Army blanket in the cold woods, but he *had* thought it would be soon, somewhere.

She stroked his hair and then his mustache. "I was thinking about a motel, if you want."

"Oh, I want," Joe assured his girl. "I *want*."

Just beyond the bend of the fire trail, a pair of stadium binoculars was trained on them.

"Nigger-loving bastard," Mimi McKinley cursed to herself. She was furious over what she had seen.

43. Averytown

Joe and Denise rolled off I-65 at the exit marked *Averytown/ Old Uncle Jed's*. That was the way it was in Kentucky, the local bourbon distillery sharing roadside billing with an entire town. They followed the GPS on Denise's phone, drove on past malls and homes, office buildings and chain restaurants. In a matter of blocks, they were looking at payday loan walk-ins, fast food boxes, pawn shops and liquor stores.

"Here we are," Denise said, as soon as they drove past West Fourteenth St. "Where all the black folk live."

At 18th, Joe shook his head and said, "Bernie's parents wouldn't have lived around here."

That callous remark surprised her. "You never went to her house?"

"Never made it," Joe said. He didn't elaborate. He felt her eye on him and realized he'd made a careless put-down of the neighborhood. "What I mean is, Mister Armstrong was retired Army. They would have had a nice place somewhere."

"Maybe *this* was really nice back in the day," she came back at him.

""Did I tell you Bernie's half-Korean?"

"*What?*"

"Yeah. That's where those eyes came from. Her mother."

"Why didn't you tell us that before?"

"No reason."

"Big reason," she told him. She wanted to know everything she'd be up against, if they found her. "If I ever run into the mother, there's no reason for me to stand and gawk, just because I can see for the first time that she's Asian."

"That's a point," Joe shrugged. But he didn't see it as any big deal.

"Black daddy, obviously," she said.

"Correct," Joe said.

Denise registered that factoid. That explained Bernie's eyes. She put those genes together, military and mixed. Good chance Girlfriend was one tough sistuh.

"There it is!" Her head swiveled to the bungalow they just passed. She read the stenciled sign out loud. "'N'ella's B. S.' That's it!"

Joe found a parking space on down the street. While he walked around to get her door, she quickly snapped her vest shut. Joe was the only one she was giving that show to.

They looked the place over as they approached. The wide front porch of the old house had been glassed in and it now served as a waiting area for customers. Denise read the sign out loud again and shared it with Joe. "If a girl can't get her fill of b.s. at a beauty shop," she said with a hearty laugh, "where *can* she?"

Two women were sitting out there, waiting for appointments. A toddler—probably a grandson—was sitting at the feet of one of them, working at the video game in his hands. Beyond them, through sliding patio doors, three salon chairs held customers. There was a stylist at each of them.

"Dis mus' be da place," Denise said. She turned to Joe and saw that his eyes were trained through the patio doors at the customers, searching. Surely, she thought, the man didn't think he was going to stroll in and find his Nubian Prin-*cess* under a hair dryer, waiting for him to show up. They were making a nice entrance so far, she thought. Good-looking white man opening the door for her, going into a shop full of sistuhs. She put her hand on his arm and said something in his ear. The only reason she did it was to make the sisters wonder what kind of thang was going on between them. In reality, her sexy sweet nothing was, "Remember, Joe, I start this off."

The two of them nodded hellos and received stiff nods back. Just inside the patio door, they walked past a tiny table occupied by a thin sister punching numbers on her cell phone. The name *C'eruh* was tattooed up and down along her neck in stacked vertical letters. A hand-printed sign on the wall behind her read **C'eruh's NAILS $15-up**. C'eruh looked up, saw the couple and stopped dialing.

As soon as they entered the working salon, all of the chatter stopped. The only sounds left were the R&B oldies coming from the radio and the water gurgling loud in a sink. The women found themselves looking at a sister with kickin' hair and clothes. She was well put together, they saw—if you looked past the extra pounds. The white man, the shiny face, had a righteous stubble on his face and—*oh, yes*—clothes that cost some healthy paper.

"Whew, this place is jumpin' to-*day*," Denise gushed to nobody in particular.

Joe nodded and smiled, "Hello, Ladies." Denise had warned him to keep a low profile, knowing that most women wouldn't exactly be overjoyed having *any* man march in and see them all wetted and matted-down and shampooed.

The older hairdresser took one more snip-snip of her customer's moistened hair and then stepped around the chair to deal with them. "Help you with something, Dah'lin?" she said to Denise.

"Wow," Denise said, "You look busy."

"You noticed," the woman replied sarcastically. Hand on hip, she impatiently waited on the girl to get to it.

Denise knew what the crowd was about. *Saturday morning. Place getting slammed for hairdo's for Sunday.* "My name's Denise Jackson," she told the woman. She gestured toward Joe and added, "and this gentleman's name is Mister Joe Normal."

"I'm Miz N'ella Washington. This is my place." She gave the white man a skeptical eye.

"We're kind of looking for somebody," Denise said.

N'ella stiffened. "You the law?"

Before Denise could shake her head *No*, Miz N'ella was laying it down for her.

"We don't play that," she said, her voice turning harder. "Don't do child support, restraining orders, EPOs, none of that. All we do's hair, Lady. All hair, no hassles."

"Oh, Lawd, no!" Denise said, trying out ethnic to win some points back. "We're not the law. We're just trying to find a woman who might have lived around here. A sister." She saw him out of the corner of eye and jolted. Joe was stepping toward the woman and pulling something out of his coat pocket.

"Haven't seen her for awhile," he said. He held a blow-up copy of Bernie's yearbook picture, preserved in plastic. He held it up to the room, like a badge. "Here's what she looked like thirty-five years ago."

A blow dryer fell to the floor. Women gasped. One of them gave out a coarse sound and exclaimed, "He said thirty-five years ago!"

Denise went stiff.

"Name's Bernie," Joe told the room. "Bernadette Armstrong."

Miz 'N'ella gave the old photo of the black girl a cursory blink.

"Look familiar?" Joe asked her.

Miz 'N'ella looked up at the white stranger, trying to figure out what kind of crazy he was.

Denise felt sharp pains shooting through her. She said an urgent prayer, *Please don't tell them she's your Nubian Princess.*

Miz N'ella let out a mocking laugh. "In a *while*," she snorted. "You need to check your watch, Man." She glanced at the photo again. "Been longer than any *while*."

"I doubt if she's changed all that much, Ma'am," Joe added helpfully.

Miz N'ella scanned the man's pupils for drugs. She turned to Denise and lowered her voice. "*Honey,*" she said, "You two got ta go."

That was fine with Denise. She was ready to punch Joe right in his big mouth. "We'll try another place, Miz N'ella." She gave the old woman a friendly smile. "Thanks anyway."

Joe wasn't finished.

"Bernadette Armstrong's her name," he repeated to the eight women. He held Bernie's freshman picture higher. He even walked in a small circle, so all could see the picture. "Her parents were Harold and Mi-Cha Armstrong. Mother was Korean, and..."

"*That's* it," Miz N'ella butted in. She looked at the white man's friend and motioned toward the wall. "You're free to put up a business card."

Denise, Ms. Preparation, had several cards in her vest pocket, ready to go. She found an empty spot near the edge of the corkboard and thumbtacked it in place. That done, she turned just in time to catch one of the middle-aged clients taking a long, nervy once-over of Joe's bod, head to toe.

As soon as they reached his Jeep, Denise let it go. "What was *that* all about?" she yelled, voice high and strained.

Joe gave her a puzzled look. "Finding Bernie?"

"You tell'em you're looking for somebody. Giv'em a name. That's all. You can't just go up to sistuhs and tell them you're trying to find your black girlfriend from college. They'll think you're weird."

He came back at her, still happy. "Personally, they should give me points for just trying. Besides, people find their soul mates all the time. Just look at you and Rudinski."

Denise could have done without *that* comparison. After six months' worth of shackin' with Rudolph, her bottom line assessment was this: A little company, a lot of sex. *Big damn deal.*

"Let's get out of here," she said.

44. Second Wind

There were nine more stops that day. They all produced the same wonderful results:

"Never heard of her."

"I used to know some Armstrongs, but none of 'em had any foreigners in the family."

"No, but let me get your number. You know, just in case I run into somebody." (The man wanted the hot sister's number, not Joe's.)

Denise and Joe also struck out at that second beauty parlor (*Brenda B's Cuttin' Up*), two liquor stores, a tavern (they stayed just long enough to hear a, "Hey-ho, Oreo," and make a u-turn), a drug store and the local Walmart. Denise made a point to scribble down the names of three churches. They were all locked up on Saturday afternoon but she could try them some other time.

After checking out the last one, a Methodist church, she tried something different. Since theirs was the only vehicle in the lot, she gave out a blow and said, "Joe, I don't know about you, but I'm whupped." She casually unsnapped her vest and started finagling with the electric seat buttons. She hit the one that tilted her back, putting her chest on full display for him.

"Darn, wrong way!" she said. "How in the world do I get it back up, Joe?"

He responded matter-of-factly. "Just keep working the levers until you get the one you want."

Denise fumbled around, making sure she didn't press anything that was going to work right. She pushed her neck hard against the headrest and gave out a little guttural complaint to get his attention. Her bosom rose for a full display. She looked over at him, helpless. "Can you try it, Joe?"

Joe reached across her, but he stopped when he realized his face would wind up in her chest. He got out of the car, and while he came around to her side, she allowed herself a tiny, exasperated grunt. She had never had a man act *this* damn respectful toward her. He squatted next to her seat and pushed a lever that brought her back to an upright position.

Her voice was flat when she thanked him.

"What are friends for?" Joe smiled amicably to Rudinski's girlfriend.

As he pulled into the traffic, he said, "I guess we need to look at it this way—there'll be a dozen fewer places for us to check out next week."

"Next week?" she said.

"You're coming with me again, aren't you?" he asked. Joe assumed they would keep searching until they found her.

Denise didn't bother checking her phone calendar. "I'm game if you are."

"Done!" he said. "Now let's go get something to eat." Joe had been so caught up with beating the bushes, they hadn't even stopped for lunch. Missing a meal hadn't bothered Denise, either. Being with Joe, she hadn't even thought of food. Besides, she was eating so much lighter these days she'd begun to put her weight gain in reverse. Before they got out, Denise battened down her vest again. She wasn't going into a restaurant looking like a white man's rental goods, even it the man was Joe.

Denise experienced a wonderful thing as soon as they stepped into the classy *Dion's*. The black hostess, looking like a young Oprah, acted as if there was *nothing at all wrong* with her being with the white man. It may have been Denise's imagination, but she thought she even saw a *You Go Girl* in the sister's eyes.

To Denise, a good number of the early evening crowd appeared to be military, judging by their reserved behavior and stiff seating posture. That was reasonable, since *Dion's* was only a fifteen-minute drive from Fort Knox. Here was another surprise—there was a sprinkle of mixed couples. There were different combinations—Hispanic-white, Asian-black, Asian-white, Hispanic-Asian. She and Joe were the lone black-white pair. She was amazed that the two of them barely rated more than a brief look-over.

She didn't put up a fight when he ordered red wine for the two of them.

After they selected their Italian dishes, Denise phoned Rudy to tell him they'd had no luck, but that she would be late getting back. Joe had insisted on buying her dinner.

"Dinner, huh?" Rudy replied. The man would have bet good money on her showing up back home by the middle of the afternoon, after handholding Joe all day. "Well...I guess I trust you," he joked.

She had her questions ready to go, but Joe beat her to it.

"Tell me about yourself," he said, after trying the dry, tart cabernet.

"Oh, there's not much to tell," she said, trying to flip the focus back on him.

"I know better than that," he smiled. "You work with interesting people all day. People from all over the country."

Now *that* Denise enjoyed, being flattered by a nice-looking man asking her about herself. She kept herself low-key. "You already know lots of things about me, Joe," she told his green eyes. "I like to take power walks, as you know...and I've got a dog, as you know...and I work at the Hotel Kentuckian..."

"Which I know," he chuckled, breaking in. "And you and

Rudy have been together a good while now—which I know."

"Right."

"Yah," Joe said. "Rudolph is a good guy."

Denise gave a small nod. There was a lot more she could have laid on Joe. Her fatherless childhood. Her busted relationships. Growing up in her Mama's Section 8. But those kind of life markers certainly wouldn't score any points with the man. She turned the conversation back on him. *Gently.*

"I know it's still painful," she said, "but...how have you been since your wife died? I mean, *really*, Joe."

Joe looked away for a second, as if he were looking for a cue card to read. "I'm fine," he said came back to her.

"It must have hurt a great deal, losing her the way you did."

"Sure," he said. "You spend a couple of decades with somebody, then have her all of a sudden *removed* from your life, yeah, it hurt," He reflected. "No kids, so we took a lot of trips."

"She must have been something," Denise said, hoping she wouldn't come off as patronizing. She scarcely knew anything about the woman, other than what Rudy had passed on. But she also knew in her heart that Joe wouldn't have married any junk. "Did you meet her in college?" she asked, thinking *on the rebound after Bernie.*

He shook his head No. "Three years after I graduated," he said. "Woman I worked with at my first job introduced us."

Denise hoped her show of interest would keep him rolling on his own.

"Franki had a good head on her shoulders," Joe went on. "And she was pretty." When Joe added, "dark hair, dark skin, brown eyes," she felt a sexy tingle. And then he really poked her hot wire. "Believe it or not," he said, "in the summertime, when her tan came in, she was almost *your* shade."

She felt the heat build under her vest. "I'll take that as a compliment," she said, smiling. She unfastened it.

"You should," he said, again sounding straight as an arrow.

She waited until they finished their lasagna, and then came out with the question she'd been saving for just the right time.

"Do you think a person can fall in love with an idea, Joe?"

"What do you mean, *idea*?"

"I was just thinking, you know, people get caught up in their old memories sometimes, old loves. And it's like if they're not careful, they can make them bigger than life—if that makes any sense." *God*, she hoped he wouldn't be insulted.

He surprised her again. *Amazed* her.

"Oh," he said, "I think *love* is an idea, anyway."

Her wide, steady eyes encouraged him to go on.

"I think that whenever you fall in love with somebody," he said," it's *always* with an idea. The idea that that person is *it*, the answer for the rest of your life. Something that's almost too good to be true. But *is* true, right there in front of you. Right?"

Denise took her first full swallow of her wine, just to allow herself some time to appreciate what he'd just said. She wasn't about to shake his tree any more about Franki, or True Love, or this Bernie Fantasy of his. A fantasy that wouldn't have a snowball's chance of jiving with reality, if somehow they *did* find her.

"Wow," she smiled. "This is getting way too deep for me, Joe."

"How about dessert, then?" he smiled. "They're really pushing the Chocolate Avalanche."

"Just what I need," she laughed back at him. It was that very moment the inspiration came. If she really worked at it, dieted *and* exercised big-time, she could make herself almost the size Bernie appeared to be in her picture. Reasonably close, anyway. She *knew* she could.

During the drive back to Louisville, Denise kicked herself for focusing so much on him during their meal. When Joe asked her about herself, she *could* have told him a lot of good stuff. Stuff that maybe he would like. Could've mentioned that she liked strolls at sunset and smooth jazz and laughing. And sci-fi and dogs and working out and meeting new people on behalf of the HK. She stopped to say goodnight at her door. She didn't want to share her goodnight to him with Rudy.

"Next Saturday, then," he said.

"I'm all yours, Joe."

He gave her another of his grateful, hammy pecks on the cheek and headed back down the stairs. Denise, with that mental note of hers recalled before he left, had this observation: *Joe didn't wear cologne at all.* What she smelled was all him.

45. Creeping Thoughts

She stepped in and saw Rudy on the couch, settled in with one of his little poetry books. He looked up, smiled and said, "Some day, huh?"

"I'll tell you all about it after a hot soak. A *long* one."

Denise plodded to the master bedroom and took off her vest and shoes, then stepped into the adjoining bathroom and drew a nice, steaming bubble bath for herself. Sir Pepi, after being deprived of his mistress for an entire Saturday, was allowed to lie next to the tub. The dog seemed to be as relieved as Denise was when she unhooked her bra. She took one breast in each hand and lifted them a couple of inches, up to where they hung in her younger days. She quit torturing herself and eased herself down into the water. She wanted to let everything from her neck down absorb the moist, pink heat. Five minutes in, the random questions came to her: *What if Mystery Girl asked her what Joe had been up to all this time—other than him not looking for her? And if Joe actually hooked up again with Bernie, where would that leave her?*

A good half-hour later, she patted herself dry and pulled on the long thick, luxurious white robe bearing the gold letters *HK.*" She stepped into the bedroom and saw that Rudy was already in bed, everything shut down for the night. He was sitting up, wearing one of his new V-neck undershirts. He'd decided to switch styles a month or so back, after every mirror in the apartment let him know he didn't belong in a young person's undershirt any more. His old ribbed "beaters" amplified his growing bulges, from his man-boobs to his love handles.

He was thumbing through a magazine he'd just started receiving in the mail. *AARP*, for 50s and up. The thought of being a subscriber made him feel old, but after a quick flip-through, he'd discovered it had information he could use, instead of stories like, "My Life with Prune Juice" or "Moving In with The Kids and Loving It." It even had a good number of black seniors sprinkled through it, from celebrities on down.

He was about to ask Denise to began her recap of the day when she abruptly changed course and veered deep into her closet. After some rustling around, she emerged holding a high-necked white blouse and her navy skirt. She hung them on the knobs of her closet door, ready to throw on in the morning.

She noticed him staring at her.

"Just getting ready for tomorrow," she explained. She had one knee on the bed before she caught herself. "Lawd...Did I just say *tomorrow*?"

"Sho did."

"And tomorrow's only Sunday. *Mercy*."

Rudolph grinned. "I was about to ask you about Joe's trippin' day, not yours."

She got silly and calling over to the clothes, "Take another day off, guys." After she climbed into bed next to him, she said, "Well, you have to admit, this isn't my typical Saturday night routine. Or yours." She looked at her clock. "Not even ten-thirty and here you are."

"Just thought I'd be here for your play-by-play," he said. "If there's anything to tell."

Denise almost felt like she was getting a two-fer. No pressure from the man for sex, plus she was being invited to talk about Joe. She pulled her legs up, and while she massaged her feet, she got to it.

"Not only did we not find her, nobody even *heard* of her."

"Hmm," he said.

"But I left my business cards all over," Denise said. "Just in case."

"Play the lottery while your at it," he said, being cute. "No hassles from anybody?"

"Nothing big."

She took up the day's highlights, starting with Miz N'ella's. "You should have seen the females eyeballin' that white man. Especially after they found out he was on the hunt—looking for a sistuh!" Her energy level was coming back up, Denise was enjoying herself again, talking about her and Joe. "But they had to be cool, know what I'm sayin'? 'Cause they don't know if I'm his little helper or his woman or what." She laughed, not bothering to worry about how Rudy took that last part. She reached over to the nightstand and grabbed an HK notepad and matching pen. "I need to know lots more about Joe."

"Not tonight you don't," he said in a firm voice.

"C'mon, Rudy" she said. "Just a few questions."

He let out a heavy breath. "Like what?"

Denise readied her pen. "Like did he ever tell you how long it took him to get over Bernie?"

"I thought that's where we came in," he said.

She reset. "Did you and Doris ever socialize with them, Joe and Franki?"

Rudolph could have done without her bringing up his ex-girlfriend. "If you want to call it that. We sat together at the employee Christmas party, at employee picnics. It was all work get-togethers, whenever the four of us got together."

"What was his wife like? Pretty?"

"I'd give her an 8," he said.

"I didn't get anything much out of him about her," she said.

"You won't," Rudolph said. "It's like he closed the book

on her. Totally." He looked her over. *All ankle-length robe and do-rag.* "You're a 10, by the way. Naw, make it a 20."

Denise waved his bull off.

"Interesting," she said. "Gave up on the college sistuh, married a white woman, and now he's trying to do the black thang again."

"Yup," he said. The other thing still played on him. He distinctly remembered that Denise's vest was snapped tight when she left home with Joe. Tonight, when she walked back in the door, it was open. She must have given Joe Cool a real eyeful.

46. Almost Done

Joe stood on the side lawn of McAfee Hall and gave their blanket a snap. With the leftover dead leaves and twigs from the fire trail shaken out, he went creative. He held it up high above his head and lowered it. It draped over his skull and hung tent-like, down to his knees.

"C'mon in," his muffled voice called to her from inside. "I'll be a human tent pole." Then, as more incentive, he added, "You won't believe how warm it is in here."

"You are so *silly*," Bernie laughed. In a flash, she was under it with him.

"You in here, Bernie?" he played in the dark. " I can't see a thing."

He felt her hands on his hips.

"Does it *feel* like I'm here, Baby?" she said in the dark. She gave him a long, tantalizing kiss. Then, "How many poles did you say you have holding this up?" She didn't see anything wrong with talking dirty to her boy. While he couldn't do anything about it, she brought her hands up under his shirt and stroked his chest. "How long do you think you can keep your pole up? All night?"

"Uggh, my arms feel like they're about to break off already."

"I'll take it," she said. Her hands followed his arms as high as she could reach and he lowered the blanket onto them. Her voice came to him seductively. "While I'm doing my job, maybe you could find something else to do, Baby."

That, Joe could. He brought his hands under her sweatshirt and lightly squeezed her breasts. She gave a twitch from the coolness of hands, but let him keep them there as they warmed.

They took turns back and forth, one holding the blanket and while the other did the kissing and fondling, until the snickers from somewhere on the outside grew too loud to ignore. Blanket removed, they saw that the two couples who were amused by the four-legged blanket batting around in the shadows. Joe walked her to the porch, gave her his polite lip smack and then took a hard kiss at her. She gave it back.

Bernie hopped up the stairwell to her room, where the sisters were waiting. They all expected to see a newly-minted woman walk in the door.

Jelise had already laid out her early views, as darkness fell and still there was no Bernie. "Well, girl's got herself done up, by now," she announced to the others. "She'll either come in here cryin', already kicked to the curb, or she'll be on Cloud Nine."

"Aw, stay cool Jelise," Ameya had come back at her. "At least the girl's using some protection."

"How do *you* know?" Jelise said. Then, after thinking about it, "You give her some rubbers?"

"'Stuck'em right in her hand," Ameya shot back.

Jelise was ready to get bitchy. "Hope they weren't old enough to bust."

"Laughing my head off," Ameya said icily.

Kym jumped in, getting hot herself about Jelise's attitude. "Well, at least they're in love, Roomie," she lectured. "A blind-ass beggar can see that. You got a better reason for doin' the nasty than that?"

Jelise sniffed. "Shit, first piece in her whole life. She don't even know what it's about yet."

"Well, I'd rather throw her a party than a damn funeral," Ameya said, looking down from her bunk. "At least now she can *really* enjoy her man."

"Said the girl who gets her stuff part-time from a seminary student," Jelise purred.

Ameya was about to drop to the floor and shut Jelise's stupid mouth when the door swung open. There was Bernie, new, short hair a wreck. Makeup smeared, jeans and sweatshirt all wrinkled.

Bernie gave them a cool, stingy, "Hey."

"Drop the 'Hey' shit, Shirley Temple," Jelise huffed at her. "You feelin' all special?"

Bernie ignored that prying remark. "Now *that* was some kinda day."

"Girl didn't say no," Jelise said, voice rising, as if she were marking a Bernie Scorecard.

"Mmm-hmm," concurred Kym.

Bernie's eyes went to the top bunk and fixed on her roommate. She gave a little smile and nodded her head. Ameya let out a joyous shriek. She slid down off her bunk and grabbed her roommate in a huge rocking hug. "Oh, I'm so happy for you, Girl!"

Kym hustled over to do her own hug on Bernie. "Woman now," she smiled. "Love you, Girl."

Jelise held onto her sour, examining smirk, and said under a dubious stare, "I guess that's a yes." Then, to no one in particular, "What did I tell ya. I *knew* white boy had chocolate stuff all up his nose."

Close enough, Bernie stood there and told herself. Now maybe they would get off her case.

47. Phone Calls

Denise was in her sales office, fiddling with the button on her red silk blouse—third one down—when her cell phone rang. Instantly, she thought, *Bottle Boys*. She always waited until the last minute before flicking that third button open, and she'd always done it with her door closed. She unfastened it and put her unofficial Site Visit Cleavage on display.

The plan was, as soon as the bottle collectors' plane landed at Noon, they were to call her to pick them up. She checked the time—*12:14*—and looked at the I.D.—*Private Caller.* Not Anson Huey's name this time, but she assumed it was him, maybe on a company phone.

"Denise Jackson," she said, pumping up her voice.

"My name is Kym Suggs." She pronounced her name as if it were a question. "You called a few days ago? Left a message for me?" The dusky-soft voice suggested she was a sister.

Denise, with the bottle collectors on her brain, had no idea who Kym Suggs was. *Somebody wanting to reserve the banquet room? Maybe book a reunion?* The Hotel Kentuckian's sales manager had no choice but to say, "May I help you?"

Suggs' voice came back peevish. "You called *me*. Said you were looking for a Bernadette Armstrong."

The air left Denise's lungs.

"Yes. Yes!" I *am* looking for Bernadette Armstrong!"

The woman let out a rude chuckle but then let herself turn friendly. "*Now* we're on the right page. Suggs is my married name. It used to be Kym Whaley." She waited for Denise's questions.

Denise racked her brain over the list of Joe's school contacts until it clicked. "Kym Whaley—yes! I understand you went to Rolling Flatts State College, Mrs. Suggs."

"Just call me Kym."

Denise heard a faint boop. *Call coming in.* She ignored it.

"I remember the girl you're talking about," Kym said. "Freshman year, both of us. I lived right down the hall from her."

The incoming call booped again. While the Suggs woman talked on, Denise pulled her phone from her ear and checked the ID. *Huey. Damn.* She blurted into the phone, "I'm terribly sorry, Kym. You called my work number and I just *have* to take this call. I'm *really* very sorry. Can you hold?"

There was a pause on the other end, and then a frosty, "All right."

"Be right back, promise," Denise said. She felt a tight pull in her stomach as she clicked over and cranked herself into Super Sales Manager Mode for Huey.

"Denise," she smiled. She gave herself a command. *Do not get into another gabfest with this man.*

"Denise! Anson Huey. We're on the ground. Nancy Pat says you're gonna be our chauffeur."

"Right," Denise said. "I've been waiting for your call. On my way."

"Delta," he reminded her.

"Right. On my way," she repeated.

"Weather was kinda bumpy," he said.

Oh God, Denise thought to herself. *Here he goes.*

"Yah. Even had to buckle up the ol' seat belts back over Indiana. Turbulences. Air pockets make a bottle collector kind of jumpy, know what I mean?" He responded to his bottle humor with a machine-gun laugh.

Denise swallowed hard and then let out a goofy "Ha-ha-ha!" She needed Kym to stay on the line for just thirty seconds more. "I *know* you're right," she told the corny guy. I'll be right..."

"Glad ya like bottle jokes, Denise," Huey interrupted. "If we wind up here in Louisville you're gonna hear'em from three thousand people."

"On my way, Mister Suggs," she said for the third time.

"Suggs?" he asked. "Who in tarnation is *Suggs?"*

Denise's brain was doing flips.

"I mean...(finally remembering up his name)...Mister Huey." She felt a bitter taste in her mouth thinking about Suggs, who she had already dissed by not remembering her name. Girl would be long gone.

"Anson," he said. "I told you before. From now on it's Anson." He gave her a folksy reprimand. "Now don't you come to the airport lookin' for any Mister Suggs instead of Mister Huey," he laughed kindly.

"No, I won't, Mr. Huey—Anson. Be right there," Denise said.

As soon as he hung up, she clicked over. *Dead air.* She yanked her door open, but not before letting out a loud curse. Denise barely broke stride as she hurried past Nancy Pat's office and shouted duty-bound, "They're here. On my way."

"Go get'em, Girl!" Nancy Pat yelled back. Denise didn't hear it, her mind was weighed down by her screw-up with Suggs.

As soon as Denise slid behind the steering wheel of the Hotel Kentuckian's shuttle van, she punched the Suggs number on her phone. The woman's voice mail message came on. Denise hung up, frustrated enough to spit. She had no choice but to deal with these bottle guys now and worry about Suggs later.

There at the terminal, she picked up not only Huey but his

second-in-command, Vice President Albert "Al" Zielinski. They were expecting to be wined and dined by the HK sales staff as soon as they got checked in. A half hour after the men were shown to their adjoining suites and had freshened up, that was exactly what happened. Nancy Pat, Denise and Chip Petersen were waiting down in the lobby. They and the Bottle Boys all rode the elevator up to the third floor, to the HK's breakfast-and-lunch restaurant, *Louis-Louis.* Signature dish: *Cordon Bluegrass.*

Petersen was there by way of Nancy Pat's well-honed business instincts. These Bottle Boys, she shrewdly anticipated, might be like some other male negotiators from the Dark Ages—guys who still had a problem with Women Power. She didn't need these two bottle fanatics to take this as any Boys vs. Girls thing, two-on-two. She decided to tweak the situation by throwing in Petersen. The HK's only male sales manager wasn't expected to do anything other than play bobblehead for his boss.

At six o'clock that evening, Denise trudged up the stairs to her apartment, stomach stuffed with Angus-fed beef and half a stein of stout, ingested at the insistence of the Bottle Boys.

Rudolph was lying back on the couch reading his very first Langston Hughes collection. A depleted carton of *chicken lo mein* and a drained *Corona* bottle was on the coffee table in front of him. Joe had put him onto the dude, thinking Rudinski might appreciate the way Hughes sassed the White Man through his poems.

When Sir Pepi heard the key rattle in the door, the dog shot toward it, wagging his furry behind off. Denise clunked in on her high heels and used her plump backside to thump the door closed.

"Lord *Jesus*," she said, slumped back against the door. She brought a high heel up as far as she could—which wasn't far—and reached down to pry it off with a finger.

"Sign'em up?" Rudolph asked. He snapped his fingers to tell Sir Pepi to back off Denise's ankles and let her get into the room. Sir Pepi didn't care about the man's snapping fingers. He licked Denise's ankles and then tongued her shins to let her know he was there.

"Official walk-around, first thing in the morning," she exhaled to Rudy. She used her booty to push herself off the door and into the room. "Gotta make a phone call."

"You're kiddin'!" he said. "More business, after all *that*?"

"Woman named Suggs called me this afternoon—about Bernie. I had to tell her I couldn't talk."

Rudolph's brow wrinkled. "Couldn't talk? *Hell*." His face grew darker with the thought of Denise passing on a Bernie call.

Denise sank to the arm of the sofa. "Had to put her on hold, and by the time I could finally click over—gone."

Rudy got heated. "That was our contact, Baby!"

Before the man could go ballistic, she said, "Soon as I get out of these clothes, I'm gonna call her again. I checked my phone. Maysville, that's where she called from." She bent down to kiss his head but he backed away.

"Don't tell me they got to see all that," he said, taking in her chest. She'd forgotten to button back up. Here Rudy was being all possessive with her again, even if he knew this was just business.

"Un-did it on the way home," she lied. "Got too hot in

the car." She tried to appease the man. "Let me go see if I can make this Suggs connection right now." She started toward the bedroom. "Keep your fingers crossed."

His eyes followed the rocking booty that was at least one size too big for her skirt. Sir Pepi bounced along behind her, wagging his own tail.

In the bedroom, Denise took off her sexy sales manager clothes and pulled on her Rudy, Don't Even Think About It horse blanket of a robe. She dialed Suggs' number.

48. Looking for A Break

At 10 p.m., after listening to Suggs's voice message tell her for the third call to *'Have a blessed day,'* Denise gave up for the night. She would try again tomorrow, after the Bottle Boys were out of her hair and back on their plane to Illinois. She set her phone on her nightstand and she and Sir Pepi padded back to the living room.

Rudolph was standing there, as if he were making a speech, but nodding his headphones as he mouthed out Hughes' poem, *Memo to Non-White Peoples.*

As soon as it closed--*It's the same way from Cairo to Chicago*—he looked up and asked, "No luck with the callin'?" He didn't need a spoken answer after he saw her expression.

"Woman's life is nothing but a recording," she said. "I'm turning in." She put a cool stamp of a kiss on his cheek, and headed back to the bedroom.

After seeing her in her long robe, Rudolph went ahead and grabbed the dog's leash from the wall hook next to the door. Outside, he told himself to cool it. The next day was going to be a real butt-kicker for her. Her site visit with the bottle collectors was scheduled for nine-thirty a.m., sharp. The bottle guys weren't on CP Time, so they would be there on the dot, if not before. No Colored People's Time for them. Starting twenty minutes late might be acceptable to some black groups, like Denise's church people, but no way would it fly with her Midwest white folk.

Ten minutes later, Denise heard the apartment door thump, and here came Pep. The dog went up on its hind feet to its Mama to get its goodnight hug. That done, he veered into his cage in the corner and settled in for the night. "Pep go sweepy now," she told him. When Rudolph came to bed a few minutes later, she surprised the heck out of him.

"Okay, tell me more about Joe," she said, sitting up. "What's the story with him?"

Her prodding over Joe was starting to get old with Rudolph, now that he pictured her traveling around with that open vest of hers in front of the man.

"What do you mean 'story'?" Rudolph came back, being obstinate.

"Well, I'm supposed to be making connections," she said. "If we ever find this long-lost Girl, she just might ask me a question or two about him, y'know."

Her fatigue made her go loopy on him. "Play in a band? Take up for the March of Dimes? Raise a herd of cattle?'" She gave in to an overpowering yawn.

Just to amuse her before she blanked out on him, he put his fingers to his temples and closed his eyes, answering her questions psychic-style. 'Don't know...Maybe...I doubt it.'"

He opened his eyes to her. "How's that?"

"Real cute," Denise said, sticking out the tip of her tongue at him. "Thanks for the help." She turned her reading light out and lay down with her back to him. Before sleep took over, she thought about it again. Rudy could be fun, but it seemed like he was doing his own thing more often than ever, what with his ballgames and now this damn poetry. The man had no use for most of her TV shows, or joining her for her neighborhood walks. Of course, there wouldn't be any children, too late for that scene. The heavy, sinking truth returned to her. *Forget about Mister Right showing up. It wasn't going to happen.* Behind her, she felt Rudy spoon himself into her curves and scoop up a handful of breast. She imagined that the man's warm body lying next to her belonged to Joe. Shocked by her own sinning imagination, she asked the Lord to forgive her. Then, when the sobering, hammering truth returned, the one that assured her that Rudy would never marry her, she allowed herself to let go. Until she fell asleep, she would imagine that it was Joe lying next to her.

49. Mimi Makes Her Plans

Mimi McKinley could out-fuck Little Black Bitch, she knew that much for sure. She suspected it all along, and the episode up at Fightin' Pioneer Lake just confirmed it for her. Up there on the top of the hill, the black girl hadn't even gotten out of her jeans for him. Even if the fool had been on her period, she could have at least unzipped him and made him happy.

At dusk, behind the blackberry thicket along the fire trail, Mimi had watched the murky couple head back down the hill. Joe led the way down in slow, cautious steps—not the excited, anxious ones he'd used on the way up. Mimi had found out months ago that the black girl's name was Bernadette. Not that it mattered. *Black Bitch* worked fine for her.

When the couple reached the bottom and continued their walk along the gravelly, deserted beach, Mimi slowly began working herself down the hill. The lake had become a dull mirror, reflecting a charcoal-blue, darkening sky. The pair, now barely visible, was too busy getting in their last-minute intimate clutches and squeezes to notice her. Joe and Bernie walked back up the the slope that led to the street, arms around one another.

As soon as they disappeared over the rise, Mimi picked up her pace. When she reached the top, she'd had to duck quickly behind a tree. The two of them had slowed to share their last grabbing embrace. That done, they had gone back to their private handholding under the folded blanket. Mimi pulled down her black ball cap—the one with the pink lettering that read, in swooping cursive, *Girl Power*—to cover her eyes. She scoffed to herself. All that dry humping on each other, and now they were acting all *respectable*.

"Joe Normal," she hissed a few minutes later, as she watched them walk up the steps of McAfee, "you are such a dumb-ass." If she had been his partner, people would have heard her getting him off all the way over in West Virginia.

She left the two in the shadows and started back to her upperclassmen dorm, Williams Women's Hall. By the time she entered her suite, her head was filled with a dull, pounding. She'd been straining her brain ever since she followed them to the lake, trying to come up with a plan. There *had* to be a way to break the spell that the evil Black Bitch had put on him.

It cost her a restless night and then some, but by mid-day on Monday, two days before Valentine's Day, her plan was literally in motion.

Mimi lay on the burping waterbed in 165-B—the left side of the duplex. Man Two arched above her, pumping away. He had a real name—Butch Yenowine—just as did Man One, the guy she'd just finished balling. His real name was Alan Pintorini. He was now an exhausted spectator, just a crawl away from the other two, back propped against a wall. He was taking a hit on a joint and slowly recuperating.

They'd become Man One and Man Two at the flip of a coin. The winner, Man One, would have first go at her. Mimi had given them nicknames, she told them, simply because she liked fun party names. Her real reason, which she kept to herself, was she didn't want to make her threesome with these two Roscoes any more personal than it had to be.

She'd met Pintorini at an off-campus house party her freshman year. They had wound up in the last unoccupied bedroom. He thought he was doing a great impression of a drunken jackhammer until she'd made a startling roll of her hips and was suddenly on top of him, doing her own jackhammering. The next day, Pintorini told his buddy Yenowine all about Mimi.

"So what if she looks like Rocky?" Pintorini howled after Yenowine complained about her face. "Best lay ever, Man. Tits bigger than your head."

Neither one of the wild boys was exactly intoxicated by the academic life. The only reasons they were in school at all were because (A) their folks were paying their way, and (B) college was, as Pintorini so succinctly put it, "the best place ever invented to get free pussy."

Mimi had lain there and let the two airheads go at her. In return, all they had to do was beat the hell out of Joe Normal— and then let him know why. Mimi knew Joe wasn't retarded like these two clowns. Some serious pain would teach him to drop Black Bitch like a hot rock.

Yenowine's second go-around with her didn't last long. After ten minutes' worth, he'd fallen off of her looking like a spent Saturn rocket booster. He lay there staring up at the ceiling, trying to re-focus his eyes.

"Everybody get enough?" Mimi asked the two screwballs. She sounded like a young mother making sure the kids got enough ice cream and cake at the birthday party.

While Yenowine lay there and waited for his heart rate to slow down, she sat up and crossed her legs Indian-style. Her size DD boobs, which were porcelain white, had been sucked and whisker-scratched into angry, mottled globes. Her pink nipples were fire-red from all the mouth work the guys had given them. There wasn't a mark on her face. She didn't mind. This little party was all about motivating the two jerk-offs, not jumping on The Love Boat with them. She felt a little tender at her pelvic bone, but she could live with it. The heated, undulating waterbed helped soothe her haunches.

She turned her head at Man Two and saw that Yenowine was slowly getting his pathetic mind out from between his legs. On the other side of her, Pintorini had relocated and was sitting buck-naked in his ratty armchair, lighting up another of her joints. Mimi patted the patch of duct tape that covered a pinhole leak on the brown vinyl bed.

"Man One, come on down!" she commanded with a heavy throat. "And bring us a fresh toke."

Pintorini obediently left the chair and lowered himself to the bed. For extra incentive, she nudged closer to him, nestling her perspiration-slicked boob against his arm. She held out two split fingers. He inserted the joint between them. After taking a puff, she began her final pep talk.

"Creep screwed over me," she reminded them. "I need you two studs to put the fear of God in 'im."

"What his name again?" Pintorini asked.

Mimi rolled her eyes at him. She said it again, with as hard a stamp as she could put on Joe's name.

"Normal. *Joe Normal*. And don't worry about what dorm he lives in, he's never there."

One last time, she threw out her race-card motivator.

"If he's not in class, he's always sniffin' around this nigger girl of his. Dude is actually going with her, if you can believe that."

"Yeah, you told us already," Yenowine said. Disgust registered in his voice. "I seen them two around campus."

"*Who ain't?*" Pintorini chipped in, speaking to her prodigious breasts. "Paradin' around campus with a nigger. Talk about one messed-up motherfucker."

"Amen," Yenowine seconded. He took the weed from Mimi's fingers and squeenched his eyes together. As much to please Mimi's eye-popping rack as anything else, he groused, "Oughta have his nigger-lovin' ass run out of town."

It was that kind of talk that convinced Mimi that these two morons were the right guys for the job. *Racist as hell—and lovin' it.*

"Beat him up as in...*what*?" Yenowine said. He used his finger to trace one of the thin blue veins that was beginning to reappear on Mimi's milk-white breast. He moved his finger slowly, as if he were following a major river on a world globe. "Break his balls or throw him off a bridge or what?"

Mimi patiently let his fingers play with her.

"Do enough to put him in the hospital...but just for a day or two," she said. "Ribs, I guess, mainly. Something that heals back and don't show. Just make sure you mention the *why*." She gave that directive a few seconds to sink in and emphasized the point again. "You have to tell him *why* you're kicking his ass. And you'll do it again if you have to. Otherwise, he's just going to think you two are a couple of punks who want to rob him."

"Ain't you the ballbuster," Yenowine said with a low chuckle. He marveled over how an elementary education major could dream up shit like *that*.

"More than anything," she said, "this has to be a *learning experience* for him." She brought a hand under each huge breast and juggled them for the morons. "Got a pair of sore ones, thanks to you two," she said, knowing the two airheads would love a compliment like that. Sternly, she told them, "I know he's got to be doing something with her on Valentine's night, go up to the lake or something. You two need to do it to him right after he gets out of his four o'clock class. Soon as he gets off by himself, see to it." She paused for that mountain of information to sink in on the two. "If you can't get him alone, one of you go up to him and tell him his girlfriend's been hurt. Then take him behind a building and go to it."

"Didn't I tell you she had a brain, too?" Pintorini grinned to Yenowine.

Mimi let the idiots think whatever they wanted to.

"Be there by four-thirty so you don't miss him," she ordered them. That detail passed on, she massaged her tender left tit. Why, she complained to herself, did guys always go for the one on their right first? Must be like a driving thing, she decided. Stay on the right side of the road. "His class lets out at four-fifty. Spanish. Just get to the Language Arts building early and follow him."

"Which building is that?" Yenowine asked vacantly.

Mimi heard the question and was instantly pissed. "Which one is *that?*" she snarled. She stared at him, astonished by his stupidity. Here it was, *only* the middle of freakin' February.

"*Well?*" Yenowine said. He could afford to get huffy with her, since he'd just fired off his second round and was done for the day. "The Language Arts building," he repeated. "Which one *is* it?"

"It's the Abraham Lincoln and Terryella P. Bottoms Language Arts Building," she recited in a condescending voice. "You can't miss it. There's a big statue out front of Lincoln, and another one of Terryella Bottoms. "Lincoln's the one with the beard."

"I know which building it is," Pintorini said. He slowly pulled his eyelids down and held them closed, as if he'd just dispensed some great wisdom.

"Righteous," Yenowine chipped in.

Mimi clenched her jaws to keep from screaming her head off. She waited a few seconds to gather herself and plowed ahead.

"I guarantee you he's got *something* planned for them on Valentine's Day. *Surely.*"

"And don't call me Shirley," Yenowine said like a space cadet—still using the line from the *Airplane!* movie. He cackled at his own wit.

"You two stay with him and get it done before he meets up with her," she repeated. She pushed her hands behind her hips to let them admire her bobbing breasts one more time. Pintorini's open mouth went to her left tit like a baby robin. She swung herself away from him.

"Everybody gets to play some more," Mimi said. "*After* the job's done. You two studs teach that nigger-lover his lesson and I promise you, I'll screw both of your brains out." She figured that should take about fourteen seconds. She got dressed before the two bozos came up with enough energy to get grabby again. When she opened the door, she turned back to say, "Let me know as soon as you're done. I gotta get to class."

As soon as Mimi pulled the door behind her, Pintorini got up, pulled on his jeans and went to the bathroom. After he emptied his bladder, he opened the medicine cabinet and pulled down the small Band-Aids tin. He lowered two fingers down into it and tweezered out one of the three joints inside. He fired it up, smug as he could be. As long as Big Tits was supplying the weed, there was no reason to deplete their own stash.

He returned to the bedroom, dropped himself into the old, lumpy chair, and with a snippy tongue said to Yenowine, "Why didn't you just ask *me*. I know where the goddam Language Arts building is."

"Take a chill pill, bro," Yenowine said, voice nearly flat-lining.

"It doesn't get dark until what, five, five-thirty?" Pintorini calculated as he took a hit. He held it as long as he could, blew it out and asked, "You think we can pull this off, Man?"

"*Think?*" Yenowine said, as he seized the joint from his buddy's hand. "Hell, Man, that's the beauty of this whole thing. There's no thinkin' to it!"

"Be sure to wear the panty hose she gave you, Yeno," Pintorini added.

"*And* you," Yenowine came back at him.

"That was pretty slick," Pintorini said. "Her telling us that the whole time we've got her pantyhose on, we'll be smelling her stuff."

"This prick won't be able to ID us in a hundred years," Yenowine said. "Pantyhose makes *everybody* look fuckin' weird."

"Just remember what she told you to say," Pintorini said.

Before she left, Mimi had gone over two lines for each of the guys. Any more than that and she figured she might as well expect them to memorize the Gettysburg Address.

Yenowine recited his two lines. His voice was rigid as a board, as if he was trying out for a grade school play, 'White girls ain't good enough for you, *MAN*?' And...and...(the second line finally came to him) 'Happy Valentine's Day, Joe!'"

"Right," Pintorini said. "You use *his* name. And I've got: 'This is for *you*, nigger-lover.' And then, 'Stay away from Bernie if you know what's good for ya.'"

They gave each other high-fives. Pintorini gave Yenowine's torso a disapproving glance and said, "You gonna cover up your dingle or *what*?"

50. Alone

Bernie was curled up, thinking over the *how* part of Valentine's Day. Directly above her, Ameya was sucking air like a machine. It was going to happen, that was for sure. Indoors. And in a real bed, too, not on an old blanket or in a funky bunk like the one she was lying in. She couldn't believe how lucky— no, *blessed*—she was to have already found her boy. Not even a year out of high school, and here she had a white boy—no, a white *man*—who really loved her.

All they had to do was borrow a car from somebody. Joe could check with one of his Loud Crowd buddies for that. Ameya had suggested the *Whispering Springs Motel,* just out of town. "They don't hassle students," Ameya had passed on to her roomie. "They'd lose too much business." She pointed out that the place had another big advantage—an outside entrance to each room. "Out of the car, in the door. You won't be paradin' around in any lobby."

Joe had done a double-take when she mentioned finding a motel room for Valentine's Day, and then he pulled her to him so hard she couldn't breathe. On Valentine's Day, she would call her parents early—by six. She knew the parents would grill her about her and Joe's plans. She would give them a generic response. Joe would give her candy and take her out to a dinner and then probably a movie.

Her mind went back to lunch in the Student Union the day before. It had been so deliciously *obscene* to sit there, immersed in the din of a couple of hundred other students, and have a conversation between each other over how many condoms they would need. Ameya had counseled her roommate weeks ago, before Bernie's afternoon up at the lake, that it might hurt at first, and there probably would be a little blood. "But after that," she had smiled to her roomie, "You'll be a one hundred percent woman."

Bernie felt like she was going to explode.

51. Trouble

Denise huffed to a stop on the elliptical in the HK's Fitness Center. Workout over, she returned to the women's locker room. Although her legs felt like melting rubber bands, she didn't go straight into the shower. Since she had the place all to herself, she sat on one of the low benches, mopped her sweaty neck with her exercise towel and punched in Kym's number.

She jumped the gun as soon as she heard the phone pick up.

"Kym!" she said sincerely, "Denise Jackson. I am *so* sorry."

"Excuse me?" the man said.

Denise felt like she was snake bit, letting herself go totally unprofessional like that *again*. "I'm so sorry," she said. "Kym Suggs, please."

The man's voice sounded away from the phone. "Kym! Yo!" And then, fainter, "Woman apologizing about something, I dunno."

Denise got back up on her feet, too hyper to sit. She could feel the stiffening. She would pay for this all day long, her not jumping straight into the shower. While she waited, she looked in the floor-to-ceiling wall mirror and saw again why she was doubling up on the elliptical. Fat squeezed out from of the edges of her sports bra. Her belly rolled up and over the waistband of her tights. Her butt looked as wide as a cattle gate.

She heard the sound of a phone being picked up. A woman's icy voice said, "This is Kym."

"Kym! This is Denise Jackson calling back. I am *so* sorry about yesterday." She heard measured breathing. The woman apparently was letting her know she was still annoyed over being dissed. "Yesterday just turned crazy on me," Denise said. "Like

I said, I'm a sales manager at a large hotel in Louisville. I really did have a *very* important call yesterday."

"Well..." Kym said.

Denise kept groveling. "A client called in while I was talking to you. I had to pick him up at the airport right away." *More silence on the other end.* "It's a long story."

That was enough twisting-in-the-wind to satisfy Kym. With that, the veteran fourth-grade teacher was ready to show her charitable side. She even doctored up her own language a little to make it sound more sister-friendly. "Okay, Denise" she said, "I feel ya. Sometimes it jes' be that way. Tell you the truth, in a way I'm glad we got interrupted. Gave me a chance to go back and do some mental excavating."

"I understand," Denise said.

"Bernie A.," Kym said, reflecting. "It's been a minute since I thought of her. "I just knew her one year, anyway. Freshmen year."

Denise felt her shoulders sag. *Dead End.* Suggs hadn't kept up with Bernie.

"We lived on the same floor," Kym said. "In fact, she was in the room right next to me." She paused a beat. "Now *why* are you looking for her?"

Denise dropped her understanding with Rudy over not giving the *Why* to any of Bernie's friends. Kym, she saw, wouldn't be doing any talking to Bernie, anyway.

"Friend of mine is trying to find her," Denise said. Says Bernadette—Bernie—was his girlfriend back in college. His name is Joe Normal, if that rings a bell."

"It does."

"You know him?"

"White guy, right?"

"Yeah. White guy."

"Tell you the truth, when I thought back on Bernie, I couldn't help but dredge up her boyfriend, too. Those were weird times. Bernie 'n' Joe. They were like Siamese twins, the whole year."

"Really," Denise said.

"And he's out looking for her—after all this time?"

"Joe's a recent widower," Denise explained. Now that she was getting her footing with Suggs, she threw out her prompt. "I understand he broke up with her." Maybe, she thought, Kym could supply the reason for that. *Love child?*

Kym didn't do anything of the kind.

"Wow. White widower out beating the bushes for his black college sistuh. Somebody call Hallmark. Put it on TV."

Denise heard a chair creak.

"Gonna have a seat." Kym informed her. "You lucked out, Ms. Jackson. No school today. I can give you a little back story. Okay?"

"Oh yeah."

"Bernie was a sweet thing," Kym began. "Different from a lot of girls. She was from a military family. Very respectful. If that wasn't enough, she had foreign blood, mother was Vietnamese or something, as I recall. Black father." She stopped for a few seconds. "Slight little thang, kinda cute."

Denise congratulated herself. So much for Rudy's "Plain Jane" assessment from that *Splenditus* photo.

Just to get the woman's opinion, Denise said, "Mixed couple in Nineteen Eighty. Crazy."

Kym went her one better. "And in *Kentucky*. She was sure ahead of the curve on that one. Girlfriend had stars in her eyes from Day One. We all saw it."

"Can you remember why they broke up?"

"Can't say. But it was him who broke it off, I know that for sure. Bernie, Oh Lordy—she would have hung onto him 'til the Rapture." She gave out a little chuckle. "You realize we're talking about a college romance that happened half a lifetime ago?"

"Oh yeah."

"There was something else," Kym said in a halting voice. "There was some kind of trouble there at the end."

Denise got a catch in her throat. *Baby.*

"Trouble, Kim?"

"A fight, an attack, *something*," Kym said. "Yeah. Joe wound up in a hospital. That's when Bernie left school, right after that. Didn't even bother to finish out the semester." She went silent for a moment. "If you're wondering, she wasn't pregnant. Somebody would have got word on that and passed it on, no matter if Bernie *was* gone from school."

With nothing else to add, she wrapped her story up with, "And that was The Legend of Bernie 'n' Joe, as far as I knew. God-*awful* flame-out."

Before Denise could ask any more questions, Kym came back with a laugh. "That's all I've got for ya, Denise. I'm lucky I remembered what I did, after all this time." Shortly after that, Kym was done with Nineteen-Eighty. She wished Denise good luck and hung up.

Denise sat there, body stiff and cold, and added it up. Nubian Prin-*cess* had out of the blue left school—but she wasn't pregnant. And *he* wound up in the hospital.

52. Valentine Plans

Heavy had a car, a previous bright orange '72 Duster that years and years of the sun's rays had faded to cantaloupe. Joe could live with that; all it had to do was roll him and Bernie to the Whispering Springs Motel, not win the Indy 500. He went to Heavy's dorm room two days before Valentine's Day and asked.

Ugly images came to Heavy right away. If the wrong people spotted Joe 'n' Bernie ducking into a motel, it wouldn't matter if the Springs was just three miles from campus. Joe 'n' Bernie's friends wouldn't be able to protect them.

"You need your Valentine that bad, huh, Jedi?" Heavy said.

"Come on Heavy, this is *really* important." Joe had caught him at a good time, in the middle of the day, when the dorm was virtually deserted. "If you and Stick have plans, I'll drive Bernie to the motel, drop her off, and bring your car back to you. I can hitch myself back out there."

"Wouldn't that be too coo fa scoo," Heavy said.

Joe smiled.

"Not really," Heavy said with a pointed look at his friend. "Sit down, Mister Hot Pants, and let's talk about this." Heavy steered Jedi to his own single bed—no upper bunk attached to it—and sat him down. Heavy stayed on his feet so his friend had to look up at him and pay attention.

Joe had proven to Heavy just how real he was their freshman year. It was on a Thursday night. Heavy's room was occupied by six brothers who were blowing off steam at the end of the class week, jawing with each other while they played Spades. Joe had dropped in to socialize.

Twenty minutes later, the early Spring thunderstorm rolled in. It rampaged its way along the valley, booming and flashing into Pine City. With an enormous window-rattling charge of thunder, everything in the room went black.

Heavy's voice jumped in between rolls of reverberating explosions of energy in the mountains. "Now we're all the same color, Jedi." He made sure it came out cool and collected. The other brothers knew Heavy was ridiculous-nervy with the rap he laid on Joe, but this was off the charts. They all waited to hear what the white dude would say to *that*.

Joe kept Heavy and the rest of the room wondering for a few seconds. Finally, he pointed his mouth into the blackness, in the direction Heavy's voice had come from, and asked, tongue-in-cheek, "Is that a *good* thing?"

Silence amid the rumbles.

Then came the laughter, cascades of it. Jedi had kept his cool, hadn't done the expected white thing and gotten himself all pissed off for feeling like he was being lowered to the same level as the brothers.

"It's a *damn* good thing, Jedi! " Heavy answered with a shout back into the dark. With that one answer, Heavy was assured that Joe Normal was *solid.*

So here Heavy was, with Valentine's Day two days away, grilling Joe about his big plan to head to a motel and lay himself down with a young sistuh. Joe 'n' Bernie were super-tight, everybody knew that. The whole world could blow up around the Joe 'n' Bernie Show and the two of them wouldn't even notice the fireball.

"Am I *sure*?" Joe repeated Heavy's question. He looked up at Heavy as if his friend had been brain-dead the past five months.

Heavy joked his message on to his friend. "You know if some rednecks see you two, the first thing they'll do is torch my ride. Who's gonna pay me back for that?"

Joe blew out a big laugh. "Fire wouldn't hurt it. I've seen it."

"Watch out," Heavy grinned. He loved this, playing back-and-forth with the dude. "How 'bout I *really* class up this date of yours. Drive you two to the motel and drop you off? People'll think you got your own black chauffeur."

After they both had their laughs, Heavy cut the comedy and said, "You gonna cover up, right?"

"Of *course*," Joe said.

"You best hustle yourself downtown to the P.C. Apothecary pronto, then. They might run out of rubbers, with Valentine's and all."

"You can keep this on the QT, right?" Joe asked.

"Oh yeah," Heavy said. He made his next line as dry as he could. "Can't be more than five hundred people on campus who know about y'all's date at the Springs."

"Funny," Joe said. Truth be told, he didn't care. Let everybody at Rolling Flatts know he was crazy in love with Bernie.

"Intercourse between the races is now legal in Kentucky," Heavy noted, just for the record. "Only trouble is, a lot of white folk don't believe it. Don't you go anywhere shoving your romance in people's faces, unless you want some of your body parts rearranged."

"So Dad," Joe whined in a make-believe teen voice, "Can I have the car or not?"

"Yeah, you can have it." Heavy wasn't finished messing with his friend. "Got three whole gallons of gas in the tank. You don't plan on driving around all night sight-seeing, do you?"

"Ha-ha. I've got my sights picked out." Heavy gave him a hand slap on that one. Joe thought of something else. "What about you and Stick?"

"Had our honeymoon last year. This year we're going to a party just on the other side of the tracks. We'll walk. She won't mind."

Heavy took a key off his key ring and handed it to Joe, then gave his friend a four-part soul shake and a bear hug.

"I owe you one, Dad," Joe said gratefully.

"Get it back to me first thing in the morning of the fifteenth," Heavy teased. "Five a.m. sharp."

Joe left with a laugh and hustled out into the hall, almost colliding with two liberal-minded guys he knew who didn't seem to mind if Joe got himself tangled up with black friends or not. Heavy saw another audience he could play to.

"I mean it, Bro," he yelled down the hallway. "Don't you knock up my main squeeze!"

The two guys looked at the two of them and gave it a hoot. Heavy thought of another line. Shouting four doors down before Joe made it back to his room, he yelled, "May The Force be with you, my bru-tha."

On the afternoon of that same day, Bernie kept the shopping bag folded over and closed until she got back to her room. She was thrilled to see that Ameya was the only one in the room, although the door was wide open. After her last class of the day, Bernie had made a beeline to Cassandra's World. It had the town's biggest assortment of clothes that were anywhere close to stylish, other than Jacque Pe-nays, which was out of walking distance. Bernie had been totally up for shopping, after Joe told her at lunch that he'd gotten the keys to Heavy's car. Joe would furnish the wine, the room, the chocolates and, of course, dinner—two Big Mac combo meals, to be picked up on their way out of town. Bernie would supply a romantic Valentine's card, two condoms and herself.

"Show you a couple of things my emergency money got for tomorrow night," she said shyly to Ameya. "But you have to shut the door." Bernie didn't need hateful Jelise barging into their room unannounced.

Ameya saw the fancy shopping bag that Bernie set on her desk and left her bunk, grinning big. She gave the door a hard-enough shove that it *whammed* shut, then put her hands at the back of her hips and smiled, "Let's see how our naughty little Bernie plans on gettin' down."

Bernie smiled sheepishly. As Ameya looking on, she pulled out a tiny spray bottle.

"*Charlie*," Ameya ooo'ed. "All right, Girl. Let's have a whiff."

Bernie squirted a mist of it on her wrist and held it out to Ameya.

"Yay-yuh," Ameya said, sniffing it in. "You go, Girl."

"And..." Bernie said. This time she withdrew a long, red satin robe. "I'm going to come out of the bathroom wearing this." Ameya gave the sexy thing a "*Woo!*" and an approving nod. Bernie set it to the side.

"I'll let him enjoy that for a minute..." Bernie grinned coyly at her roomie. "And then I'll pull it off, nice and slow, and he'll see *this*." She held up a sheer white baby doll. It had a dainty little pink tie at the throat that would make her look downright busty.

"And *finally*..." she said. With a self-conscious giggle, she reached into the bottom of her bag and brought out a hot pink bikini bottom. It had a red satin heart at the crotch.

"Oh, you bad *Girl!* " Ameya yelled, giving Bernie a high five.

"Do you think Joe'll be interested?" Bernie said, hungry for some more flattery.

"*Girl*," Ameya said. Her eyes went to her roommate and stayed there. "Let me take one last look at you right now."

Bernie wondered what Ameya's joke would be.

"Ain't ever gonna see you again—man's gonna eat you *up*."

"Ameya," she said blushed, not knowing what else to say.

Ameya took the baby doll and panties in her hands, held them up and admired them and said, "Of course, you know you'll only get about a minute and a half of wear out of these numbers. Joe sees you in this and it'll be chocolate-and-vanilla swirl, Baby. Motel gonna have to replace the mattress after you two set fire to it."

She felt good about pumping her roomie up over her big night, but then took in the faraway look in Bernie's eyes and dialed herself back. "I can't believe you're not on the pill yet," she said. "You be sure and use some protection, like you did up at the lake." In a meaningless afterthought, she asked. "You *did* have him wear one at the lake, right?"

Bernie didn't see any reason to come clean about that. "He stayed covered up," she said. She gave Ameya an assuring smile. "He's buying lots more."

"Damn better," Ameya said. She started toward the bathroom, had another thought, and turned to pull something out of her purse. She showed the plastic bag to Bernie and handed it to her. "As long as you're lettin' yourself go crazy, you might as well try some weed, too," she said.

Bernie shook her off but then took it when Ameya pressed it hard into her hand.

"Don't tell me you ain't done weed before."

"No."

"Then this is the perfect time. You might just *like* gettin' mellow between rounds."

Bernie turned and set the bag on her bookshelf.

"No you *didn't!*" Ameya gasped, then lowering her voice, she said, "Out of sight, rookie. In your purse."

Bernie went to the drawer she'd emptied out to make room for her special Valentine's things.

Ameya noticed how carefully, how thoughtfully, the girl put each item away. Her roomie was so happy, so anxious, so in love. It scared the living hell out of her.

53. Done

By two-thirty in the afternoon on Valentine's Day, everybody's plans were coming together. Joe had driven the Duster to the motel and reserved the room. He had worked up enough nerve to ask at the front desk for "Room 14, if it's not too much trouble—Sir."

"No such number," the gray-haired man informed him. The owner of the Whispering Springs saw the kid at least had a little romance to him instead of the typical college guys, young-and-dumb-and-full-of-enough seed to re-populate China. *Asking for room number 14 on Valentine's Day.* He cut the young man some slack and explained things.

"Everything starts with a *one* on the first floor. You know, 101, 102. That's why we don't have a 14. Some folks just beat you to 114, but you can still have 214—how's about that?" Seeing the look of disappointment in the kid's green eyes, the desk man offered some good news. "It's in the back."

The man's big-heartedness evaporated when he watched the kid sign the register with what was likely a joke name—*Joe Normal.* You'll like it, Mr. *Normal*," he said sarcastically. "Two double beds, good night's sleep for everybody."

Joe shelled out what was left of his weekly food budget, minus what he had set aside for the combo meals, and paid the man his $24.99 plus tax. With his biggest job done, he returned to campus and parked Heavy's car exactly where he'd found it, on the back row of Student Lot C. As soon as his Spanish class was over, he would walk to the drugstore on Main Street, buy the condoms, and then hustle back and get the Duster. And then it would be him, Bernie and one red-hot bed.

At 4:45, Mimi McKinley's Man One and Man Two went

into action. Pintorini and Yenowine stood across College Blvd. and watched Joe emerge from the building with the statues of Lincoln and Trophyella in front of it. They followed him, keeping a good distance back. They saw the guy was in a big hurry to get to wherever it was he was going. Enough of a hurry that both of them found themselves booking it, just to keep up.

"Dude's got *something* going, that's for sure," Pintorini panted to his buddy. They followed Joe across a good chunk of the Rolling Flatts campus, ducking and dodging behind telephone poles and mailboxes, as if they were tailing somebody in a jokey spy movie. There wasn't any reason for it; Joe didn't know them from Adam. When they crossed over into town, they watched him enter the *Pine City Apothecary.* He was back out in five minutes, stuffing a small paper bag into the slash pocket of the goofy-looking jacket he wore. Joe crossed the street, preoccupied by something, and almost got hit by an old man in an Oldsmobile. "How about *that* shit," Pintorini complained to his buddy. "Old Fart almost did our job for us."

Yenowine broke into a laugh. "Yeah, let's see *him* do a round with Big Tits."

When Joe did double-time back toward campus, the two figured their chances were drying up fast. Pretty soon, they would have to go with Mimi's Plan B. They were relieved when, a block and a half before Joe reached campus, he veered to the right and crossed the street. There were only two things in that direction—the Bottoms Equine Research Center and the student parking lots. With that, the two guys gave each other wary looks and slightly curled smiles.

Joe speed-walked until his sneakers crunched into the big, rough rocks of Student Lot C. At five-thirty in the afternoon, one-third of the lot was already in the deep purple shadow cast by the steep hill beside it.

Pintorini eyeballed the area. A couple of cars were headed out of the lot and toward the street, students done for the day. As soon as they disappeared, the two of them would have a clear shot. He slapped Yenowine's coat with the back of his hand and, in a low, rasping voice, said, "Perfect. Showtime."

As Joe crunched through the pointed rocks, he stuck his hand into his jacket pocket to make sure the two packages of Trojans were still there. He considered the weird, deceitful irony of it, rubbers in the jacket that Bernie's father had passed on to him. Rubbers he was soon going to use on the man's own daughter. If he hadn't loved the girl, he would have felt like a sleaze. But he *did* love his Nubian Prin-*cess*.

The faint amber security lights had been on for several minutes. Even at their full brightness—still a good ten minutes away—their amount of candlepower would be pitifully low for dissuading a thief who wanted to pop a door lock and rip off a student's cassette deck. Or—although such things were rarely reported—discourage the assault of a coed.

Two rows in, Pintorini and Yenowine squatted down and stretched Mimi's pantyhose over their heads. "Man's got pussy on the brain, all right," Yenowine told his buddy. "Hasn't even looked back." The two of them did a good job of timing their crunching steps to match Joe's own. They worked themselves ahead of him, staying below the height of the car windows, and then split up.

One row away from Heavy's sun-faded Duster, Joe's head blasted apart.

Pintorini had waited for Joe to approach the blue Mustang. As Joe went past him, Joe slammed his *College Algebra* book viciously at the back of the guy's head. Joe fell face-first into the rocks. Joe's right hand, which he had instinctively flung in front of him to brace his fall, took most of the force. As Joe yelled out with pain, Yenowine ran up from the other side and walloped the side of Joe's face with his *U.S. History to 1865*. He'd swung it with two hands, like a baseball bat. It made a resounding *thwop* against Joe's nose and blood spurted. The book came apart in his hand.

The books were Mimi's inspiration, cheap purchases from a second-hand book store. She thought the two losers could just use them as props, make themselves look like typical Rolling Flatts students while they stalked Joe. But when she discovered their hefty weight, she realized the books would be as good as fists—even better, since they wouldn't leave any knuckle marks or ring cuts. Her two goofs could lay some short-term damage on Joe and leave it at that.

Yenowine barked out the pair of lines Mimi had rehearsed with him.

"White girls ain't *good* enough for you, Man?" he shouted. "Happy Valentine's Day, Joe!"

Pintorini followed up. He was halfway through his first line when he realized he'd screwed up and was actually delivering a mash-up of both lines. So it came out, 'Stay the hell away from that bitch Bernie if you know what's good for ya."

"Congratulations," Pintorini called out to Yenowine in disapproval. "Cocksucker's nose is broke now for sure." Yenowine was holding only the cover of his dry-rotted book. The pages were down on the gravel with Joe.

"Shouldn't 'a give us books this big," Yenowine snorted.

When Yenowine reached down to pick up the thick chunk of ripped-out text pages, Joe swung wildly at him with his good arm. Yenowine smacked it away with a *whap* from his dangling back covers and sent a glancing kick to Joe's ribs. Joe rolled on his stomach, arms over his head to shield himself from what was next.

"Fucker tried to *hit* me," Yenowine snickered to his friend.

Pintorini dropped to a knee and delivered his own personal message. In the descending darkness, from behind his pantyhosed mask, he told Joe, "Yeah, we know all about your little black-ass girlfriend. Bernie, right? You stay the hell away from Bernie, or next time we'll give *her* a little surprise party. Make what we did to you look like patty-cake. Even take a few turns with her. *Got it*, Joe?"

Yenowine wasn't expecting Pintorini's little add-on, but he liked it. He grunted down at the guy, "I'll back door her, Joe, just so I won't have to look at her nigger face. Whaddaya think of that?"

With that, the two of them left. Just before the two walked out of the lot and back on the sidewalk, they yanked the stifling pantyhose off their heads. Back on campus, the two tossed what was left of the schoolbooks into a dumpster behind the RFSC library.

"Done," Pintorini said under his breath to his friend. He pulled Mimi's pantyhose from his pocket, rolled it up and tossed the thing in.

Yenowine followed suit. "What if somebody finds this stuff?" he asked.

"Yeah, *that'd* be awful," Pintorni snarked at him. "Worn-out school books and a bitch's used pantyhose. Real suspicious in college." He sent a backhand against his partner's chest and said, " Let's go settle up with Big Tits. I got a hard-on so big it ain't funny."

Yenowine gave out a burst of a short laugh, thinking his best bud was joking. He wasn't.

At six o'clock, Bernie peered out her window and searched the street in front of McAfee. She walked over to her bed and fiddled with her packed shopping bag. Ameya, who had decided not to hang out at the grill but come back to the dorm and see her roomie off, was hoping Bernie could keep herself together. She made a lame suggestion. "Maybe he couldn't get the car started."

"But he's already used it once today," Bernie said. "He went and got the room."

"Oh yeah. What time did you say he was he supposed to be here?" Ameya asked.

"Five-thirty at the very latest," Bernie repeated.

Ameya had a dark thought. Maybe Joe really *had* gotten all he wanted from Bernie that day up at the lake. "Give him a few more minutes," she suggested. She puttered around their room, trying to look busy while she sneaked glances at Bernie. She expected to see tears any second. A whole tidal wave of them.

At quarter after six, Ameya touched Bernie's shoulder. "Want me to go next door and see if Kym or Jelise know anything?"

Bernie fingered her shopping bag. "Not them," she said. "Joe had to go back to the lot and get Heavy's car. Maybe Heavy knows something. He lives on the same floor as Joe."

Ameya imagined how pleasant *that* would be. Call Heavy and inform the brother that both his car *and* his white friend were missing. She didn't see much choice. "I'm on it," she said. She headed toward the pay phone at the staircase landing.

She was back in minutes, taking nervous breaths that she couldn't hide.

"Called the dorm. Nothing. Then the Grill. Heavy was there. He doesn't know what's going on, but he said he'd check the parking lot to see if his car is there."

Bernie grabbed her coat. "I'm going, too," she said in a tight voice.

"I knew you'd say that. I told him we'd be out front."

It was almost six-thirty by the time their scramble brought them to Lot C. The girls followed Heavy toward the back, where he'd left his car for Joe. Heavy saw his Duster, and felt the stab in his chest. It was still on the back row, right where he'd left it for Joe.

He almost tripped over the body on the ground. As soon as Ameya saw Heavy's heels dig into the rock, she looked down and saw the human shape, too. Her arm swung behind her to hold Bernie back.

"I think it's Joe," Heavy said, trying to keep his raised voice under control.

Bernie pushed past them, wild to get to the guy on the ground. The three of them went to their knees, pulling at the guy who lay on his stomach in the rocks. Taking heed to the groans, Heavy slowly turned him over. Even by the faint security light, they recognized the fair skin wet with blood. It was Joe.

Bernie let out a terrible, shattering scream.

54. Weigh-In

"Nobody ever told me about a fight," Rudolph said at Denise's dinette table.

Denise believed him. "All I know is, this Kym Suggs said there was some kind of (she made air quotes) 'trouble.' Said Joe wound up in the hospital and Bernie wound up quitting school."

"*Get out.* She quit school?" Rudolph couldn't believe Joe didn't mention that little tidbit.

"That's what her college friend said. She hung up on me right after that, so that's what we've got to work with."

Denise dished the chunks of skinless grilled chicken into the plastic bowl and mixed them in with lettuce and some other vegetables. Her body re-shaping was now officially on, seven days a week. Rudy had a choice. He could share her salads with her, or stop on his way home from work and buy all the heart-clogging sludge he wanted from Taco Bill's. Rudolph made a face at her meal. It deepened after she suggested—again—that Bernie "might have had a bun in the oven."

"Quitting school don't automatically make a girl pregnant," he sniffed. "I told you, Denise. My boy ain't gonna ditch a girl carrying his baby. His Nubian Prin-*cess*? *C'mon*, Denise."

"Sounds like he should be wearing a halo," she said. "Except Kym said in no uncertain terms that he *did* ditch her."

"But she didn't say anything about Bernie being knocked up, now did she? Hell, he already admitted he broke it off." Rudolph looked over Denise's rabbit food and reluctantly forked some of it onto his plate. "My bet is, Joe got either roughed up by some KKK wannabe's, or he got hospital sick—strep throat or something—and just flat cooled off for her. And then she did what a few other school girls have been known to do after a break-up—just ran on back home."

Denise shrugged. Getting pregnant wasn't totally out of the question. Bernie had still been a teenager, eighteen or nineteen years old. Lots of girls that age did whatever it took to please their boyfriends.

Right now, she was on a path to pleasing Joe herself. With her weight loss plan in place, there would be no red meat, no junk food and very little booze, unless it was work-related—and she could always do her routine of spitting it most of it back in her glass. She'd gone out and bought herself a treadmill—a big, expensive one. Between her dieting and morning/evening walk-jogs on her tread, she intended to lose twenty pounds. The Saturday morning walks were history, no more subjecting herself to Scootie's never-ending pumping about Joe.

"What's the point with the play food?" he asked.

"I'm getting heavy, Rudy. I know you can see it."

"Aww, just barely."

"Barely, nuthin'. I'm gonna lose twenty pounds. Get myself back to a Size 10. Maybe even an 8."

Rudolph sucked back his breath. *"Twenty pounds,"* he said, making a face. From his experience, when women lost that much weight, it was all from the wrong places.

"Three months, Rudy. By the first of September, I expect to be down to at least a Size 10."

"How about our partyin'?"

""We can still party. Just no liquor and chips and all that. Half-glass of wine for me, max."

"Damn, Denise!"

She was determined. By the time she hit her forty-sixth birthday, she would look as good as she did in her thirties. When

Joe finally gave up on his Bernie Fantasy, she might even be down to a 8. Joe would like her at that size.

55. Speechless

By the wavering flame of Heavy's Bic lighter, the three of them saw that Joe's nose had been broken, slammed out of place. A long, dark stain of blood ran down the front of his jacket. His face was punctured in several places from falling onto the rocks.

"God, look at his hand," Ameya said. Heavy brought the flickering yellow light over to see a grotesquely-swollen right wrist.

"Joe? JOEY! It's me." Bernie wailed his name, then said it gently. She put her fingertips to his face but his immediate groan made her jerk her hand away.

"Can you hear me, Jedi?" Heavy said. Joe gave out a weak grunt.

Ameya pushed against Heavy's huge arm. "We gotta get him to the hospital."

"No way," Heavy said. "We don't know what-all got torn up."

"Yeah," Ameya agreed, trying to think straight. "Was he run over?"

"No way," Heavy said. "Clothes would've been ripped up somewhere."

Ameya's hand was shaking as she rubbed Bernie's shoulder and agreed.

Bernie swiped the tears off her face and said, "We've got to do *something*." She unbuttoned her cable sweater, the one she'd planned to replace with her baby doll as soon as she got in their room. She put it under her boy's head.

Heavy watched her shake from the cold and he pulled his enormous jacket off. He draped it over the girl.

Ameya turned to him. "Give me your key. I'll get back to

campus and flag down security." When he didn't respond, she made her voice sharper. "You said you had a spare key, right?"

"Yeah," he said, grateful that Ameya was keeping her cool. He brought his extra Duster key out of his pants pocket and set it in the tall girl's open palm. "Take Bernie with you. I'll stick here."

"I'm not going *anywhere*," Bernie said, eyes fixed on Joe.

"Go on, Ameya," Heavy said. "Both of us'll stay here with him." He yelled after her, "Keep the gas all the way to the floor when you crank it." After a couple of stubborn tries, the car kicked over and Ameya pulled away, crunching through the rocks. As soon as she hit the street, she kicked it. The car went squealing toward campus.

Heavy turned back and flicked his Bic again. Bernie was pulling at the drugstore bag that sagged out of Joe's jacket pocket. She opened it, looked inside, and shoved it down into her own jeans pocket. From Joe's other jacket pocket, she delicately pulled out two keys. One was to the Duster. The other was attached to a plastic tab that read *214* and below it, *Whispering Springs Motel.* She looked intently at the worthless, magical room key, and then shoved it into her jeans pocket. As soon as she handed Heavy's car key back to him, he took the flame back to Joe's face and left Bernie to her thoughts. It occurred to Heavy to check to see if Joe still had his wallet. He went to his friend's back pocket and felt for it. It was still there. Heavy wiggled it out and brought his lighter to it. He squinted inside while Bernie looked on.

"Student I.D., driver's license—not hardly any money, though."

"He didn't have much to begin with," she said. "Just enough for dinner and...some other stuff."

He looked at her solemnly. "Then it doesn't look like they took *anything*."

They thought the same thing. *Haters.*

At 7:14 that evening, the phone rang in the upperclassman's dormitory suite that Mimi shared with Evelyn Baker. Mimi could speak as freely as she wanted. Baker, a music major, never showed up until at least ten, thanks to having a graduate-student boyfriend who had a key to one of the rehearsal rooms in the Bottoms Performing Arts Building.

Mimi seized the phone. *"Well?"*

"Mission accomplished," Pintorini's reported from his duplex.

"Where?" she asked.

"C Parking Lot. Nobody else around, I promise."

"No blood?"

There was a pause.

"Hardly any," he said, his voice drawing back.

"*Shit.* You didn't break anything, right?"

"Tried not to. Let's just say he got a free nose job." He laughed. "Good thinkin' with the books."

She didn't need a compliment from an idiot sociopath. "And you got rid of them, right? The books?"

"Of course. Big dumpster behind the library."

"And you said what I told you to say?" Mimi pressed. *"Both* of you?"

"Just like we rehearsed it," Pintorni hedged. He pulled up a vision of her on top of him, with those humongous, hot jugs of hers smushing down into his face.

"And you left him there?"

Pintorini got cute. "We weren't supposed to bring him back

in a limo, were we?" When he got nothing but cold silence for his brilliant wit, he added, "Left him right there on the rocks."

"Okay," she said. "I'll call security, tell'em somebody came to the dorm and said they saw a guy lying on the ground in the C Lot. I'll tell him it sounds like an OD and the poor guy might freeze to death. That should make somebody hustle out there. See you two later."

"Hold the phone," Pintorini cut in. "What about our deal?"

"What about it?"

"You said you'd fuck our brains out, remember—when we finished the job?"

"Are you *insane*?" she hissed, barely able to check herself. "I said *after*, not *when*. You just beat up a guy on damn Valentine's Day. You need to give that prick of yours a rest."

"Well, *when*?"

One more time, Mimi promised herself. She'd do them one more time, and then these two losers would be history. "I think I'm getting my period, anyway," she lied. She made it sound as disgusting to the idiot as she could. "Way too messy for you to have any fun. Make it next week."

Pintorni stood there playing with himself. "So we're just supposed to *wait* on you?"

Mimi was sick of his sorry-ass whining. "Go stick it to your buddy, if you can't wait," she suggested. "*Next week.*" She hung up and called campus security.

As Officer Johnny took her information down on the phone, the old Duster lurched to a screeching stop outside his glass booth.

Within the hour, Joe was in the emergency room of the Pine City/Rolling Flatts Medical Center. By nine o'clock that night, the Dean of Student Affairs, Billy Ray Settles, had called

Joe's parents in Booneville and given them the news about the "extraordinarily-rare campus incident" involving their son. "The folks at the Med Center say it's not as bad as it looks," he assured Benjamin and Sharon Normal. "Broken nose and hairline fracture of the wrist." Another student, he informed them, had ridden with their son to the hospital. In a dubious tone, Settles said, "She identified herself as your son's girlfriend."

Since the Normals had never met their son's girlfriend in person, they couldn't even conjure up an image. Practically all they knew from Joe's phone calls from school was the girl's name was Bernie and that she was a pretty freshman, with a "crazy sense of humor" and brown hair. And that Joe thought she was really special, in some vague way.

56. In the Hospital

At 12:45 a.m. on February 15th, the phone in Harold and Mee'ch Armstrong's bedroom went unanswered for the first three rings. They had been knocked out by their huge Valentine's dinner at the *West Texas Steak House*. Bernie's agitated voice was already crying to him as Harold fumbled the phone to his ear.

"He's in the hospital!"

"What? *Bernie?*"

"Joe!" Bernie's crying picked up.

After making several attempts to understand his daughter, Harold handed the phone over to the girl's mother. His dark, familiar scene immediately flashed into his head. The boy had rejected the warm jacket he'd given to his daughter and had come down with pneumonia, thanks to that little nuthin' jungle coat of his. That meant Bernie would be playing nursemaid to him—and missing her classes. He put his head close enough to the phone that they could both hear.

"Joe was attacked," Bernie blurted out, voice strung out tight. "They jumped him. He's in the hospital here." Hearing the words come out of her own mouth made Bernie break into heaving sobs.

Harold sent a sharp bark back at her. "Jumped him? *Who* jumped him?" He was surprised, but not shocked by the news.

"They don't know," Bernie said between catches of breath.

"Oh my God!" It was Velvette's voice, from the extension in her bedroom.

"'Vette!" Harold shouted. "Who told you to get on the line?"

"She's my sister, Daddy!"

"Let her listen," Mee'ch said, thinking Velvette's voice would help calm her sister down.

Bernie told them all about it, about searching for Joe when he didn't show up for their Valentine's date, and then finding him lying in the back of the student parking lot. She settled down as she relayed what the emergency room doctor told her—most of the blood was from a broken nose, but he also had a broken wrist and maybe some cracked ribs.

There it was, Harold told himself. *Bernie's boyfriend had went and got his ass whupped good for crossing the line.*

Bernie wasn't about to give her father a reason to say *I told you so.*

"The campus police said some guy, or maybe more than one, was trying to steal the car from him. Said they must have gotten surprised by some other students and ran off."

Horse hockey, Harold thought. He relayed that message to Mee'ch with a slow shake of his head and a disagreeing look. Mee'ch bit her lip.

Bernie began to weep between her sentences and now Velvette was swept along with her. "Joe was on his way to borrow a friend's car," she said. "He was going to take me out to dinner." She couldn't hold back a sharp cry.

"Now Bernie, calm down," Mee'ch said, her words even and under control. *"Calm down."* When she heard Bernie's heaving begin to ebb, she said, "This is a sad thing, but Joe will be all right. And so will you."

"I love him," Bernie snuffled. It was the first time she'd used the L-word around them.

A high-pitched whimper came from 'Vette's phone.

"We'll be there first thing in the morning, Bernie," her

father assured her. "First thing."

When 'Vette pointed out, "It's *already* morning," he let out a blow and said sharply, "Nine, nine-thirty."

"Soon, Bernie," Mee'ch said softly. "Everything's going to be all right."

Harold tried to think of something helpful to say. "Hang in there, Honey. He'll be okay."

"Am I going, too?" Velvette asked her parents.

"Hell, no," the Master Sergeant gruffed in a sound that discouraged any possible debate. "You're going to school."

After Bernie hung up, she said a prayer, thanking God for her family. Then, for the hundredth time, she checked the clock on the wall. It read 1:27. Right now, they should have been in bed with each other, lost in each other. She should have been a woman by now. Joe's woman.

Five hours later, at seven o'clock, Harold and Mee'ch were dressed and ready to go. The early start didn't bother them. They were right on their weekday work schedule. He yelled up the stairs to make sure Velvette was awake for school before he and Mee'ch hit the road.

"I'm up, I'm up!" 'Vette had yelled obediently from the top of the steps.

Harold ripped away at his Juicy Fruit. "Hold down the fort while we're gone." He passed on another thought. "Call the hospital if you have time, before you leave for school. Your sister might need somebody to talk to before we get there."

'Vette was up for that, thankful that her father gave her some responsibility. As soon as they pulled out, she was on the phone.

The horrific night and her fatigue had weakened Bernie's

determination not to let her little sister in on her big night. When she heard her sister's voice, she let it go, told her all about the incredible night she and Joe were supposed to have at the motel. They cried together.

In the car, Harold was in the mood to unload on somebody. As soon as he pointed his Lincoln east on Interstate 64, he turned to his wife and said, "Girl had herself all puffed up over having a white boyfriend, and see what it got her."

Mee'ch had anticipated a tirade from her husband, once they were in the car. "Korean girls have been known to fall for men they're not supposed to, too." This time she didn't say it sweetly, like a daydreamer.

Harold shoved in another stick of gum. "Girl's in her first year of college and already talking about being in love. *Please.*"

Mee'ch reminded him again. "You did."

"I was in the Army. That was different."

"How does that make it different?"

"You know why. I had to decide fast." He went to his other point again. "Hell, Mee'ch, she's just a freshman."

"Love doesn't wait for graduation, Dear."

He went hard to the other thing.

"You know that wasn't any attempted '*carjack.*' Or robbery—which one would think would go hand-in-hand. Bernie said his wallet was still in his pocket, with everything still in it. Besides, if you're in a hurry to steal a car, you don't stop and work somebody over like that. You just disable the person—hit the kneecaps, throat—and go."

Mee'ch put her hand to her mouth and gazed out her window, taking in the frost that painted the beautiful bluegrass pastures dusty-white. Such beauty, she thought, and such a sickening thing, for these race-haters to live in it.

Harold had something else to get out of his craw. "Surely to hell you don't want to see Bernie get hurt, on account of that boy."

Mee'ch turned on that remark so quickly she alarmed her husband.

"She's *already* hurt, Harold. "Didn't you hear her going to pieces on the phone? Crying her heart out?" She let out a sigh for her daughter. "Do you really think she would abandon him *now?*"

Harold knew the sad answer to that one. The boy got himself beat up for her. Now their daughter had herself a bona fide hero.

Just after nine that morning, Ben and Sharon Normal's blue Chrysler minivan pulled into the two-level hospital parking garage. Shortly after a stop-in at the front desk, they stepped into Room 335. They were just in time to take in a sight that was so bizarre they were momentarily frozen by it. A black nurse was leaning over the young man in bed—their son—and *kissing him on the mouth.* Ben, working off two hours' sleep, could only think to give out a sharp, cutting, "*Hello?* "

The startled girl flinched at the voice behind her and turned around. The Normals took the stranger in. She looked horrible for a hospital employee. Jelled hair sticking out all over, smeared lipstick, eyes red-rimmed, with dark brown pouches beneath them. Her sorry, wrinkled, uniform didn't even have an ID badge pinned to it.

"We're Joe's parents," Sharon said. "I'm his mother." Then she realized what she'd said and her frayed nerves kicked out a laugh. "Of *course* I'm his mother if I'm his parent."

The girl stared at them a few seconds, as if she were in a

daze. A look of relief suddenly came over her face.

"Mister and Mrs. Normal," she said. "Oh God." She put a hand to her chest. "I'm Bernie."

The Normals kept staring.

"Joe's girlfriend. Bernie."

They were stunned. Joe hadn't bothered to tell them his girlfriend was black.

"Really," Ben said, absorbing the news. "*That* Bernie." He groped for words. "We didn't know you were a...nurse."

Bernie groggily looked down at her clothing, stopped, and made a dopey chuckle. "Oh, these. They gave me these to sleep in. My clothes had blood on them." With the mention of blood, Sharon moved next to her son's bed and Ben hurried to the other side. Bernie teared up again as she said, "When they brought him in last night."

The parents saw that the left side of their son's face was one large purplish bruise. An ice pack rested against it. His nose was taped in place. His face was pocked with small scratches and punctures that were covered with dots of orange antibacterial solution. His right hand was in a splint and propped up on a large pillow.

"Joey, it's Mom and Dad," Sharon said softly. Joe opened his eyes to see her and shut them again. She bent down to kiss him and noticed there was lipstick already there. She kissed his cheek. Ben moved in to gently pat his son's chest. Joe closed his eyes again.

Bernie leaned in to give her boy a touch on the arm. They saw the girl was exhausted, close to falling down.

"They said he was going to be okay," Bernie told them. "But it would be hard to talk, because of his jaw."

Sharon kept her eyes on her son and smiled, "So this is

how we get to meet your girlfriend, huh, Joe?" Joe responded with a weak smile, but kept his eyes shut. Sharon put a friendly hand on the black girl's shoulder, and when Bernie's body went limp, she took the girl into a hug. In the comforting embrace of the older woman, Bernie gave way to her sobs. Sharon found herself joining her, and the two of them had a long, teary cry with each other. When they were both over the shared emotion, Bernie stepped back and said, "I'm so sorry. I didn't know how to get in touch with you guys." She noticed that Joe's father's eyes were as dazzling green as his son's.

Ben shook off the girl's apology. "The school called," he said. "Don't worry about that, Bernie. Thanks for being here for our son." He gave her shoulder a stiff patty-pat.

Silently Bernie replayed that promise to herself, the one Joe had made about taking her home for Spring Break to meet his parents.

"Joe is very special to me," Bernie told them.

Joe's mother looked down again at her son. "This girlfriend of yours is really loyal," she said.

Ben took a closer look at Joe's face. "Do you know when the doctor is due in, Bernie?"

"By eight, they said," Bernie said. Joe's parents looked up at the clock. It was going on ten.

"Maybe he came in while you were sleeping," Ben suggested.

"No Sir," Bernie said. "I didn't miss anybody."

Ben wanted to believe her, but the girl was dead on her feet. He looked the room over and spotted the leather recliner in the corner.

"You need to get yourself some sleep, Bernie," he told her. "Let's get you in that big chair over there."

Bernie hardly realized that Joe's father had her by the arm and was guiding her. She lay back, head nestled on a pillow, and Ben covered her with a blanket. She told herself she wasn't supposed to meet his parents like this, barely awake and one hot mess. She didn't hear Joe's father tell her, "We'll keep tabs on Joe for awhile." She also didn't hear Joe's father huff low to his wife a few minutes later, "Attempted car theft. And I'm the King of Siam."

Ben pushed a chair up to the bed for his wife. Sharon caressed her son's head and kept her hand there.

"You're going to be fine," his mother assured him. Joe again acknowledged her with a wincing smile, but continued to keep his eyes closed.

"Let's let him get some rest," Ben suggested. He thought of the black girl in the recliner. "Let *both* of them rest." He had a seat on the wide window sill.

Joe lay there, grieving.

57. The Folks Meet

A little over an hour later, the Armstrongs arrived at the hospital room listed for Joe Normal, looking for their daughter. They saw a white woman, apparently Joe's mother, sitting on one side of the bed, running her hand through the boy's hair. A white man sat next to the window. They spotted their Bernie in the recliner. She was on her side, knees up high, lying in the same little girl position she took at home when she napped on the couch in front of the TV. Her brown face was barely visible above the hospital blanket, short hair shooting out every which-way.

The incoming footsteps shook the Normals out of their lull. They looked toward the door, thinking the doctor had finally arrived. Instead, they took in a tiny Asian woman wearing a black velour tracksuit. Closing in behind her was a husky black man in his 40s, wearing a black ball cap labeled SECURITY.

Mee'ch spoke first. "Mister and Mrs. Normal?" The Normals nodded at the visitors. Mee'ch smiled. "We're Bernie's parents. Mee'ch and Harold Armstrong."

Ben and Sharon, presented with yet another surprise, took a second to get their bearings before they returned the other couple's cordial smiles. The men exchanged handshakes.

"How is he doing?" Mee'ch asked Joe's parents, as she and Harold checked out the damage done to their daughter's boyfriend.

"We're still waiting on the doctor," Sharon said. "The nurse came and pretty much repeated what your Bernie told us when we got here. He's going to be all right."

"Thank God," Mee'ch said. She went up on her toes and took another look across the room at her daughter. She looked back at the boy's parents, "Bernie thinks a lot of your Joe."

"Well, Joe's gone on for months now about this special girl of his," Sharon reciprocated. "Our son absolutely raves over your Bernie," She immediately wished she hadn't said that—absolutely raves. *Way too snobby-sounding.* She didn't bother bring up the little race situation Joe failed to pass on.

Harold's gum-chewing slowed considerably, now that he could see with his own eyes that his daughter was safe and resting. He volunteered, "We met your son when we brought Bernie back to campus after Christmas break." He kept his cool easy enough, after dealing with all kinds and colors at the VA hospital. "Joe's a fine young man," he said, leaving it at that.

With the Armstrongs' arrival, Room 335 soon became an attraction. Workers came from as far away as West Virginia— by way of having jobs in the cafeteria—just to mosey by and rubberneck the rare scene. There they were—blacks, whites and Asians, all mixed together, seeming to get along just fine.

The room became a *real* ethnic casserole when the Indian doctor finally showed up. Dr. Samir Manohar stepped into the room at 11:38 to wrap up the last of his morning rounds. Employed at the regional hospital for just over a year now, Samir ("Just call me Sammy") Manohar had comprised the facility's entire international staff. For that reason, plus the fact that he was a fountain of corny jokes, he'd become the Med Center's reigning celebrity.

Dr. Manohar took in the rare multi-racial, multi-ethnic landscape and went straight into his stand-up.

"Ah," he said, showing a big, toothy smile. "I see we have a roomful of Mexicans." When he was met with awkward smiles, he dropped the humor bomb and introduced himself. Formalities over, he stepped in to get a closer look at the young man in the bed.

All the commotion woke Bernie. When she batted her eyes open and saw her parents, she scrambled out of the recliner and went to them. After brief, intense hugs, she returned to the side of Joe's bed.

Dr. Sami saw the girl's lips shape the words *Baby* as she rubbed his shoulder. He could spot the concerned gaze of a girlfriend from here to Bombay. "Is this a friend of yours?" he teased the girl.

"*Boy*friend," she said, keeping her eyes glued on her Joe.

"Time to wake up, Joe," Dr. Sammy said. He pressed the button on the bed frame and brought Joe up nearly to a sitting position, Joe reluctantly opened his eyes. Relief filled the room. "There's our Joe," the doctor smiled.

"Hi Baby," Bernie greeted him, Joe gave her a friendly smile.

Let's take a look at our Fighting Pioneer," Dr. Sammy said. He shone a small flashlight into Joe's eyes.

"How is he?" Bernie asked impatiently.

"Not bad at all," Dr. Sammy said as he looked Joe over, "for having a couple of cracked ribs, multiple facial punctures, a broken nose, a slightly but nonetheless fractured wrist and a technicolor mandibular contusion." He substituted the everyday name for that last item. "bruised jaw." He dispensed a comforting smile. "He will heal. Helps if you're twenty years old." He smiled warmly at the exotic-looking girlfriend wearing her college-fad hospital scrubs. "He's already on the mend, young lady." He looked over the unlikely pair again, the white student and his Asian-eyed black girlfriend, right here in Pineville, Kentucky, and thought, *amazing*. "He may also have a bit of a concussion, as hard a blow as he took to his head. That's why we're taking our time here." He looked back at Joe. "Big Joe. Can you move your jaw just a little bit for me?"

Joe gave out a weak, "Umm."

Bernie jumped and squeezed her boy's good hand.

"What's your name?"

The words came out faint and slurry through a half-opened mouth. "Normal, Joseph."

Chuckles all around.

Dr. Sammy appreciated the student's sense of humor. He filed the line away for future use.

"Normal Joseph. Excellent," the physician said. "Are your parents in this room, Normal Joseph?"

"O' there," Joe mumbled, motioning toward his parents.

Dr. Sammy tipped his head toward the young black girl. "And this pretty young lady, I'm guessing, is your girlfriend? I'm only saying that because she said you were her boyfriend."

"Yes," Joe said. He didn't elaborate.

Bernie squeezed Joe's hand harder.

"And where do you go to school?"

"Harvard."

Dr. Sammy laughed with the others. "Most likely no concussion for you, Man," he said, straightening up. "If you had a concussion, you would have told me Yale."

After the titters, Dr. Sammy got back to business. "The only thing you have to do is lie here and let us watch you for a day or two. Then you can get yourself back to class...and this devoted girlfriend of yours."

As soon as the doctor left, Bernie let it go. "Oh, I love you, Baby!" she chirped to her Joe. She kissed his good cheek and kept her face next to her boy.

With that scene playing in front of them, Mee'ch asked Joe's parents, "Would you like to go down to the cafeteria for a cup of coffee? Or lunch?" Then, in a wifey tone, "I know my husband has got to be hungry enough to eat a horse, after that drive. *Aren't* you, Harold?"

Harold took a couple of seconds to process the question. "Sure thing," he said. He was already preoccupied about *the next time.*

The Normals and the Armstrongs went down to the cafeteria and made chit-chat over lunch. It was Harold who had to say it to Ben and his wife. With his daughter so close to danger, he was compelled to say it.

"You know that wasn't an attempted car theft, don't you?" he asked Ben.

"That's what the school officials said," Ben replied.

"And you believe that?" Harold said, skeptically.

"Not now," Ben said. "Not after seeing him."

"They're walking a fine line," Harold told them.

"Harold," Mee'ch said, saying it in a way that told him to drop it.

Harold shoved a new stick of gum in his mouth.

"If our son is as taken with your daughter as she obviously is with him," Ben said, "then they've got some kind of relationship."

"Agreed," Harold said. "And we all get to lose sleep over it."

"Young love," Sharon offered up, smiling and swaying her head. It helped that she and Ben had been liberal coffee house fixtures in their own youth. Questioning the status quo. The only snag was, their coffee house had been all white. Their neighborhood, when they later immersed themselves in middle class society as parents, also happened to be white. Ninety-nine percent of their friends were white. But here—now—one of their three kids had certainly turned rebel.

The Armstrongs stayed the night in town, at the Holiday Inn. The next day, they headed for home, with an agitated Harold predicting to his wife en route that her oldest daughter was getting herself into "one helluva mess." The Normals left a day later. By then, after they finally saw Bernie rested and cleaned up, they were heartened to see that Joe's love interest was a nice-looking, well-mannered, intelligent girl.

On the afternoon of February sixteenth, after allowing the campus hubbub about the student attack to settle down, Mimi McKinley went to the hospital. She wanted to see the finished product in person. She had walked down the third-floor hallway, hidden in a headscarf and sunglasses, and slowed down to shoot a sly gaze into the open door of Room 335. She saw a couple of old white people in there—probably Joe's parents—plus a few black hoodlums—one a really big one. Black Bitch was in there too, hovering over Joe like he was her little baby. Before she got all the way past them, she spotted the cast on Joe's right hand. Pintorini hadn't mentioned that little injury when he called in his report to her. *Bastard.*

Pissed over seeing Nigger Bitch hanging around, Mimi decided to reinforce the message. She went down to the gift shop and bought a Get Well card. It had a religious message, one with an ironic warning attached to it. It read in blue, soothing script, "You'll Never Walk Alone." She took it to the lobby and had a seat. Just under the words *Get Well Soon*, she had printed, with the ugliest penmanship she could create with her non-writing left hand, "Remember us, Buddy Joe?" Out of writing space,

Mimi had made a crude arrow with the words, "See bak." On the back of the card, continuing to speak for the two retards, she added, "If you don't stay away nigger Bernie, next time around we'll give *her* a surprise." It was followed by a *???* And then a, "TRUST us."

It took a good amount of time for her to scrawl it all out. She finished up the barely legible card and slid it in its powder blue envelope. Joe would *have* to think the sorry thing came from the two Neanderthals who kicked his ass. If the beating wasn't enough of a persuader, this card should be. Hell, she thought, Joe would see this card and be sure to think they were right there in the hospital, keeping tabs on him. If Joe cared anything at all about the nigger girl's health, he'd drop her like a hot brick, right?

Mimi decided right then to cancel her final payment to the two jerk-offs, thinking bitterly about Joe's hand winding up in a damn cast. She walked to the information desk across the lobby and handed the card to the old retiree she saw manning the house phone. The card was addressed to *Joe Normal, Room 335*. Then she split.

58. Coke Bottle

On Friday, Anson L. Huey was in town to sign his three-year contract with the Hotel Kentuckian. With it, the American Antique Glass Bottle Collectors Association's annual convention would be locked in. Huey and vice president Zielinski had flown back into Louisville to formally seal the deal after Nancy Pat sweetened the pot by lowering the daily room rates from one hundred-and-five dollars per room per day to ninety-nine, based on a four thousand room-night minimum.

"Now I've got a surprise for you ladies," Huey told Denise and Nancy Pat in the hotel's well-appointed conference room. He gave his VP a nod and said hammily, "Drum roll." Al obediently rapped his knuckles rapid-fire on the table in *booda-booda-booda* style. He quit when Huey made a *slash* sign across his own throat.

"And the news is..." Huey said melodramatically, "Ambeca is joining us!"

Whoopie damn woo, Nancy Pat said to herself. She was ahead of the man on that one. The assistant director at the convention bureau had alerted her to that little tidbit two days earlier. The addition of a few hundred milk bottle groupies wouldn't exactly set the town on fire, but she'd take it. Take it and fake it.

"Well all right!" Nancy Pat shouted, juicing up her joy over Huey's pint-sized bulletin. She stretched her arm across the board room table and gave a high-five to Huey. They all yucked it up. Denise produced a mid-level, "Woo!"

Huey didn't bother to tell Nancy Pat he was adding the Antique Milk Bottle Collectors Association as insurance, just in case his organization couldn't hit that room-night minimum on its own.

So it had been a good day for Denise—new business assured. And she'd had to put up with barely a flirty look from either one of these Illinois guys. Around one o'clock, signing done, the four of them went to celebrate with lunch and cocktails in the HK's own *At the Post Lounge*. It was perfect for killing the hour and a half that remained before Denise drove them back to the airport to make their flight home. At three, after nursing her one Old Fashioned, there she was, pulling the HK shuttle bus over to the drop-off curb.

"We'll be talkin' at ya, Denise!" Huey bellowed from the shuttle's shotgun seat, as the Delta commuter prop came in overhead.

She did the professional thing, sliding out—carefully—in her tight skirt, to give each of the men a big smile and a businesslike hug. The eyes of both men were still on her when she pulled away.

Huey elbowed Zielinski and said, "We gotta have a nickname for that girl."

Zielinski must have already given it some thought.

"*Coke Bottle,*" he said. "No doubt about it. Look how she's built."

Huey agreed. The woman had an hourglass. Indeed, she was a nice match-up with one of Coke's old-time favorites. "The 1915," he told his VP. "Either that or the '57."

"Oh, the Fifteen," Zielinski said. The classic 1915 bottle was heavy on the curves, with a thick middle. "*Definitely* the Fifteen."

Huey gave his righthand man a hearty midwestern smile. "*Coke Bottle*. Perfect." They headed into the terminal, having settled that.

Denise had spent the rest of her work day feeling free as a bird. Contract signed and legal, Nancy Pat had taken the rest of the day off. Her sales managers, other than Denise, followed their boss' example soon enough. Denise would stay another hour, just in case any more business dropped in the HK's lap like that. It wasn't likely, but you never knew.

Denise leaned back in her chair, which brought on a light-headed rush. She got up and retreated to her love seat. Although she'd milked her drink for over an hour, she wasn't used to much alcohol in the past few weeks. She draped her legs over the end of the armrest, lay back and imagined herself being in shape again. *Sugary beach, some place, say, like Jamaica. Her feet would be planted wide in the sand. She would pull the brilliant white cover-up off to let Joe admire the sexy aquamarine tankini she was so impressively packed into. She'd dare him not to want her in that curve-hugging number.*

A reflexive belch forced her out of her gauzy daydream and she found herself looking over at the photo on her desk. The one with her and Rudy, taken down in Atlanta. That unsettling feeling returned, the one that told her that the man in the picture was turning into more of a roommate than a life partner. He wouldn't be the kind of man who would chase after her, not like Joe was pursuing his Bernie. She thought back to that first time she met Joe. It was over a year ago, at Max-It's annual company picnic. She'd looked up from her barbecued ribs to see Rudy heading directly at her with his white buddy and Franki in tow. Rudy was literally tugging the couple toward the all-black table,

anxious to show off his new white pal to her as much as he was
to introduce her to him.

"This is my friend, Denise Jackson," Rudy had told Joe. He
hadn't even bothered to use the word *girlfriend*. She remembered
it like it was five minutes ago.

She stretched out on the furniture as best she could and once
again admonished Rudy *in absentia*. He could've pitched her
to Joe 'way better than that. Could've said to him what he told
her in private—that she was the first girl he had ever been with
who had looks *and* brains. Rudy could've bragged that she was
his confidant and counselor. Could've mentioned that she had a
good sense of humor. Could have—hell—gone to the trouble to
call her his *soul mate*, like he did when they were alone. But he
hadn't done any of those things in front of his white friend, or
for that matter, in front of any of his friends, as far as she knew.
She'd sat there at that picnic table and given her cool smile to
the weird white guy who didn't mind hanging out with a crowd
of black folk.

Shortly before five, Denise started to stand up, but even the
small amount of bourbon she'd had was still working on her. Her
body came back down so hard, she almost flipped the sofa. When
she righted herself, she laughed out loud. Now *that* would have
been comical in front of room full of bottle collectors, legs up
high and wide for all to see. She settled back and looked again
at that selfie on her desk. Her and Rudy's very first weekend
trip together. What a wild, fun weekend that was.

Girl, she thought, you've got it better than most of the sisters out there, you know you do. Denise kicked the arm of the
love seat hard with her heel. She would *never* be Rudy Barnes'
Nubian Prin-*cess*.

59. Crushed

Joe was dressed and sitting on the side of his hospital bed, waiting. The clock on the wall read 2:46. Soon, Bernie would be out of her freshman English class and here to help him check out. He knew if he waited until they got back to campus, it would be the Bernie 'n' Joe Show all over again, until they hurt her. And they *would* hurt her.

The Get Well card from the haters was folded in half and shoved in his back pocket, where Bernie wouldn't see it. Joe had his head down, fingering the cast on his wrist, when she charged into the room, wearing her very best smile for him.

"Big, blessed day, Baby!" she cheered him. She was bouncing on her toes, happier than ever. She wedged between his legs and put her hands on his shoulders to balance herself. When he parted his lips to speak, her tongue went into his mouth. She kept it there, feeling the erotic tingle deep inside her. That was her official hello to him. She pulled back at the waist. "I almost didn't recognize you with your clothes on," she played, halfway hoping somebody out in the halfway would hear her talk that way with her man. Bernie didn't care what anybody saw or heard. They wouldn't be coming back here.

Joe knew she could be his tonight, tomorrow night—anytime he chose to get her to that motel. When she came in harder against him, he felt the stiff corner of the Get Well card poke into his rear end. He tried to take a deep breath, hoping she wouldn't tongue him again. He needed to say this in one big breath. It would be the only way he could do this thing and not give in. He eased away from the bed, gently pushing Bernie aside, and slowly stepped over to close the door.

Bernie first thought *private feel*. She was more than willing to let Joe give her a *Whispering Springs* preview.

As the door clicked shut, she said, "I like the way you think, Mister Normal."

She went to him to give him another deep kiss and was startled when he brought up both hands, cast and all, and held them in front of her. She gave a chuckle—*Silly Joe playing hard to get*—but then her laugh broke apart as she took in his eyes. Joe was wearing an expression she'd never seen before.

"I think we need to take a break from each other," he said. The voice was cool and flat.

When she said nothing back to him, only stared, he went on with it. "I've been thinking about this for quite awhile."

Still playing, she thought. Of course he was playing with her. Bernie let out a short burst of a laugh to get her rhythm back. She started to reach for him again but this time he straightened out his good arm and stiff-armed her away.

"I mean it," he said. "I...think we're moving too fast here."

His face was so forlorn that it frightened her. Something yanked hard in her stomach. Joe, standing there with her lipstick on his mouth, was somehow *serious*. He was still Joe, but he *wasn't* Joe. He almost looked like a stranger to her.

"What are you *talking* about, Joey?" she wailed. "I came to get you."

Joe recited what he'd gone over in his head.

"I just think we should see other people," he said. And then, he knifed the pain home. "You'll always be a special friend to me."

Bernie realized he hadn't said her name since she came in.

"*Special?*" she heard herself say. Her eyes were on him,

stunned. She tried to get close to him again, thinking a kiss would turn this person into her Joe again, the Joe she knew.

This time, his arm pushed her away.

"What's going on, Joey?" she screamed, looking into his green eyes. Somewhere in her head, the voices said, *The world's not ready for that...he'll get a sample...dump ya like yesterday's paper.*

Joe said something she never dreamed she would hear from him.

"See any other couples like us around here?" he asked. "You don't, do you?"

With that, the floor dropped out from under her. The tears came, dripping off her trembling chin as she looked dumbly at him, bewildered. She thought of something that made no sense at all. "We can do it right now, if that's what you want, Baby. I can give it to you right now."

Joe forced himself to shake his head at her. He realized what horrible power he held, the power to cut deep into her. *God help me,* he told himself. He said it.

"It's over, Bernie."

Hearing him finally say her name, it came out like a profanity to her. She took her eyes away from him, feeling the flame of humiliation overtake her. She let out an awful cry and ran from the room. She kept her head down nearly all the way back to her dorm. She was wounded again when she reached McAfee's front steps and one of her sister friends greeted her with a, "Hey, Ms. Normal."

She charged past, went into her room and locked the door behind her. Through her tears, she looked upon things that didn't mean anything to her anymore. Text books, Army blanket, the wall calendar with the big red star marking February

14th. Through the rivulets of tears, she went to her closet. She opened it, reached to the very back, and pulled out Joe's skimpy safari jacket. She brought it to her face and smelled him, the boy she would have sworn was going to marry her. Then came the uncontrollable weeping. Bernie thought of the other precious, meaningless keepsake. She went to the shelf just below her wall mirror, and, from the small jewelry box, pulled out the key. *Room 214 Whispering Springs Motel.* She slipped it into one of his jacket pockets, folded the coat up neatly and placed it in the bottom of her trash can.

Before the day was out, anybody who cared anything about the two of them had heard the big news. Jedi Joe, the super-cool white dude, had ditched his black girlfriend. The Bernie 'n' Joe Show was over. Another shock wave hit the very next day, when Bernie's parents came to Rolling Flatts to take their daughter and all of her things back home.

60. The Rev Calls

Even from the second bedroom that Denise had converted into an office, Rudolph could hear the squeak of the front door being opened. He stepped into the hall, holding his phone to his ear, and waved for her to join him.

"I'm putting this on speaker, Rev," Rudolph said in a raised voice. "My friend Denise is helping me look for Bernie, too."

She heard the word but she made herself focus on the matter at hand—Rudy calling somebody "Rev." Now that was comical. In the time she'd known him, Rudy had never got loose enough around *any* preacher to call him, "Rev."

A black man's high-pitched voice greeted her from the phone. "Sister Denise."

She looked at Rudy, curious. "Hey, Reverend," she came back tentatively, tilting her head in a *whatever* gesture to Rudy. She pointed to her office chair and Rudy spun it around and held it for her as she sat.

Rudolph clued her in as he talked to both of them.

"Got a call at work today from one of Joe's college friends. Guy named Hurtt. He didn't help us much, but then he got in touch with Reverend Williamson here. The Rev called just before you came in."

"Brother Barnes here tells me you're on a missing persons search, Sister Denise," the reverend said.

Brother Barnes, she repeated silently to herself. Not hardly.

"I went to school with Joe back at Rolling Flatts," the preacher said. "Of course, I wasn't a minister then. Everybody knew me by my nickname, 'Heavy.'"

Denise cut in. "Do you know where we can find her—his old girlfriend?"

"In a word—no. I was just explaining to your friend Rudolph, when she left school, that was it. Nothing after that."

"No reunions, get-togethers, that sort of thing?" Denise asked.

"Oh no," Williamson said. "I mean..." His voice went more deliberate. "Can I tell you two a story?"

Denise and Rudolph traded glances.

"Go for it," Rudolph said. "We'll take any information we can get."

They heard him take a swallow of something. "Sorry," Williamson said. "Better wet up my whistle before I get into this." He took a big breath. "First of all, Joe's good people, okay? Just so you know where I'm coming from. Now, Brother Barnes, I..."

"Call me Rudolph, Rev," Rudolph interrupted.

"Fine." He reset. "Joe and I were freshmen together at Rolling Flatts. Isaiah too. Now you two got to know this, right up front: Back in the day, Joe was a different kind of cat, he was so cool with everybody. In fact, we wound up giving him a nickname—'Jedi Joe.' You know, from the *Star Wars* movies." The Rev chuckled with that tidbit.

"Jedi Joe, " Denise said out loud. This time the name put an amused smile on her face.

"Anyway," Williamson said, "In our sophomore year, ol' Jedi got himself a little shawty of his own. That's the Bernadette Armstrong you're out huntin' for. Cute little sister."

Cute, Denise mouthed over to Rudy. He sent back a disagreeing scowl. "So they fell for each other?" she asked.

Williamson gave that question a big, high laugh. "Fell, tripped, collapsed, capsized, you name it," he giggled. "Joined at the hip, hear me tell it. It was crazy for the times—or at least for Rolling Flatts. A white boy and a black girl hooked up with each other."

"Crazy," Denise echoed to nobody in particular.

"Here Joe was, white as a wedding cake," Williamson said, "and here was this sister who not only had chocolate skin but was half Oriental. Korean, or Vietnamese, I think they said."

"Oriental, yeah," Rudolph said.

"So this Hurtt guy was jealous?" Denise blurted out, throwing out a guess.

"Oh no," Williamson said. "None of us peoples gave Joe 'n' Bernie any trouble, as I can recall. None of the whites did, either, not 'til Valentine's Day. That's why I remember it. Valentine's Day. That's when all the bad stuff went down."

Denise sensed a long, complicated back-story. "'Scuse me, Rev. But could the three of us get together and go over this face-to-face?"

"Love to, Sister Denise," Heavy laughed. "Only-ist problem with that is, I'm calling from Oakland. After 9/11, I decided to tack on a divinity degree. Wound up in California."

"So what happened on Valentine's Day?" Rudolph said, anxious for the man to get back to his story. "That's when they broke up?"

"Technically, no," Williamson said. "Valentine's Day was the exact day that Joe—pardon my French here—got the hell beat out of him. They split up...well, let me finish this part first... it was Bernie and me, plus Bernie's roommate, who found him."

"Oh wow," Denise said. *"Beat up?"*

"Big-time," Heavy said. "Whupped him bad enough to put him in the hospital."

Denise and Rudolph looked at each other and nodded. Kym was right on, on that part.

"Jedi was going to borrow my car, have a big romantic night with his sista-girl. They never found out who did it. Joe said they were wearing panty hose over their heads, like small-time hoods. The Lord was with him. Had a broken hand and broken nose, but things could have been a lot worse. They didn't steal nuthin', didn't even touch his wallet, and they had all the time in the world. So it was a racial thing, no doubt about it. Anyway, that undid everything, no doubt about it."

"What do you mean *undid*?" Denise asked.

"That's why I said that technically that's the day they broke up. Joe did the actual splittin' up two days later at the hospital."

Gave her back. Denise said to herself again.

"That threw everybody," Williamson said. "Here they'd been hooked up the whole school year. And then—*boom*—everybody thought he turned it off, went cold as ice."

Denise played dumb. "She must have been a real basket case after that. I mean, seeing him on campus every day until the school year was over."

Rudolph started to correct her but she waved him off. He looked at her, curious.

"Well, that's the thing," Williamson said. "She up and quit school that morning, the very day he broke it off. She didn't go to another class."

"Wow," she played along.

"I'll be damned," Rudolph said, forgetting himself.

"'Damned' is pretty close, actually," Williamson said, "After that, Joe was a Judas, as far as the black folk were concerned. Some of 'em even did a Matthew 27:4 on him."

"Which is..." Rudolph cluelessly asked.

"Judas said," the Rev quoted, "'I have sinned in that I have betrayed the innocent blood.'"

"Amen," Denise said.

"So that was it for Joe, as far as him having any credibility left with the brothers. They'd even cross the street when they saw him coming. It hit Joe hard, being dropped cold by all of them like that. And the sisters—*watch out.* They all gave him *real* hard looks, after what he done to their own. Would've been nasty for a while if he'd been a brother, but here he was, white man crossing the line, making everybody believe in him, and then he went and did that to a *sistuh.* So he was a pariah beginning that very day, know what I'm sayin'?"

"Poor Joe," Denise said.

Right on," Rudolph said.

"I wasn't one of 'em, by the way," the Reverend said. "I *knew* there had to be more to it than Joe cooling off to her. Caught some grief from going on hangin' out with him. And there was *more* to it. When Jedi got out of Dodge—last day of the school year and the last time I ever saw him—he came to my room and told me the whole thing. Said the punks who jumped him told him what they'd do to his black girlfriend if he didn't drop her."

"Which was," Rudolph asked.

Denise bit her lip, dreading the answer.

"Guess the worst," Williamson said. "I mean, some *really* ugly stuff."

"My God," Denise said. "And he didn't fight to keep her?"

"The way I saw it, and still do," Williamson said, "Joe was a young buck then, white guy new to dealing with haters. I like to think he was 'way more scared for her than himself. So he cut her loose. He didn't come back to Rolling Flatts the next year or ever again, as far as I knew. Transferred."

"But now he's going after her again," Rudolph said. "Widower, like I told you."

Denise horned in. "Do you think he's more mature, Rev, and that's why? Or he has some kind of guilt trip over the whole thing?"

"I can't say," Rev. Williamson said. "All I know is, it sure looked like love in Nineteen-Eighty-one. If he ever finds her, I'd say they've got a lot better chance of being left alone than they did back then. We can all see how the world's changed."

"Or not," Rudolph said.

"Or not," the Rev repeated.

"And you don't know how to get in touch with her," Rudolph asked the man again, just to be sure.

"I'm afraid not, my brother," the Rev said. "God's going to have to work this out, if that be his plan."

"But if you hear anything about her..." Rudolph said.

"Absolutely," Williamson said.

Phone call over, Rudy looked over at Denise and said, "Damn, what do you think of that? *Joe* quit, too!"

Denise looked away from him, and said it herself, as much as to Rudy. "Kicked her to the curb to *save* her."

61. Twisted

At seven-thirty the following night, Joe pulled into the parking lot of the Valley Vista apartments. He turned off the engine but left the key on so he could listen to one more song from his favorite CD, *Truckin' to the 80's.*

The bumping disco beat caught Scootie's ear. She was sitting on her bed, smoothing up her nails for church tomorrow morning—and doing it with a sour attitude. Church was her second option. With no Saturday night action, she had to hope that some Baptist brother might notice her fine nails and then get interested in all the rest.

She twisted her window blinds open just enough to see the fancy Jeep, with Joe all alone in it. She tossed aside her nail-buffing tool and hot-footed it out of her bedroom. She was wearing a white T-shirt, shorts and no bra.

After the final bars of *I'm Your Boogie Man* faded away, Joe switched it off and headed toward the building. By then, Scootie was waiting in the foyer, with her hand on the doorknob. And as soon as Joe started in, she pulled in hard. His forward momentum brought him crashing into her, his hand breaking his fall against one of her breasts. She kept her grip tight on the doorknob, while her right hand grabbed onto him.

"Ooof!" she pretended. The girl had never said "Ooof!" in her life.

Joe saw where his hand landed and quickly yanked it away. Scootie held her grip on him.

"Hey!" he exclaimed, facing Denise's friend with an embarrassed grin. When he stepped back to take himself off of her, she had no choice but to turn him loose.

"I am so *sorry*," she coo'ed. "You're Denise and Rudy's friend, right? Jim, Jack?" She set her gaze on his sexy green eyes and batted her eyelashes.

"Joe," he grinned good-naturedly. "And you're...don't tell me..." He tapped his temple with his fingertip. "Starts with an 'S'..."

"Wow, I'm impressed!" Scootie flattered him. She wasn't about to wait until Hell froze for the damn man to come up with the rest of the letters. "Add a cootie and you've got it," she joked.

"S...coo...Scootie! Right!"

"There ya go," she beamed. She sucked in her belly, and used both hands to pull down hard on bottom of her shirt. Despite the weak light overhead, her half-dollar-sized nipples appeared under her shirt. He smiled back at her and thought, *super*-friendly woman. Realizing he was holding her up from leaving, he stepped aside.

Scootie didn't budge. "We never got our power walk in, you know it, Baby?" she said. While Joe drew a blank, she arched her shoulders back like a beaming TV game show model, sexing it up in front of a new washing machine.

"Yeah, that's right," he said as it came to him. "The Saturday morning walks with you and Denise."

"Well, if she ever *makes* it again." She released her shirt and then yanked it down a second time, in case he missed anything. "I never know about the girl anymore, Joe," she said with a straight face. "Half the time she gets tied up doin' something else." She let her voice go helpless. "I don't *mind* going by myself but, you know, single girl walking around all by herself in the 'hood..." She tried to penetrate those green eyes of his. "Know what I mean?"

"Yeah, a partner would give you a sense of security," Joe

offered.

Clueless, she told herself. "Some men'll jump you, tear your clothes off in no time to get what they want. Don't matter if it's broad daylight." She let her eyes give him an up-and-down. "Think somebody would try that on me, Joe? Come on out from behind a building and just jump me?"

"Oh yeah," he said. He shook his head as if he were talking to a neighbor about a newspaper being stolen. "You gotta be careful."

Unreal, she told herself. Man couldn't recognize an invitation the size of a billboard.

"I'll get on Denise about that right now," he said in a playful, chastising voice. "Gotta get up there anyway for a meet-up." He started up the stairs. "Catch you next time, Scootie."

Scootie saw she had no choice but pretend she was really headed somewhere.

"Okay, later," she said. "This Saturday, promise?"

"You got it," he said.

She stood outside on the porch and waited until she heard Denise's open and bang shut again. She returned to her apartment, more pissed than ever. Here was a single man just above her head, going to total waste on a Saturday night.

"You'll never guess who I ran into downstairs," Joe grinned to Denise and Rudinski. "I mean, literally."

"Who?" Rudolph asked.

Denise couldn't resist. "Michelle Obama?"

"Scootie!" Joe said.

"What a coincidence," Denise came back.

Rudolph swung his head toward her with a look that said,

Cool it with the Scootie crap.

"I was coming in the door and she was going out," Joe said. "I nearly ran over her."

Connivin' B., Denise thought.

"It was pretty funny," Joe said.

Not only for her own pleasure, but to get his mind off Scootie, Denise eagerly offered her cheek to Joe. The three of them went to what was becoming their customary spot, Denise's dinette table. Rudolph poured out two beers. Denise had water.

Denise informed Joe that her phone conversation with the college roommate, Ameya, had been a real wash-out. The girl apparently had some real dementia issues. Rudolph went next with his news.

"Talked to an old college buddy of yours today," he said. "Heavy. He said he goes by *Reverend* Williamson these days. Doesn't have any idea where Bernie might be."

"Heavy, a preacher? Really?" Joe smiled. "He was something else."

"Here's a question for you, Mister Joe," Denise said. She tapped Rudy's foot to let him in it. "How'd you get through the end of the year? I mean, seeing her around school after you broke up with her?"

"Yeah," Rudolph said, jumping in. "How'd *that* play?"

Joe took a sip of his beer on that question. "Never was an issue. She left school right after that. Withdrew."

Rudolph and Denise glanced at each other. *Preacher Man was right.*

Joe looked at the two of them. "I didn't tell you this, but I left Rolling Flatts myself. Waited until the end of the year, but, yeah, I left.."

"Really," Denise said.

Seeing that the couple was waiting for more information, Joe said, "Let's just say I lost my fan base."

"Wow," she said.

Rudolph was happy to see Denise show the man a little compassion. In his day, Rudolph had ditched a few women himself, with the same results—the sister's friends had dogged him, too.

Joe's face brightened again. "I can make it right," he said. Then, with even more conviction—*the trippin' kind,* as Denise and Rudolph might have described it—he added, "I *know* I can."

62. The Big News

On a Monday night three weeks later, Denise didn't trouble herself to pick up the call on her phone. She was right in the middle of her routine on her new treadmill—her two-mile evening power walk, just like the one she took in the mornings. Her exercise was done to the catchy, energizing beats of people who could really crank it up, Bruno Mars and Nicki Minaj. This so beat Saturday mornings, she thought, instead of dealing with Scootie's mouth harping over Joe. "How much money does he make? What kind of black women is he into? Light? Dark? Lots of bounce? *What?*"

When her thirty-minute regimen was over, she went straight to the bathroom scale. She was thirteen pounds lighter already. The tread would turn things around, get her back down to a 10. Maybe even back to that magic 8.

Feeling strong and somewhat lithe—her thighs no longer rubbed each other when she walked—she picked up her phone and dialed the caller she'd ignored during her workout high. *Jelise Strader.*

"Jackson?" The woman came at her hard, almost as an accusation.

"Yes, this is Denise."

"Girl that tried to call me a few days ago?"

"A week and a half ago, yes. This is Denise. Is this Jelise?"

"Right. I'm Jelise Strader. You said something about trying to find a girl from way back in college named Bernie. I went to school with her."

Denise's heart rate, which had been in the process of slowing, revved up again.

"My last name was Henry, back then," Jelise said. "You say you're helping out a guy named Joe Normal. I knew both of' em, Bernie and him."

"Really."

"You can tell your Joe Normal he can quit looking," Jelise said.

Married, Denise instantly thought. Amen.

"Girl's dead."

"Ex*cuse* me?"

Jelise drily spelled it out for the girl. "D-e-a-d. Dead. Passed about a year ago."

Bernie couldn't get anything to come out of her mouth. Jelise had more to say, anyway.

"He's a little bit late."

"My God," Denise said to herself. "That's unbelievable."

"Believe it," Jelise said. Anticipating the next question, she told Denise, "Cancer, that's what I heard. No reason for you to look any more." She said it with a *Don't bother me anymore* tone in her voice. As she hung up, she added a snide, "You're welcome."

Jelise had been an eyewitness, on that sad day when Bernie's parents came to school to pick up their daughter. The Mama's face was puffy and wet, looking almost as devastated as Bernie's. The Daddy was stone-faced and smoking like a chimney. After Bernie left school, Jelise had used the girl as her own private poster child. "That's why you don't trust *any* of them white motherfuckers," she raged back then, right there on the front steps of McAfee, to any blacks who cared to listen. She got a good number of "Amens" and "Right on's."

When Rudy got in from running his errands, Denise met him at the door. Sir Pepi stood just behind her. Her dark, uncertain expression did the initial talking.

"What," he said, his smile turning into a straight line.

"Got a call from somebody from Rolling Flatts. Got bad news for Joe."

"What is it?" His first guess to himself was *married*.

"Bernie's passed."

"What?"

"Passed. I'm serious. That's what I was told."

You mean *dead*?"

"I mean dead."

He stared at her as the news took hold. "I'll be damned," he finally said.

"Cancer. Said it happened about a year ago."

Unreal, Rudolph thought. First Joe's wife and now this. The only two women who, as far as he knew, Joe had ever been in love with. Rudolph jingled the keys in his hand, trying to hear something familiar, to settle his nerves.

"I found the girl's picture in the yearbook," Denise said. "Henry was her maiden name. Jelise Henry. She's the, 'Yo white boy girl...'"

"Yeah, yeah, got it," Rudolph said curtly.

"Sister was cold as ice," Denise said. She fingered her lip apprehensively. "So how do we tell Joe?"

Rudolph stood there, thinking. "Have him come over, the sooner the better."

"Yeah," Denise said, nodding. "I agree. Tomorrow night. Do it here. We don't know how he's going to react."

"I'll give him a call and tell him we've got an update for him."

"Don't play it up," Denise said. "He'll come in flying high if you play it up."

Rudolph wasn't in any mood to be bossed. "Ain't gonna play *any* damn thing up," he snapped.

Denise didn't need him biting her head off like that. She let her thoughts shift. Joe would *really* be needing a woman now. A flesh-and-blood woman.

That same evening, in the storage locker of her Nashville condo, Velvette Armstrong-Bradley, two months retired from the Tennessee Army National Guard, was digging out the ancient copy of the *1980 Splenditus.*

63. Tweeted Out

Velvette Armstrong-Bradley yanked the padlock on the storage locker so hard she tore the hinge off its wood frame.

"That sonofa*bitch*" she screeched from down in her condo building's shared basement.

She'd just received another message from C'eruh Stiles, a girl she'd once mentored at the Averytown Boys & Girls Club. The first text that C'eruh had sent to her nearly a month ago had been bad enough. It read:

Unbeleevable. Shiny face just come n w a sistuh. Lookin 4 Bernie. Said Bernie was his GIRL from college!!! Name Joe Normal. Everbodyz like, IDK. Crazy r whut?

Velvette had blown that note off with a one-word **Thnx.** And now she'd received this:

Update: JNormalz frien Denise Jackson jus tex th shop. Said pls take her bizcard off wall. Jus foun out Bernadette Armstrong passed! Herz her phone#297-7929.

Irresponsible as hell, Velvette had complained to herself. Especially since she just called Seattle three days ago, where her older sister seemed alive enough to run in a mini-marathon—on her forty-ninth birthday.

"Fuck Denise Jackson," she yelled, not caring if any of her condo-neighbors heard her or not. "Fuck both of' em." It hadn't taken ten seconds for the retired Captain in the Guard to connect the dots. It was their Mama who died a year ago, not Bernie. This Jackson had gotten her Armstrong women mixed up. Now Velvette was down in the dim basement with a single objective: *Know your enemy.* Determine what the enemy looks like, even if you have to go to a thirty-year-old photo to get a rough idea.

She gave herself twelve minutes to get this done. Then she'd have to beat it back upstairs to her father. After Mama died, the old man had tried to stay in the house they'd lived in for more than half a century, back in Averytown. But that turned into a no-go when Harold had finally resigned himself to his COPD and his oxygen tank. He took 'Vette up on her invitation to move in. The company was good for both of them. Her own girls were finally both out of college and out of the house. Veldra was in her first year of teaching third-graders 'way across the state in Knoxville. Venisha, the aspiring M.D., was up to her neck here in town, interning at Vanderbilt College Medical Center. Their father, Army Capt. Romeo Bradley, was winding down his third and final deployment to Afghanistan. When 'Vette's husband packed for home at the end of the year, that would be it. No more Romeo being stuck 'way over on the other side of the world. No more teary Skype videos.

Velvette turned on the clamp light that hung to an overhead shelf. She found the two large plastic containers that her mother had filled and added to over the years, one for her and one for her sister. She lugged the one marked "Bernie" out in the open, flipped the lid aside and dug in. 'Vette wasn't in the mood for a stroll down Memory Lane. She hastily set everything to the side: old snapshots and hair bobs, dolls, and gnarly hats. Brittle teen magazines. One featured Peter Frampton on the cover, another played up a Michael Jackson pic with the caption, "Michael Sings 'Ben'." At the very bottom of the box was Bernie's *Splenditus.*

In her old fatigues, 'Vette had a seat on the floor. Even with her strong hands, it took a minute for her to pull the pages apart.

She found him soon enough. The sight of his green eyes and blond hair forced Velvette back to that Sunday after Christmas break, when she and her parents had taken Bernie back to school. Bernie had been so busting-proud to show off her white boy. Velvette stared at the picture and thought, Devil in Disguise. She felt the painful ache for her sister, all over again. There hadn't been a hint in the prick's face to show he was about to play Bernie like he did. Velvette tried to imagine him with three decades' worth age on him. Wrinkles, white hair, no hair. If he ever showed up at her door, she wanted to be ready for that face.

Just to finish on a positive note, she turned the pages and revisited Bernie's picture. Her older sister's face was fresh, and so very naive. 'Vette couldn't help but break out in a smile after she spoke the words, "What a kid." With that, she smacked the book shut and assured herself that tomorrow, she was going to be making one hell of a phone call.

64. Breaking the News

Rudolph had the snacks set out, good to go. Corn chips here, M&M mix there. He flipped his notepad on the dinette table and squinted at the pitcher of ice water. Denise had told him that he and Joe could have their beers, but she was going with her damn water—with lemon.

Denise came in from the bedroom, wearing black leggings and a tunic top that was cinched around her waist with a belt. No way was she going to look around Joe again. The leggins were relatively loose, no longer squeezing at her thighs like a snake. She'd lost an inch off her bust, but it actually appeared larger, now that she'd trimmed two and a half inches off her waistline and played it up with a tight, wide belt. Thanks to her tread and her diet, her middle was flat again, no more belly suggesting an early baby bump. She placed her iPad close to his notebook so both of them would be facing Joe when they broke the news.

At seven-thirty, right on schedule, they heard the tinny clank-clank of the cheap door knocker. With a low, "Here we go," Rudolph went to the door.

Joe stood there in slacks and a dress shirt, big smile on his face.

"Whoa, Mister GQ," Rudolph smiled, surprised by the dress-up.

After Rudy and Joe did their soul brother hug and shake, Denise stepped up for her turn. As he always had done, Joe kissed her cheek respectful as a judge. She put her hands on her hips to bring Joe's attention to her melting waistline.

As soon as Rudolph set the beers down, Joe was ready with his guesses. "Don't tell me," he said. "You found somebody who's still keeping up with her. And you got Bernie's phone number." He smiled hopefully. "*Right*, Rudinski? Got a number?"

Rudolph took a swallow of his Corona so he wouldn't have to answer right away. Denise took a drink from her water glass.

Rudolph thought of that Kipling poem about the British soldiers galloping themselves into one hell of a fight. Being *brave*. Being *determined*. "Uh, I've got some bad news, Man," he said. He glanced at Denise, who'd already shifted her gaze to Joe. "Real bad news."

Joe broke ahead of him. "Married."

Rudolph shook his head no.

"Living with somebody," Joe guessed.

Rudolph popped his knuckles and said it. "Girl called and told us...Bernie's passed."

Denise softly said, "I'm so sorry, Joe."

Joe stared at them skeptically, not budging. After several long seconds, he said, "She's younger than I am."

Rudolph didn't know what to say next. "Well," he said, making the word sound as indisputable as he could.

Denise glanced down at her iPad. "Girl from Rolling Flatts called me to tell me. Jelise. One of her college friends."

"Some kind of cancer," Rudolph added.

"My God," Joe said. He let out a huge breath and stared up at the ceiling.

They were surprised when his head came down and Joe reached to the floor. He brought Sir Pepi up to his lap. Then, just as rapidly, he surprised them again by setting the dog back down on the floor.

"I need to go home," he told them.

"Oh, no," Rudolph told him. "No way you're going to be by yourself tonight, Man." He meant it in a convincing ass-kicking way. "You're staying here tonight."

Joe said it to the two of them. "On one condition. We're going out."

"*Out?*" Rudolph said, puzzled.

Joe looked at Denise, the beautiful girl Rudinski was lucky enough to have. "I want to go to a place Bernie would have liked. You know, oldies music, dancing."

"You mean an old-school club," Rudolph said.

"Yeah," Joe said in a measured voice. "Old school club."

Denise didn't like this, them taking Joe out before the news had a chance to sink in on him, but she swung her head to Rudy. He gave her a nod.

"I have to change clothes," Denise said.

"Yeah, me too," Rudolph said, standing up. Denise was already padding toward the bedroom. "Back in five, Cool." Rudolph assured him.

As soon as Rudolph and Denise were in their bedroom, door shut behind them, she whispered to him, "Man's in shock."

He conceded that possibility and then thought of the man's wife Franki.

"Might be thinking of losing his wife again, too," he suggested. "Double trouble. Let's not fight him, though. Maybe music can help."

Rudolph *was* back in the living room inside five minutes. He wore slacks and a silk-blend casual shirt. A thin gold chain dangled from his neck.

Denise wasn't *about* to be back in five. As soon as Rudy left the room, she stripped off everything but her panties and went to her closet. She pulled out her black jumpsuit, the one with the gold sequins. She hadn't been able to stuff herself into it since her early days of good-timin' with Rudy. She stepped into it, and when the zipper slid smooth and easy all the way up, she nearly let out an exhilarated squeal. She checked herself in her three-panel floor mirror, pivoted to look over her backside, and saw something that would *not* do—her panty line was showing. Time to get young and get nervy, she told herself. She peeled the jumpsuit off, took off her underwear and zipped up again. This time, she saw nothing but pure, smooth backside. Her spikes went on last. The added height made her look almost trim. She let her longest necklace cascade down into her cleavage. Last thing: she applied rose lip gloss that jumped against her mahogany skin.

Denise stood there and congratulated the forty-five-year-old sistuh in the mirror, and then she strutted herself out the door. Before she got to the living room, she dialed her swing back, reminding herself that Joe just found out about long-lost Bernie. Dead, for God's sake.

Rudolph's head snapped when he saw his woman return. He couldn't resist curling one arm around her waist. Where Joe couldn't see, he let his hand slide down her fine, full booty slope.

She didn't want the embarrassment of slapping his hand away in front of the other man, so she turned her eyes to Joe and waited for his compliment.

"You look great, Denise," Joe said, as if she was showing him a new purse. "Ready to go?"

No *Yowza* from Joe, she observed. Not even in his eyes.

"Let's hit it," Rudolph said.

"Suh Pepi he be guh bouy," Denise called to the dog, just before Rudy slammed the door in the mutt's face.

Scootie didn't have any problem hearing the door wham shut. She left her living room and climbed on her bed, hustling on her knees to the window. The three of them were all dressed up, walking to Joe's Jeep. That damn Denise, Scootie grumbled to herself. She didn't need one of each color. The Girl could've asked *her* to come along and even things up. She went back to her living room to stare sullenly at BET.

65. Release

They headed over to *Groovin*, an old school/jazz club in the West End.

By the time they rolled into the lot, Rudolph saw that Joe's face hardly looked party-loving. As they walked in, with Joe trailing behind, Rudolph leaned over to Denise and whispered, "Says he wants to have fun, but check him." That move of Rudy's irritated Denise. She didn't like Rudy cozying up to her like that; it could give Joe the impression she was happy. She gave a slight lean to Rudy, but didn't make it nearly as close to him as he had come to her. "Let's just watch him," she whispered back.

They took a table. As usual, the crowd was ninety-five percent black, with one or two white women mixed in. The middle-aged sisters in the house noticed the shiny face who dressed like he had money. The question was, was the white man going solo or were they going kinky and sharing the Sistuh or what. As soon as the female DJ called out, "Electric Slide, y'all! Everybody up!" Rudolph and Denise joined the surge that headed for the dance floor. They hadn't been out on the town doing the Slide more than twice since Rudolph moved in.

"You sure we should leave him alone?" Denise asked, glancing back. There at the table, Joe was nodding to the beat and appeared to be cool.

Rudolph picked up his game of playing things off. "He don't look like no basket case to me."

To Denise, this was risky business, and not only in the way Rudy thought. Denise saw Joe all alone in the ocean, surrounded by manless sistuhs trolling the water.

Halfway through the *Slide*, a panting Rudy surprised her

by pulling her off the floor. Denise didn't expect him to head to the bar already, but there they were, with Rudy holding up three fingers to the bartender. "Tres Coronas, amigo," he said.

"Make mine a chardonnay," Denise shouted over the music. Whether Rudy took her serious or not, she was more determined than ever to lose weight, now that she could back into clothes she'd had on standby for a year. What better incentive than the very jump she was wearing? A glass of chard, with a little discipline, she could work all night.

Rudolph took a gulp from his longneck and then pointed the bottle toward the room. "He should be able to find somebody here to cheer him up, don't you think, Baby?"

"Don't push it," she cautioned him. "Not tonight. Let his Bernie-grieving run its course."

She was so pissed over him trying to play matchmaker for Joe she took in a whole mouthful of her wine. She caught herself just in time and let most of the chard drain back into her glass. Silently, she congratulated herself.

"You know what I almost told Joe back at the apartment while we were waiting for you to get dressed?" Rudolph grinned, elbow on the edge of the bar.

"Tell me," Denise said, bracing herself for one of his outrageous Rudy-isms.

"I was going to tell him," he laughed, "the only problem with treating a woman like a princess is, after a while she starts *acting* like one!'"

She couldn't believe he said that to her face. Slap me again, she told herself. She took another pretend-sip of her drink and spit it back. Lord, he was so clueless.

"Thank God you didn't say that," she said. "That would've really torn it with you two."

Rudolph shrugged. As the *Slide* wound down, he added, "I seen women treated like that turn around and run over their man like a bulldozer."

The organ riffs of Blondie's *Call Me* started up and they headed back to their table. "Joe and his girlfriend were kids," he reminded her. "The color thang gave them a new toy to play with. What kind of true love was that, for real?"

Denise gave the man a cool shrug. With an adoring man like Joe, she thought, she would've been a Bernie at nineteen. Swear to God she would have been.

Back at the table, she asked Joe if he was okay. Joe's head was still bopping mildly to the beat. "Sure," he said. "Why wouldn't I be?"

Rudolph handed him a Corona. The three of them small-talked, with Rudolph and Denise keeping a close eye on him. When George Benson's *Give Me the Night* came up, Rudolph got an idea.

"Yo Joe," he said, "why don't you take Denise for a whirl?"

Denise's eyes shot straight to Joe.

Rudolph thought getting Joe to dancing with sexy Denise might loosen the man up enough to get him interested in one of the sisters out in the room. If not tonight, *sometime*.

"Don't think so," Joe smiled.

"Go *on*, Cool," Rudolph pressed. "You'll be with the foxiest girl in the house." He looked over at Denise. She had ignored his flattery and was eyeballing Joe, waiting for his answer. "Don't tell me you're going to insult my woman right in front of me," he chuckled. He fought off a belch. "If I was an Eskimo I could kill you for that." He laughed at his own joke and tacked on a, "Unless you're waiting for one of these hongry sistuhs out here to grab hold of ya instead."

With that chilling image, Denise seized Joe's hand and tugged him out of his chair. "This doesn't have to be *Dancing with the Stars,*" she assured him. " I promise."

Rudolph sent Joe off with a, "Just stand there if you have to. Make all the brothers jealous."

As Denise towed Joe toward the dance floor, a tantalizing thought came to her. She was giving him a nice view back there, with her booty jacked up in the air, jiggling all free 'n easy. She felt a special tingle. It grew, now that she could feel all the other eyes on her and the white guy. She found an open spot on the floor and turned to him, ready to do a slow groove. Joe was standing somewhere on the other side of the Grand Canyon. She wasn't about to let him get by with that.

"Aren't you supposed to put your hand at the lady's back?"

When he gave her a courteous smile and placed a light hand at her shoulder blades, she closed the space by taking a step into him, bringing her body close enough to touch his. She began moving slowly from side to side, setting him in motion with her. She wondered if he could feel the heat of her hand and know she felt the same heat all through her body.

Ask, she ordered herself.

"I've been wondering," she said, "What exactly was it that made you go hunting for Bernie after all this time? I mean, what triggered that?"

It was as if he'd been waiting to be asked.

"I was alone one night," he said simply. "So I wound up thinking about the other women in my life. It was a natural, going all the way back to Bernie. It was unreal how close I felt to her. He smiled a melancholy smile at her. "Why wouldn't I go looking for that again?"

Denise wished she could pull her zipper down to her navel.

Not to come on to Joe—although that was a delicious thought—but to cool herself down. She didn't know how many more chances she would get like this. Her eyes checked Rudy back at their table. He waved.

"What if you found another girl like that today?" she said. She caught herself. "Well, not *today*, but..."

She was astonished when Joe lowered his head to her shoulder and went into a sudden, convulsive weeping.

"It's over," he said, head still against her. "I'll never feel that way about any woman again."

"I'm so sorry, Joe," she said. She absorbed his trembling until her own tears came.

"Listen up!" the DJ's voice rang out. "This place is hotter than Three Mile Island, Y'all! Gonna get even hotter with Earth. Wind. Aaannd...Figh-ya!"

Fantasy cranked up and suddenly here was Rudolph standing beside them. "You all right, Cool?"

Joe quickly pulled away from Denise and he saw she had been weeping as well. "Yeah," he said, getting himself together. "Okay, Rudinski. Just hit a little snag." He backed away so his friend could re-join his girl. Denise stayed long enough to see Joe was okay and went to the ladies' room to clean herself up. As Rudolph watched his woman's super-fine bottom wiggle away from him, a thought came to him. As far as he knew, Joe hadn't had any since Franki died. It was time—past time—to pitch Joe again.

"Ladies been scouting you out, Main," he smiled, trying to flip Joe back. "Me pairing you up with Denise must have scared 'em off, though. My bad."

They left around one-thirty, just as a skinny sister made her move toward the white guy. Along the way, she was lip-synching to Whitney Houston's swoony *Saving All My Love for You*. Just twenty feet from him, the white dude and the couple he was with got up and headed for the door. The skinny sister made an abrupt u-turn and returned to the other sisters she was sitting with. They busted out laughing at her.

An hour later, the three of them turned in for the night. Sir Pepi was in his cage. Joe was bunked down on the couch in the living room. Rudolph lay close to Denise's backside. He kept seeing Joe in that tight clutch with Denise. Any other man, and he would have been jealous as hell.

66. Lap Dance

Rudolph walked into the second bedroom to see Denise down on the floor, doing some cool-down stretches after putting in her latest workout on her tread.

"I think it's time I had a long talk with Joe," he announced.

Denise looked up at him. It had been a month since their trip to *Groovin'* with Joe. It was almost as if Rudy was carrying some kind of attitude toward his friend. Rudy reported to her every now and then that he had talked to Joe at work, but it was always that—small talk. She felt a sting when Rudy told her, "The guys at work still call him 'Joe Cool,' but now they do it to be sarcastic. He's back in his fog again, like he was after Franki." That was a bummer, especially now that all her exercising and dieting were showing some dramatic results. With her three-month deadline less than a month away, she thought she really *did* have a chance to get down to that Size 8. She lay back on her exercise mat and, without making eye contact, asked Rudy a sex question. She attempted to put a detached, clinical spin on it.

"Just wondering," she said. "How can a healthy man like Joe not want to...be with a woman?"

Rudolph was more than happy being extended an invitation to discuss a man's carnal needs. "Still trippin'," he answered. "Man's spent all of his sexual energy trippin' out over women he can't have anymore."

"But he must have his *needs*," Denise pushed. "You go without it for more than three days and you turn into Frankenstein."

He considered the accusation a compliment. "Aw, I can take it or leave it," he kidded nonchalantly. He got an eye roll from her with that nonsense.

"For one thing," he said, "the man doesn't have to torture himself having your fine self spread out in front of him." He took in the curves straining against her sports bra and leggins and gave her an appreciative leer. He began making play windmills with his outstretched arms, mocking the girl's exercising. "Like I told you, women at work can't even get to first base with him."

Denise ignored the silliness with his gyrations but was relieved to hear *that* update.

Rudolph shrugged. "I dunno. Maybe he gives himself a hand every now and then, if you know what I mean."

"Gross," she said. She hoped that was much true.

Rudolph's face crinkled into a wry smile as he recalled something. "After word got around that the girl Joe was looking was black, the white women dropped him like a hot rock, anyway."

Denise almost shouted out a *Yay* on that one. At least that would eliminate *some* of the competition.

Rudolph finally got to the reason he dropped in on her workout. "I was thinking I could take him to the club,"

The suggestion made the slick of sweat on Denise's bare midriff turn cold. "You mean *Bumpy's?*" She wasn't smiling.

Rudolph had this all thought out. "You know, go right after work."

"*Why?*"

"I'm thinking, if I can get a few beers in the man, get him in a social setting, it might pull him out of his damn funk."

Denise saw the man wasn't waiting for her seal of approval.

He was gonna do what he was gonna do, anyway.

"It didn't work at *Groovin'*," she pointed out. With no rebuttal from him, she huffed, "You two have fun, then." She got up from the floor and made a beeline into the bathroom. She *bammed* the door hard to let him know she was pissed.

"Anything else you'd like to say, Rudy?" Rudolph stood there and asked the door, ticked off himself.

The next day, just before it was time to clock out, Rudolph called Joe's work phone.

"Hey Cool," he said, nice and easy, "Whadda ya say we go wild tonight. Go get a couple of brews after work." He was braced to argue with the man when he heard Joe say, "Sure, Rudinski. Why not? You're a fun couple."

"Time out," Rudolph said. "Denise ain't going. Just you and me."

Joe's voice dropped. "Oh."

"You sound disappointed, Cool."

"Denise is a fun person, that's all," Joe said. "Just assumed you were including her."

Rudolph let that go.

"It can't be like the last place," Joe said. "Women looking at me like I was a fresh piece of meat."

"Well, why wouldn't they?" Rudolph said. "They don't get a white man in their club every day. Besides, since when being looked at like a piece of meat a problem? *Hell!*" He laughed when he said it. "Are you on or not?"

"On," Joe said. Then stronger, "I'm on, I'm on."

Rudolph's "club" was outside the county line by no more

than a quarter of a mile, but it was stuck so far out of the way that nobody would just chance across it. It was at the end of a snaking backroad that weaved through a stand of cedar trees down in a floodplain. There were the regular patrons and very few others.

The unmistakeable smell of ignited marijuana was in Rudolph and Joe's noses before they got through the door. "One thing about Bumpy's," Rudolph told Joe, "You don't have to pay for any any weed—just breathe the air."

Rudolph knew he'd get a mean-mug or two for dragging a white guy into the place, but he also knew his friends wouldn't show out over it. Before he'd taken up with Denise, Rudolph had practically been a fixture at Bumpy's. That was before the stabbing. It hadn't been much more than a week after he moved in with her. Denise had seen the story on the eleven o'clock news, the piece about the murder at Bumpy's. It happened on one of the nights Rudy was there. Rudy Barnes wasn't the stabber or the stabbee, but it didn't matter to Denise, not after it hit the local TV stations. The voice on the news intro blared out, "Tavern fight over woman in Shelby County leaves one black man dead and another behind bars." With that, fresh move-in Rudolph went from being a familiar face at Bumpy's to an infrequent visitor, per Denise's insistence. But tonight, for Joe, he'd done it, right in her face.

"Well lookee here—*Barnesy!*" The bearish man bellowed it out from the far end of the bar. He folded his bar rag and waited for Rudolph to come to him. "What up, dawg? Where you been?" Bumpy noticed the white guy trailing in behind Rudolph, and a big, amused grin came over his face.

Rudolph was about to tell him *What up* using one of his smart-alecky answers, but the wrinkled beanpole who was sitting on a nearby bar stool beat him to it.

"He been *married*, that's where he been," the beanpole cracked.

Wary laughs came from a few of the patrons. They all waited for Rudolph to explain the white stranger.

Rudolph was rarely vulgar in public, but he made an exception for the beanpole. He turned to the man, Ado Poussaint, and flashed a middle finger high enough for everybody in the room to see. "I don't see a ring. Do you, Piss-ant?" he joked. "Do you see anything on my finger, huh?"

This time the laughs from the customers came easier. White buddy in tow or not, Rudolph Barnes was still the old, wise-cracking Rudolph Barnes. That was all the invitation Rudolph needed to play comedian.

"Hey," he said, panning the crowd. "Somebody take my picture with Bump. I'm the only one in here using cash instead of food stamps."

More laughs. "Watch it!" somebody mildly called out.

Bumpy Freeman reached across the bar and gave Rudolph a loud, popping, hand clasp. Rudolph returned his grin, tipping his head toward Joe. "Big Bump, meet Joe Normal. I work with him at Max-It."

Bumpy didn't have more than two or three white dudes show up in his joint in any given month, and when they did, they came in as a guest of a brother—definitely not on their own. He gave Joe a standard handshake. "You ain't going to act like your Black Panther buddy, are ya?" he teased, nodding over at Rudolph.

Joe played along. "I just follow Rudins—Rudolph's lead."

"Lord help us with *that* shit," Poussaint cracked.

"Drink your whiskey, P," Bump said. He turned back to Joe.

"Any friend of Barnsey's is a friend of mine." Knowing what Rudolph drank, he pulled out a couple of Coronas and handed them over.

Rudolph showed off for Joe. "What did I tell ya? VIP treatment all the way." He led Joe through the tables to the back of the room, where the light was even weaker behind the black lattice divider.

Rudolph grinned to Joe as they pulled their chairs up to the tiny table. "Not a single cougar to come on to you back here."

About thirty feet away, a pair of young shorties gave Rudolph and Joe a good long look from their high table. The girl with the muscular shoulders wore a bright orange halter top that popped against skin that was almost African blue-black. The other girl was a thin, high-yellow thing. Her top was so sheer her small nipples pointed against the material like arrowheads. Both of the women wore Daisy Dukes and platforms. The dark-skinned female whispered something to her BFF. The petite girl looked through the lattice at Joe and lifted her chin.

The juke box fare was loud and nonstop, everything from Delta blues to Marvin Gaye.

"I got the next round, Rudinski," Joe said.

"Damn right you do," Rudolph joked. He took another sip and got to it. "We've—Denise and me—been worrying about you, Man."

Joe gave him a shrug. "Don't have to," he said. "Like Yogi Berra said, 'It ain't over 'til it's over.' And now it's over."

Rudolph dropped the sensitive approach. "Come on, Cool. Don't you think it's about time you got real? Look at all the time you've been spending by yourself since we got the word on Bernie."

"Don't sweat it, Rudinski," Joe said. "I'm dealing with it."

Rudolph stared at him and in a loud, aggravated voice delivered the line he'd been waiting to say without Denise around. "How long's it been since you had some chicken?"

"Some *what*?"

""Puddin'. Cobbler. Pussy, Man!"

Joe's eyes went to the other side of the lattice to see if anybody heard Rudinski's vulgar mouth. The only two people who seemed to care were the two 20-somethings at the high table. They looked at the two guys and grinned.

"It was Franki, if you just have to know," Joe said defensively. "You know, my *wife*?"

"Time to let her go, Man," Rudolph said. "Bernie, too. You need to take care of your immediate *needs*, before you get any freakier on us. Then after you straighten yourself out you can go find yourself somebody special."

"Easy for you to say," Joe said. He threw out a kidding crack on his friend."You flat lucked out with Denise."

Rudolph was glad to hear the man talk back to him, at least. And acknowledge that Denise was his. "She ain't the only one out there, Main," he said. He took another drink. "Dig this. By the time a sistuh hits, say, forty, the smart ones are locked in, making damn good pay. And—*and*—most of 'em are looking for a dependable man. Don't matter what color his skin is, for real. Not no more."

"I'm happy for you, Rudinski."

"We're not talking about *me*, dammit," Rudolph came back, exasperated with the man.

"My turn to buy the beer," Joe said. He pulled a twenty out of his wallet and started to stand up. Rudolph pushed him back in his chair, stood up himself and plucked the bill from Joe's hand. "I'll make the beer run," he said.

"It's all yours," Joe said. He didn't want to hear a lecture on that, too.

When Rudolph headed back from the bar, he was carrying four beers. He stopped at the high table long enough to hand a beer each to Ms. Poppin' Orange Top and to the other girl. That done, the skinny girl uncrossed her legs, slid off the pleather-topped stool and walked with Rudolph back toward the guys' table.

Joe was looking away from them, seemingly following the beat of the song.

Rudolph raised his voice to break Joe away from his private thoughts. "Say hey to Latisha."

Joe looked up. The girl was backlit by the glowing beer signs at the bar and he could barely make out her face.

"Latisha's an old friend of mine," Rudolph smiled, handing Joe his beer. "Mind if she sits down and says hi for a minute?"

Joe started to pull another chair over.

"Leave it, Cool," Rudolph said. "I need to go talk to her roadie for a few." Rudolph pulled his own chair out for the girl and she demurely lowered herself to the seat. Her shorts rode up to her crotch.

"This is Joe Cool," Rudolph said, looking down at her. "Practically a brother." He looked at Joe and pointed his beer in the direction of the orange-topped girl. "Be right over there."

Before Joe could ask him why, Rudinski was gone, on the other side of the lattice and talking to the other girl. Joe's attention was broken by the light tap of fingernails on his thigh.

"So you're Joe," Latisha said in a voice that was deep for her age. She gave him a big smile. "Rudolph told me all about you."

Her face was easier for him to see, now that she was out of the line of the bar lights. She had straight black hair and small white teeth. Even in the shadows, Joe could see the girl didn't have enough years on her to be anybody's *old* friend. He guessed early 20s. The girl looked slightly familiar to him.

"Larisha, is it?"

"Luh-TEE-sha," she gently corrected him. She scooted her chair closer to him. "I hear you like to dance."

Joe gave her a small upturn of his mouth. "You must have been talking to Rudinski," he said. "He knows I'm pathetic."

She went bug-eyed. *"Rudinski?* Is that what you call Rudolph?" She let out a little gasp and then laughed hard enough that her small bosom shook for him. "Oh God, that's hilarious." Her upright nipples caught his eye, but Joe quickly brought his gaze back to her face. "That's okay," she said. "We can just sit here and talk."

Latisha fed the generic questions to him. *Had he ever been to Bumpy's before. What kind of music did he like? What kind of work did he do?* In the middle of one of his answers, she startled him by placing her sharp fingernails—two purple, three yellow—on his forearm. He flinched.

"Oh, I'm sorry," Latisha said. She pulled her hand away and looked into his eyes.

"No, it's okay," Joe said. "My fault."

She put her nails back on him.

"Mercy, Joe, I know girls who would kill for eyes like yours," she went on. When he smiled gratefully, she gave a little tremble. "Brrr, it's cold back here, and me in my nuthin' top and these Daisies on." She made sure his eyes followed her own gaze down to her lotioned thighs. They didn't disappear in her shorts until they were nearly at her juncture. "See any goosebumps, Joe?" He didn't say anything. She rubbed her arms as if she were in a blizzard. "Mind if I sit a little closer to you until I warm up? Just for a minute?"

Before Joe could suggest that they get a warmer table, she raised slightly from her chair and in one smooth motion swung herself onto his lap. He let her stay there. Latisha placed her hand behind his neck. "Oh, yeah," she said close to him, "That's a *lot* warmer, Joe. Thanks." She made a little wiggle with her hips. "Gotta get just right." Her words were barely more than a breath. When she was sure the old white dude wasn't going to get stupid and throw her off of him, she turned to straddle him and began a slow, rotating grind.

Joe closed his eyes and inhaled the sweet, rich goodness rising from her top. His hands went to her hips and he began pushing himself against her. With that, she pushed harder.

"You like me, Baby?" she asked softly.

The question from the stranger broke his illusion. Joe's pelvis went still.

"*What*, Baby?" she asked, startled that he'd broken her rhythm.

"You're not Bernie." he said, voice rigid. "You're not her."

Latisha couldn't believe it. The man was serious as a train wreck. Here he was going ice cold and comparing her to some other bitch. Before she had a chance to brush that insult off and get him cranked up again, he very gently lifted her off of him.

"Sorry, Latisha." He looked down at his beer and took a sip. "I've got another girl on my mind."

In all her twenty-four years, Latisha had never had a man cut her off, not after she got into full grind. She recovered from her astonishment and went to her feet, yanking her Daisies down far enough to cover her privacy. She followed his put-down with a face-saving diss of her own. "You ain't exactly Justin Bieber yourself, Baby," she sneered.

She made a quick strut back to her own table, where she huffed low to her wide-eyed roadie, "Let's get the hell out of this hole, Melvina." While she was at it, she gave Rudolph a snitty face and said, "News flash, your honkie pal just might be a homo."

Rudolph had seen Joe push the girl away, but he didn't need to hear any trash talk. He kicked it back. "Guess you're not his type."

"Bullshit," the Latisha grumped. She patted her hair. "You don't want this thing back, do ya?" She said it in a pissy tone that dared Rudolph to tell her *Yeah, give me the wig back.* She was out twenty bucks as it was, since Rudolph had promised her an extra Jackson if she got Joe to shoot his shot.

"Keep it," Rudolph said in a cold voice.

On the way out, Latisha slid Bumpy a ten. He gave her a wink and said, "Be careful out there, Ladies."

As soon as they got outside, Latisha yanked the wig off and fanned herself with the thing, spouting, "Damn, that motherfucker was hot!" Underneath it was a super-tight Afro.

"He didn't act like it," her friend said.

Latisha gave her friend a hard look. "I'm talking about the damn *wig.*"

As they stepped through the grass on the way to Latisha's car, Melvina fired up a joint and told her friend, "What can I say? Rudolph told me the guy's wife was dead. Said the dude would be pumping it out like a fire hose."

Melvina had a crazy thought to cool her friend down. She came to a hard stop and swung Latisha around by the arm. Then she gave the girl a scrutinizing once-over and yelled, "Girl!"

"*What?*" Latisha said, not in the mood for any more bad news. "Another zit?"

Melvina's hand swiped at something on Latisha's face. Barely able to hold back her grin, she held two fingertips up in front of her friend's eyes. She gave it a beat and said, "Some white rubbed off on ya."

Latisha gave her roadie a long, rude stare. "Fuck *you*," she said.

Back inside, Joe stared at Rudinski as the man eased back in his chair. "Why did you do that?" he asked sedately.

"Do what?" Rudolph said, playing dumb.

"*Do what.* Come up with somebody who just happened to look like *her.*"

Rudolph wasn't about to apologize.

"Because Bernie's dead and that girl's alive, that's why." He softened up his tone—a little. "That was a livin', breathin' girl workin' on your business, in case you didn't notice—and I think you did."

Joe went silent. Then he said, "Thanks for going to the trouble, anyway."

Rudolph frowned at Joe's Mr. Nice Guy routine. "Be a monk, then. Just thought you'd like to be reminded of what you're missing."

"Bernie," Joe said wistfully. "Having *her* on my lap. Now *that* was something else."

"More of your trippin'," Rudolph told his friend to his face, making it come out disgusted. He was tempted to scream at the man, *Your Nubian Prin-cess is gone for good, Man!* But he held back.

"I'm done with it," he said.

67. Fireworks

Denise bolted up in bed. "You bought the man a *what?*"

Over in his cage, Sir Pepi's ears crinkled and he lay as low as he could.

Rudolph thought she'd be pleased. Here he found a girl who more or less matched up with Bernie in the *Splenditus* photo. Even had her wear a wig to finish it out.

"You put a wig on a *bar hustler?*"

Rudolph returned her yelling. "Community college!" he said. He didn't believe the girl either, but defending her made sense at the moment. "She said she goes to a community college!"

Her anger made Denise's eyes look like ping pong balls with big brown dots in the middle.

"So that she could look like his dead girlfriend? Were you out of your *mind*, Rudy?"

Rudolph stood there and felt his seething anger build. He couldn't believe she was attacking this great idea of his.

"I don't believe you," Denise railed. "Don't you know how fragile Joe is right now?"

"At least I tried," he came back. His voice sharpened. "You almost sound like you're jealous, Denise."

"Don't even think about going there," she answered. She made herself sound as offended as she could.

"Nothing happened, anyway," he said. "Even with girlfriend in her Daisy Dukes sitting on his lap. He didn't do anything, for real. I saw the whole thing." Then, in an afterthought, he added, "from across the room." He thought of one positive takeaway she'd have to agree with. "At least the girl reminded him of what he's been missing out on."

"I thought you said he didn't do anything."

"He didn't—after about three minutes."

"*Jesus.* What stopped him? I know it wasn't you."

"Joe just got up and pushed the girl off of him." There was a hint of pride in his voice when he explained, "she had him going for awhile, with him being in his little Bernie World. Then he snapped out of it, saw she wasn't the real thing."

Denise was relieved by that much, anyway. Just to put him back on the defensive, she asked "You get a lap, too?"

"Behaved just like you knew I would," he said.

Denise took that as a *No* and pulled the sheet up over her nightshirt. She assembled the pieces in her head. *She* could've put on a Bernie wig and lap-danced Joe, if that was all it took to shake the man out of his funk. "Great therapy," she told him, being snide again. "Hook him up with a total stranger who doesn't care a thing about him."

Stung by Denise again, Rudolph retaliated, "You didn't have any problem wearing that paint-on number around him the other night. Busting all out of your jumpsuit."

"I wasn't 'busting out' of anything," she yelled back. "And I sure wasn't doing a lap dance on him, now was I?"

The bedroom went silent for several minutes. At last, Denise got brave enough to say it. "I think we need a break from each other." As soon as she said it, she felt some of her anxiety leave her.

"That makes two of us," he said, trying to sound as determined as she had. "I'll take the couch." He headed out of the room, muttering in a hurt tone, "Goddam. That's what I get for trying."

In a sinking voice, Denise said back at him, "Don't take the Lord's name in vain."

Back in the living room, Rudolph snatched his book of Kipling poems off the coffee table. Onward rode the six hundred, he thought to himself. *Strong in battle.*

Below them, Scootie lay in her bed, putting it together. At first, she thought they were getting it on again and just being extra loud about it. But as she concentrated on the noise, she realized she was listening in on a blow-up. A *big* one. A faint smile came over her face.

68. In Motion

The day after her lap-dance fight with Rudy, Denise's office phone rang. The I.D. read, *Velvette Armstrong-Bradley.* Denise didn't have a clue what a *Velvette Armstrong-Bradley* was, but she answered it anyway. That's what you did if you were in the heads-in-beds business.

She gave a cheery, "Mornin! Denise Jackson, Sales Manager."

"Jackson?" the no-nonsense voice came back. "This is Master Sgt. Velvette Armstrong-Bradley, Tennessee Army National Guard, Retired."

It was the heavy, rich voice of a black woman. Denise reached for her pen and scribbled the name on her HK memo pad. Military reunion, most likely.

"May I help you, Sgt. Armstrong-Bradley? Beautiful day here in..."

"Cut the b.s.," Armstrong-Bradley said, in a strained voice. "I understand you've been looking for my sister. You and some friends of yours."

Denise felt a flutter in her stomach. *Armstrong? Bernie's sister?* The woman must have been contacted by somebody who told her about their fruitless Bernie Search.

She felt the air leave her lungs. Not knowing what else to say, Denise offered a tender, "I am so sorry about your sister. We just got word."

"You just got word about *what*, ma'am?" Armstrong-Bradley demanded.

"You know, about her passing."

The sergeant's voice flattened. "And who the hell told you

she was dead, Lady?"

Denise felt a yanking twist in her gut. *Something was wrong.*
"One of her old college friends," she answered. "Lived in the
very same dorm, as a matter of fact. She told us about Bernie
just a little while back."

"Jesus fuckin Christ!"

"Excuse me?" Denise said. She heard the woman make a
derisive laugh.

"One phone call and you took it for *gospel*? Are you that
fuckin' *gullible*, Lady? My sister's not even sick, let alone dead."

Denise felt like she'd been flipped upside down. "We...just
never ran across anybody who told us otherwise."

"Pathetic, Miss Jackson," Velvette said. Her hot words
sped up as she vented. "You go tell that fool of yours you call a
"contact" that I *talked* to Bernie yesterday—in person. For your
information, it was our mother who passed, not Bernie. Your
little news girl screwed it up. And then she was nice enough
to pass on her fucked-up information to you so you could *keep*
fucking it up."

Feeling like she was about to fall down, Denise braced her
hand against her office chair.

"You tell your goddam friend I'm not playing here," Bernie's
sister said. "Stop spreading all of your shit around."

"I will," Denise answered obediently.

"And something else, Miss Jackson." Velvette said.

"Ma'am?"

"Just to be generous with you, I'll clue you in on this, since
your boy probably didn't tell you. Thanks to your Joe Normal,
my sister was messed up for a long, long time."

"I'm so sorry.'

"Yeah." Velvette's next words came out as she intended

them to, an ominous threat. "You and your pals stop looking for her. Right *now*."

"I...we will," Denise said. She meant it from the bottom of her heart.

"And FYI, Ms. Denise Jackson, *Sales Manager*—Bernie's living a great life. Husband, kids, even a grand baby on the way. You tell your Joe his Bernie *is* dead, as far as he's concerned. Got it?"

"Got..." The phone clicked hard in Denise's ear.

She lowered herself onto her chair. She didn't move for half an hour, not until she made her decision. Bernie *would* stay dead. And not only to Joe, but to Rudy, too. As long as nobody else came out of the woodwork—and the odds were close to zero, on that happening, since their strongest contacts hadn't even come through—she wasn't going to change a thing.

69. Trippin'

After a few lousy nights of sleeping by herself, Denise allowed Rudy to come back into her bed. With her Bernie secret all to herself, she felt a strange kind of freedom to bide her time with Joe.

She remembered that lecture Nancy Pat gave not long ago to her court of female sales managers. "You best keep your man happy," Denise recalled the divorcee saying, "When single women hit middle age, it's a stampede to find a decent one."

Denise had felt like Nancy Pat's message was aimed right at her, since she was now the HK's senior sales manager, with a decade of service under her belt. In five short years, she'd be fifty. Just two days ago she'd changed her hair for him, had it cut in sort of a Bernie-style. She'd followed that up by downloading some poetry on her pad. Joe wouldn't drop her like he dropped his precious Bernie. Joe was a man now, not some green college boy who let himself get scared off by some punks, haters.

70. Shape Up

Scootie was familiar with Denise's new rotating work schedule—one Saturday half-day on, the next off. After she brushed her teeth and took a bath, she put on a pair of panties. Going nude from the waist up, she picked one of her son's shirts, making sure she got the one that fit tightest across her chest. She let the long shirttail cover her up. That done, she dabbed some perfume behind her ears and—*why not*—between her breasts. Then it was a quick dash of make-up, followed by some lotion on her arms and face to get rid of the chalky look. All done, she punched up Rudy Barnes' number. By then, it was nearly ten o'clock.

Upstairs, Rudolph was watching *The Rifleman* on a cable station that specialized in old TV westerns. When the phone rang, he saw Scootie's name and number pop up just above the face of Lucas McCain. In the past, he would've just let the phone ring, thinking *girl-talk for Denise.* But with Denise gone and hot-to-trot Scootie on the line, he saw a play he could make on Joe's behalf. One get-together with Scootie, he projected, might just get the man's head out of the Year 1980 for good.

"'Zup, Scootie?" he answered.

"Somethin'," she said. "Mind coming down here for a minute?"

"Not at all," he said.

As soon as he got to Scootie's apartment, she shoved what she jokingly called an "energy drink,"—a Bloody Mary—into his hand. Rudolph wasn't a morning drinker, but he took it, thinking he and Scootie were on the same wave length—how to arrange her hook-up with Joe.

"Let me guess," he said. He was so sure about it, he got jokey with her. "You wanted to go walking with Joe today but you were afraid he'd take advantage you."

"Now that's silly," she said, fluffing off that picture. "That Caucasian boy of yours needs to be led to the well by his—nose." She walked Rudy to her lumpy couch. "You think you could put in a good word for me?"

"Be glad to."

His answer didn't have enough of a kick to suit her. "Hell," she said. "Tell white boy I just *love* horizontal dancin'. What the hell, fib about it—tell him you're a witness."

"You're so bad, Scootie," Rudolph said, giving her a crooked smile. He took a sip of his drink. With Bernie gone for good, he thought, maybe a roll with somebody who definitely *didn't* look like her was just what the man needed. Show the man once and for all he didn't need his precious Bernie to make his loins feel like it was the Fourth of July. Scootie would sure see to that.

"Why not," she said. "I mean, since he can't seem to find this old girlfriend of his, anyways."

Rudolph pulled back. "Didn't Denise tell you?"

"Tell me what?"

"She's passed. Bernie's passed."

Scootie gave him a long look. "I'll be damned."

"Yep. Died last year. We found out a little ways back."

Scootie snorted. "Denise must have been preoccupied with, um, other, things," She looked away, thinking, and then turned back to give the man a sly smile. "Hate to tell you this, Bro, but I think the rooster's in the henhouse."

Rudolph's brow wrinkled. "Come again?"

Scootie licked some of the thick tomato juice off the side of her glass and this time took it to the man. "I said, I think there's some heat between Denise and your boy Joe."

Rudolph gave her a small, dismissive laugh. "Girl! Better put that Bloody Mary down and get yourself some coffee." He waited for her to give him some more information.

"Oh yeah?" she said. She didn't have any problem twisting a couple of facts. "Denise been talkin' a *whole* lot to me lately about your Caucasian friend, uh-huh. About how much fun she had traipsin' off with him to help him look for his long-lost girlfriend—if there ever was one. About him calling her at work all the time. She got that tread of hers for a reason, y'know. Who you think she's shapin' it up fa? You never wondered what *that* was all about?"

Rudolph *had* wondered. He still thought she was full of it, but he gave a little agreeing nod to let her run on.

"She just changed her hair, I know you saw that, got it cut a lot shorter. That wasn't your idea, was it? Did you ask her to check in with the guy every day, which she does do, by the way? She tells me her and Joe text each other all the time."

Scootie stood up and went to her kitchen counter to give him time to think about all that.

"Want another drink?" she asked.

"I'm good."

She poured herself another round. As long as the man wasn't telling her to shut up, she she kept playing her hand. She came back and stood bare legged right in front of him. "Seems like lately she's talking to me more about him than you," she said. Drink in one hand, she used her other hand to adroitly release her highest button, the one at her breastbone. Her naked breasts surged toward the opening like boulders edging their way into a landslide.

"Think Joe would like these?" she asked Rudy. She went down to the next button and undid it. Her breasts rolled toward the opening. Rudolph was looking at the inner hemispheres of sizable boobs that rose and fell.

"Probably so," he underplayed it. Very nice, he told himself. But Denise's were better. And without the drama.

Scootie wasn't finished seducing Denise's man. She undid her last two buttons and pulled her shirt to the sides, releasing her breasts from their cloth cage. "Do you think they're too big, Rudy? I mean, for Joe?"

Rudolph put her off with the best compliment he could bring to mind.

"If he don't like those, he doesn't have any blood flowin' in him," he told her. He gave her chest and then her face an appreciative look, but then wiggled the fingers of his left hand up in the air, playing like he wore a wedding ring.

A shadow went over her face. While she buttoned her shirt back up, she said, "You know, hookin' Joe up with me just might mean more Denise for you. Look at it like that."

"I'll work on Joe," he said. He set his glass on the end table. "Gotta go, Scoot."

"Give us a hug, then." He allowed the girl that much. She nudged her pelvis against him, then pulled back her head and asked, "No hard feelings?"

Rudolph played it cool. "No hard feelings." Physically, he had hard feelings, all right. She could tell it herself.

Five minutes after he left, she was still incredibly horny. "Damn Denise," she told herself. It wasn't fair. Here Denise was pulling a double for herself while she got nothing.

71. Dog Talk

Rudolph didn't think Joe would go behind his back with Denise, but, on the other hand, he could see that she was changing. The next week, coming home from running errands, he saw more evidence of it. There was Denise, curled up on the couch reading a freakin' book of poetry. She'd never cracked a poetry book in front of him before, not once. But there it was. *Maya Angelou.* So Scootie hadn't been making *everything* up.

His greeting came off as more of an accusation than a question. "When did you get into poetry?"

Absorbed with Angelou, she finished her verse before she raised her head to him. "Week or two ago. Girl's good. *Damn* good."

He tightened up and played his guess, which didn't take much. "So Joe's gone and put you onto poetry?"

"Yeah. I called Joe and asked about women writers, and he told me to check her out. I figured there must be something to it, since he got you hooked." She waited for Rudy to buy that. When he gave her a gratuitous nod, she piled it on. "Gives me some brain food, you know? After spending all day selling."

Rudolph turned to lock the door and Sir Pepi's leash, hanging next to the door, caught his eye. He felt the driving need to bust away from Denise and her Poetry-by-Joe, even if it meant using her yappin' dust mop as an excuse. He went to the fridge, grabbed a Corona and slid it in a plastic grocery bag. Back at the door, he lured Sir Pepi away from Denise by waving the spring-loaded leash in the air.

"Takin' the dog to the park," he told her. Denise didn't know what *that* was about—Rudy voluntarily going on an outing with her dog—but she relaxed after he snapped the leash on the dog and gruffed, in his more familiar Rudy-style, "C'mon, mutt."

Rudolph tugged the dog out of the apartment building and down the sidewalk. Sir Pepi did his business in the usual grassy spot, but then was thrown off when, instead of heading back toward home, they crossed the street. With his twelve whole pounds pitted against the human's mass, the dog had no choice but to hustle and keep up. Rudolph was so preoccupied by Denise's instant love of poetry that he didn't realize how fast he was walking. By the time they reached the park, Poor Pep was panting like a marathon runner at the finish line.

The man went straight to one of the old gnarly picnic tables and sat on its top, bringing his feet up on the long plank seat beneath him. He let out enough leash that Pepi could lie under the table in the shade while he enjoyed his beer.

"Helluva note," he sniffed down to the dog. "Your Mama, all of a sudden a big poetry lover." He gathered his saliva and made a tape-measure spit toward the closest garbage barrel. His spittle hit the nearly empty thing—empty despite all the litter around it—and made a loud, hollow *ping*. Sir Pepi crouched under the table to stare mystified in the direction of the sharp sound. Rudolph peered down at the buggy brown eyes, set in the shaggy head that rotated up at him. "*Yo* Mama." He took himself another swallow. The dog kept his head cocked up at him. The man had never given him this much attention before. Its brain work over, the dog began working against the leash, anxious to go exploring. Rudolph was fine with that; he pressed the button release, and Pepi gradually snuffled his way over to the swing set. When he reached its closest metal pole, he sniffed at it and let go with another leak.

A gray-haired man with deep wrinkles and a wild tangle of a dirty white beard showed up on a sorry-looking bicycle.

He was trying to peddle and at the same time balance on the handlebars what was left of an abandoned shopping cart—the valuable caster wheels already stripped off of it. He gave the husky man with the beer and the prissy dog a wary stare that said, Don't even think about it, this basket's *mine*.

Rudy reeled the dog back in so he would have an audience for what he was about to say.

"It don't make no sense," he told Sir Pepi. "Joe's head's stuck on his Nubian Prin-*cess*. *Period*. So who's frontin' on me? Scootie or your Mama?" He reached down to pet the dog, but here the animal ducked again, expecting the same low-grade violence the man had shown him in the past. Rudolph flushed with embarrassment after realizing what behavior the animal expected from him.

"Oh, I'm not gonna hurt you, Pep," Rudolph said. He tried it again, this time extending his hand slowly. Pep ducked again. Rudolph let it go. He remembered how he'd petted the dickens out of the dog to impress Denise when they were dating, back when it made sense to pretend to like the thing, if it meant getting in its Mama's pants.

With his rear end starting to feel like needles were stuck in it, Rudolph shifted his weight on the tabletop. He had more to tell the dog.

"You know what Cool said to me, Pep? More than once?" Sir Pepi continued to sniff at the weeds. Rudolph reeled the leash in so tight the dog's head was pointed up like a fish on the hook. Sir Pepi had no choice but to gawk up into the man's eyes. "He said, 'You're some kind of lucky, Rudinski—you've got Denise.'" He bent down closer for emphasis. "Me don't think Joe he do dat, come onto yo Mama." The man sat there and thought and sipped at his Corona. He resumed. "Me doan think yo' Mama would do that, either." Rudolph let his eyes roam over the park. Then he returned to the dog, whose eyes nervously tried to shift away but had nowhere to go. "Me think Scootie need to get rocked bad, you know dat? You know what *rocked bad* mean? Huh? Doan even haffa worry about having a litter no mo, either."

With no feedback from Sir Pepi, he finished his beer and threw the bottle toward the barrel. He missed and it bounded on by. Just to be a good example, in case anybody was actually paying attention to him, Rudolph picked it off the ground, and before he stood all the way back up, he slam-dunked the thing into the can. The loud *clang* made all four of Sir Pepi's feet leave the ground. As the two of them started for home, he told Denise's beloved dog, "Yo Mama somethin' else. You wememba dat, Pep."

72. Found

For the next few weeks, Rudolph and Denise coasted along, acting more like roommates than lovers. She'd told him her calling Joe with her poetry questions was a way for her to check in on Joe every now and then, just to make sure he was all right. "You know, ask him what Angelou meant by this poem or that one," she explained to Rudy. "Use that for an excuse to keep an eye on him."

She kept up her workouts, too, and crossed her fingers that Joe wouldn't snap out of it one fine day and get himself smitten with the first good lookin' woman he ran into.

In September, she bought her first Size 8 in years. In fact, she'd happily purchased two more new outfits, after she saw how well the first one fit. Soon after that, on a Wednesday, she'd walked downtown on her lunch break, wearing her favorite one. She saw she was passing her pre-Joe test with flying colors. Her spankin' new two-hundred-dollar charcoal skirt-suit was turning heads all up and down Lincoln Avenue. Her phone rang, and when she pulled it out of her pocket, she felt an overwhelming rush and told herself, *God Thang*. It was Joe. She into the empty alcove of an abandoned drug store, out of the foot traffic and general street hubbub. She didn't want to miss a single word of his.

His voice came at her, huge and energized.

"Denise! I've got to tell you something."

She jumped the gun. "I'm at work. Do you want to meet later on?"

"I can't wait that long."

Denise nearly swooned, hearing that. "Now you've got *me* excited," she said. She nearly went euphoric, imagining how he would react when he took her in, in the Size 8 she scored for him.

"I just talked to her," he said. His voice was soaring. "Just a little while ago!"

An alarm bell sounded out of nowhere. Oh God, she thought. *Not Bernie.*

"Angel!" Joe shouted into the phone.

"Who?"

"Girl from my high school," he said. "Angel French. She belonged to the same sorority that Franki did."

Denise felt herself sinking in some strange, unknown swamp. Joe was acting even more excited than he'd been when they were out on their Bernie search.

"Really?" she threw out, dreading what was next.

"Really. She saw the announcement about Franki in her sorority's newsletter. Tells me, 'When I saw Franki's husband listed as Joe Normal, well—that just had to be you. So I went online and *voila!* There you were, still living around Louisville!'"

A couple of businessmen approached. They slowed to take in the voluptuous black woman, and then, seeing that she was on the phone and wearing a shaken expression, kept going.

"Divorced, a couple of kids in college," Joe said, as if she'd begged him for the details.

"Oh?" Denise said. She tried to make herself sound interested for him. What she honest-to-God wanted to do was throw her phone against the building so hard that the whole thing with Joe in it would shatter into a thousand pieces. In her expensive new suit, she slumped against the, smeary, filthy window.

"She wants to come down here from Chicago and visit," Joe announced to her. He caught his breath and kept going. "You know, talk about old times at Squire Boone High and all that. How about *that*, Denise? Talk about out of the *blue*."

Denise swallowed hard. She didn't know how much longer she could keep listening.

"First black girl I ever knew." Then Joe stabbed her in the heart. "Nothing romantic back then, but boy, did I like her."

Denise snapped open her purse, found her sunglasses and put them on before her eyes welled up. Such a fool, she thought. *I am such a fool.* When Joe finally calmed down, she said, in a wobbling voice, "Gotta get back to work, Joe. I'll tell Rudy when I get home tonight."

"Negatore," Joe came with his goofy slang. "I went out on the floor as soon as I finished talking to Angel. Told him all about it. It think he was almost as happy as I was!"

Of course Rudy was, she told herself. It looked like His Buddy Joe had his Nubian Prin-CESS after all. The two men would be buds again, no doubt about it.

"It's almost like I've been forgiven," he said.

She had no idea where *that* came from. "Forgiven for what?" she asked, not that she cared anymore.

"You know. For dropping Bernie. Maybe if I'd hung with her back then, she'd still be around."

"Don't go there," Denise said in a harsh voice. "That was a long time ago, Joe." She kept to her secret promise. "Maybe Bernie had a good life, anyway—as long as it lasted."

"How's that for karma?" he said, wonder in his voice. "That girl could really make me laugh. Angel, I mean."

Denise couldn't listen to any more of it. "Gotta go, Joe" she said. She punched her phone off. She stood in the alcove and shook her head ineffectually. Joe sounded like a silly teenager bragging about his first big crush. Just like he'd done with his wonderful, one-of-a-kind Bernie.

She bolted into the HK, ignoring the smile of Brent Williamson, the new black staffer working the registration desk. She'd lobbied hard to get the brother in his out-front job. She hurried into her office and shut the door. She didn't believe that Joe's *Angel*, whoever the hell the girl was, came by way of forgiveness or karma or any other made-up nonsense. She took off her shades and looked in the mirror at her reddened eyes. She stayed alone in her office just long enough to get her face put back together. When she called Nancy Pat to ask for the rest of the day off— *"bad, bad headache"*—Nancy Pat was so surprised by her workhorse that she didn't hesitate to tell her to get on home.

On the way back to her apartment, Denise stopped at the supermarket and bought a quart of ice cream. It was a calorie bomb of chocolate and dark fudge. Before she walked five feet from the display case, she spun back to grab a second one. Back home, she peeled off her stupid, smudged Size 8 office suit and went straight into the biggest, sloppiest sweats she owned, which was now her Steelers outfit. In front of her dressing mirror, it seemed big as a tarp on her. Then it was on to the kitchen and her ice cream. She'd let it all out, she told herself. Drop off her little health grid and *enjoy* herself for a change. As soon as the first spoonful of sugar hit her tongue, she retched with its taste. She lurched to the sink and violently spit it out, then threw the container in the trash. She snatched open the freezer and did the same thing to the second quart. With that, she retreated to the bedroom, crawled into bed and cried.

Denise woke up two hours later. She lay there on her back,

contemplating the funk that had forced her to betray herself. She stretched her body out hard. The hard tightening and releasing of her supple muscles felt glorious to her, from her scalp to her toes. Her well-conditioned body was telling her it was ready for its evening workout. She sat upright and pulled her floppy sweatshirt away from her belly. Flab gone, she was eighteen pounds lighter than she'd been when she'd started all this. Denise Jackson had really *done* it. "Not me," she said out loud. She clamored off the bed and went to the bathroom to wash the dried tear-tracks from her face. Back in the bedroom, she opened her dresser drawer and grabbed the weight-loss clothes she'd awarded to herself—brand new top-of-the-line sports bra and tights. She felt a sublime joy with the way they pulled on with ease and supported her, almost like good friends. The girl went to her music dock and cranked up the heaviest bass-thumping work-out tunes she had. She stepped onto her treadmill, hit the *ON* switch and began walking, pumping her arms across her body to warm up. "Tread, you ain't seen nothing yet," she declared. She got into her rhythm, breathing easy, energetic steps matched to the big bass beat. In the middle of her fourth song, she felt a sudden, slowing drag. The tread's belt had slowed down. She thought something had broken.

"Need an exercise partner?"

Denise had been concentrating so hard on her workout that the sound of a man's voice frightened her into a sharp, alarmed chirp. She twisted around to see Rudy right behind her, walking on the tread with her. He had both arms behind him, trying to keep his balance. She hit the *OFF* button. The sudden halt made Rudolph bump against her. He courteously pulled himself back, still managing to keep his hands behind him.

"It's just me," he said. The smile she saw was a tentative

one, but one that was poised to get bigger if she encouraged him. He brought his right hand toward her and showed her the bouquet of yellow roses.

"For me?" she asked. She wasn't being coy. Before he could answer, she stepped off the tread and shut down the music. He'd given her roses only once, last Valentine's Day.

Denise took them from his hand as he got off the machine and took a cautious motion toward her.

"My favorite color," she said, which of course he knew. "Thank you." She had no idea what she would do next.

"You're welcome, M'Lady," he said, playing it silly-formal. Encouraged by her smile, he brought his other hand around and held out the three lustrous new books. They were all by Maya Angelou, and bound by a frilly yellow ribbon. Her eyes went wide.

"Thought you'd like these," he said.

"I do." She took them from him.

"I went out and bought some exercise duds of my own," he told her. "I can join you—if you want me to."

Her eyes left the books and came up to study his face. "You have to be serious about it."

"I am," he said.

She offered her cheek to him. He kissed it.

When he came back to the room, Denise saw soft brown flesh squeezing out from every hem of his stretchy new gear. He smiled sheepishly. "I got some work to do, don't I, Baby?"

"That you do," she answered. Denise turned the music back on and they climbed on her tread, him behind her again. She grasped one handle grip and used her other hand to push the *ON* button. There was too much weight on the rolling belt for it to turn as fast as it should, but she'd put up with the drag this time. The next time, they could take turns. Or maybe even buy a second tread so they could walk together.

"Hang on," she shouted above the happy music.

With Rudy at her back, Denise walked, enjoying her private tears.

the end

CPSIA information can be obtained
at www.ICGtesting.com
Printed in the USA
FFOW04n1650090616
24883FF